The Random House
Book of
Fantasy Stories

The Random House Book of

Fantasy Stories

Edited by
Mike Ashley

Illustrated by
Douglas Carrell

Random House 🏠 New York

Contents

Foreword:
A World of Wonders

MIKE ASHLEY

Are there things that you believe in that your friends or parents don't?

You know, like monsters or dragons or trolls? The imagination is a wonderful thing. Even if these things don't really exist (and who knows? they might have once) you can conjure them up in your imagination and to you they're as real as this book. Do you remember that moment in *Peter Pan* where if even just one person believed in fairies, then Tinkerbell came back to life? That's the power of the imagination. If you believe, anything can happen.

And that's what you'll find in this book—tales of the imagination. Adventures into worlds of fantasy where anything and everything can happen.

What do you want to believe in? A way through to another world? You'll find plenty of those like "The Door to Dark Albion" or "The Bone Beast," although beware—that other world might be rather more dangerous than you'd hoped, as you'll find in "The Closed Window" or "The Hoard of the Gibbelins."

Where are these other worlds? Maybe they're in the past, as in "Atlantis" or "A Pattern of Pyramids" or "The White Doe." Maybe they're a mirror world, as in "The Last Card" or "Mirror, Mirror . . ." or through a painting, as in "The Dark Island." Or maybe they're all around us and we just don't know it. Try out "The Invisible Kingdom" or "The Secret of Faërie" or "Troll Bridge," and you'll see what I mean. We breathe in wonder all our lives, but don't always realize it.

You'll find many of our best fantasy writers in this book. You may have seen some of their work else-where. Diana Wynne Jones has written many fantasy novels and short stories, and her story here opens the book in more ways than one. Have you heard the story of the newspaper publisher who, when asked whether he should print the facts or the legend, said, "Print the legend"? That's what stories are and that's what Diana Wynne Jones showed. You might like to check out other books by her, such as *Charmed Life*, *Archer's Goon*, *Fire and Hemlock,* and *The Magicians of Caprona*.

Joan Aiken should be no stranger to you, as the author of *The Wolves of Willoughby Chase,* and *Black Hearts in Battersea*. And I'm sure you'll know the works of Edith Nesbit and Garry Kilworth. Garry has very kindly provided his own personal introduction to the book.

J. R. R. Tolkien is the biggest-selling fantasy writer in the world, and I wouldn't mind betting that *The Lord of the Rings* has been read by more people than any other fantasy series. You'll find here an extract from *The Hobbit*, which is the book that takes place a few years earlier than *The Lord of the Rings*, and tells of Bilbo's quest to help the dwarves recover their gold from the dragon Smaug. In this extract Bilbo has an encounter with some murderous trolls.

You probably also know the book *The Lion, the Witch and the Wardrobe*, which introduces us to the world of Narnia. C. S. Lewis wrote other books about Narnia, and one of the most exciting is *The Voyage of the Dawn*

Treader, which takes us on a journey beyond Narnia.

You'll find that in most of these stories the main character is on some kind of quest, searching for something, whether that's treasure, fame, safety, knowledge, understanding, a way home . . . almost anything. Some might be successful, but even if they don't achieve their aim, they all learn something en route. Get ready to start your journey. I hope you have some fun and enjoyment, and find something at the end of it. Good luck.

Mike Ashley
January 1996

Introduction:
Into Your Dreams

GARRY KILWORTH

We are living in an age of marvels. Those of you who read this anthology of short stories, each dealing with some kind of fantasy, are surrounded by real wonders. I am talking of television, film, and computers. These three forms of entertainment can entrance us with visual stories. In the case of interactive computer games, we can even become involved and influence the outcome of the tale. We can follow the quest for treasure, or take part in it, become one of the searchers. This can be a wonderful and exciting experience.

However, because these forms of entertainment are quicker and easier than reading, they can just as swiftly become boring. Thus fantastical new creatures are in demand all the time; even as we grow tired of last year's wizardry we are looking around for something fresh to enchant us. Once it was Ninja Turtles, then it was Jurassic beasts, after which came Power Rangers. They come and they go, absolutely magical for a time, but losing their luster and glamour as quickly as they captivated us.

However, there are some fabulous beings who have been with us far longer than these fleeting wonders: creatures who bewitched our great-grandparents and their great-grandparents before them. They still fascinate us because no one has ever been absolutely sure they have never existed. They come out of the darkness of the distant past, from a world without machines, and they haunt us on the edge of our memories. In our sensible moments we tell ourselves that fairies, giants, dragons, elves, trolls, hobgoblins, and all the other mythical figures of fantasy stories are not real, yet they must be important to us in some way or they would not be there at all.

If we did not need such creatures as giants and fairies, if we totally stopped believing in them, we would not write or want to read about them. We would cut them out of our stories and forget them. After all, if they do not really exist, what would it matter if we burned all the stories in which they appear and wiped them from our minds?

It would only matter if we felt we would lose something valuable by doing so; something we cannot properly name but know is important to us; some magical world just out of reach, some place just behind the shadows, some half-forgotten land where strange beings sit and ponder on whether humans are real creatures or whether they have been invented by storytellers.

When we open the pages of a book such as the one you have in your hand, we are going in search of those creatures. (At the same time they in turn are searching for us, for they need you and me as much as we need them.) We go on a voyage of discovery, into their various worlds, looking for excitement and adventure, not knowing whether around the next corner the heroes and heroines with whom we travel might meet some adversary. Sometimes our companions have to use magic, or trickery, or even force to overcome the odds. We are tied to them through the story, so their fate becomes our fate for the unfolding of the tale. We need them to succeed in their quest because we are with them and want to win, too.

The quest does not need to be a physical one, traveling over land and sea, over mountains and through forests, to reach the desired object. It might be a spiritual quest, where the hero or heroine goes on a search for something missing within themselves—love, kindness, happiness—and becomes a better person at the end of the trail. Always, though, something wonderful happens on the road. Some marvelous creature shows us the path, or lights the way in the darkness, or gives us the strength to find courage in ourselves.

I have always loved reading fantasy stories because they come from deep within us, below our everyday ordinary thoughts, from some misty hidden sea of dreams. They take me closer to the soil, to the roots of the natural world, to the pungent woody, mossy, mushroomy, leafy mold out of which we first came onto the earth. Never, in this age of technology, has there been a more urgent need to cling onto the creatures who live in the hollows or rocks, in the dark holes of trees, in the remote valleys and high mountains. These things are inside us, unlike the technological wonders that remain outside, and we can only find our way down to them through tales of wonder.

What you hold in your hands at this moment is a map and guidebook to such a place.

Virtual reality is with us; we cannot send it back whence it came, nor should we want to. Everything has its place in the world, whether newcomer or with us since the beginning of time. All should be treasured equally and we should not put aside one because the other has arrived. We need new fantasy fiction just as much as computer games. There are dark forests in our souls, full of fabulous beasts and strange beings, and we should go inside and look for them occasionally.

That's what these stories are for, to help you find your way into your dreams.

Garry Kilworth, 1996

The Green Stone

DIANA WYNNE JONES

The heroes were gathering for the Quest in the inn yard. It was chaos. Since this was my first Quest as recording Cleric, I was racing around among them trying to get each hero's name and run down my checklist with them. They tell me more experienced Clerics don't even try. Half of them were barbarians who didn't speak any language I knew, large greasy fellows in the minimum of leather armor, with a lot of hairy flesh showing. Most of them were busy waxing and honing at a variety of weapons: gigantic swords, whose names they insisted on telling me instead of their own, monstrous cudgels, ten-foot spears and the like. Every one of them was also shouting for provisions and equipment and running about for last-minute extras. There was a constant, tooth-splitting din from the grindstone, where a squat person with a long gray beard was carefully putting a surgical edge on an axe blade as wide as his own shoulders.

"Rono?" I screamed over the din at a tower of muscle in a leather loincloth. "Is that your name or your sword's name?"

He was in a bad mood. He had been waiting half an hour for his turn at the grindstone. He glowered and fingered what looked like a shrunken human head dangling from his loincloth. "No. Name secret!" he snarled.

I wrote ?Rono? on my tablets and went on to my

checklist. "And are you aware of the nature of the Quest? We travel in search of the Green Stone of Katta Rhyne—"

"Yah, yah. We go now," he snarled.

"Not quite now," I bawled. "We wait until the King comes to give us his personal blessing." In view of the screaming chaos in that yard, I was rather glad the King hadn't arrived yet. "And you are properly aware of the difficulties and dangers? The Green Stone is in the hands of a powerful wizard and can transform fatally anyone who touches it—"

"I *know*!" he bawled. "I hero!"

"Yes, yes," I said hurriedly. His hand was meaningfully caressing that shrunken human head of his. I went on down my list. "And you have proper equipment, weapons, armor, warm clothes? It will be cold in the mountains." He glared at me. I gulped, "Well, you ought to have a warm cloak at least. And transport. Have you horse, dragon or other means of conveyance?"

Here I was rudely interrupted by a very large female who plucked me by the shoulder and spun me away from ?Rono? Apart from the fact that she had added a leather bra with knobs on, she was dressed just like him, mostly in a big sword and shrunken human head. I stared into her grubby navel, shaken. She was big. "You try coddle my little brother?" she demanded.

"No, no," I said. "This list. I have to make sure everyone has what's on it. Name, please."

"Name secret. We walk. We carry nothing," she said.

I hoped that keeping up with the horses would warm them up in the mountains and scuttled quickly on to the next hero. He was a suave young man in a

turban who had brought a camel to ride. The creature was something like a moldy hearthrug on long knobbly legs, out of which stuck a long neck with a temper worse than ?Rono's? on the end of it. It made three attempts to bite me while I was finding out that the young man was called Haroun and that he carried a talisman of some kind. He didn't actually *say*, but I assumed he was our statutory magic-user. I wrote down ?Magician? and dodged away among the crush, worrying about it. We really *had* to have a magic-user. I couldn't control this lot on my own.

I made another attempt to collect the name of the person monopolizing the grindstone, but he couldn't hear me for the noise he was making. So I wrote down Dwarf, because he obviously was, and reckoned that with that axe he was certainly properly equipped. I skirted an argument, two horses, and an aggressive griffon, and found we had a harpist at least. He was seated on the horse trough, strumming inaudibly, a very pleasant young fellow with curly hair who said his name was Trouvere. There was a smiling man with white teeth next to him, carrying a pack, but when I tried to take this one's name he turned out to be a tinker, come to see his friend the harpist off. Embarrassing. But I felt better when I spotted a tall figure in a cowled cloak a little way off beside one of the store sheds. That *had* to be our magician.

I hastened up to him. "Name, please."

His hooded head turned, giving me a glimpse of a piercing eye staring at me across a hooked nose. "Why?" he said. "Does it matter?"

"I have to have you all down in my records," I explained.

"How diligent," he said. "Then I am Basileus for

your records." His tone was deeply sarcastic. I knew it was a false name, but I wrote it down—with the usual query.

I was just turning away, when a tall pallid figure leapt out through the door of the shed. "Don't go without me!" he said breathlessly. "I won't be long now."

He was wearing some kind of apron and long gloves, both of which were dripping with something greenish. His right hand clutched a knife, also dripping green. "Er—who are you?" I said faintly.

"Pelham," he said. "I'm your healer. You'll need me."

"Oh," I said.

"I'll be about ten minutes," he said. "I'm just finishing a postmortem." And he added to the cowled Basileus, "You were right. The creature was definitely human once." After which he dived back into the shed.

I wrote him down, too, wishing I had not eaten breakfast, and went back to the rest of the chaos. To my surprise, it was beginning to sort itself out. The Dwarf backed away from the grindstone, lovingly stroking his axe, and ?Rono? dived forward for his turn. Everyone else began climbing up onto their mounts. As recording Cleric, I had been allotted a cart to ride in which had a cunning desk-attachment I could swing over my knees, so that I could go on writing down all things at all times. The cart was drawn by a highly opinionated mule. But nobody had thought of providing it with a driver.

It was my turn to make some chaos. "How on *earth* am I supposed to write *and* drive?" I screamed. "This mule is a full-time job! Am I expected to make an exact

record of everyone's deeds while controlling the brute with one hand, or something?"

Every hero there stared reprovingly and then turned away. Clerics are not supposed to fuss. I was eventually rescued by the harper Trouvere, who pushed through the crowd and climbed smilingly into the driving seat. "I'll deal with the mule," he said. "I'm no hand at riding and—to be frank—I can't afford a horse anyway." While I was gushing grateful thanks at him, Trouvere dumped his harp beside me and collected the reins as if it was something he'd been doing all his life. The mule stopped trying to kick the front of the cart in and stood still. Now we were only waiting for the King to arrive and give us his blessing.

In the sudden hush, Pelham emerged from the shed again, without the gloves and apron this time. Looking pallidly smug, he whispered to Basileus and passed him a small bag. Basileus was clearly delighted. He patted the healer on the shoulder. Then, deliberately and jauntily, he climbed to a high mounting block by the inn door, where everyone could see him, even those, like me, who had Haroun and his bad-tempered camel in the way. Basileus threw off his hood and flung back his cloak. There was a crown on his head and the rest of his clothes were purple and ermine.

"I am your King," he said. Everyone gave an uncertain, muttering sort of cheer. He smiled. "I was coming here," he said, "to bless this Quest on its way, when I was attacked by a strange green man. I was fortunate enough to kill him. And when I examined the body, it reminded me very strongly of the hero Seigro, who went in search of the Green Stone a year ago. So I brought it here and asked my Royal Healer,

Pelham, to dissect the corpse. This is what we have been waiting for. Pelham cut the creature open and discovered that, in place of a heart, it had the Green Stone of Katta Rhyne. Here it is." He held up the bag. "It only remains for me to thank you all very much for answering my call and to tell you that there is now no longer any need for the Quest."

There was an instant of thunderstruck silence. Then a growl arose in a dozen languages. Such words as I could pick out were "recompense!" "Something for our trouble!" and "Cost of travel!" mixed with cries of "Swindle!" and "Cheat!" Axes and swords were waved. I did not blame them for feeling cheated. This was my first Quest. Though it had promised to be nothing but trouble, I found I was furious to be deprived of it. Haroun's camel seemed to have the same feelings. It

vented bubbling howls and plunged about. My mule was not the animal to take noises from a mere camel. It went for the camel, dragging my cart with it, Trouvere wrestling at the reins, Haroun wrestling at *his* reins—both laughing for some reason—myself screaming, every hero in the yard roaring . . . I had a glimpse of the King with the bag in one hand and the other making soothing gestures. The next glimpse I had of him, the bag was gone from his hand. The tinker leapt nimbly up beside me, flourishing a bag that looked just the same. "Got it! Let's go!" he shouted.

Trouvere whipped on the reins. The mule forgot the camel and dashed for the yard gate. "Cover our backs, Haroun!" Trouvere shouted as we thundered out into the town. And we galloped madly from under the noses of heroes.

We have been galloping almost ever since. Haroun caught us up after an hour, laughing heartily.

"The heroes didn't know what hit them," he said. "Never seen an angry camel before. Aren't you going to throw that whining Cleric out?"

"Oh, no," said Trouvere—if that is his name. "She can stay and do her job. Let her write down how we get on against all the heroes the King is going to send after us."

"Not to speak of the wizard who had the Stone in the first place," said the tinker. "Don't forget *him*."

"Then write, woman!" Haroun laughed. "Write, or my camel may get angry."

So I write . . .

The Hoard of the Gibbelins

LORD DUNSANY

The Gibbelins eat, as is well known, nothing less good than man. Their evil tower is joined to Terra Cognita, to the lands we know, by a bridge. Their hoard is beyond reason; avarice has no use for it; they have a separate cellar for emeralds and a separate cellar for sapphires; they have filled a hole with gold and dig it up when they need it. And the only use that is known for their ridiculous wealth is to attract to their larder a continual supply of food. In times of famine they have even been known to scatter rubies abroad, a little trail of them to some city of Man, and sure enough their larders would soon be full again.

Their tower stands on the other side of that river known to Homer—ὁ ῥόος ὠχεανοίο, as he called it—which surrounds the world. And where the river is narrow and fordable the tower was built by the Gibbelin's gluttonous sires, for they liked to see burglars rowing easily to their steps. Some nourishment that common soil has not, the huge trees drained there with their colossal roots from both banks of the river.

There the Gibbelins lived and discreditably fed.

Alderic, Knight of the Order of the City and the Assault, hereditary Guardian of the King's Peace of Mind, a man not unremembered among the makers of myth, pondered so long upon the Gibbelins' hoard that by now he deemed it his. Alas that I should say of so perilous a venture, undertaken at dead of night by a valorous man, that its motive was sheer avarice! Yet upon avarice only the Gibbelins relied to keep their larders full, and once in every hundred years sent spies into the cities of men to see how avarice did, and always the spies returned again to the tower saying that all was well.

It may be thought that, as the years went on and men came by fearful ends on that tower's wall, fewer and fewer would come to the Gibbelins' table: but the Gibbelins found otherwise.

Not in the folly and frivolity of his youth did Alderic come to the tower, but he studied carefully for several years the manner in which burglars met their doom when they went in search of the treasure that he considered his. *In every case they had entered by the door.*

He consulted those who gave advice on this quest; he noted every detail and cheerfully paid their fees, and determined to do nothing that they advised, for what were their clients now? No more than examples of the savory art, mere half-forgotten memories of a meal; and many, perhaps, no longer even that.

These were the requisites for the quest that these men used to advise: a horse, a boat, mail armor, and at least three men-at-arms. Some said, "Blow the horn at the tower door"; others said, "Do not touch it."

Alderic thus decided: he would take no horse down to the river's edge, he would not row along it in a boat, and he would go alone and by way of the Forest Unpassable.

How pass, you may say, by the unpassable? This was his plan: there was a dragon he knew of who, if peasants' prayers are heeded, deserved to die, not alone because of the number of maidens he cruelly slew, but because he was bad for the crops; he ravaged the very land and was the bane of a dukedom.

Now Alderic determined to go up against him. So he took horse and spear and pricked till he met the dragon, and the dragon came out against him breathing bitter smoke. And to him Alderic shouted, "Hath foul dragon ever slain true knight?" And well the dragon knew that this had never been, and he hung his head and was silent, for he was glutted with blood. "Then," said the knight, "if thou wouldst ever taste maiden's blood again thou shalt be my trusty steed, and if not, by this spear there shall befall thee all that the troubadours tell of the dooms of thy breed."

And the dragon did not open his ravening mouth, nor rush upon the knight, breathing out fire; for well he knew the fate of those that did these things, but he consented to the terms imposed, and swore to the knight to become his trusty steed.

It was on a saddle upon this dragon's back that Alderic afterward sailed above the unpassable forest, even above the tops of those measureless trees, children of wonder. But first he pondered that subtle plan of his which was more profound than merely to avoid all that had been done before; and he commanded a blacksmith, and the blacksmith made him a pickaxe.

Now there was great rejoicing at the rumor of Alderic's quest, for all folk knew that he was a cautious man, and they deemed that he would succeed and enrich the world, and they rubbed their hands in the cities at the thought of largesse; and there was joy among all men in Alderic's country, except perchance among the lenders of money, who feared they would soon be paid. And there was rejoicing also because men hoped that when the Gibbelins were robbed of their hoard, they would shatter their high-built bridge and break the golden chains that bound them to the world, and drift back, they and their tower, to the moon, from which they had come and to which they rightly belonged. There was little love for the Gibbelins, though all men envied their hoard.

So they all cheered, that day when he mounted his dragon, as though he was already a conqueror, and what pleased them more than the good that they hoped he would do to the world was that he scattered gold as he rode away; for he would not need it, he said, if he found the Gibbelins' hoard, and he would not need it more if he smoked on the Gibbelins' table.

When they heard that he had rejected the advice of those that gave it, some said that the knight was mad, and others said he was greater than those that gave the advice, but none appreciated the worth of his plan.

He reasoned thus: for centuries men had been well advised and had gone by the cleverest way, while the Gibbelins came to expect them to come by boat and to look for them at the door whenever their larder was empty, even as a man looketh for a snipe in the marsh; but how, said Alderic, if a snipe should sit in the top of a tree, and would men find him there? Assuredly never! So Alderic decided to swim the river and not to go by the door, but to pick his way into the tower through the stone. Moreover, it was in his mind to work below the level of the ocean, the river (as Homer knew) that girdles the world, so that as soon as he made a hole in the wall the water should pour in, confounding the Gibbelins, and flooding the cellars rumored to be

twenty feet in depth, and therein he would dive for emeralds as a diver dives for pearls.

And on the day that I tell of he galloped away from his home scattering largesse of gold, as I have said, and passed through many kingdoms, the dragon snapping at maidens as he went, but being unable to eat them because of the bit in his mouth, and earning no gentler reward than a spur-thrust where he was softest. And so they came to the swart arboreal precipice of the unpassable forest. The dragon rose at it with a rattle of wings. Many a farmer near the edge of the world saw him up there where yet the twilight lingered, a faint, black, wavering line; and mistaking him for a row of geese going inland from the ocean, went into their houses cheerily rubbing their hands and saying that winter was coming, and that we should soon have snow. Soon even there the twilight faded away, and when they descended at the edge of the world, it was night and the moon was shining. Ocean, the ancient river, narrow and shallow there, flowed by and made no murmur. Whether the Gibbelins banqueted or whether they watched by the door, they also made no murmur. And Alderic dismounted and took his armor off, and saying one prayer to his lady, swam with his pickaxe. He did not part from his sword, for fear that he met with a Gibbelin. Landed the other side, he began to work at once, and all went well with him. Nothing put out its head from any window, and all were lighted so that nothing within could see him in the dark. The blows of his pickaxe were dulled in the deep walls. All night he worked, no sound came to molest him, and at dawn the last rock swerved and tumbled inward, and the river poured in after. Then Alderic took a stone, and went to the bottom step, and hurled the stone at the door; he heard the echoes roll into the tower, then he ran back and dived through the hole in the wall.

He was in the emerald-cellar. There was no light in the lofty vault above him, but, diving through twenty feet of water, he felt the floor all rough with emeralds, and open coffers full of them. By a faint ray of the moon he saw that the water was green with them, and, easily filling a satchel, he rose again to the surface; and there were the Gibbelins waist-deep in the water, with torches in their hands! And, without saying a word, *or even smiling*, they neatly hanged him on the outer wall—and the tale is one of those that have not a happy ending.

A Harp of Fishbones

JOAN AIKEN

Little Nerryn lived in the half-ruined mill at the upper end of the village, where the stream ran out of the forest. The old miller's name was Timorash, but she called him uncle. Her own father and mother were dead, long before she could remember. Timorash was no real kin, nor was he particularly kind to her; he was a lazy old man. He never troubled to grow corn as the other people in the village did, little patches in the clearing below the village before the forest began again. When people brought him corn to grind he took one-fifth of it as his fee and this, with wild plums that Nerryn gathered and dried, and carp from the deep millpool, kept him and the child fed through the short bright summers and the long silent winters.

Nerryn learned to do the cooking when she was seven or eight; she toasted fish on sticks over the fire and baked cakes of bread on a flat stone; Timorash beat her if the food was burned, but it mostly was, just the same, because so often half her mind would be elsewhere, listening to the bell-like call of a bird or pondering about what made the difference between the stream's voice in winter and in summer. When she was little older Timorash taught her how to work the mill, opening the sluice-gate so that the green, clear mountain water could hurl down against the great wooden paddle-wheel. Nerryn liked this much better, since she already spent hours watching the stream endlessly pouring and plaiting down its narrow passage. Old Timorash had hoped that now he would be able to give up work altogether and lie in the sun all day, or crouch by the fire, slowly adding one stick after another and dreaming about barley wine. But Nerryn forgot to take flour in payment from the villagers, who were in no hurry to remind her, so the old man angrily decided that this plan would not answer, and sent her out to work.

First she worked for one household, then for another.

The people of the village had come from the plains; they were surly, big-boned, and lank, with tow-colored hair and pale eyes; even the children seldom spoke. Little Nerryn sometimes wondered, looking at her reflection in the millpool, how it was that she should be so different from them, small and brown-skinned with dark hair like a bird's feathers and hazel-nut eyes. But it was no use asking questions of old Timorash, who never answered except by grunting or throwing a clod of earth at her. Another difference was that she loved to chatter, and this was perhaps the main reason why the people she worked for soon sent her packing.

There were other reasons, too, for, though Nerryn was willing enough to work, things often distracted her.

"She let the bread burn while she ran outside to listen to a curlew," said one.

"When she was helping me cut the hay she asked so many questions that my ears have ached for three days," complained another.

"Instead of scaring off the birds from my corn patch

she sat with her chin on her fists, watching them gobble down half a winter's supply and whistling to them!" grumbled a third.

Nobody would keep her more than a few days, and she had plenty of beatings, especially from Timorash, who had hoped that her earnings would pay for a keg of barley wine. Once in his life he had had a whole keg, and he still felt angry when he remembered that it was finished.

At last Nerryn went to work for an old woman who lived in a tumbledown hut at the bottom of the street. Her name was Saroon and she was by far the oldest in the village, so withered and wrinkled that most people thought she was a witch; besides, she knew when it was going to rain and was the only person in the place who did not fear to venture a little ways into the forest. But she was growing weak now, and stiff, and wanted somebody to help dig her corn patch and cut wood. Nevertheless she hardly seemed to welcome help when it came. As Nerryn moved about at the tasks she was set, the old woman's little red-rimmed eyes followed her suspiciously; she hobbled around the hut watching through cracks, grumbling and chuntering to herself, never losing sight of the girl for a moment, like some cross-grained old animal that sees a stranger near its burrow.

On the fourth day she said,

"You're singing, girl."

"I—I'm sorry," Nerryn stammered. "I didn't mean to—I wasn't thinking. Don't beat me, please."

"Humph," said the old woman, but she did not beat Nerryn that time. And next day, watching through the window hole while Nerryn chopped wood, she said,

"You're not singing."

Nerryn jumped. She had not known the old woman was so near.

"I thought you didn't like me to," she faltered.

"I didn't say so, did I?"

Muttering, the old woman stumped off to the back of the hut and began to sort through a box of mildewy nuts. "As if I should care," Nerryn heard her grumble, "whether the girl sings or not!" But next day she put her head out of the door, while Nerryn hoed the corn patch, and said,

"Sing, child!"

Nerryn looked at her, doubtful and timid, to see if she really meant it, but she nodded her head energetically, till the tangled gray locks jounced on her shoulders, and repeated,

"Sing!"

So presently the clear, tiny thread of Nerryn's song began again as she sliced off the weeds; and old Saroon came out and sat on an upturned log beside the door, pounding roots for soup and mumbling to herself in time to the sound. And at the end of the week she did not dismiss the girl, as everyone else had done, though what she paid was so little that Timorash grumbled every time Nerryn brought it home. At this rate twenty years would go by before he had saved enough for a keg of barley wine.

One day Saroon said,

"Your father used to sing."

This was the first time anyone had spoken of him.

"Oh," Nerryn cried, forgetting her fear of the old woman. "Tell me about him."

"Why should I?" old Saroon said sourly. "He never did anything for *me*." And she hobbled off to fetch a pot of water. But later she relented and said,

"His hair was the color of ash buds, like yours. And he carried a harp."

"A harp, what is a harp?"

"Oh, don't pester, child. I'm busy."

But another day she said, "A harp is a thing to make music. His was a gold one, but it was broken."

"Gold, what is gold?"

"This," said the old woman, and she pulled out a small, thin disk, which she wore on a cord of plaited grass around her neck.

"Why!" Nerryn exclaimed. "Everybody in the village has one of those except Timorash and me. I've often asked what they were, but no one would answer."

"They are gold. When your father went off and left you and the harp with Timorash, the old man ground up the harp between the millstones. And he melted down the gold powder and made it into these little circles and sold them to everybody in the village, and bought a keg of barley wine. He told us they would bring good luck. But I have never had any good luck and that was a long time ago. And Timorash has long since drunk all the barley wine."

"Where did my father go?" asked Nerryn.

"Into the forest," the old woman snapped. "I could have told him he was in for trouble. I could have warned him. But he never asked *my* advice."

She sniffed, and set a pot of herbs boiling on the fire. And Nerryn could get no more out of her that day.

But little by little, as time passed, more came out.

"Your father came from over the mountains. High up yonder, he said, there was a great city, with houses and palaces and temples, and as many rich people as there are fish in the millpool. Best of all, there was always music playing in the streets and houses and in the temples. But then the goddess of the mountain became angry, and fire burst out of a crack in the hillside. And then a great cold came, so that people froze where they stood. Your father said he only just managed to escape with you by running very fast. Your mother had died in the fire."

"Where was he going?"

"The king of the city had ordered him to go for help."

"What sort of help?"

"Don't ask *me*," the old woman grumbled. "You'd think he'd have settled down here like a person of sense, and mended his harp. But no, on he must go, leaving you behind so that he could travel faster. He said he'd fetch you again on his way back. But of course he never did come back—one day I found his bones in the forest. The birds must have killed him."

"How do you *know* they were my father's bones?"

"Because of the tablet he carried. See, here it is, with his name on it, Heramon the harper."

"Tell me more about the harp!"

"It was shaped like this," the old woman said. They were washing clothes by the stream, and she drew with her finger in the mud. "Like this, and it had golden strings across, so. All but one of the strings had melted in the fire from the mountain. Even on just one string he could make very beautiful music, that would force you to stop whatever you were doing and listen. It is a pity he had to leave the harp behind. Timorash wanted it as payment for looking after you. If your father had taken the harp with him, perhaps he would have been able to reach the other side of the

forest."

Nerryn thought about this story a great deal. For the next few weeks she did even less work than usual and was mostly to be found squatting with her chin on her fists by the side of the stream. Saroon beat her, but not very hard. Then one day Nerryn said,

"I shall make a harp."

"Hah!" sniffed the old woman. "You! What do you know of such things?"

After a few minutes she asked,

"What will you make it from?"

Nerryn said, "I shall make it of fishbones. Some of the biggest carp in the millpool have bones as thick as my wrist, and they are very strong."

"Timorash will never allow it."

"I shall wait till he is asleep, then."

So Nerryn waited till night, and then she took a chunk of rotten wood, which glows in the dark, and dived into the deep millpool, swimming down and down to the depths where the biggest carp lurk, among the mud and weeds and old sunken logs.

When they saw the glimmer of the wood through the water, all the fish came nosing and nibbling and swimming around Nerryn, curious to find if this thing that shone so strangely was good to eat. She waited as long as she could bear it, holding her breath, till a great, barrel-shaped monster slid nudging right up against her; then, quick as a flash, she wrapped her arms around his slippery sides and fled up with a bursting heart to the surface.

Much to her surprise, old Saroon was there, waiting in the dark on the bank. But the old woman only said,

"You had better bring the carp to my hut. After all, you want no more than the bones, and it would be a pity to waste all that good meat. I can live on it for a week." So she cut the meat off the bones, which were coal-black but had a sheen on them like mother-of-pearl. Nerryn dried them by the fire, and then she joined together the three biggest, notching them to fit, and cementing them with a glue she made by boiling some of the smaller bones together. She used long, thin, strong bones for strings, joining them to the frame in the same manner.

All the time old Saroon watched closely. Sometimes she would say,

"That was not the way of it. Heramon's harp was wider," or "You are putting the strings too far apart. There should be more of them, and they should be tighter."

When at last it was done, she said,

"Now you must hang it in the sun to dry."

So for three days the harp hung drying in the sun and wind. At night, Saroon took it into her hut and covered it with a cloth. On the fourth day she said,

"Now, play!"

Nerryn rubbed her finger across the strings, and they gave out a liquid murmur, like that of a stream running over pebbles, under a bridge. She plucked a string, and the noise was like that a drop of water makes, falling in a hollow place.

"That will be music," old Saroon said, nodding her head, satisfied. "It is not quite the same as the sound from your father's harp, but it is music. Now you shall play me tunes every day, and I shall sit in the sun and listen."

"No," said Nerryn, "for if Timorash hears me playing he will take the harp away and break it or sell it. I shall go to my father's city and see if I can find any of

22

his kin there."

At this old Saroon was very angry. "Here have I taken all these pains to help you, and what reward do I get for it? How much pleasure do you think I have, living among dolts in this dismal place? I was not born here, any more than you were. You could at least play to me at night, when Timorash is asleep."

"Well, I will play to you for seven nights," Nerryn said.

Each night old Saroon tried to persuade her not to go, and she tried harder as Nerryn became more skillful in playing, and drew from the fishbone harp a curious watery music, like the songs that birds sing when it is raining. But Nerryn would not be persuaded to stay, and when she saw this, on the seventh night, Saroon said,

"I suppose I shall have to tell you how to go through the forest. Otherwise you will certainly die, as your father did. When you go among the trees you will find that the grass underfoot is thick and strong and hairy, and the farther you go, the higher it grows, as high as your waist. And it is sticky and clings to you, so that you can only go forward slowly, one step at a time. Then, in the middle of the forest, perched in the branches, there are vultures who will drop on you and peck you to death if you stand still for more than a minute."

"How do you know all this?" Nerryn said.

"I have tried many times to go through the forest, but it is too far for me; I grow tired and have to turn back. The vultures take no notice of me, I am too old and withered, but a tender young piece like you would be just what they fancy."

"Then what must I do?" Nerryn asked.

"You must play music on your harp till they fall asleep; then, while they sleep, cut the grass with your knife and go forward as fast as you can."

Nerryn said, "If I cut you enough fuel for a month, and catch you another carp, and gather you a bushel of nuts, will you give me your little gold circle, or my father's tablet?"

But this Saroon would not do. She did, though, break off the corner of the tablet that had Heramon the harper's name on it, and give that to Nerryn.

"But don't blame me," she said sourly, "if you find the city all burned and frozen, with not a living soul to walk its streets."

"Oh, it will all have been rebuilt by this time," Nerryn said. "I shall find my father's people, or my mother's, and I shall come back for you, riding a white mule and leading another."

"Fairy tales!" old Saroon said angrily. "Be off with you, then. If you don't wish to stay I'm sure *I* don't want you idling about the place. All the work you've done this last week I could have done better myself in half an hour. Drat the woodsmoke! It gets in a body's eyes till they can't see a thing." And she hobbled into the hut, working her mouth sourly, and rubbing her eyes with the back of her hand.

Nerryn ran into the forest, going cornerways up the mountain, so as not to pass too close to the mill where old Timorash lay sleeping in the sun.

Soon she had to slow down because the way was so steep. And the grass grew thicker and thicker, hairy, sticky, all twined and matted together, as high as her waist. Presently, as she hacked and cut at it with her bone knife, she heard a harsh croaking and flapping above her. She looked up, and saw two gray vultures

perched on a branch, leaning forward to peer down at her. Their wings were twice the length of a man's arm and they had long, wrinkled, black leathery necks and little, fierce yellow eyes. As she stood, two more, then five, ten, twenty others came rousting through the branches, and all perched around about, craning down their long black necks, swaying back and forth, keeping balanced by the way they opened and shut their wings.

Nerryn felt very much afraid of them, but she unslung the harp from her back and began to play a soft, trickling tune, like rain falling on a deep pool. Very soon the vultures sank their necks down between their shoulders and closed their eyes. They sat perfectly still.

When she was certain they were asleep, Nerryn made haste to cut and slash at the grass. She was several hundred yards on her way before the vultures woke and came cawing and jostling through the branches to cluster again just overhead. Quickly she pulled the harp around and strummed on its fishbone strings until once again, lulled by the music, the vultures sank their heads between their gray wings and slept. Then she went back to cutting the grass, as fast as she could.

It was a long, tiring way. Soon she grew so weary that she could hardly push one foot ahead of the other, and it was hard to keep awake; once she only just roused in time when a vulture, swooping down, missed her with his beak and instead struck the harp on her back with a loud, strange twang that set echoes scampering through the trees.

At last the forest began to thin and dwindle; here the tree trunks and branches were all draped about with gray-green moss, like long, dangling hanks of sheepswool. Moss grew on the rocky ground, too, in a thick carpet. When she reached this part, Nerryn could go on safely; the vultures rose in an angry flock and flew back with harsh croaks of disappointment, for they feared the trailing moss would wind around their wings and trap them.

As soon as she reached the edge of the trees, Nerryn lay down in a deep tussock of moss and fell fast asleep.

She was so tired that she slept almost till nightfall, but then the cold woke her. It was bitter on the bare mountainside; the ground was all crisp with white frost, and when Nerryn started walking uphill she crunched through it, leaving deep, black footprints. Unless she kept moving she knew that she would probably die of cold, so she climbed on, higher and higher; the stars came out, showing more frost-covered slopes ahead and all around, while the forest far below curled around the flank of the mountain like black fur.

Through the night she went on climbing, and by sunrise she had reached the foot of a steep slope of ice-covered boulders. When she tried to climb over these she only slipped back again.

What shall I do now? Nerryn wondered. She stood blowing on her frozen fingers and thought, "I must go on or I shall die here of cold. I will play a tune on the harp to warm my fingers and my wits."

She unslung the harp. It was hard to play, for her fingers were almost numb and at first refused to obey; but while she had climbed the hill, a very sweet, lively tune had come into her head, and she struggled and struggled until her stubborn fingers found the right notes to play it. Once she played the tune—twice—

and the stones on the slope above began to roll and shift. She played a third time and, with a thunderous roar, the whole pile broke loose and went sliding down the mountainside. Nerryn was only just able to dart aside out of the way before the frozen mass careered past, sending up a smoking dust of ice.

Trembling a little, she went on up the hill, and now she came to a gate in a great wall, set about with towers. The gate stood open, and so she walked through.

"Surely this must be my father's city," she thought.

But when she stood inside the gate, her heart sank, and she remembered old Saroon's words. For the city that must once have been bright with gold and colored stone and gay with music was all silent; not a soul walked the streets and the houses, under thick covering of frost, were burned and blackened by fire.

And, what was still more frightening, when Nerryn looked through the doorways into the houses, she could see people standing or sitting or lying, frozen still like statues, as the cold had caught them while they worked, or slept, or sat at dinner.

"Where shall I go now?" she thought. "It would have been better to stay with Saroon in the forest. When night comes I shall only freeze to death in this place."

But still she went on, almost tiptoeing in the frosty silence of the city, looking into doorways and through gates, until she came to a building that was larger than any other, built with a high roof and many pillars of white marble. The fire had not touched it.

"This must be the temple," she thought, remembering the tale Saroon had told, and she walked between the pillars, which glittered like white candles in the light from the rising sun. Inside there was a vast hall, and many people standing frozen, just as they had been when they came to pray for deliverance from their trouble. They had offerings with them—honey and cakes and white doves and lambs and precious ointment. At the back of the hall the people wore rough clothes of homespun cloth, but farther forward Nerryn saw wonderful robes embroidered with gold and copper thread, made of rich materials, and trimmed with fur and sparkling stones. And up in the very front, kneeling on the steps of the altar, was a man who was finer than all the rest, and Nerryn thought he must have been the king himself. His hair and long beard were white, his cloak was purple, and on his head were three crowns, one gold, one copper, and one of ivory. Nerryn stole up to him and touched the fingers that held a gold staff, but they were ice-cold and still as marble, like all the rest.

A sadness came over her as she looked at the people and she thought, "What use to them are their fine robes now? Why did the goddess punish them? What did they do wrong?"

But there was no answer to her question.

"I had better leave this place before I am frozen as well," she thought. "The goddess may be angry with me, too, for coming here. But first I will play for her on my harp, as I have not brought any offering."

So she took her harp and began to play. She played all the tunes she could remember, and last of all she played the one that had come into her head as she climbed the mountain.

At the noise of her playing, frost began to fall in white showers from the roof of the temple, and from the rafters and pillars and the clothes of the

motionless people. Then the king sneezed. Then
there was a stirring noise, like the sound of a winter
stream when the ice begins to melt. Then someone laughed—a loud, clear laugh. And just as outside
the town the pile of frozen rocks had started to move
and topple when Nerryn played, so now the whole
gathering of people began to stretch themselves and
turn around and look at one another and smile. And
as she went on playing they began to dance.

The dancing spread, out of the temple and down
the streets. People in the houses stood up and danced.
Still dancing, they fetched brooms and swept away the
heaps of frost that kept falling from the rooftops with
the sound of the music. They fetched old wooden
pipes and tabors out of the cellars that had escaped the
fire, so that when Nerryn stopped playing at last, quite

tired out, the music still went on. All day and all night, for thirty days, the music lasted, until the houses were rebuilt, the streets clean, and not a speck of frost remained in the city.

But the king beckoned Nerryn aside when she stopped playing, and they sat down on the steps of the temple.

"My child," he said, "where did you get that harp?"

"Sir, I made it out of fishbones after a picture of my father's harp that an old woman made for me."

"And what was your father's name, child, and where is he now?"

"Sir, he is dead in the forest, but here is a piece of a tablet with his name on it."

And Nerryn held out the little fragment with Heramon the harper's name written. When he saw it, great tears formed in the king's eyes and began to roll down his cheeks.

"Sir," Nerryn said, "what is the matter? Why do you weep?"

"I weep for my son Heramon, who is lost, and I weep for joy because my grandchild has returned to me."

Then the king embraced Nerryn and took her to his palace and had robes of fur and velvet put on her, and there was great happiness and much feasting. And the king told Nerryn how, many years ago, the goddess was angered because the people had grown so greedy for gold from her mountain that they spent their lives in digging and mining, day and night, and forgot to honor her with music, in her temple and in the streets, as they had been used to do. They made tools of gold, and plates and dishes and musical instruments; everything that could be was made of gold. So at last the goddess appeared among them, terrible with rage, and

put a curse on them, of burning and freezing.

"Since you prefer gold, got by burrowing in the earth, to the music that should honor me," she said, "you may keep your golden toys and little good may they do you! Let your golden harps and trumpets be silent, your flutes and pipes be dumb! I shall not come among you again until I am summoned by notes from a harp that is not made of gold, nor of silver, nor any precious metal, a harp that has never touched the earth but came from deep water, a harp that no man has ever played."

The fire burst out of the mountain, destroying houses and killing many people. The king ordered his son Heramon, who was the bravest man in the city, to cross the dangerous forest and seek far and wide until he should find the harp of which the goddess spoke. Before Heramon could depart a great cold had struck, freezing people where they stood; only just in time he caught up his little daughter from her cradle and carried her away with him.

"But now you are come back," the old king said, "you shall be queen after me, and we shall take care that the goddess is honored with music every day, in the temple and in the streets. And we will order everything that is made of gold to be thrown into the mountain torrent, so that nobody ever again shall be tempted to worship gold before the goddess."

So this was done, the king himself being the first to throw away his golden crown and staff. The river carried all the golden things down through the forest until they came to rest in Timorash's millpool, and one day, when he was fishing for carp, he pulled out the crown. Overjoyed, he ground it to powder and sold it to his neighbors for barley wine. Then he returned to the pool, hoping for more gold, but by now he was so drunk that he fell in and was drowned among a clutter of golden spades and trumpets and goblets and pickaxes.

But long before this Nerryn, with her harp on her back and astride of a white mule with knives bound to its hoofs, had ridden down the mountain to fetch Saroon as she had promised. She passed the forest safely, playing music for the vultures while the mule cut its way through the long grass. Nobody in the village recognized her, so splendidly was she dressed in fur and scarlet.

But when she came to where Saroon's hut had stood, the ground was bare, nor was there any trace that a dwelling had ever been there. And when she asked for Saroon, nobody knew the name, and the whole village declared that such a person had never been there.

Amazed and sorrowful, Nerryn returned to her grandfather. But one day, not long after, when she was alone, praying in the temple of the goddess, she heard a voice that said,

"Sing, child!"

And Nerryn was greatly astonished, for she felt she had heard the voice before, though she could not think where.

While she looked about her, wondering, the voice said again,

"Sing!"

And then Nerryn understood, and she laughed, and, taking her harp, sang a song about chopping wood, and about digging, and fishing, and the birds of the forest, and how the stream's voice changes in summer and in winter. For now she knew who had helped her to make her harp of fishbones.

The Selkie's Cap

SAMANTHA LEE

Donal came up from the bay, shook himself like a dog, and headed off in the direction of town. He crunched purposefully over the gravel, eyes flicking right and left, searching out a marker in the sand dunes that divided the beach from the patchwork fields beyond.

A hundred yards down he found what he was looking for, a hump of bladder wrack, dark as a beached whale. The perfect hiding place. Taking off his cap, he tucked it into the belly of the mound. Then he set off again.

The early autumn breeze held the promise of a hard winter to come. It ruffled his short dark hair and made his eyes smart. Under his Fair Isle pullover, relic of a long drowned sailor, he shivered, half in cold, half in fear.

It was the first time he'd been away from home alone, and he wondered whether his relatives weren't right when they said he wasn't old enough for such a quest. But Gregor would not last the winter, and his wish was to see his wife again before he died. No one else in the family would speak her name, let alone volunteer, and so eventually they'd let Donal go.

As he hit the high road, a dirt track bordered by dry stone walls and scrub grass, the weathercock on the distant steeple winked like a lighthouse in the setting sun. Lowering his head against the wind, he trudged on.

Over the brow of the first hill a boy sat astride a wooden stile, aimlessly throwing stones at a dandelion. He was younger than Donal by about three years and had the emaciated look of the half-fed and often beaten.

He and Donal sized each other up.

"Where did you spring from?" the boy said.

Donal waved vaguely in the direction of the shore. "I'm looking for my mammy," he said. "She's been gone a while and my da's not well and he thinks she might be being kept against her will."

"Held for ransom, eh?" said the boy. "Is she a princess, then?"

Donal shook his head.

"I didn't think so," said the boy. "Not by the state of your jersey anyway. Would you like some tea?"

"No, I'll need to get on."

"All the more for us." The boy pointed to the rough stone croft that clung like a limpet to the barren hillside. "But if you change your mind, that's our house. I'll ask my mammy if she's heard of any kidnapping hereabouts," he said. And with a final wave, he raced off up the slope.

Donal waited until the dark came down in earnest, then followed him up the heather-covered drumlin to the pinpoint of light that was the cottage window.

Inside, a woman in a worn dress stood stirring a panful of porridge with a wooden spoon. The boy from the road was washing his hands in an old iron sink. Two other children, about three and five respectively, sat at a table, spoons at the ready. A baby, not yet walking, played in the hearth with a collie pup.

"I met a laddie in the lane," said the boy. "His mammy's been kidnapped. She's a princess."

"Whist, Rory," said the woman. "You're worse than your da with your stories."

"It's true," protested the boy. "He said she'd been gone a good while and that she was being kept against her will. His da is on his last legs," he added dramatically. "And he's been sent to find her."

The woman turned, almost upsetting the porridge. Donal, nose pressed to the pane, felt his heart lurch in his chest.

It was his mother. He had not hoped to find her so soon, but there she was, her hair somewhat faded with the passage of years but her face still beautiful enough to stop hearts. She turned her limpid brown eyes to the window and Donal raised an arm in greeting.

"What're you up to, you skulking devil?"

A rough hand grabbed him by the collar, shaking him like a rat. The whiskey breath almost overpowered him as he struggled to extricate himself from the vise-like grip. But the man was twice his size and had the brute strength born of years of back-breaking work done in all weathers.

He swung Donal toward him, hand raised to strike, then his face blanched as he took in the dark eyes and the small pink ears set close to the head. His grip loosened momentarily and Donal, taking his chance, squirmed free and hared down the hillside as fast as his feet would carry him.

"Come back you thieving throwback." The harsh voice sliced through the night like a harpoon. But Donal was well away, leaping the wall into the lane, legs pumping like pistons all the way back to the beach.

Coming to rest at last by the bladder wrack hummock, he crouched down, breath like fire in his lungs, and scrabbled beneath the soft damp weed for his cap.

What was his mother doing with such a man? Why didn't she come home?

He thought of his own father, gentle, protective, as different from that cruel bully as chalk was from cheese. Anger bubbled up inside him. Whatever the danger, he must face his mother and ask her for an explanation. He owed Gregor that at the very least.

Tucking the cap into its hiding place once more, he rose and began the long trudge back to the cottage.

Hugging the wall for safety, he climbed the hill at a crouch, moving from the shadow of one boulder to another until he stood in the lee of the window sill. There he waited, heart pounding, gathering his courage. Then slowly, slowly, he stood up and peeped inside.

The table had been cleared, the children put to bed in a curtained alcove. The man lay, mouth ajar, snoring on the rocker. He had the red hair and freckles of a native islander. His skin, once eggshell pale, was veined by whisky and weather.

The woman sat by the fire, a half-knitted sock held loosely in her lap, staring vacantly into the dying embers of the turf. There was a cruel bruise on her right cheekbone. As Donal made to tap, she laid her work aside and, wiping her eyes with the back of her hand, tiptoed to the door and stepped out into the silence of the pale, Hebridean night.

Down below, the still sea glittered under a waning moon. Gathering her shawl around her shoulders, the woman eased the door shut behind her and walked a few paces down the hill. Then she tilted her face to the sky and gave a small, shrill bark.

Donal barked in reply, moving to his mother and

wrapping his arms around her, burying his face in her waist.

"Whist," she said, stroking his sleek head. "We dinna want the man to hear us."

"Gregor's dying," said Donal fiercely. "He needs you. You must come."

"I cannot."

"Why can you not? How can you stay with that monster? Why did you leave us?" And much to his chagrin, for he had not wept in years, he began to cry.

His mother continued to stroke and to soothe.

"I never left you, bairn. There has not been a moment these last seven years when I have not thought about you both."

"Then why?"

"I was young and foolish. And the man was handsome then. A wordsmith, a poet. He charmed me with his fine verses and tales of the dancing in the town. I only meant to look. But he had seen me hide the cap. And he stole it. And though I have searched high and low I've never been able to find it. And so I am trapped here. And there's nothing I can do."

"I'll find it," promised Donal. "And then you'll come home."

"Then I'll come home."

"What about the bairns?" Donal, suddenly contrite, remembered the desolation he had felt after his mother had gone.

"Someone will take them in," said his mother sadly. "Wherever they go they'll be better off. But I doubt if it'll come to that. The cap has vanished. I fear he has destroyed it."

For a full week Donal stalked the soul stealer. Like an

otter after a sea trout, he slithered facedown in the heather, lurking behind walls, following in the man's wake each day as he took the coracle out to the fishing grounds. During these expeditions he just managed to replenish his food store. But he dared not close his eyes for fear that his quarry might choose that time to return to the scene of the crime.

At night, while the island slept, he scoured the hillside, upturning every stone, exploring every cave and cranny. When that was done he searched the beach, end to end.

But of the cap there was no sign.

Eventually, on the seventh day, dog-tired and weary to the bone, he made his way into town, to the tavern, where the man and several of his cronies were swilling beer and singing raucous songs.

Shivering with cold, Donal kept vigil in the street outside, watching through the window, straining his ears for a word or sign that would lead him to the thing he sought.

Around dusk it began to rain. Not the sudden, fresh downpour that sweeps the streets and clears the air, but that steady, bone-drenching drizzle that knows neither beginning nor end.

After an hour of it, Donal, asleep on his feet, decided to take refuge in the large gray church whose steeple had beckoned to him his first day ashore. Finding it locked, he dodged into the building next door. There was lettering over the lintel that he could not decipher. Six runes in all, the first and last identical. Like twin peaks of a magic mountain.

Inside there were many wonderful things on display, and for the first time in several days he felt at home. Here was the skeleton of a shark, there the jawbone of

a whale, shells and stones and round gold coins, the sort that littered the seabed where the old Spanish treasure ship had sunk. There was a coracle, too, and a ship in a bottle. Donal was just wondering how they got such a large rig through such a small opening when a voice behind him nearly made him jump out of his skin.

"You're dripping all over my nice clean floor," it said.

Donal turned to find a pleasant-looking woman in tweeds, gray hair pulled back in a bun, regarding him with an exasperated expression through horn-rimmed glasses.

"You're not from hereabouts," she said. "What are you doing in the museum?"

Donal flattened himself against the wall. "It's raining," he faltered.

"I can see that, said the woman. "You've brought most of it in with you. Where's your mother? Why aren't you at school?"

Donal shook his head, wordlessly.

"Well, you can't stay here. We're just about to close."

The woman took a large umbrella out of a stand by the door and made to lock up.

"I want to go home." Donal drooped with fatigue.

"Are you lost?"

Donal nodded.

"Poor boy." The woman patted him on the head, drew back a saturated hand. "Heavens, you're soaked. If you don't dry off soon you'll catch your death. I'll tell you what, you wait here and I'll pop across and check at the station. Your mother's probably over there worried sick about you. While I'm gone you can have a look at our prize exhibit. It's over there in the corner."

39

Donal dragged unwilling feet across the room to the glass case resting on a fat plinth beneath an arched window. Inside, nestled on a bed of red velvet, lay a small, gray, conical object made of animal fur.

"It's a Selkie's cap," said the woman, as though he didn't know. "They say that the seal people can change into humans at will. But if they lose the cap they can't get back. It's only a legend, of course, but it makes a nice story, don't you think?"

"Where did you get it?" Donal tried not to sound too interested. The cap might be anyone's. Might be a hundred years old. Might not be his mother's at all.

"A man brought it in. A local. About seven years ago. Said he found it on the beach."

That settled it.

Donal grinned. Such cunning. Hiding it in plain view.

"Can I touch it?" he asked, trying the lid.

"Certainly not." The woman was outraged. "Don't touch anything. I'll be right back."

And she darted off into the rain.

Donal looked around for something with which to prise open the lid, found nothing. Finally, in desperation and because time was short, he lifted a large marble bust of some long-dead notable and crashed it through the glass. Then he grabbed the cap and fled from the building.

He was half-way down the road when he heard the familiar voice, bellowing "Stop, thief." Never halting in his stride, he looked over his shoulder. The woman was dancing up and down in the gathering dusk, gesticulating frantically to a man in a dark blue suit and a peaked cap who stood by her side. Curious onlookers were beginning to emerge from adjacent

shops to see what the commotion was about.

And then the tavern doors burst open and a red-headed man staggered out, swaying on drunken legs, crowded on to the rain-drenched pavement by a quartet of equally inebriated companions. A word from the woman and he was suddenly sober, lurching off down the cobblestones in hot pursuit.

Donal ran as he had never run before, the gathering mob howling after. Past houses and shops, stores and garages he raced, till the dwellings dwindled and he was once more in open country.

Still the rain pelted down. He shut his eyes against its ferocity, running blind, trusting to his instinct to keep him from stumbling, while behind him his pursuers bayed their bloodlust to the darkening sky.

Down the road he fled, fording the stone wall at a

breach in the masonry where the fallen stones made a handy step-over. Cutting across country, he powered toward the solitary cottage, his mother's passport home clutched in one sweating hand.

Bursting into the house he grabbed the startled woman by the arm, dragging her down the hill toward the sea and safety. Behind her, the baby began to cry and she half-turned to look back.

Then the crowd rounded the corner, armed to the teeth with sticks, stones, broken bottles, anything they could lay their hands on along the way.

Donal climbed the stile and his mother followed, catching her apron on a spur of wood, worrying it free, following him across the dunes and along the beach to the hillock of seaweed and the second cap.

When, moments later, the crowd crested the dunes, blood up to batter and bruise, woman and child had gone.

The man with the red hair and the biggest stick dropped to his knees and howled his loss into the approaching storm.

"Moraaaaag."

The guttural human cry echoed across the water, almost obscuring the thrumming of the rain. As if in answer the sky threw back a bolt of lightning, electrifying the air, illuminating the coastline.

Out in the bay two sleek gray heads bobbed side by side, swimming strongly for the sanctuary of the open sea.

The Back of the North Wind

GEORGE MACDONALD

The following story comes from the novel At the Back of
the North Wind. *It was written over a hundred years ago,
so it is set in Victorian times. It's the story of a young boy
called Diamond, who is the son of a coachman to the
wealthy Mr. Coleman. Diamond befriends the North Wind,
who takes him on many adventures. In this extract,
Diamond travels to the home of the North Wind itself.*

When Diamond went to breakfast, he found
his father and mother already seated at the
table. They were both busy with their bread
and butter, and Diamond sat himself down in his
usual place. His mother looked up at him, and, after
watching him for a moment, said:

"I don't think the boy is looking well, husband."

"Don't you? Well, I don't know. I think he looks
pretty bobbish. How do you feel yourself, Diamond,
my boy?"

"Quite well, thank you, Father; at least, I think I've
got a little headache."

"There! I told you," said his father and mother both
at once.

"The child's very poorly," added his mother.

"The child's quite well," added his father.

And then they both laughed.

"You see," said his mother, "I've had a letter from my sister at Sandwich."

"Sleepy old hole!" said his father.

"Don't abuse the place; there's good people in it," said his mother.

"Right, old lady," returned his father; "only I don't believe there are more than two pair of carriage horses in the whole blessed place."

"Well, people can get to heaven without carriages— or coachmen either, husband. Not that I should like to go without *my* coachman, you know. But about the boy?"

"What boy?"

"That boy, there, staring at you with his goggle eyes."

"Have I got goggle eyes, Mother?" asked Diamond, a little dismayed.

"Not too goggle," said his mother, who was quite proud of her boy's eyes, only did not want to make him vain. "Not too goggle; only you need not stare so."

"Well, what about him?" said his father.

"I told you I had got a letter."

"Yes, from your sister; not from Diamond."

"La, husband! You've got out of bed the wrong leg first this morning, I do believe."

"I always get out with both at once," said his father, laughing.

"Well, listen then. His aunt wants the boy to go down and see her."

"And that's why you want to make out that he ain't looking well."

"No more he is. I think he had better go."

"Well, I don't care, if you can find the money," said his father.

"I'll manage that," said his mother; and so it was agreed that Diamond should go to Sandwich.

I will not describe the preparations Diamond made. You would have thought he had been going on a three months' voyage. Nor will I describe the journey, for our business is now at the place. He was met at the station by his aunt, a cheerful middle-aged woman, and conveyed in safety to the sleepy old town, as his father had called it. And no wonder that it was sleepy, for it was nearly dead of old age.

Diamond went about staring with his beautiful goggle eyes, at the quaint old streets, and the shops, and the houses. Everything looked very strange, indeed; for here was a town abandoned by its nurse, the sea, like an old oyster left on the shore till it gaped for weariness. It used to be one of the five chief seaports in England, but it began to hold itself too high, and the consequence was the sea grew less and less intimate with it, gradually drew back, and kept more to itself, till at length it left it high and dry: Sandwich was a seaport no more; the sea went on with its own tide-business a long way off, and forgot it. Of course it went to sleep, and had no more to do with ships. That's what comes to cities and nations, and boys and girls, who say, "I can do without *your* help. I'm enough for myself."

Diamond soon made great friends with an old woman who kept a toy shop, for his mother had given him twopence for pocket money before he left, and he had gone into her shop to spend it, and she got talking to him. She looked very funny, because she had not got any teeth, but Diamond liked her, and went often to her shop, although he had nothing to spend there after the twopence was gone.

One afternoon he had been wandering rather wearily about the streets for some time. It was a hot day, and he felt tired. As he passed the toyshop, he stepped in.

"Please may I sit down for a minute on this box?" he said, thinking the old woman was somewhere in the shop. But he got no answer, and sat down without one. Around him were a great many toys of all prices, from a penny up to shillings. All at once he heard a gentle whirring somewhere amongst them. It made him start and look behind him. There were the sails of a windmill going around and around almost close to his ear. He thought at first it must be one of those toys that are wound up and go with clockwork; but no, it was a common penny toy, with the windmill at the end of a whistle, and when the whistle blows the windmill goes. But the wonder was that there was no one at the whistle end blowing, and yet the sails were turning around and around—now faster, now slower, now faster again.

"What can it mean?" said Diamond aloud.

"It means me," said the tiniest voice he had ever heard.

"Who are you, please?" asked Diamond.

"Well, really, I begin to be ashamed of you," said the voice. "I wonder how long it will be before you know me; or how often I might take you in before you get sharp enough to suspect me. You are as bad as a baby that doesn't know his mother in a new bonnet."

"Not quite so bad as that, dear North Wind," said Diamond, "for I didn't see you at all, and indeed I don't see you yet, although I recognize your voice. Do grow a little, please."

"Not a hair's breadth," said the voice, and it was the smallest voice that ever spoke. "What are you doing here?"

"I am come to see my aunt. But, please, North Wind, why didn't you come back for me in the church that night?"

"I did. I carried you safe home. All the time you were dreaming about the glass apostles, you were lying in my arms."

"I'm so glad," said Diamond. "I thought that must be it, only I wanted to hear you say so. Did you sink the ship, then?"

"Yes."

"And drown everybody?"

"Not quite. One boat got away with six or seven men in it."

"How could the boat swim when the ship couldn't?"

"Of course I had some trouble with it. I had to contrive a bit, and manage the waves a little. When they're once thoroughly waked up, I have a good deal of trouble with them sometimes. They're apt to get stupid with tumbling over each other's heads. That's when they're fairly at it. However, the boat got to a desert island before noon next day."

"And what good will come of that?"

"I don't know. I obeyed orders. Good-bye."

"Oh! Stay, North Wind, *do* stay!" cried Diamond, dismayed to see the windmill get slower and slower.

"What is it, my dear child?" said North Wind, and the windmill began turning again so swiftly that Diamond could scarcely see it. "What a big voice you've got! And what a noise you do make with it! What is it you want? I have little to do, but that little must be done."

"I want you to take me to the country at the back of the north wind."

"That's not so easy," said North Wind, and was silent for so long that Diamond thought she was gone indeed. But after he had quite given her up, the voice began again.

"I almost wish old Herodotus had held his tongue about it. Much he knew of it!"

"Why do you wish that, North Wind?"

"Because then that clergyman would never have heard of it, and set you wanting to go. But we shall see. We shall see. You must go home now, my dear, for you don't seem very well, and I'll see what can be done for you. Don't wait for me. I've got to break a few of old Goody's toys: she's thinking too much of her new stock. Two or three will do. There! Go now."

Diamond rose, quite sorry, and without a word left the shop, and went home.

It soon appeared that his mother had been right about him, for that same afternoon his head began to ache very much, and he had to go to bed.

He awoke in the middle of the night. The lattice window of his room had blown open, and the curtains of his little bed were swinging about in the wind.

"If that should be North Wind now!" thought Diamond.

But the next moment he heard someone closing the window, and his aunt came to the bedside. She put her hand on his face, and said:

"How's your head, dear?"

"Better, Auntie, I think."

"Would you like something to drink?"

"Oh yes! I should, please."

So his aunt gave him some lemonade, for she had been used to nursing sick people, and Diamond felt very much refreshed, and laid his head down again to go very fast asleep, as he thought. And so he did, but only to come awake again, as a fresh burst of wind blew the lattice open a second time. The same moment he found himself in a cloud of North Wind's hair, with her beautiful face, set in it like a moon, bending over him.

"Quick, Diamond!" she said. "I have found such a chance!"

"But I'm not well," said Diamond.

"I know that, but you will be better for a little fresh air. You shall have plenty of that."

"You want me to go, then?"

"Yes, I do. It won't hurt you."

"Very well," said Diamond; and getting out of the bedclothes, he jumped into North Wind's arms.

"We must make haste before your aunt comes," said she, as she glided out of the open lattice and left it swinging.

The moment Diamond felt her arms fold around him he began to feel better. It was a moonless night, and very dark, with glimpses of stars when the clouds parted.

"I used to dash the waves about here," said North Wind, "where cows and sheep are feeding now; but we shall soon get to them. There they are."

And Diamond, looking down, saw the white glimmer of breaking water far below him.

"You see, Diamond," said North Wind, "it is very difficult for me to get you to the back of the north wind, for that country lies in the very north itself, and of course I can't blow northward."

"Why not?" asked Diamond.

"You little silly!" said North Wind. "Don't you see that if I were to blow northward I should be South Wind, and that is as much as to say that one person could be two persons?"

"But how can you ever get home at all, then?"

"You are quite right—that is my home, though I

never get farther than the outer door. I sit on the doorstep and hear the voices inside. I am nobody there, Diamond."

"I'm very sorry."

"Why?"

"That you should be nobody."

"Oh, I don't mind it. Dear little man! You will be very glad someday to be nobody yourself. But you can't understand that now, and you had better not try; for if you do, you will be certain to go fancying some egregious nonsense, and making yourself miserable about it."

"Then I won't," said Diamond.

"There's a good boy. It will all come in good time."

"But you haven't told me how you get to the doorstep, you know."

"It is easy enough for me. I have only to consent to be nobody, and there I am. I draw into myself, and there I am on the doorstep. But you can easily see, or you have less sense than I think, that to drag you, you heavy thing, along with me, would take centuries, and I could not give the time to it."

"Oh, I'm so sorry!" said Diamond.

"What for now, pet?"

"That I'm so heavy for you. I would be lighter if I could, but I don't know how."

"You silly darling! Why, I could toss you a hundred miles from me if I liked. It is only when I am going home that I shall find you heavy."

"Then you are going home with me?"

"Of course. Did I not come to fetch you just for that?"

"But all this time you must be going southward."

"Yes. Of course I am."

"How can you be taking me northward, then?"

"A very sensible question. But you shall see. I will get rid of a few of these clouds—only they do come up so fast! It's like trying to blow a brook dry. There! What do you see now?"

"I think I see a little boat, away there, down below."

"A little boat, indeed! Well! She's a yacht of two hundred tons; and the captain of it is a friend of mine; for he is a man of good sense, and can sail his craft well. I've helped him many a time when he little thought it. I've heard him grumbling at me when I was doing the very best I could for him. Why, I've carried him eighty miles a day, again and again, right north."

"He must have dodged for that," said Diamond, who had been watching the vessels, and had seen that they went other ways than the wind blew.

"Of course he must. But don't you see, it was the best I could do? I couldn't be South Wind. And besides it gave him a share in the business. It is not good at all—mind that, Diamond—to do everything for those you love, and not give them a share in the doing. It's not kind. It's making too much of yourself, my child. If I had been South Wind, he would only have smoked his pipe all day, and made himself stupid."

"But how could he be a man of sense and grumble at you when you were doing your best for him?"

"Oh! You must make allowances," said North Wind, "or you will never do justice to anybody. You do understand, then, that a captain may sail north—"

"In spite of a north wind—yes," supplemented Diamond.

"Now, I do think you must be stupid, my dear," said North Wind. "Suppose the north wind did not blow, where would he be then?"

"Why then the south wind would carry him."

"So you think that when the north wind stops the south wind blows. Nonsense. If I didn't blow, the captain couldn't sail his eighty miles a day. No doubt South Wind would carry him faster, but South Wind is sitting on her doorstep then, and if I stopped there would be a dead calm. So you are all wrong to say he can sail north in spite of me; he sails north by my help, and my help alone. You see that, Diamond?"

"Yes, I do, North Wind. I am stupid, but I don't want to be stupid."

"Good boy! I am going to blow you north in that little craft, one of the finest that ever sailed the sea. Here we are, right over it. I shall be blowing against you; you will be sailing against me; and all will be just as we want it. The captain won't get on so fast as he would like, but he will get on, and so shall we. I'm just going to put you on board. Do you see in front of the tiller—that thing the man is working, now to one side, now to the other—a round thing like the top of a drum?"

"Yes," said Diamond.

"Below that is where they keep their spare sails, and some stores of that sort. I am going to blow that cover off. The same moment I will drop you on deck, and you must tumble in. Don't be afraid, it is of no depth, and you will fall on a roll of sailcloth. You will find it nice and warm and dry—only dark; and you will know I am near you by every roll and pitch of the vessel. Coil yourself up and go to sleep. The yacht shall be my cradle, and you shall be my baby."

"Thank you, dear North Wind. I am not a bit afraid," said Diamond.

In a moment they were on a level with the bulwarks, and North Wind sent the hatch of the afterstore rattling away over the deck to leeward. The next, Diamond found himself in the dark, for he had tumbled through the hole as North Wind had told him, and the cover was replaced over his head. Away he went rolling to leeward, for the wind began all at once to blow hard. He heard the call of the captain, and the loud trampling of the men over his head, as they hauled at the main sheet to get the boom on board that they might take in a reef in the mainsail. Diamond felt about until he had found what seemed the most comfortable place, and there he snuggled down and lay.

Hours after hours, a great many of them, went by; and still Diamond lay there. He never felt in the least tired or impatient, for a strange pleasure filled his heart. The straining of the masts, the creaking of the boom, the singing of the ropes, the banging of the blocks as they put the vessel about, all fell in with the roaring of the wind above, the surge of the waves past her sides, and the thud with which every now and then one would strike her; while through it all Diamond could hear the gurgling, rippling, talking flow of the water against her planks, as she slipped through it, lying now on this side, now on that—like a subdued air running through the grand music his North Wind was making about him to keep him from tiring as they sped on toward the country at the back of her doorstep.

How long this lasted Diamond had no idea. He seemed to fall asleep sometimes, only through the sleep he heard the sounds going on. At length the weather seemed to get worse. The confusion and trampling of feet grew more frequent over his head; the vessel lay over more and more on her side, and went roaring through the waves, which banged and thumped at her as if in anger. All at once arose a terrible uproar. The hatch was blown off; a cold fierce wind swept in upon him; and a long arm came with it that laid hold of him and lifted him out. The same moment he saw the little vessel far below him righting herself. She had taken in all her sails and lay now tossing on the waves like a sea bird with folded wings. A short distance to the south lay a much larger vessel, with two or three sails set, and toward it North Wind was carrying Diamond. It was a German ship, on its way to the North Pole.

"That vessel down there will give us a lift now," said North Wind; "and after that I must do the best I can."

She managed to hide him among the flags of the big ship, which were all snugly stowed away, and on and on they sped toward the north. At length one night she whispered in his ear, "Come on deck, Diamond"; and he got up at once and crept on deck. Everything looked very strange. Here and there on all sides were huge masses of floating ice, looking like cathedrals, and castles, and crags, while away beyond was a blue sea.

"Is the sun rising or setting?" asked Diamond.

"Neither or both, which you please. I can hardly tell which myself. If he is setting now, he will be rising the next morning."

"What a strange light it is!" said Diamond. "I have heard that the sun doesn't go to bed all the summer in these parts. Miss Coleman told me that. I suppose he feels very sleepy, and that is why the light he sends out looks so like a dream."

"That will account for it well enough for all practical purposes," said North Wind.

Some of the icebergs were drifting northward: one was passing very near the ship. North Wind seized Diamond and with a single bound lighted on one of them—a huge thing, with sharp pinnacles and great clefts. The same instant a wind began to blow from the south. North Wind hurried Diamond down the north side of the iceberg, stepping by its jags and splintering; for this berg never got far enough south to be melted and smoothed by the summer sun. She brought him to a cave near the water, where she entered, and, letting Diamond go, sat down as if weary on a ledge of ice.

Diamond seated himself on the other side, and for a while was enraptured with the color of the air inside the cave. It was a deep, dazzling, lovely blue, deeper than the deepest blue of the sky. The blue seemed to be in constant motion, like the blackness when you press your eyeballs with your fingers, boiling and sparkling. But when he looked across to North Wind he was frightened; her face was worn and livid.

"What is the matter with you, dear North Wind?" he said.

"Nothing much. I feel very faint. But you mustn't mind it, for I can bear it quite well. South Wind always blows me faint. If it were not for the cool of the thick ice between me and her, I should faint altogether. Indeed, as it is, I fear I must vanish."

Diamond stared at her in terror, for he saw that her form and face were growing, not small, but transparent, like something dissolving, not in water, but in light. He could see the side of the blue cave through her very heart. And she melted away till all that was left was a pale face, like the moon in the morning, with two great lucid eyes in it.

"I am going, Diamond," she said.

"Does it hurt you?" asked Diamond.

"It's very uncomfortable," she answered; "but I don't mind it, for I shall come all right again before long. I thought I should be able to go with you all the way, but I cannot. You must not be frightened though. Just go straight on, and you will come out all right. You'll find me on the doorstep."

As she spoke, her face too faded quite away, only Diamond thought he could still see her eyes shining through the blue. When he went closer, however, he found that what he thought her eyes were only two hollows in the ice. North Wind was quite gone; and Diamond would have cried, if he had not trusted her so thoroughly. So he sat still in the blue air of the cavern listening to the wash and ripple of the water all about the base of the iceberg, as it sped on and on into the open sea northward. It was an excellent craft to go with a current, for there was twice as much of it below water as above. But a light south wind was blowing, too, and so it went fast.

After a little while Diamond went out and sat on the edge of his floating island, and looked down into the ocean beneath him. The white sides of the berg reflected so much light below the water, that he could see far down into the green abyss. Sometimes he fancied he saw the eyes of North Wind looking up at him from below, but the fancy never lasted beyond the moment of its birth. And the time passed he did not know how, for he felt as if he were in a dream. When he got tired of the green water, he went into the blue cave; and when he got tired of the blue cave he went out and gazed all about him on the blue sea, ever sparkling in the sun, which kept wheeling about the sky, never going below the horizon. But he chiefly gazed northward to see whether any land were appearing. All this time he never wanted to eat. He broke off little bits of the berg now and then and sucked them, and he thought them very nice.

At length, one time he came out of his cave, he spied, far off upon the horizon, a shining peak that rose into the sky like the top of some tremendous iceberg; and his vessel was bearing him straight toward it. As it went on the peak rose and rose higher and higher above the horizon; and other peaks rose after it, with sharp edges and jagged ridges connecting them. Diamond thought this must be the place he was going to; and he was right; for the mountains rose and rose, till he saw the line of the coast at their feet, and at length the iceberg drove into a little bay, all around which were lofty precipices with snow on their tops, and streaks of ice down their sides. The berg floated slowly up to a projecting rock. Diamond stepped on shore, and without looking behind him began to follow a natural path that led windingly toward the top of the precipice.

When he reached it, he found himself on a broad table of ice, along which he could walk without much difficulty. Before him, at a considerable distance, rose a lofty ridge of ice, which shot up into fantastic pinnacles and towers and battlements. The air was very cold, and seemed somehow dead, for there was not the slightest breath of wind.

In the center of the ridge before him appeared a gap like the opening of a valley. But as he walked toward it, gazing, and wondering whether that could be the way he had to take, he saw that what had appeared a gap was the form of a woman seated against the ice front of the ridge, leaning forward with her hands in her lap, and her hair hanging down to the ground.

"It is North Wind on her doorstep," said Diamond joyfully, and hurried on.

He soon came up to the place, and there the form sat, like one of the great figures at the door of an Egyptian temple, motionless, with drooping arms and head. Then Diamond grew frightened, because she did not move nor speak. He was sure it was North Wind, but he thought she must be dead at last. Her face was white as the snow, her eyes were blue as the air in the ice cave, and her hair hung down straight, like icicles. She had on a greenish robe, like the color in the hollows of a glacier seen from far off.

He stood up before her and gazed fearfully into her face for a few minutes before he ventured to speak. At length, with a great effort and a trembling voice, he faltered out:

"North Wind!"

"Well, child?" said the form, without lifting its head.

"Are you ill, dear North Wind?"

"No. I am waiting."

"What for?"

"Till I'm wanted."

"You don't care for me anymore," said Diamond, almost crying now.

"Yes, I do. Only I can't show it. All my love is down at the bottom of my heart. But I feel it bubbling there."

"What do you want me to do next, dear North Wind?" said Diamond, wishing to show his love by being obedient.

"What do you want to do yourself?"

"I want to go into the country at your back."

"Then you must go through me."

"I don't know what you mean."

"I mean just what I say. You must walk on as if I were an open door, and go right through me."

"But that will hurt you."

"Not in the least. It will hurt you, though."

"I don't mind that, if you tell me to do it."

"Do it," said North Wind.

Diamond walked toward her instantly. When he reached her knees, he put out his hand to lay it on her, but nothing was there save an intense cold. He walked on. Then all grew white about him; and the cold stung him like fire. He walked on still, groping through the whiteness. It thickened about him. At last, it got into his heart, and he lost all sense. I would say that he fainted—only whereas in common faints all grows black about you, he felt swallowed up in whiteness. It was when he reached North Wind's heart that he fainted and fell. But as he fell, he rolled over the threshold, and it was thus that Diamond got to the back of the north wind.

The Pit of Wings

RAMSEY CAMPBELL

Since before dawn Ryre had been riding through the forest. Except that he disliked sleeping on the move, he would have trusted himself to his steed. Instead he sought calm at the center of himself, as he'd begun to learn to do. But the oppression of the forest clung to him. Time had drowned in the green depths.

Great leaves sailed by above him. Each was shaped like an inverted ribbed umbrella spiked on a massive trunk, and each was broader than the stretch of his body from toes to fingertips. As the trunk mounted, so the leaves dwindled; the highest would be no wider than Ryre's head. But he could see none of this. Beneath the unbroken canopy of the lowest leaves, even the dawn had been no more than a greening of the dimness.

The forest road was a tunnel formed by cutting leaves; once cut, they never grew again. They rustled, withered, beneath his steed's pads. The constant sound distracted him as he listened for a hint of the sea, a breeze to stir the stagnant air.

Sometimes, especially before dawn, he'd heard a flapping high above him. It must be the gliders—the highest leaves that, having shed scales of themselves, drifted away bearing seeds. But could those leaves make such a large, lethargic sound?

Now he was caged by a lingering clamor of rain.

He'd heard the storm coming, high and distant at first, advancing and descending through the forest. He could only shelter close to a trunk while the deafening rain poured down the trees, turning the leaves into basins of fountains. Above him the great leaf had shivered repeatedly beneath the onslaught; he'd feared drowning. Though the storm had moved on hours ago, its sounds remained. Drips seeped through the foliage to water the roots, to tap Ryre on the shoulder, to stream down his face, to coat and choke him with humidity.

He shook his head, snarling like a trapped beast— like the beast whose emblem was the V-shaped mane that widened from his shaved crown to his shoulders. He felt helplessly frustrated by the eternity of forest, the suffocating luxuriance that seemed triumphant as a mocking conqueror, the sounds whose sources he could never glimpse. He yearned for an adversary to fight.

Suddenly he put his hands over his mount's eyes. The creature halted obediently. Ryre strained his ears; impatience gripped his brow. Yes, he had heard the sound. Amid the creaking of leaves, the soft plop of rain on the decayed forest floor, the chorus of descending splashes as high leaves drooped beneath the weight of rain, there was a distant, jaggedly rhythmic thudding: axes cutting trees.

So he was nearly free of the forest. Yet the sound was not altogether heartening. As he rode forward he began to hear the dragging of chains, the cut of a whip. The oppression was lifting with the leaves, but now it was anger that shortened his breath.

Where the road dipped, he saw them. Young men whose arms looked massive as the trunks they chopped,

older men whose skin was more scarred, a few brawny women, all naked except for a strip of hide protecting the genitals: there must have been a hundred of them, toiling in small groups at the edge of the forest. From their fetters, long chains trailed toward the town that Ryre glimpsed beyond the trees. Beyond the town the sea burned calmly as sunlight trailed over the horizon.

Men, dressed like the slaves but bearing whips and swords, stalked about or squatted in shade. Most looked bored, and flicked their victims as they might have lazily fingered an itch. One stood over a fallen slave. A fresh weal glistened rawly on the victim's back; his ankles were bruised by a tangle of chain. He looked old, exhausted, further aged by suffering.

Ryre hated slavery as only a man who has been enslaved can. Fury parched his throat. Yet he could not fight a town, nor its customs, however deplorable. He made to ride by, past the corpse of one of the immense, almost brainless crawlers of the forest, which must have wormed too close to the swordsmen. Chunks of its flesh had been stripped from the bone; its eye gazed emptily at Ryre from the center of the lolling head. The slaves must have eaten the flesh raw.

The standing man grew tired of kicking his victim. He said loudly, "I'm wasting my strength. You're past your usefulness. Tonight you'll ride above the trees."

The effect of his words was immediate and dismaying. His victim soiled himself in terror. The other slaves glanced upward and shuddered; Ryre heard a distant flapping. All at once, unable to bear his inability to intervene, he urged his steed to canter.

But the slave driver had seen his glare of contempt. "Yes, ride on, unless you're seeking honest toil. We've a place for you, and chains to fit." His slow voice was

63

as viciously caressing as a whip. As he gazed up at Ryre, he licked his lips.

Ryre's grin was leisurely and mirthless. Though he could not battle slavery, he would enjoy responding to this challenge. He stared at the man as though peering beneath a stone. "Ridding the world of vermin? Yes, I'd call that honest."

The man's tongue flickered like a snake's. His smile twitched, as did his hand: nervous, or beckoning for reinforcements? "What kind of swordsman is it who lets his words fight for him?" he demanded harshly.

"No man fights with vermin. He crushes them."

Swordsmen were advancing stealthily. "Perhaps his words are a sheath to keep his sword from rusting," one said. Let them think Ryre's awareness was held by the duel of words. He would cut down his challenger when he was ready, together with anyone else who dared attack him. Unhurriedly he withdrew his sword from its sheath.

A third man spoke, drawing Ryre's attention to the far tip of the advancing crescent of men. "He'll wear our bracelet well."

His steed's uneasy movement warned Ryre. He glanced back in time to see why they were trying to distract him: a man was creeping carefully over the decayed leaves, ready to drag Ryre down and club him with a sword hilt.

Discovered, the man leapt back—but not swiftly enough. The quick slash of Ryre's blade failed to cleave his skull; instead, the sword bit lower. The man staggered away moaning, trying to hold his cheek to his face.

The others rushed at Ryre. When the original challenger flinched back from the whooping arc of the sword, however, they retreated, too. The man seemed wary not only of Ryre but also of the darkening sky. "Let him go," he snarled, trying to sound undaunted. "We've no time to waste on him—not now."

The drivers tugged the chains. It was clearly a signal, for the chains drew loudly taut and dragged their victims into the town like strings of struggling fish. Ryre saw the old man stumbling to keep up. The slaves were pulled staggering into a large wooden barn, which resounded with an uproar of metal links. The great doors thudded shut.

The sight infuriated Ryre. He was scarcely heartened by the agony of the slave driver, clutching his face as companions aided him into a structure like a barracks next to the barn. Shrugging beneath the weight of his frustration, Ryre rode into the port of Gaxanoi.

In the streets men were lighting lamps. Flames fluttered in vases of thick glass which dangled from poles sprouting next to the central gutters. The entire small town was built of wood; the dim narrow streets reminded him of the forest. But at least a chill salt wind blew through the town, which creaked like an enormous ship. Above the forest the flapping was louder.

Like the streets, the dockside was almost deserted. Ryre's mounted shadow accompanied him, jerking hugely over logs that formed walls. Seamen were entering taverns beside the wharf. On the dock, next to a lone ship, timber lay waiting to be loaded in trade for, among other commodities, chains. He grinned sourly. Gaxanoi had summed itself up.

Eventually he found the harbor master's house, overlooking the wharf. The man proved reluctant to open his door, and taciturn when he did so. At last he admitted grudgingly that there might be ships tomorrow on which Ryre could work his passage. "Stay near the wharf," he advised, already closing the door.

Ryre did so, in a tavern, once he had stabled his steed nearby. The streets resembled decks of a ship of the dead. The only sounds of life were the clatter and panting of a boy who ran from tavern to tavern, apparently bearing a message. As Ryre entered the tavern the boy ran out, flinching wild-eyed from him.

A few sailors sat on benches, drinking morosely. Each stared into the steady flame in the glass vase before him. Frequently one or another of them would glance up like a wary beast. They seemed to resent having to spend a night in Gaxanoi—or, Ryre suspected, this particular night. He wished he knew more about the town than its name.

Was it their resentment that made the seamen dangerous? One demanded of the taverner why the door was unlocked. When his companions tried to restrain him he fought savagely; the floorboards made it sound like giants were wrestling. The fight spilled out of the tavern, and Ryre observed that the sailors quickly stunned the drunken man and dragged him hastily inside.

"What is out there?" Ryre asked one—but the man glared, seeming almost to blame him for the fracas. When Ryre asked the question of the taverner, he shook his head nervously. "Nothing that I care to speak of."

Ryre had his wooden tankard refilled, and sat by a window. Let whatever was abroad in the night stay out there—but he wasn't about to blind himself with drink and glassed flame: if a threat was approaching, he meant to see it before it came too near.

Still, there seemed to be little to see. Beside the ship,

vases flickered on their poles. Waves lapped sleepily at the dock; light snaked in the water. A thin, chill wind swung the vases. Shadows of poles danced, advancing, retreating. The ship rocked; it creaked, muffled and monotonous. Ryre shook himself free of its wooden lullaby—for suddenly there was something to watch.

At first he could hardly make out the swimming shapes below the far end of the wharf: a pack of white rats, advancing through black water? The vases swayed, and showed him the figures whose cowled heads he'd glimpsed reflected in the sea.

Their robes were pale as fungus. They emerged two by two from a wide, dark street at the edge of the dock. The slow, pallid emergence reminded Ryre of worms dropping from a gap. There seemed no end to the procession; surely it would fill the wharf.

Despite its size, the procession was unnervingly silent. A distant flapping could be heard. But there was violence amid the ceremony: figures struggling desperately but mutely, which seemed to hover in the air among their robed captors. Ryre distinguished that the victims were bound and gagged, and kept aloft by taut ropes held by robed men. The sight made him think of insects in a web.

As the vanguard came abreast of the window, Ryre saw that the first victim was the slave whom he had seen struck down. The old man looked too exhausted to struggle; he hung slack in the air—but his eyes were lurid with terror. The procession halted as though to display him. A seaman muttered nervously, "What do they want?"

At once Ryre knew, and sprang to his feet, cursing. He drew his sword as the tavern door crashed open. Six hooded men came in, swift and silent as predators.

67

Only their robes whispered, and glimmered like marshlight in the dimness. One man pointed at Ryre and his companions imitated him. The foremost and tallest intoned, "He is to fly."

His voice was low, yet seemed as massive as the creaking that had caged Ryre in the forest. No doubt his ritual words terrified slaves, and perhaps the whole of Gaxanoi. But to Ryre the six were only men who had to hide their faces in cowls—and one of them, the man who had pointed him out and whose cowl now sagged back treacherously, was the slave driver who had challenged him.

The high priest—presumably the tall man called himself something of the kind—stood aside. Three men stepped forward; swords sneaked from beneath their robes. The slave driver and another man hung back, ready with ropes to bind their victim.

One swordsman advanced, while his companions began to circle their prey. They meant to trap Ryre in the cramped maze of tables and benches, which were fastened securely to the floor. But the furniture helped Ryre. He leapt backward onto a bench; then, as his adversary lunged at him, sprang onto the bench behind the man. Before the swordsman could react, a blow of Ryre's sword had split his skull. He sprawled over a table, his head spilling like an overturned tankard of blood.

Ryre leapt from table to table, heading for the door. Wood thundered around him. As he reached the door, the priest retreated hastily along the wall. One stroke of the blade severed the web of ropes—but four men came running from the procession, swords gleaming eagerly.

Could Ryre hold the priest hostage? Perhaps—but as

he made to seize the man, a blade came hissing toward Ryre's neck. Only a desperate leap sideways saved him from the blow, which bit deep into a log of the wall. He whirled; his movement added force to his blade's sweep. The second swordsman crumpled, bowing his half-severed head.

Ryre had been driven back into the tavern. He stared about wildly. The seamen had withdrawn into the shadows and clearly wanted no part of the fight; the same appeared true of the taverner. Beyond the vats of wine, Ryre glimpsed a rough staircase. If he reached an upper window, he could escape through the alley—if it was unguarded.

He dodged backward between the tables. His scything blade cleared a space around him. By the time the swordsmen saw his plan and rushed toward the stairs, Ryre was nearly at the vats. As he reached them, the taverner grabbed a heavy wooden scoop from beside a vat. Before Ryre could turn, the taverner had clubbed him down.

The swordsmen were on Ryre at once. One knocked the sword from his hand, another inserted the point of his blade beneath Ryre's chin to lever him to his feet. "Come," he said with cruel tenderness. "They are hungry. Can't you hear them?"

Ryre heard only the taverner's fearful muttering. "Take him out. I got him for you. Take him out and let me lock the doors."

Belatedly Ryre understood why the boy had been running from tavern to tavern. He turned on the taverner, snarling—but at once four sword points pricked his neck. The points, a lethal collar, urged him out onto the wharf.

The procession and the bared swords closed around

him. His captors unbelted their robes, which they had gathered up in order to pursue him. The gliding robes helped muffle the advance of the procession. Ryre was silent too: not from awe, but because all his being was alert for a chance to make his escape.

If he so much as moved his head to ease his cramped neck, a sword point drew his blood. At least they had been unable to remove his armor, whose leaves would simply tighten about him unless he first relaxed. He trudged onward, a puppet strung by its neck. Vases swung their lights and made the town sway. Houses floated by, rocking with shadow, locking up fear. The flapping was closer, and sounded impatient.

Soon they entered the forest. At the edge of the town, robed men had seized vases; the light groped amid the gigantic leaves, or wandered away vaguely into the reaches of the forest. This was not the road that Ryre had followed, and that he had assumed to be the sole track. Where did this road lead, and to what evil purpose?

The multitude of trees rose above him. They glistened like pillars of a submerged temple, secret and threatening. Smells of warm luxuriance and decay oppressed him. Huge, dim leaves twitched as stored rain fell; the dark, dripping avenues sounded like an infinity of moist caves. Somewhere was a leathery fluttering, sluggish and restless. Once he had heard such a clamor deep in a cave that stank of beasts and blood.

Far down the leafy tunnel the dimness was shifting. It fluttered pallidly. Ahead the leathery restlessness grew louder, peremptory. Sword points bit into Ryre's neck. Were his captors ensuring that he could not escape, or making him the scapegoat of their own fears?

They prodded him forward into the open. As he stumbled from beneath the trees, he saw that the pale stirring was only of moonlight and shade. The moon had risen above distant, forested mountains, and showed him a wide glade, bare except for unstable shadows. Above the trees hovered a host of dry, eager flapping.

Ryre felt a sword reach for his jugular vein. He tensed: if he was to die here, he'd leave a few agonizing memories among his captors. But the sword relaxed as the slave driver said, gloating, "Save him for last. Let him watch."

The trussed victims were carried into the glade. Ryre saw how hastily they were dropped, and how the robed men scurried out of the glade, glancing fearfully at the sky. Despite the size of the procession, there were only four victims. One did not struggle—because he was already dead, Ryre saw; he looked days dead. Presumably this rite served as funeral in Gaxanoi.

All at once the flapping was violent above the glade. Ryre could not lift his head to see, but he glimpsed nightmare shadows roaming over the ground. "Now," the slave driver hissed.

As swords rose to tap his veins, Ryre sprang. He had slumped a little, bending his knees, as though crushed by despair. Now he leapt to his full height, a head taller than any of them, and launched himself at the slave driver. Sword points ripped tracks down his neck—but his shoulders knocked two blades aside, while the others thudded against his armor, bruising his torso. Before the man's exultant grin had time to collapse into panic, Ryre had smashed his fist into the slave driver's face.

The man staggered backward into the glade, flailing

the air with his sword, and fell. But the shock failed to jar the hilt from his grasp. Ryre rushed at him to grapple for the weapon. The sword sprang up. Had Ryre not dodged aside, he would have been emasculated.

The hooded men hung back, daunted by the flapping. How much time had Ryre to gain himself a weapon? The sound of great, dry wings descended; shadows swallowed the glade. As he circled the prone man, staying just out of reach of the sweeps of the sword while he tried to dizzy his victim, Ryre glanced up—and gasped, appalled.

Flapping down from the pale sky, in a flock that stank of caverns and worse, came wings. Their span was greater than the spread of his arms. They were the blotchy white of decay; between their bony fingers, skin fluttered lethargically as drowned sails. All this was frightful—but there was no body to speak of between each pair of wings, only a whitish rope of flesh thin as a child's arm. Yet as a pair of wings sailed down near him, Ryre saw a mouth gape along the whole length of the scrawny object. Its lips resembled a split in fungus, and it was crammed with teeth.

The slave driver scrabbled backward toward the trees, mumbling in terror. One pair of wings settled on a bound victim, like a carelessly flung shroud; then they rose, lifting their prey toward the moon. Ryre's spirit sickened, for the mouth was embedded in the length of the man's chest. The lips worked, sucking.

Enraged and dismayed, Ryre forced his adversary away from the trees. But neither could Ryre flee that way, for the shade bristled with swords. The man twisted on the ground, moaning—then made a vicious lunge with his sword. It was too violent. It hurled

the sword from his grip, to impale the ground beside
Ryre.

Ryre seized the hilt. Now he could defend himself as
best he might, though the weapon was less well-
balanced than his own, and heavier. He heard the thud
of another sword, thrown to his adversary. The watch-
ers barred the way into the forest. They intended the
man to finish Ryre, rather than risk combat themselves.

Somewhere behind him, far too numerous and close,
Ryre heard wings. They would be enough to contend
with when he tried to cross the glade. Before the slave
driver could reach the thrown sword, a slash of Ryre's
blade hamstrung him.

Ryre was turning, ready to dash for the far side of
the glade, when a shadow engulfed the earth around
him. He had no time to react before he was flung to

the ground. Once, onboard ship, he had been crushed by a fallen sail. He was as helpless now—but this burden felt as though it had been dragged from a swamp. A stench as of something dead and disinterred filled his nostrils. Though he had clung to the sword, his sword arm was pinned down, useless. He could only snarl and writhe impotently as teeth bit through his armor and fastened in his back, beside his spine.

He felt the lips tear his armor like paper, widening the gap. He lay in wait and forced himself to suffer the sucking of the mouth embedded in his flesh. As soon as the wings lifted him, he began to chop at the nearest. But they were tougher than his armor. The sword hardly marked them.

He was being lifted as he might have caught up an infant. The glade whirled away below him; the forest was a moonlit whirlpool, dizzying. He felt himself dangling from teeth clenched deep in his flesh. He hacked at the wings, haphazardly and frenziedly—until he felt the sword grow heavier. The feaster was draining his strength with his blood.

The shrieks of the slave driver afforded Ryre grim satisfaction. He saw the man borne upward, struggling by avid wings. But the sight dwindled; Ryre's wings were carrying him above the trees. He hurled himself about, trying to force the wings toward the leaves, to entangle them. But he could not control their flight; he was merely wasting his strength.

The forest plummeted below him. Deafening winds grabbed his breath. A chill seized him—because of the giddy height, or the leathery fans of wings, or the ebbing of his vitality? The swaying moon steadied; it seemed unnaturally close, perhaps because the wings crowded the sky with its color.

Beneath him, the world consisted of nothing but trees. The shrunken forest drifted by, a dense mosaic formed by countless concentric patterns of leaves. It looked unreal; his sense of perspective was floating away, into something like a dream. Among the flock of wings, a few seed-bearing leaves glided by.

Was the mouth poisoning him as well as drinking his blood? Perhaps, for as his wings swooped higher he was possessed by a kind of insidious delirium. He felt he had sprouted wings that obeyed his dreams. They had transformed him. No longer was he doomed to earthbound plodding. He was a creature of the air, with only the approaching moon, the gliding leaves, the rest of his flock for companions.

A glimpse of that flock pierced his delirium. Around him airborne mouths gaped, hungry for the leavings. His wings lifted him greedily. They were gaining height thanks to his blood, and because he was growing lighter. The other feeding pairs of wings rose exultantly. As their victims turned moon-pale, the gorged wings glowed blotchily pink. Like remains in a web, the victims hardly struggled now.

All at once Ryre saw his chance. The moon swayed like a spider's cocoon shaken by the gusts of the wings; the dwarfed forest looked insubstantial as the blanched sky. Sly waves of vertiginous ecstasy crept over him, blurring his vision further. But he had seen a broad leaf gliding toward him. If it drifted sufficiently close—

It did, and at once was impaled by an upward thrust of his sword. The additional burden had no effect on his headlong flight, but that was not his plan. Instead, he thrust the leaf among the fingertips of one wing, to hinder them. The wing struggled; off balance, the feaster dropped toward the trees—and the leaf ripped, almost wrenching the sword from his grasp. He had to cling to the hilt with both hands to prevent the weapon from falling with the torn leaf.

He grew frenzied. Ramming the sword into his belt, he seized the bony arms of the wings, either to break them or to wrench the mouth out of his flesh. Why had he waited so long? Though his muscles trembled with his gathered strength, the wings brushed his hands aside. In any case he would achieve only a fall to his death; but he preferred a clean death to suffering the hunger of the wings. Ahead he could see their lair.

It was a blotch of darkness, roughly circular and perhaps a hundred yards wide, among the trees. Wings circled above its rim, like witches dancing a delirious ritual. Was it another glade? As the foremost pair of burdened wings dropped its victim—the bound corpse—into the circle, Ryre saw that the lair was a pit.

His own wings bore him helplessly closer. He glimpsed the depths, and nausea giddied him. He clutched the sword hilt. Rather than fall conscious into that pit, he would take his own life. Even that ultimate hopelessness was preferable to what waited below.

The rocky sides of the pit were dry. The place resembled the socket of a skull, a desiccated cavity amid the profusion of forest. Its floor was invisible, for the pit was piled with skeletons, tangled indistinguishably. Some of the bones were awesomely gigantic. Atop the pile lay the dropped corpse, as though on a mockery of a pyre.

As Ryre watched, aghast, the enormous bony heap stirred. The corpse toppled down its slope. Had the surrounding fecundity possessed the jumble of skel-

etons, united them into a monstrous parody of life? Ryre's brain whirled, bereft of sense. Then he saw what was crawling out from beneath the bones.

Very slowly and feebly, old wings emerged. They were discolored as corpses, and looked as though they should have died long ago. A stench of decay welled upward. Dust, no doubt from skeletons, clung to the wings. Their groping reminded him of worms in meat.

They clambered on their fingertips over the bones, toward the corpse. They resembled pairs of senile hands, skeletal and webbed. Their lips sagged open, exposing teeth and stumps of teeth. The wings fumbled blindly up the shifting heap; they slid back and clambered again. One by one they reached the corpse and fastened on it. Soon it was entirely covered by a heaving of wings, which divided their victim raggedly and crawled away with their prizes.

Ryre dragged his sword free. The burdened wings hovered above the rim. He knew they were draining their victims before dropping the remnants into the pit. He saw the slave driver fall, clenched and empty.

The sword felt leaden. Ryre clutched the hilt with his other hand, in case it fell from his enfeebled fingers. Then, snarling at his vindictive fate, he turned the point toward his belly. He meant to drive the blade upward. Mouths hovered close to him, baring their teeth. He hoped he was weakened enough to die quickly.

Then—though perhaps it would serve only to make his death more ironic—he glimpsed his chance. Was it worth trying? Might he not use up his strength, and be unable even to die cleanly? But he refused to die while he yet had a chance to fight. Without warning, he lunged with the sword at the nearest pair of empty wings and stabbed at the mouth.

He felt the sword pierce flesh within the lips. Yes, the flesh was vulnerable there! He dug the blade deeper, embedding it—and the hilt was almost torn from his hands as the wings flapped convulsively. He managed to keep hold, though his agonized fingers were audibly straining. The hilt was his last hold on life.

Then, as he had prayed inarticulately might happen, the wounded wings became entangled with his own. The leathery struggle caged him; he choked on gusts of decay. He was falling amid the tangle of wings. But as he glimpsed the landscape he roared, enraged by the taunts of his fate. He was falling straight into the pit.

His rage twisted the sword deep in the flesh of the mouth. He heard and felt teeth grind on the blade; he clung grimly to the flailing hilt. The uninjured mouth writhed in his own flesh. For a moment the struggling wings disengaged. He was borne upward, over the rim of the pit.

A few trees sailed by, close enough to grab. But they were withered, and might break. In any case, he dared not let go of the sword. He soared away from the pit, above the denser forest. His strength was still dwindling; the hilt shifted dangerously in his hands. He had no time to choose his moment. Closer to the pit than he would have wished, he dragged the blade toward him with all his remaining force and entangled the wings.

Convulsed by their struggles, the hilt smashed against his fingers, bruising them. He felt his back tear as the embedded teeth gnashed. But the wings had ensnared one another, and were falling toward the trees.

They crashed through leaves. Cupped rain inundated them. Ryre was deafened by the battle of wings and the ripping of leaves. The trunks grew close here, as though to wall off the aridity of the pit. The wings smashed through another flooded layer, and were caught between trunks. Ryre snarled with gasping mirth as he heard the struggling fingers break.

Still the canopy of leaves gave way. The twitching wings continued to fall. Ryre let go of the sword and, embracing a trunk, swung his body with all the violence he could summon. He felt skeletal fingers break. Even then the mouth refused to let go of his flesh. Not until he and the wings had crashed through the lowest leaves to the ground did the teeth part, jarred open by the shock of the fall.

Half-stunned and giddy with the draining, Ryre nonetheless forced himself to his feet. The pairs of wings were hobbling away in the direction of the unseen pit. He wrenched his sword out of the injured mouth and pursued them, stabbing and hacking. But the wings would not die. Though he chopped at the joints of the fingers, and thrust the blade again and again into the mouths, the wings still dragged themselves unevenly toward their lair. Long after he had exhausted the last of his strength and was sitting propped against a tree, with the sword dug into the ground before him to prevent his toppling forward, he heard a ragged flapping and saw pale things crawling lopsidedly away from him, into the dark.

He pressed his back against a drooping leaf, which was cool as balm. His back felt raw and withered as a mummy's, but seemed to be losing little blood. He dozed, waiting for the dawn and for a hint of his strength to return to him. Nearby there might be leaves whose healing power was greater. He could hear the serpentine denizens of the forest worming their way through the dark arcades. Surely one would be stupid enough to come within reach of his blade. When he could, he would walk—and if his wanderings took him toward Gaxanoi, a few buildings might blaze and a few chains break.

A Spell for Annalise

PARKE GODWIN

On an obscure island surrounded by an unimportant body of water, there lived a young girl named Annalise who lay under a spell, the dismal nature of which had never been clarified for her, though it seemed to render Annalise strikingly unattractive. At least her mother never said she was anything else and her father was too busy to notice her much.

Annalise searched her mirror for an answer, finding only imperfections. She was told the pimples would depart in the fullness of time, but that didn't help now. Her nose seemed to grow larger with each worried inspection. True, she was a loser, but she would not surrender without a fight.

"I'll make myself brilliant," Annalise conceived. "My searing intellect will dazzle merely beautiful people and they'll never know how I feel inside."

That worked all too well. They never guessed, went away, and left Annalise in her brilliance.

"My hands are worst of all," she schemed. "I'll play music, beautiful music, so soulfully and swiftly, no one will notice my fingers are large and warty."

Right again. People admired her talent but left her alone with it.

"I won't care," Annalise whispered terminally to her pillow. "They'll never see my heart."

And so they didn't.

One summer day when she was sixteen, walking by the sea and feeling as lonely as sixteen could feel, which is considerable, she came upon an odd-looking stranger carving letters into a driftwood log. He wasn't much for company, but Annalise didn't feel she could be picky.

"What are you carving?" she asked.

"What I am." He blew the wood crumbs from the last letter. "There, finished." The sign read:

GOBLIN.

So far as Annalise knew, he might be one. Homely enough, his bushy gray hair wind-blown and salt-stiffened, skin leather-brown, dressed as if he'd hurried through a closing down sale in a charity shop. But hardly malicious as one thought of goblins; more like a leprechaun at the frayed end of his whimsy and quite ready to throw in the towel. Annalise was understandably skeptical.

"A real goblin?"

"Real as we get," he acknowledged with better grace than most of his unpredictable kind. "And at your service. Make a wish."

"Wish?" Annalise stared at him. "You can do magic?"

"When needed." The Goblin looked her through and through. "The usual: mud into gold, that sort of thing."

"Father would like that." Annalise's father had a good deal of money that seemed to require his constant attention. His liver had enlarged from worry over losing it.

"Words into music," the Goblin went on invitingly, "darkness into light."

Annalise hardly dared say it. "Ugliness?"

"Into beauty," he finished, smiling. "I thought you'd never ask."

Annalise discovered a new problem with her hands; they wanted to cover her face. She denied them. "I don't believe you. You're an old fake!"

The Goblin appeared unfazed. "And how real are you, girl?"

That was a crusher, considering all she'd done to cover and revise herself. "I can't help it. I'm bewitched."

"Besieged," he agreed. "Anyone can see that. There's a high, thick wall about you. Alas, demolition's not my specialty. When you get tired of living inside, let me know."

"Don't hold your breath," Annalise prophesied from dreary experience. "Boys run from me, dogs shiver in their sleep when I pass, and an over-the-hill goblin isn't going to help. Try wood carving. Goodbye." And she went.

Still, lying in bed late in the summer night, Annalise thought sometimes she could hear the Goblin's voice speaking or singing, since one was the other coming from him: *mud into gold, words into music . . .*

"Magic," Annalise grumped into her pillow. "Nothing but a weird old man."

Ugliness into beauty.

Couldn't be. Never happen. But if it could . . .

One awful morning the sun rose glaring and horrid as the way Annalise felt, and her mirror outdid itself in frankness. She walked the streets of the town, surer than ever of the spell that clung to her like the suggestion of eggs past their prime. *Had* to be hopeless, then. She saw girls homely as herself laughing with handsome young boys. One was even in a wheelchair, which piled insult on injury. Annalise glowered at their happiness until the pain was a weight dragging on her heart and the corners of her mouth. In her chest a great dark bubble was swelling tight, and when it burst, she felt as if the bitterness would flood in a poisonous torrent through all of her for all time. Frightened, she ran away, out of the town to the safety of solitude and the beach. Then it happened.

"Someone must love me," she whispered. The words sounded strange. "Goblin? Goblin, where are you!" She turned about the beach, wild, desperate. The sand was deserted. A gull jeered at her. *Alone*, the surf breathed as it slid in over the sand. *Alone*, laughed the hovering gulls. Then Annalise felt a hand fall lightly on her shoulder. The Goblin grinned at her, impish and inviting as ever.

"Don't be alone, Annalise."

Perhaps it was the sun's glare, but he seemed younger and much more presentable than she remembered. "Goblin, did you mean it? Can you make me beautiful?"

"You can."

"Me?"

"Of course you can."

Her hands strayed to her cheeks. "Will it hurt?"

Something like sadness clouded the indeterminate color of the Goblin's eyes. "Always does eventually. Nothing's free."

Frightening to have to change, even the notion of it. "Will you be with me?"

"Always," the Goblin promised.

Annalise took the hand he held out to her. She thought he smiled; she couldn't see his face clearly. In the sun's hard dazzle, it seemed to shift and change. Yes . . . he was much younger than Annalise had thought at first. She steeled herself. "I'll do it. Hurry before I lose my nerve."

"Then close your eyes and tell me what you want most."

She knew, but the painful truth stuck in her throat. "I can't."

"You have to try. That's the beginning."

Annalise found it easier to get out all in a rush. "Iwishsomeonelovedme."

With her eyes closed tight, the Goblin's voice was

near and soft as her own wish. "Turn it around, Annalise."

That made no sense all. "Me loved someone wish I. That's silly."

"Oh dear," the Goblin sighed, settling on the log with his name carved on it. "Far too rational. Absolutely sodden with intellect. Don't try to go it all at once. Relax. Find out how you feel."

That was harder than Annalise would have suspected. All her life she'd been mindful of what she should feel, not what she did or might. She faltered. "I feel . . ."

Once more the bubble swelled in her chest, but now the pain was softened a shade as the mellowed sunlight lit the sea and sand around her.

"When it comes," the Goblin read her thought, "listen to what it tells you."

Lis-ten, the surf whispered.

And the gulls hovering over them advised, *Lis-ten*.

Annalise listened, very still, still enough to know how she felt. "I must love someone," her self said. "Goblin, did you hear?" Like most determined intellectuals, simplicity astonished Annalise. "I *want* to love someone . . . but there's no one around."

Just her luck: things were going beautifully, the urge and the need overflowing in her heart like three pounds of molten, pure gold in a two-pound mold—and no one to lavish it on. On his log, her casual magician chuckled.

"No one but us goblins."

The glare was quite gone, the sunlight slanting soft on the sand, driftwood shadows east of the afternoon just beginning. Annalise blinked. Her benefactor was still a goblin, still gray-brown, though in the warmer light he seemed—no, he *was* the handsomest of all

possible things to go bump in the night or even at high noon. And the new, lighter sensation about her lips was a smile.

"I do love you, Goblin. It must be the magic."

"Wrong," he corrected gently. "You have until sunset to find the answer."

"But you said you'd be with me always."

"In a manner of speaking, like confidence and knowing yourself. But the wind's breezed it to the sandpipers: there's someone like you on the other side of the island with the other side of your problem. A girl who's always been beautiful, far as that goes, but not much else. Emergency case. And then, if I can squeeze it in"—the Goblin consulted an antique pocket watch that tinkled "Time on My Hands" when opened— "there's a politician in whom I must seed a conscience like a migraine. Can't even stop for lunch."

The watch vanished into a frayed pocket; he held out brown fingers. "Take my hand, Annalise. There's all the time in the world, or none. That's not magic, just life. You choose."

Later, when the sun had risen and gone down many hundreds of times, Annalise had only a dim picture of walking with the Goblin by the sea, through the sea grass, along the streets of the town. They told each other big, little, or secret things, and as time passed or seemed to stand still, Annalise forgot herself and saw only the Goblin. She felt a lightness and warmth about her whole being, young and wise and happy all at once, painful joy and delicious hurt like a sad song flourished from a clown's banjo. Men turned their heads, stopped and stared. Some who knew Annalise rubbed their eyes or polished their glasses and goggled again. Walking hand in hand with a goblin, unique in himself, was the most stunning young woman any of them had ever overlooked.

"Fantastic!" breathed one phrasemaker, salivating.

"Unbelievable," another gasped.

"Beautiful," said a third, simpler than the rest.

"Beautiful?" Annalise wondered. "Me?"

Their walk had brought them to the beach and the sea again. In her companion's hand something shimmered as it caught the setting sun. He held a small mirror before both of them. "Are you beautiful?"

"I don't know," Annalise cried out, older than when they started. "All I see is you."

"You must know," the Goblin urged, glancing at the sun. "Hurry."

"I don't believe it. I can't. The love was all your magic."

"No." He began to fade, grow older.

"Goblin, don't leave me!"

"Turn it around . . ."

The sun was gone. Annalise was alone by the log where he'd carved what he was into the wood and perhaps into her as well. She sat by the sea for a long time while the sky evening-dressed in indigo and hung itself with stars. The bubble swelled one last time in her breast, broke, and ran its secret through her.

The magic was the love. Not Goblin's but her own.

Like all truths, a kind of sadness came with it, and loss, but the Goblin had told her there would be that. Then and later and many times over when Annalise had to remind herself of the lesson again and again. And, since no wisdom comes free, she wondered what it might have once cost the Goblin himself—wondered while young, that is. When older, she didn't need to ask. For now, Annalise blew a kiss to the stars.

Sometimes when she was sad, she could feel the Goblin's hand on hers, and when she laughed there might be some echo of his. And since Annalise never forgot how or why or when to love, one assumes she laughed full and often.

The log still lies on the beach with GOBLIN cut deep into its grain and the name ANNALISE beneath, visited often by the sea and stars, happy people, and those still hovering and hunting like the gulls.

The Secret of Faerie

PAUL LEWIS

Every night for the past few weeks, Kevin Jackson had found himself in a strange other world. His dreams were so vivid, they seemed as real to him as the life he returned to each morning when he woke.

Sneaking past a sleeping dragon to steal the gold and jewels it guarded with flaming breath . . . Climbing a high tower to a room where a princess slept for a hundred years . . . Striking bargains with fairy folk, who gave him wonderful gifts in exchange for the stories he told . . .

At first this other world had seemed idyllic. As the weeks passed, however, Kevin sensed a cold and evil darkness setting in. . . .

He was walking through the bustling streets of a country town when a group of armor-clad knights galloped through at speed, their horses looking tired enough to drop. A few people around him gave halfhearted cheers. Everyone else seemed afraid . . .

One night Kevin was shaken out of sleep to find a woman more beautiful than any he could have imagined staring down at him.

"What—?" was all he could say before a perfumed hand was pressed to his lips.

"Please be quiet," whispered the woman. "I won't hurt you."

Kevin struggled weakly for a moment, convinced he was still asleep. When he realized it was no dream, he forced himself to relax.

"That's better," said the woman, smiling and nodding her head in approval. "Do you promise you'll be quiet?"

Kevin nodded, and the woman took her hand from his mouth.

He wanted to ask her what she was doing in his room so late at night, but was so shocked that the words refused to come.

"W-who are you?" he managed.

"My name is Rowan. I'm here to ask for your help, Kevin."

"How did you know my name?"

"I know a lot about you," said Rowan, smiling.

Kevin reached out and switched on the bedside lamp. He could see the woman's hair was fiery red and her eyes shone like bright emeralds. The long skirt and tunic she wore appeared very old fashioned, and were made from some kind of drab green cloth. "I'd love to talk to you more, but I'm afraid time is against us," she said.

Rowan padded across the room before pulling back the curtains and staring out into the night. "You have to give me the book. I'll be on my way before they know what's happened."

"What book?"

"The book of power. We know you have it. Its magic leaves traces."

"I have no idea what you're talking about," said Kevin. "Besides, if we keep talking we'll wake my parents and then there'll be trouble."

Rowan murmured something, then clicked her fingers.

Kevin's ears popped. "What was that?" he asked, voice muffled.

"A silencing spell. Nobody will hear a word we say. Please, give me the book. You'll be in terrible danger if they find you."

"For the last time, I don't know anything about your stupid book!"

Rowan stared at him, sadness in her eyes. Then she sighed. "I believe you," she said. "Except it makes no sense!"

"Neither do you," said Kevin. "Why don't you tell me everything."

"Very well. Have you heard of Thomas the Rhymer? No? Well, he was a mortal man who entered the Realm of Faerie. Years later he was allowed back, on one condition. From the time he returned to your world he could only tell the truth whenever he was asked a question."

The problem, Rowan explained, was that he would tell the truth about everything. Even the spells, which he had heard in the Realm of Faerie, and some of them were very, very dangerous.

In those days stories were passed on by word of mouth, not written down, and changed with each retelling until you would hardly recognize them. "Still, some truth remained," said Rowan. "When people began writing down the stories they changed them again.

"That was fine. It kept those nasty spells hidden. Sooner or later, though, it had to happen. Someone changed the stories again—only this time, without knowing it, they turned them back into the truth."

"Real spells?" said Kevin. "They put real spells in a *book*?"

"Yes."

"Which book?"

"One you have read. In this room."

Kevin suddenly knew what she was talking about. *The Secret of Faerie*, which he had persuaded his grandfather to lend him a week ago. He frowned. It had been old and dog-eared, and a little childish.

"Okay, I know the book."

"Then you must let me have it—now."

"Can't," said Kevin. "I gave it back. Anyway, what's the rush?"

Rowan looked sad again. "There's a war in my world, Kevin. A very evil man, a sorcerer, is leading a force of darkness across our land, destroying everything and everyone standing in his way.

"We have our own magic, and we can hold him back for a while. But if he finds the book, the oldest and most dangerous spells of all will be his, and he will surely defeat us."

"You're talking about the same book? The one I read?"

"Yes. It is very rare. Few were printed, and to the best of our knowledge only one survived. Now the Dark Lord's agents are aware of it and are searching just as I am. They must not be allowed to succeed."

Kevin had actually read something that held the key to life or death in the Realm of Faerie itself! Then his thoughts grew serious. He remembered how the idyllic land he visited each night had turned dark, as though under the shadow of monstrous evil.

"I've been having these dreams . . ."

"You have been to our world," said Rowan. "The power within the book connects yours to mine. It acts like a bridge. Although you may not know it, the magic is inside you forever. That's how strong it is."

Kevin fell silent, trying to take all this in.

"I know I am asking much," said Rowan. "But will you help me?"

Kevin stared at the row of book shelves that lined his grandfather's study. Dusty old volumes stared back at him. Books on ghosts, on myths and legends, on the search for the Loch Ness Monster, on UFOs, and countless other strange topics.

When he finally spotted *The Secret of Faerie*, he took it down and examined it closely. Truth be told, it was not much to look at. Its cover was a cracked and faded cream, with its title written in fancy gold letters across the top. Below the title was a painting of a fairy, hopelessly cute and nothing at all like Rowan, whose beauty had seemed to Kevin to mask a wild and dangerous power. The author was not named.

"You've a thing about that book," said a deep voice, startling him. Grandad elbowed the study door open as he entered, carrying a tray on which stood two glasses of lemonade and a plate of biscuits.

"It's really good," said Kevin.

"Yes, well, perhaps not the most impressive in my collection, though I must admit it has a certain . . . charm. Probably not much like the real Realm of Faerie, mind you. Dangerous place, the other world."

"You sound as if you've been there!"

"Oh, I have," his grandfather replied with a broad grin. "A place of wonders, my boy. Some good, some bad. Just like our world."

He gave Kevin a curious look. "Want to read it again, do you?"

Kevin shivered. It was as if his grandfather *knew*.

"Y-yes, if you don't mind," he said.

"Then take it with you! What is a book for, if not to

give pleasure to its readers? All I ask is that you bring it back when you're done."

"Of course I will." Kevin felt terribly guilty. Grandad had never minded lending Kevin his books because they were always returned safely. It was an unspoken promise between them. Yet if what Rowan had told him was true, his grandfather would never see *The Secret of Faerie* again.

A short time later he stepped from the house into bright sunshine and began the short walk to town. A man, maybe one of his grandfather's friends, nodded cheerfully as he passed. Kevin smiled back.

It was an August morning. The crowds of people on Station Road, the town's main shopping street, seemed to be moving slower than usual, as if the sun had sapped their energy. Kevin weaved his way through them, looking back now and then to see if anyone was following.

Rowan had assured him it would take the enemy a while to locate the book. Their magic, though strong, was raw and difficult to tame.

Despite this, when Kevin reached the McDonald's where they had arranged to meet, he did not go straight inside but carried on a few yards before abruptly spinning around. While several people gave him curious looks, none attempted to duck out of his view.

The coast was clear, he decided, then pushed open the restaurant door. Rowan sat with her back to the window. Kevin slid into the seat opposite her and put the book on the table between them.

"I'll have to pretend I lost it or something," he said.

"Will you get into trouble?"

Despite her problems, Rowan was still concerned for him. Kevin felt bad about leaving her alone to do

whatever she had to do next. He had helped by fetching the book. It just didn't seem enough. "No," he said. "And if you want me to do anything else . . ."

"You are very brave," said Rowan, reaching out to touch his shoulder briefly. "But now it begins to get dangerous. I have to take the book back to my world before it is seized by the enemy."

"You could always set fire to it."

"Unfortunately not. The pages are protected by magic and would not burn. Only our most skilled magicians can destroy it."

Rowan reached out for it. For a moment the color seemed to fade from her face. She shook her head almost angrily. When she tried to pick up the book a second time Kevin was sure he saw blue sparks crackle from its cover to her fingertips. She snatched her hand away.

"Is something wrong?" he asked.

"I'm afraid to touch it," said Rowan. "The spells are so old and evil they can corrupt you, make you evil yourself."

"It hasn't made me evil."

"That's because you are young, Kevin, free of greed and envy. The magic cannot touch you while you are innocent. If we had more such as you in the Realm we could defeat the Dark Lord with ease."

Kevin blushed and looked away, only to see a man staring through the window at them. Kevin felt the grip of an icy hand. It was the same man who had passed him near Grandad's house. One of the Dark Lord's agents, no doubt, which meant he and Rowan were in terrible danger.

"Don't turn round," he told her. "But a man is watching us."

"Describe him. Quickly!"

"He's like . . . I don't know. Just an old man with gray hair."

Rowan whispered something. "Look again," she said.

Kevin did. Where the man had stood was a nightmare.

Its skin was pale green and covered in knotlike growths. The thing's arms were long, like a gorilla's. Where its nose should have been was a single eye, which glared at Kevin. Its mouth was twice the size of a man's, crammed with dozens of sharp teeth. A small, pointed tongue flicked out from between them as Kevin watched in horror.

"They use dark magic to cloak themselves," said Rowan. "My counterspell allows you to see them as they really are."

"It's *disgusting!*"

"Yes, and unfortunately it knows we are here. I have no doubt it will have summoned help." Rowan looked thoughtful. "Kevin, I have no choice but to ask this of you. As I dare not touch the book, will you take it to the gateway for me?"

"Sure," said Kevin. At once his mind was filled with the image of a clearing in the forest, the ground daubed with splashes of sunlight, a tall stone standing at its center. The place looked vaguely familiar.

"That is where you must go," said Rowan. "Remember, should that book fall into their hands we are lost forever. Run as fast as you can. I will provide a distraction. We will meet as soon as luck allows."

Kevin nodded, his heart thumping as he realized he was caught up in a real-life adventure. Only it did not feel like a game, as he had always imagined it would. It felt scary. He picked up the book and gripped it tightly,

wondering if he should simply wait for Rowan to leave before taking it back to his grandfather as he had promised.

Yet somehow he could not bring himself to do that.

He liked the place he had not only dreamed about but had actually visited. That world seemed so much cleaner than the one he lived in. It would be a terrible shame if it was lost for the sake of paper and ink.

Grandad had told him books were for the pleasure of those who read them. Perhaps, like now, there were times when they had a more important part to play. The old man would understand what his grandson was doing. He had never been to the Realm, of course, despite his joke that he had. Even so, Kevin knew he had always been fascinated by mysteries.

And the Realm was one of the greatest mysteries of all.

Rowan stood. "Wait just inside the door."

She left the restaurant and stood outside. Kevin felt surprisingly clear-headed. There was no going back. Not that he wanted to. Here was his chance to prove that he could make a difference to all those innocent lives in the Realm. If that monstrosity didn't get to him first, of course, even though it had vanished from sight.

Kevin watched Rowan closely, frustrated that she was not moving from the edge of the pavement. She seemed to be waiting for something. Then he heard the rumble of an approaching lorry. As it drew close to the McDonald's, Rowan stepped into its path.

Kevin gasped and closed his eyes, but not before he saw his friend struck down by the lumbering giant. "Rowan!" he cried. All heads in the restaurant turned to him. A few people realized what had happened and in seconds they were running outside, swiftly joined by others.

He found himself swept along with them. So dense was the crowd that he could not see Rowan, had no way of knowing whether she was alive or dead. Neither could he afford to wait to find out.

Holding the book tightly, Kevin began to run.

There was every chance the creature was right behind. Kevin had no way of knowing, and he did not dare slow down to look. He ran until his chest felt as though it was about to burst, until his legs turned to rubber. When he was certain he could not possibly run any longer, he forced himself to keep going. By now his breath was fire in his throat and he could feel sweat glue his shirt to his back. If there was such a thing as second wind he desperately wished he could find it.

The crowds parted before him as he pelted along the pavement. A few people gave him strange looks, others smiled and shook their heads, no doubt thinking he was just another child up to mischief. One old man, his dog straining at its leash to bark at Kevin as he flew past, shouted something about young hooligans in an angry tone of voice.

Just as he reached the junction with Forge Road, Kevin felt a sharp pain in his lower right leg. He stumbled to a halt, cursing his luck, and began to massage his calf muscle. He managed to hobble around the corner, hopefully out of sight, and took advantage of the enforced break to catch his breath and see if he was being followed.

There was no sign of the creature. Now seemed a good time to try to come up with a plan. Beginning with figuring out where the gateway was. Kevin knew the place, but could not *quite* remember it. Somewhere he had been years ago . . . He shook his head. Trying to force the idea would only drive it farther away. Perhaps it would come back later. All he hoped was that Rowan had survived the accident. Otherwise he would have no idea what to do when, or if, he reached his destination.

The nearest forests were a few miles away. On one side of the town was the steel plant, on the other the beach. To the west were hills and woodlands. That was the direction he needed to travel. With his leg muscles groaning at every step, Kevin began to walk. He needed to get back onto Station Road and follow it past the river until the houses and shops disappeared.

He glanced at his watch. Nearly eleven o'clock. He had told his parents he was meeting friends for the day. They would not worry unless he failed to return by early evening. Plenty of time yet.

Turning right at the junction, Kevin saw the creature on the opposite side of Station Road, staring at him. Its mouth opened to reveal dozens of teeth like small, rusty knives as it raised its arm in triumph. Don't be so sure, thought Kevin, before spinning around and sprinting up Forge Road. His one advantage was knowing this town back to front. A left turn would take him to a footbridge leading to the riverbank path, which emerged at the westernmost end of Station Road.

When he reached it he paused until his breathing returned more or less to normal. So far so good, he thought. There was no sign of his pursuer but he could not be absolutely sure he had lost it. A carrier bag was trapped in the railings flanking the bridge, and a breeze made it flap so loudly that he could not have heard the creature approach. There was nothing else for it except to keep going.

As Kevin reached the midway point, two other monsters appeared at the farthest end. These were short, but incredibly muscular, and covered in dark, wiry fur. They glared at him with red eyes. One of the things began to move forward but the other held it back, as though waiting for orders. Hearing a dull thud from behind, Kevin groaned. He turned to face the monster that had chased him and that now blocked his only escape route. "Be still," it hissed.

Kevin thought frantically, remembering Rowans' last words. If *The Secret of Faerie* fell into enemy hands then her people would be lost forever. Only it would be Kevin's fault, and he would throw the book into the river before he gave it up to the Dark Lord.

Wait a minute. The river!

He snatched the carrier bag from between the railings.

The big creature began to move toward him.

Kevin placed the book carefully into the bag, which he twisted closed and then stuffed under his shirt. One chance, he thought, one chance to get it right. He grabbed the top of the railings and pulled himself up. All three beasts began to run toward him, realizing what he was about to do. Before they could get close enough to stop him, Kevin scrambled over the edge and threw himself off, arms and legs flailing as he plunged into the river.

Despite the hot weather, the water was icy cold and punched the breath right out of his body.

The wild current swept him away, throwing him around so savagely that he began to panic. He could see nothing but chaotic swirlings of green and white, could hear nothing but a booming roar. His leg smashed against a submerged rock. As he yelped in pain, water poured into his mouth, choking him. Kevin coughed harshly as he thrashed about for what seemed like hours in a futile attempt to resist the force of the river. He was growing tired, his limbs so heavy he was sure it could only be a matter of time before they dragged him under the surface.

Just when it seemed he was lost, Kevin's shoes scraped against gravel. At once the strength of the current diminished and, despite the trembling in his legs, he found he was able to stand. Wiping his eyes clear he could see he was just a few yards from the bank. The water was only waist-deep and it was no effort to splash his way over to dry land.

The first thing he did was to check the book. Apart from a few damp patches it had been surprisingly well-protected by the bag. Kevin sighed with relief. He was so weary that all he wanted was to sprawl out on the bank and sleep, but he might not yet be out of danger. He had no idea how far downriver he had been carried. The evil creatures could be miles away, or just a few hundred yards behind.

The houses in the distance told him he had actually been swept through the center of town and out the other side. Had anyone seen him as he struggled in the river they might have called the police, and that was the last thing he needed.

Kevin noticed the banks were lined with stone buildings, many of them falling into ruin. The old industrial estate, he realized, which was a tremendous stroke of luck. He knew exactly where he was. Beyond the derelict estate was the bus station. If by the time he reached it he could remember where the forest clearing was, his journey would become so much easier. He dug into his pockets and pulled out a handful of change, which included a few pound coins.

When he got to the station, though, he was still none the wiser.

Most annoying of all was the fact that he *knew* he had been to the standing stone before. Details eluded him, and he clenched his fists in frustration. He was pretty certain he had thrown the creatures off his trail, yet they could find him at any moment.

A few people glanced at him curiously as he walked past the buses, scanning their destination plates. The hot sun had started to dry his clothes while he traveled through the old industrial estate. Even so, his jeans and T-shirt were torn in places and covered in mud from the riverbank. When he got home his mother would—

Rookwood!

The words on the front of the bus jumped out at him.

When he was younger Kevin had had a friend in the village, about three miles west. One summer they had gone exploring in the woods nearby and had found the clearing with the stone in the middle. That was a good few years ago. No wonder Kevin had virtually forgotten it.

The driver gave Kevin a dubious look as he stepped on board.

"Some bigger boys threw me in the river," said Kevin, shocked at how easily the lie came. "I have to go home."

The driver pursed his lips, then nodded. "One pound fifty."

Kevin paid. He slipped into one of the seats close to the front and looked around briefly. There were quite a few people behind him, but none seemed to be paying him the slightest attention.

Rowan's counterspell allowed him to see beyond the human guises the creatures had adopted. What he had no way of telling was whether it worked with all of them. For all he knew others immune to his friend's magic could be sitting farther back, biding their time.

The journey lasted nearly thirty minutes. Kevin held the book tightly and kept his eyes on the road ahead, not wanting to give any of the passengers a second chance to see his face again.

As they neared the bus stop in Rookwood, he went to stand before abruptly changing his mind. He waited until they had passed the stop, then swung out of his seat into the aisle. "Here, please!" he called.

He was almost pitched off his feet as the bus braked to a halt. "Sorry, I was daydreaming," he told the driver. Kevin got off quickly and began to walk back to the village. When he heard the bus pull away he paused to check over his shoulder. No one had followed him off.

Rookwood was a small place, dominated by a beautiful church. Even though it was years since he had last been here, Kevin could just about recall the route past the houses to the woods. The shade provided by the trees was a relief from the early afternoon sun. He was sure he could find the clearing if he looked long enough.

More by luck than judgment he was there within twenty minutes. The place was exactly the way he remembered it, with the standing stone rising from the ground like a giant finger. Right then it displayed no hint of its magical qualities. Perhaps someone else would come through to his world to collect the book if Rowan had been killed.

As if reading his mind, she stepped out from behind the stone.

"Rowan!" he gasped. "How did you get here? I thought you were—"

"Dead?" she said. "No. A simple shielding spell. I was never in any danger, but I had to make it convincing for the distraction to work."

"It worked, all right," said Kevin. He raised the book. "There were three of the creatures after me. I only just managed to lose them."

"You did well." Rowan began to walk toward him. "Be assured my people will be eternally grateful. But our enemies will be here soon, drawn by the book. You must take it through the gate."

Kevin did not like the sound of that. Surely it would be safe for Rowan to hold the book long enough to return to her world.

"Come on, child," Rowan shouted. "Hurry!"

This did not feel right. He thought Rowan was his friend, yet he could see by her face that she was angry with him.

"Through the gate now!" she screamed. Kevin did not see her right hand move, but suddenly there was a knife in it. Her skin began to ripple, then peel away to expose black scales. Hair fell from her head in clumps and the pupils of her eyes turned yellow. Rowan bowed her head and spat white teeth on to the ground. When she looked at Kevin and laughed, he saw two fangs curling over her upper lip like tusks.

"Fool," she snarled, taking another step forward. Kevin stumbled backward until he was pressed against the trunk of some huge tree. "Stupid *human* believing everything he's told."

She drew closer still, until her foul breath swept over Kevin and he had to turn away. As he did, he saw the creature that had led the chase across town emerge through the trees behind the Rowan-thing's back. It had a thick branch raised overhead in a two-handed grip.

Kevin almost collapsed to the ground in fear. Rowan had deceived him, had led the monster here to finish him off. The big creature began to swing the branch down. Kevin closed his eyes before the end.

He heard a faint whistling followed by a terrible crunch.

Strangely, he did not feel a thing.

He opened his eyes. Rowan lay as still as a rock on the ground before him. The creature prodded her with one of its clawed feet, then grunted as though satisfied. Next it turned its single eye toward Kevin, who tried to scramble away. The monster said something in what sounded like a foreign language and then it was gone.

In its place was the man Kevin had seen outside McDonald's. He was tall with gray hair and looked very dignified. "That's better," said the man. Even his voice had changed. It was like Obi Wan Kenobi's from *Star Wars*. "I should have guessed that foul creature would have worked her magic on you. It explains much, including why you kept running away."

The man smiled at Kevin's obvious confusion.

"My name is Silverbirch. That thing was Gahr, a servant of the Dark Lord. It was clever, I'll grant it that. Reversed our roles. Tricked you into believing it was on the side of light, when all it wanted was to deliver the book to its master."

Kevin blinked. "So why was I told to bring it here?"

"Tell me what you know," Silverbirch commanded.

Kevin did, beginning with Rowan's arrival in his room and ending with her ordering him through the gateway.

"Hmm," Silverbirch said. "Well, the book you have in your hand is by no means rare, although it *was* the last one the Dark Lord could hope to capture. You see, over the years we managed to reach the other copies first. Unlike Gahr we knew the magic protects itself from misuse. That evil creature could not touch it. You, however, as an innocent *could*. Once it realized that it had no choice but to use you."

He took the book from Kevin's hands. "My motives are not driven by greed or malice, as you can tell."

"Then the magic isn't bad?"

"Magic is neither good nor evil but can be made to work for either side. The Dark Lord would have destroyed my people with it."

"And will you use it to defeat him?"

"No," said Silverbirch. "We will merely keep it safe, along with all the other copies we recovered. Now that none remain in your world, the balance between light and darkness can be restored."

There was a rustling in the trees, and two small beings stepped into the clearing. Kevin guessed it was they who had blocked his way across the bridge, except now they were not ugly but really rather beautiful.

Silverbirch nodded at them, then turned back to Kevin. "We must leave now." The gray-haired man held out his hand. In it was an amulet, shaped like an oak leaf and made from what appeared to be gold.

"Show this to your grandfather," he said. "Tell him your story. He is a lover of mysteries. Be assured he will understand."

Kevin took it from him. "But—"

"Goodbye, Kevin," said Silverbirch. "See you in your dreams!"

The three walked behind the stone and flickered out of existence.

For a moment Kevin was too dazed to do anything. Thomas the Rhymer had a lot to answer for, he thought. Maybe telling lies was not such a bad thing. On the other hand, look what listening to Gahr had done. Were it not for Silverbirch he would be dead by now. Truth was always better.

But, glancing down at his torn and filthy clothes, Kevin decided he would allow himself just *one* more lie when he got home.

The Invisible Kingdom

RICHARD LEANDER

In a little house halfway up the mountainside, and about a mile from the other houses of the village, there lived with his old father a young man called George. There was just enough land belonging to the house to enable the father and son to live free from care.

Immediately behind the house the wood began, the oak trees and beech trees in which were so old that the grandchildren of the people who had planted them had been dead for more than a hundred years, but in front of the house there lay a broken old millstone— who knows how it got there! Anyone sitting on the stone would have a wonderful view of the valley down below, with the river flowing through it, and of the mountains rising on the other side of the river. In the evening, when he had finished his work in the fields, George often sat here for hours at a time dreaming, with his elbows on his knees and his head in his hands; and because he cared little for the villagers, but generally went about silent and absorbed like one who is thinking of all sorts of things, the people nicknamed him "George the Dreamer." But he did not mind it at all.

The older he grew, the more silent he became, and when at last his old father died, and he had buried him under a great, old oak tree, he became quite silent. Then, when he sat on the broken millstone, as he did more often than before, and looked down into the lovely valley, and saw how the evening mists came into the valley at one end and slowly climbed the mountains, and how it then became darker and darker, until at last the moon and the stars appeared in the sky in their full glory, a wonderful feeling came into his heart. The waves of the river began to sing, quite softly at first, but gradually louder, until they could be heard quite plainly; and they sang of the mountains, down from which they had come, and of the sea, to which they wished to go, and of the nixies who lived far down at the bottom of the river. Then the forest began to rustle, quite differently from an ordinary forest, and it used to relate the most wonderful tales. The old oak tree, especially, which stood at his father's grave, knew far more than all the other trees. The stars high up in the sky wanted so much to tumble down into the green forest and the blue water, that they twinkled and sparkled as if they could not bear it any longer. But the angels who stand behind the stars held them firmly in their places, and said: "Stars, stars, don't be foolish! You are much too old to do silly things—many thousand years old, and more. Stay quietly in your places."

It was truly a wonderful valley! But it was only George the Dreamer who heard and saw all that. The people who lived in the valley had not a suspicion of it, for they were quite ordinary people. Now and then they hewed down a huge old tree, cut it up into firewood, and made a high stack, and then they said: "Now we shall be able to make our coffee again for some time." In the river they washed their clothes; it was very convenient. And even when the stars sparkled most beautifully, they only said: "It will be very cold tonight: let us hope our potatoes won't freeze." Once George the Dreamer tried to bring them to see differently, but they only laughed at him. They were just quite ordinary people.

Now, one day as he was sitting on the millstone and thinking that he was quite alone in the world, he fell asleep. Then he dreamed that he saw, hanging down from the sky, a golden swing, which was fastened to two stars by silver ropes. In the swing sat a charming princess, who was swinging so high that each time she touched the sky, then the earth, and then the sky again. Each time the swing came near the earth, the princess clapped her hands with joy and threw George the Dreamer a rose. But suddenly the ropes broke, and the swing, with the princess, flew far into the sky, farther and farther, until at last he could see it no longer.

Then he woke up, and when he looked around, he saw a great bunch of roses lying beside him on the millstone.

The next day he went to sleep again and dreamed the same thing, and when he woke up the roses were lying on the stone by his side.

This happened every day for a whole week. Then George said to himself that some part of the dream must be true, because he always dreamed exactly the same thing. So he shut up his house and set out to seek the princess.

After he had traveled for many days, he saw in the distance a country where the clouds touched the earth. He hastened toward it, but came, on his way, to a large forest. Here he suddenly heard fearful groans and cries, and, on approaching the place from which they seemed to come, he saw a venerable old man with a silver-gray beard lying on the ground. Two horribly ugly, naked fellows were kneeling on him, trying to strangle him. Then George the Dreamer looked around to see whether he could find some sort of weapon with which to run the two fellows through the body; but he could find nothing, so, in mortal terror, he tore down a huge tree trunk. He had scarcely seized it when it changed in his hands into a mighty halberd. Then he rushed at the two monsters and ran them through the body, and they let go of the old man and ran away howling.

Then George lifted the old man up and comforted him, and asked him why the two fellows had wanted to choke him. The old man said that he was the King of Dreams, and had come by mistake into the kingdom of his greatest enemy, the King of Realities. The latter, as soon as he noticed this, had sent two of his servants to lie in wait for him and kill him.

"Have you, then, done the King of Realities any harm?" asked George the Dreamer.

"God forbid!" the old man assured him. "He is always very easily provoked, that is his character. And me he hates like poison."

"But the fellows he sent to strangle you were quite naked!"

"Yes, indeed," said the king, "stark naked. That is the fashion in the land of Realities; all the people, even the king, go about naked, and are not at all ashamed. They are an abominable nation. But now, since you have saved my life, I will prove my gratitude to you by showing you my country. It is the most glorious country in the whole world, and Dreams are my subjects."

Then the Dream-King went on in front and George followed him. When they came to the place where the clouds touched the earth, the king showed him a trapdoor that was so well hidden in the thicket that not even a person who knew it was there would have been able to find it. He lifted it up and led his companion down five hundred steps into a brightly lighted grotto that stretched for miles in undiminished splendor. It was unspeakably beautiful. There were castles on islands in the midst of large lakes, and the islands floated about like ships. If you wished to go into one of them, all you had to do was to stand on the bank and call:

Little castle swim to me,

That I may get into thee.

Then it came to the shore by itself. Farther on were other castles, on clouds, floating slowly in the air. But if you said:

Float down little castle in the air,

Take me up to see thy beauties rare,

they slowly floated down. Besides these, there were gardens with flowers that gave out a sweet smell by day, and a bright light by night; beautifully tinted birds, which told stories; and a host of other wonderful things. George could do nothing but wonder and admire.

"Now I will show you my subjects, the Dreams," said the king. "I have three kinds—good Dreams for good people, bad Dreams for bad people, and also Dream-goblins. With the last I amuse myself now and then, for a king must sometimes have a joke."

So he took George into one of the castles, which was so queerly built that it looked irresistibly comical.

"Here the Dream-goblins live: they are a tiny, high-spirited, roguish lot—never do any harm, but love to tease." Then he called to one of the goblins: "Come here, little man, and be serious a moment for once in your life. Do you know," he continued, addressing George, "what this rogue does if I, once in a way, allow him to go down to the earth? He runs to the next house, drags the first man he comes across, who is sound asleep, out of bed, carries him to the church tower, and throws him down, head over heels. Then he rushes down the stairs so as to reach the bottom first, catches the man, carries him home, and flings him so roughly into bed that the bedstead creaks horribly. Then the man wakes up, rubs the sleep out of his eyes, and says: "Dear me! I thought I was falling from the church tower. What a good thing it was only a dream."

"Is that the one?" cried George. "Look here, he has been to me before; but if he comes again, and I catch him, it will be the worse for him." He had scarcely finished speaking when another goblin sprang out from under the table. He looked like a little dog, for he had a very ragged waistcoat on, and he let his tongue hang out of his mouth.

"He is not much better," said the king. "He barks like a dog, and is as strong as a giant. When people in their dreams are frightened by something, he holds their hands and feet so that they cannot move."

"I know him, too," interrupted George. "When you want to run away, you feel as stiff and stark as a piece of wood. If you want to move your arms or your legs, you can't do it. But often it is not a dog, but a bear, or a robber, or some other horrid thing."

"I will never allow them to come to you again, George the Dreamer," the king assured him. "Now

come and see the bad Dreams. But don't be afraid, they won't do you any harm—they are only for bad people."

Then they passed through a great iron door into a vast space enclosed by a high wall. Here the most terrible shapes and most horrible monsters were crowded together: some looked like men, others like animals, others were half men and half animals. George was terrified, and made his way back to the iron door. But the king spoke kindly to him and persuaded him to see more closely what wicked people have to dream. Beckoning to a Dream that stood near—a hideous giant, with a mill wheel under each arm—he commanded him to tell them what he was going to do that night.

Then the monster raised his shoulders, wriggled about with joy, grinned until his mouth met his ears, and said: "I am going to the rich man, who has let his father starve. One day, when the old man was sitting on the stone steps before his son's house, begging for bread, the son came and said to the servants: 'Drive away that fellow.' So I go to him at night and pass him through my mill wheels, until all his bones are broken into tiny pieces. When he is properly soft and quivering, I take him by the collar and shake him and say, 'See how you tremble now, you fellow!' Then he wakes up with his teeth chattering, and calls to his wife to bring him another blanket, for he is freezing. And when he has fallen asleep once more, I begin it all again."

When George the Dreamer heard this, he rushed out through the door, dragging the king after him, and crying out that he would not stay a moment longer with the bad Dreams. They were too horrible!

The king next led him into a lovely garden where the paths were of silver, the beds of gold, and the flowers were beautifully cut, precious stones. Here the good Dreams were walking up and down. The first he saw was a pale young woman, with a Noah's Ark under one arm and a box of bricks under the other.

"Who is that?" asked the Dreamer.

"She goes every evening to a little sick boy, whose mother is dead. He is quite alone all day, and no one troubles about him, but toward evening she goes to him, plays with him, and stays the whole night. She goes early because he goes to sleep early. The other Dreams go much later. Let us proceed; if you want to see everything, we must make haste."

Then they went farther into the garden, into the midst of the good Dreams. There were men, women, old men, and children, all with dear, good faces, and most beautifully dressed. Many of them were carrying all sorts of things: everything that the heart can possibly wish for. Suddenly George stood still and cried out so loudly that all the Dreams turned around to look.

"What is the matter?" said the king.

"There is my princess—she who has so often appeared to me, and who gave me the roses," George the Dreamer answered, in an ecstasy.

"Certainly, certainly, it is she," said the king. "Have I not sent you a very pretty Dream? It is almost the prettiest I have."

Then George ran up to the princess, who was sitting swinging in her little golden swing. As soon as she saw him coming she sprang down into his arms. But he took her by the hand and led her to a golden bench, on which they both sat down, telling one another how sweet it was to meet again! And when they had finished saying so, they began again. The King of Dreams meanwhile walked up and down the broad path which goes straight through the garden, with his hands behind his back. Now and then he took out his watch, to see how the time was getting on; for George the Dreamer and the princess never came to an end of what they had to say to one another. At length he went to them, and said:

"That's enough, children. You, Dreamer, are far from your home, and I cannot keep you here overnight, for

I have no beds. You see, the Dreams never sleep, but have to go up every night to men on the earth. And you, princess, must make yourself ready; dress yourself all in pink, and then come to me, so that I may tell you to whom you must appear tonight, and what you must say."

When George the Dreamer heard this, he felt more courageous than ever before in his life. Standing up, he said, firmly: "My lord the king, I will never more leave my princess. You must either keep me here below or let her go up with me to the earth: I love her much too much to live without her." Then a tear big as a hazelnut came into each of his eyes.

"But George, George," answered the king, "it is the prettiest dream I have. Still, you saved my life; so have your own way; take your princess up with you. But as soon as you have got on to the earth take off her silver veil, and throw it down to me through the trapdoor. Then she will be of flesh and blood like every other child of man; now she is only a Dream."

George the Dreamer thanked the king most heartily, and then said: "Dear king, because you are so very good, I should like to ask for one thing more. I have a princess now—but no kingdom. A princess without a kingdom is impossible. Cannot you get me one, if it is only a small one?"

Then the king answered: "I have no visible kingdoms to give away, Dreamer, only invisible ones; one of the latter you shall have, one of the biggest and best that I possess."

Then George asked what invisible kingdoms were like. The king told him he would find that out, and would be amazed at their beauty and magnificence.

"You see," he said, "it is often very unpleasant to

have anything to do with ordinary, visible kingdoms. For example: suppose you are an ordinary king, and early one morning your minister comes to your bedside and says: "Your Majesty, I want a hundred pounds for the kingdom." Then you open your treasury and find not even a farthing in it! What are you to do? Or again, you wage war and lose, and the king who has conquered you marries your princess, and shuts you up in a tower. Such things cannot happen in invisible kingdoms."

"But if we cannot see it, of what use would our kingdom be to us?" asked George, still somewhat puzzled.

"You strange man," said the king, and, pointing to his forehead, he continued: "You and your princess see it well enough. You see the castles and gardens, the meadows and forests that belong to your kingdom. You live in it, walk in it, do what you like with it. It is only other people who do not see it."

Then the Dreamer was highly delighted, for he was beginning to be afraid lest the village people should look enviously at him if he came home with his princess and was king. He took a very touching leave of the King of Dreams, climbed the five hundred steps with his princess, took the silver veil off her head and threw it down. Then he wanted to shut the trapdoor, but it was so heavy that he could not hold it. So he let it fall, and the noise it made was as great as the noise of many cannons shot off at the same time, and for a moment he became unconscious. When he came to himself again he was sitting in front of his cottage with the princess sitting on the millstone at his side, and she was of flesh and blood like any other person. She was holding his hand, stroking it, and saying:

"You dear, good, stupid man, you have not dared tell me how much you love me, for such a long time. Have you been very much afraid of me?"

And the moon rose and illumined the river, the waves beat against the banks, and the forest rustled, but they still sat there and talked. Suddenly it seemed as if a small black cloud was passing over the moon, and all at once something like a large, folded shawl fell at their feet; then the moon stood out again in her full glory. They lifted up the cloth and began to spread it out. But they took a long time over this, for it was very fine and folded many hundred times. When it was quite spread out, it looked like a large map; in the middle was a river, and on both sides were towns, forests, and lakes. Then they noticed that it was a kingdom, and knew that the good Dream-King must have sent it down to them from the sky. And when they looked at their little cottage it had become a beautiful castle, with glass stairs, marble walls, velvet carpets, and pointed blue-tiled towers. Then they took hands and went into the castle, where their subjects were already assembled. The servants bowed low, drums and trumpets sounded, and little pages went before them strewing flowers. They were king and queen.

The next morning the news that George the Dreamer had come back, and had brought a wife with him, ran like wildfire through the village. "She is probably very clever," the people said. "I saw her early this morning, when I went into the forest," said a peasant; "she was standing at the door with him. She is nothing special, quite an ordinary person, small and delicate-looking, and rather shabbily dressed. What did he see in her? He has nothing, and she probably has nothing!"

So the stupid people chattered, for they could not

see that she was a princess; and in their stupidity they did not see that the house had changed into a great, wonderful castle—for the kingdom that had come down from the sky for George the Dreamer was an invisible one. So he did not trouble about the stupid people, but lived happily and contentedly in his kingdom with his princess, who presented him with six children, each one more beautiful than the other, and they were, all six, princes and princesses. But no one in the village knew it, for they were quite ordinary people, and much too silly to notice it.

The Bone Beast

SIMON CLARK

She said: "Do you want to see where the boy was taken by the monster?"

"What boy? What monster?"

"Luke knows nothing about it. He was stuck on the toilet. He's got the runs again."

"I have not."

"Don't stand too near, Lukie's down with diarrhea."

"I've told you before," Luke snarled. "Stop taking the rip."

This had been going on for the last couple of hours. Conversations kept turning into arguments. I don't suppose it was anyone's fault. Circumstances beyond our control had thrown together four people with nothing in common. Apart from our parents, that is, who were archaeologists. They were out at the dig site while we were left to entertain ourselves.

We were staying at Starreton Manor which is slap in the middle of nowhere. There was a game room in the basement so we ended up down there playing darts and pool.

As I said, there were four of us. They were Simon Pearce, age ten—he was the joker and always spoke in rhyme; then there was his fourteen-year-old sister, Rebecca, who wore black clothes and had the longest black hair you've ever seen (Luke kept calling her "the witch queen"); and then there was Luke, who was sixteen. He was cheesed off because he'd just bought a motorbike and really wanted to be at home taking it to pieces and putting it back together again. All morning he'd worn this look on his face that made you think he'd just bitten into the sourest lemon in the world.

I'm fifteen years old. My name is Pat, I own a dog called Sam, and I've got the coolest collection of videos you've ever seen. But that morning I spent all my time trying to stop arguments developing into boxing matches.

And also that morning Rebecca had told us what happened in that very basement a hundred years ago. She explained again for Luke's benefit.

We left the game room and went into the next basement room that contained nothing but old chairs stacked on the stone floor.

"There," she said pointing to the corner. "That's the well where it happened."

Simon chipped in. "Call that a well? Is it hell?"

Luke groaned. "Stop making everything rhyme."

"Can't. I'm rhymin' Simon."

The well, chopped out from the stone floor, wasn't much bigger than a kitchen sink. It was about a meter deep, with about six centimeters of water in the bottom. The bottom itself consisted of a layer of sand.

Luke's face looked sour. "Impressed . . . *not.*"

"Tell him anyway," I said.

Rebecca flicked back her long, black hair. "It all happened a hundred years ago. The boy was the son of Sir Toby Copley. Anyway, the boy was playing down here alone. The legends say the monster came up through that well, caught the boy and . . ." She moved her jaw as if munching something tasty. "They do say if you put your hand into the well, right down into

the sand at the bottom, you can shake hands with the boy's ghost."

"Rubbish," sneered Luke.

"Dare you to do it then."

"No, it's stupid."

"I'll risk it for a biscuit." Simon shoved his hand into the water. "Not nice, cold as ice."

"Feel the spook's paw?" Luke asked sarcastically.

"Nope." Simon stood up, shaking the water off his hand.

My go next. I put my hand into the water. It was colder than I expected. Also the sand only formed a thin layer. You could barely get your fingertips through it before you hit solid rock.

Rebecca tried next. Her long hair fell forward so the tips dipped into the water. She shook her head, disappointed. "Can't feel anything."

"What did you expect?" asked Luke. "To hold hands with the ghost boy or something?"

He turned to go.

"Wait," Rebecca said to him. "You haven't had your go."

"I'm not going to waste my flipping time."

"Not scared, are we?" Rebecca teased.

"Not at all," Luke said. "What do I want to stick my hand in the water for? Knowing Simon, he'll have peed in it anyway."

We all joined in, saying he was afraid.

"Oh, all right then," he grunted. "Just to shut you lot up."

He pulled up his sleeve, crouched down, and stuck his hand in the water.

"There. Satisfied now?"

"You've got to push your hand into the sand."

"Like this." He pushed hard. The water went up to his elbow. "See, there's nothing but water that smells as if Simon's done something in it, so if . . . *heck!*"

His expression altered dramatically. I actually saw him jerk as if an electric shock ran through his body. In a half-second flat he'd jumped back from the well and looked at his hand as if something had bitten it.

Simon asked, "What happened?"

Eyes goggling out of his head, he stared at his fingers.

"Luke, what happened?"

"Nothing happened." Quickly he rubbed his hand dry on his jeans. "Nothing happened at all. It's just water."

"Luke, did you feel a hand?"

"No."

"But you felt something?"

He looked at each of us fiercely in turn. He was shaking. "I'm going to play pool."

We all went into the other basement room and Luke started putting the pool balls into the plastic triangle. When Simon realized he wasn't even going to get a sniff of a game he wandered back into the room with the well.

Rebecca said, "My dad says they're going to start digging into the Iron Age tombs this morning."

"Bully for them," Luke said, chalking his cue. "Why can't we have normal parents who just go supermarket shopping on a Saturday?"

"Archaeology is important. It tells us about the past."

"Well, they won't find much out here. There's not even a decent motor bike showroom."

"You're wrong there. Starreton Manor is built on the

site of a medieval priory. In fact this basement was once the Priory kitchens. That's why there's the well."

I said, "According to what they've found so far there was a heck of a lot happening round here for thousands of years. There was the Iron Age settlement, the standing stones up on the hillside, and the remains of a Roman temple in the orchard. And there's a legend that the big pond down by the church was fed by a magic spring. In the past people used to throw coins into the pond to keep the spirits happy."

"Spirits in ponds. Monsters in wells. Ghost boys." Luke potted a green ball. "Excuse me if I don't wet myself with excitement, people. I'd rather be—"

That's when we heard the scream.

The scream came from Simon. We all rushed into the next room, thinking he'd managed to cut himself or something.

We stood and looked around in surprise.

"Where is he?"

There was no Simon.

Luke said, "He must have gone upstairs."

"How can he? He'd have to come through the game room first."

"Did anyone see him?"

"No."

Luke frowned. "Well, he should still be in here, then."

But there was only the pile of old chairs. And, of course, the well . . .

"Look at the well," I cried, "it's bubbling like lemonade."

Rebecca looked into the well. Fear made her voice tremble. "He's down there, isn't he? Oh, no . . . he's actually down there!"

Luke said, "Impossible."

"Get him out." Rebecca crouched down and peered into that fizzing water. "Get him out, please. He won't be able to breathe."

I knelt down by the well and reached in. The water came just past my wrist. Then there was only sand and rock. How could a ten-year-old boy vanish into that?

"Fetch help!" Rebecca said to Luke.

"What help? Everyone else is out at the dig."

"He might be drowning down there. We've got to get him out. Now!"

Then Simon's sister did something so unexpected that to this day I still can't believe she actually did it.

Like it was a tiny swimming pool, she stood at the side of the well and shut her eyes. Then she jumped in.

She should have stopped when she hit rock bottom, with the water just reaching above her ankles. Instead she slipped smoothly down through that hole in the floor like it was a bottomless pit. The water closed over her head and she was gone.

Luke looked at me in shock. I looked back into the well. And I knew what I had to do. Or I would have felt guilty for the rest of my life.

I followed.

Just as I'd seen Rebecca. I stood at the side of the well, shut my eyes, held my breath. Then I jumped.

I never felt the water. I was only aware of falling a long, long way . . . down, down . . . down . . .

"You can open your eyes now, Pat." It was Rebecca's voice. "We're here. Wherever here is."

I opened my eyes.

Then I shut them again. Because I couldn't believe what I was seeing.

Cautiously I opened them once more.

"Good grief," I whispered. "Where are we?"

At first I thought we'd fallen through into a huge room beneath the basement. But although there seemed to be a ceiling, there were no walls. And the ceiling itself didn't seem to be solid. It looked like a layer of mist that was a browny-gold color. Beneath my feet was hard rock. Completely flat, it stretched away into the distance.

Rebecca stood beside me, looking up. Then she said, "I know it's impossible. But is that what I think it is?"

I looked up. About ten meters above me was a silvery oblong that looked like a pane of glass set in a ceiling.

I nodded. "It's the well, isn't it? We're actually looking up at the well from underneath?"

She nodded. "And that big, darker oblong must be Starreton Manor. At least the foundations."

"But if we can see the underside of the building, what's holding it up? Why doesn't it come crashing down on us?"

She shrugged. "I think we've fallen into a place where the normal scientific laws don't exist. Just take a look at that! No, just behind you. Hanging by your shoulder."

It was a skull.

Luckily it was only the skull of a big animal, but it was still a heck of a shock. Especially as it was hanging there in midair.

"It makes no sense," I said. "What's holding it up there?"

"Do you know what I think? Not only are we underground, I think we're actually inside the soil."

"We're buried in the soil? But how can we breathe and move about?"

"She's right, you know," came a voice from behind us.

Shocked, I looked around to see a boy of about eleven. He had curly blond hair, blue eyes, and wore a white shirt with this funny high collar and a striped blazer.

I looked around, bewildered. "We're actually in the ground, but it's as if the soil is as thin as fresh air? How come—"

"Like your friend says. It's different down here. Now come with me. We must hurry."

"But where? And who are you?"

"My name is Edward Copley."

"Edward Copley? The boy who disappeared in the cellar?"

"You've heard of me?"

"Yes, we heard a story that you vanished into the well."

"That's because the Knucker took me."

"The Knucker? What's a Knucker?"

"It's the same thing that took a boy from up there just a few moments ago."

Rebecca gasped. "A boy? That will have been my brother, Simon. And you say the Knucker took him?"

I was bewildered. "Can someone tell me what the dickens is a Knucker?"

Rebecca began, "A Knucker is a—"

"Please," Edward said impatiently. "Time's running out. If we're going to find your brother, we must go now."

As we followed Edward, I happened to look up just as something strange happened to that silver square

that was the bottom of the well.

It exploded. Silver droplets sprayed down at us. Then I saw feet, legs, body, head.

It was Luke.

Quickly as we could, we explained everything to Luke—that we had somehow fallen into an underground world. He just stared goggle-eyed at the lumps of stone that seemed to hang in midair, the bones of animals, even an old Civil War cannon that floated high above our heads as lightly as a balloon.

"Hurry up, hurry up," said Edward impatiently. "We must rescue your brother before it's too late."

"Will the Knucker eat Simon?" asked Rebecca, frightened.

"No," Edward replied. "The Knucker has plans for him, though."

Luke sounded dazed. "What on earth is a Knucker?"

As we hurried through that strange underground world, Rebecca explained. "It's a creature from English mythology. Once there were dozens of different creatures, such as Wyrms, Boggarts, Nuckelaveses, Bogles, Bug-a-boos. The Knucker is a kind of English dragon. It didn't fly or breathe fire or anything like that. They were supposed to live in ponds, rivers, or wells."

Edward was worried that we were moving so slowly. "Can't you move faster? We must reach the Knucker's lair before it's too late."

"Too late? What does the Knucker plan to do to Simon?"

"You'll understand when we get there. Now, hurry . . . *please!*"

Luke said to Edward, "Once we've got Simon to safety, we'll get you back to the surface . . . you do realize you'll be famous. A boy trapped underground for a hundred years. You'll be on TV all over the world."

"TV?" asked Edward hesitantly. "What's TV?"

Luke smiled. "We'll show you once you're back on the surface."

Edward shook his head sadly. "I'm sorry, I won't be coming with you."

"You don't want to?"

"I have no choice. I must stay."

"But why?" asked Rebecca.

"You mean you've not noticed."

As we hurried along we looked at each other, puzzled.

Edward continued, "This is a place filled with magic. If you stay here too long you begin to change." He looked at each of us in turn, his blue eyes wide. "Take another look at me."

We looked at his blond hair, the old fashioned shirt, blazer and—

We gasped when we saw what he meant.

Poking from beneath his trousers, which were ripped off at the knee, were two legs.

But they were not the legs of a boy.

"Oh." Rebecca put her hand to her mouth in shock.

Edward had the legs and hooves of a goat.

He stamped and the goat hoof clicked against the rock. "I believe the name for what I am becoming is a satyr. Half human, half goat. You see now why I must stay here. Now," he clicked his fingers, "we must move faster."

"I can't," Luke panted. "I'm cream crackered."

"Pardon?"

"Exhausted," explained Rebecca.

"Look," Edward said. "See this road? It's the old Roman road and lies three meters below the surface of the earth. If you follow it in that direction you'll reach the Knucker's lair."

"But where will you be?"

"I can run far faster than you. I'll wait for you there. I must see if the Knucker has started yet."

"Started?"

"I'll show you when you get there." Edward started to run, his hoofs clicking against the cobbled road. "And whatever you do," he shouted back, "don't leave the road!"

Luke spotted the Iron Man first. "Heck, just have a gander at him."

"Wait!" Rebecca called. "Edward said we mustn't leave the road."

"Won't be a minute."

Rebecca looked at me and shook her head. "Don't blame me if he gets into trouble."

I watched Luke run across to a ring of football-size stones. In the center was what looked like a pile of old armor. On top was a huge helmet from which sprouted bull horns. Luke looked around the stone circle, pushed at a pile of stones with his foot. He saw something, picked it up, and put it in his pocket. He was still poking round the ruins when I heard Rebecca shout a warning.

"Luke! Look out behind you."

Then I saw what she'd seen. I gasped. Because slowly rising from the ruin was a man that looked as if he was made from iron. He wore the bullhorn helmet. It covered all his head, hiding his face, leaving only a narrow slit for the eyes to see through.

"Look out!" we yelled. The Iron Man lifted this huge axe above his head.

Luke jumped back just in time as the axe came down. The blade hit a stone, sparks shot out.

"Run!"

Luke ran. As soon as he reached the road the three of us legged it away as fast as we could.

I couldn't bear to look back, expecting the Iron Man to come pounding up behind us, that giant axe held high.

"It's OK," panted Rebecca, "he's too slow to follow us."

Already he was a speck in the distance. But we didn't stop running because we knew we had to reach the lair of the Knucker. But how would we save Simon? We didn't have a clue.

We ran breathlessly. Above us we saw things that are normally hidden from sight when we're on the surface. A long, straight pipe ran from left to right into the distance. "A water main," panted Rebecca, her long black hair flicking high behind her. Again the pipe seemed to hang in thin air. We passed beneath a dark shape the size of a tennis court. That must have been the pond. Here and there we saw the roots of trees hanging down toward us in long, forking fronds. Up there, too, must be our parents. But there was no way we could shout to them or make ourselves known to them—not from down here, deep within the earth.

Just then the old Roman road reached a ridge.

Edward appeared and held his finger to his lips to shush us.

"It's down there," whispered Edward. "Look."

We saw the Knucker.

And we shivered with horror.

"A slug," whispered Luke. "It's a great dirty slug."

Luke was right. Gray, and as big as a whale, it slid across the bedrock, leaving a silver slug trail as wide as a road.

"It's . . . disgusting," I whispered.

"And it's dangerous," Edward said. "More dangerous than you realize."

"What's that white building?"

"That's not a building. It's the Bone Beast."

"Bone Beast?"

Edward nodded. "For years the Knucker's been collecting bones for miles around. For a while now it's been using that silver stuff it secretes to glue the bones together."

"But the Bone Beast looks like a giant man."

"That's exactly what it is. A giant man, built out of bone, as tall as a church tower."

"But why?"

"Soon the Knucker will activate it, then it and its kind will invade the upper world—your world—and they will destroy everything they touch."

"But Simon—"

"Your brother's in the Bone Beast's head. The Knucker needs a human being to give the Beast life. So you see we need to get Simon out now. To save him. And to stop the Knucker's invasion of your world."

"But how?"

"I'll try and distract the Knucker somehow. You free your brother."

As we made our plan I heard something faintly squealing like a rusty hinge. Then I knew what it was. I looked back.

"Run!" I yelled.

The Iron Man had found us. He walked toward us holding the axe above his horned helmet.

There was nowhere to run but toward the Knucker and the gleaming white Bone Beast.

Edward shouted, "What have you done to anger the Iron Man?"

"Nothing," panted Luke, "I just looked around the ruin."

"That was the ruin of his house where he lived with his family a thousand years ago. He was cursed by the Knucker."

The Iron Man followed. He moved fast now, iron boots striking sparks from the road.

"You've taken something from him," shouted Edward, "what is it?"

"Nothing."

Rebecca panted, "You picked something up. You put it in your pocket."

"What was it?" demanded Edward.

"I don't know."

Everything was going wrong. This was going to end in disaster.

Luke pulled the apple-sized object from his pocket. "Just a stupid doll's head, carved out of wood."

"Don't you see?" Edward said. "It belonged to his child. He wants the doll's head back. And he'll stop at nothing until he gets it."

Ahead the Knucker lifted its slug body. Its mouth opened, showing row after row of teeth that were sharper than a shark's.

Suddenly I had an idea. "Here . . . Luke. Throw me the doll's head."

I caught it. Then I ran faster toward the gaping mouth of the Knucker.

I threw the doll's head. It entered the huge throat and disappeared.

"Run!" I shouted. "Back the way we came."

The Iron Man ignored us now. He rushed toward the Knucker. When he was close enough he hacked with the axe; he hacked again and again ... and again ...

The Knucker lay dead on the rock. And it wasn't long before we freed Simon from the Bone Beast's head, which was as big as a car.

Simon looked about, dazed. He seemed unable to speak. And when he looked at us each in turn, he didn't seem to recognize us.

"Simon, are you okay? It didn't hurt you?" Rebecca put her arm around his shoulder. "Simon, tell me if you're in pain."

Simon blinked, licked his lips. Then he said, "Just a scratch when I came through the hatch, but it's the dirt on my shirt that'll take some explaining when Mum starts complaining."

Luke snorted. "He's back to his old self. Worst of luck."

Simon grinned as Rebecca and I slapped him on the back, laughing with relief.

Grin widening, Simon added, "I'm Rhymin' Simon and back with the crack."

Luke shook his head. "I'm not going to make a habit of being nice to you, but it's good to see you're in one piece."

Then Edward took us back the way we had come. In the distance we could see the Iron Man walking away from us along the road.

"Why isn't he going back to the ruin?" I asked Edward.

"He's free from the Knucker's curse now. He'll start to search for his family."

"And what about you?" asked Rebecca. "Come with us to the surface. Please."

Edward smiled and shook his head. "I'm free, too. I know there are more people like me down here. I'll find them. Then I'll have a new family."

Edward pointed to a line of stones that seemed to ascend through fresh air like a flight of magic steps. "Climb those," he said. "When you reach the black stuff above your heads, push as hard as you can. But I should warn you, take a deep breath first. Goodbye, I'll miss you." Then suddenly he was gone, running with amazing speed across the rocks, goat hooves clacking.

We did as he said, then pushed upward against this black rubbery ceiling.

It all happened at once.

Suddenly I was in a mass of bubbling water. The next second I was standing chest-deep in the pond, the brilliant sunlight in my face.

Seconds later more heads appeared. Rebecca. Simon. Then Luke, puffing and blowing.

When we saw one another we all grinned. We were once more back in the world we called home.

Ice Princess

ELISABETH WATERS

It was very cold when Sharon woke up. At first she thought that the heater in her cottage had stopped working—this happened occasionally, and it got cold before dawn this high in the mountains. Then she realized that there was a lot more light in the room than there should have been, considering the fact that she was supposed to be at the rink by 5:55 a.m. and on the ice by 6:00. I guess I shouldn't have stayed out so late last night, she thought. I must have slept through my alarm. Thank God I don't have a lesson in the first session. She groaned.

"Dost thou always sleep until the sun is halfway up the sky?" The voice was that of a very young girl.

Sharon didn't have a roommate, and children under eighteen weren't allowed in the cottages. Her eyes snapped open. It didn't help much; even with extended-wear contact lenses it took a few minutes to get the world in focus in the morning. And when it was in focus, it wasn't her world.

She was still in her own bed, and her bed table was next to it, but everything else had changed. Her room was gone; the bed and table now stood in the middle of a large, round room with gray stone walls. There were four large windows at intervals in the walls, and a strong crosswind blew across the room, making Sharon's eyes feel as if the lenses were drying out and sticking to them. Fortunately she kept a bottle of saline solution on the bed table. She put a couple of drops in each eye and blinked several times. Excess salt water dripped down her cheeks, but now she could see the little girl sitting on the foot of her bed.

The child seemed to be about ten years old, and she looked exactly like Sharon herself had looked at that age. She had nondescript pale gray eyes, long brown hair, parted neatly in the middle, with a thick braid hanging over each shoulder, and she wore a long white dress with silver edging around a square neckline and a white shawl around her shoulders. She was shivering in the wind, but she didn't seem to notice.

"Art thou crying?" she asked curiously. "A princess is not supposed to cry. Mother says so."

Sharon felt as though she had fallen down a rabbit hole. "Where is your mother?"

"Our mother," the child corrected her. "Thou art my sister, Sharon, dost thou not remember?"

"I'm an only child," Sharon said. "And I've never met you before in my life. I'm sure. I'd remember anyone who talked the way you do." And I'm obviously dreaming, and I had better wake up before I do miss a lesson and my coach gets mad at me.

"The ice got her," the child said with a sigh. "The Ancient said that thou wouldst not remember, but I had hoped it was mistaken. Come, I shall take thee to it, and it can explain."

"What is the Ancient?" Sharon asked, swinging her legs over the side of the bed and feeling for her slippers. Fortunately they were there—and so was her skate bag, which she had dropped next to the bed last night. Apparently whatever had brought her here had brought along everything within a few feet of her as well. She rummaged in the bag and pulled out a pair of leg warmers and a hooded sweatshirt, a souvenir of her last skating competition.

"What dost thou?" the child asked.

Sharon stared at her. "I'm putting on more clothes—what does it look like I'm doing? You must have noticed that it's cold in here."

"But that is not proper clothing!" the child protested. "The Ancient will not like it if thou comest before it looking like a . . ." The child's voice trailed off; obviously she was unable to find a description for what she thought Sharon looked like. "Thou art a princess, and thou must dress properly," she said earnestly. "I shall help thee," she added, picking up a dress and shawl like the ones she was wearing from the foot of the bed. "I regret that we have no servants at present—"

"Don't tell me, let me guess," Sharon said sarcastically, "the ice got them, too."

The child nodded.

"Look, kid," Sharon said, "ice doesn't get people. Ice is just frozen water—it's not as if it could think for itself or anything."

"Thou dost not comprehend," the child said, pulling Sharon's nightshirt off over her head.

"That's the first sensible thing you've said yet," Sharon muttered, as the child dropped the dress over Sharon's head and tugged it into place. Sharon gasped as the cold fabric touched her bare skin. The child knelt behind her, laced the dress up the back, and put the matching shawl around Sharon's shoulders. Then she began to fuss with Sharon's hair, parting it in the middle and coiling it back away from Sharon's face.

The child stepped back to survey the full effect and smiled faintly. "Thou art so beautiful," she said wistfully. "I wish that I looked more like thee. Why dost thou have black hair and deep blue eyes whilst I have brown and gray?"

Sharon decided that there was already enough culture shock in the room without her trying to explain dyes that changed brown hair to black and contact lenses designed to change pale gray eyes to any color one desired. It's a good thing I didn't get a set in purple, she thought with some amusement. That would probably really freak the poor kid. She also decided against explaining about the hours she spent in the gym every day, lifting weights and exercising on the Stairmaster, so that she could keep in shape and look good to the judges at competitions. Keeping her weight down was a constant battle, and she needed to maintain a lot of muscle, both in her legs and in her upper body, in order to be able to do spins and jumps. But she didn't think she could explain a Stairmaster to this child. For all that the girl looked exactly like her, she seemed alien.

She followed the child up a flight of cold stone stairs that hugged the inner wall of the Tower. The heat must be off in my cottage if I'm this cold in my dreams, she thought idly. The child was breathing hard as they went up the stairs, but Sharon didn't find them particularly bothersome. Of course, Sharon was accustomed to running up and down a flight of seventy stairs, to and from the rink, several times a day.

They wound up in a room at the very top of the Tower. It had one small window off to the side, but mostly it was lit with candles, which were burning low and dripping wax all down the sides of the candle stands. The wall was the same gray stone as the rest of the Tower, but there was a design carved in a circle on

one wall. It reminded Sharon a bit of the Celtic inter-lace pattern that she had seen on someone's skating dress recently. In front of the design was a wooden pedestal, and on the pedestal was a skull—apparently the skull of a saber-toothed tiger. Sharon yawned. For some reason she was very tired today, and saber-tooths didn't interest her particularly. She had grown up near the La Brea Tar Pit, which was full of the darn things.

"Good morrow, Princess Morag, Princess Sharon," a voice said. It seemed to be coming from the skull, but the skull's jaws weren't moving. And besides, Sharon thought, skulls can't talk—especially skulls of extinct animals too dumb to stay out of the tar pits.

"Good morrow, Ancient," the child, presumably Morag, said respectfully, apparently addressing the skull. "I have brought her here, as you instructed, but she remembers nothing."

"I warned you that such was likely to be the case," the voice said calmly.

"She speaketh most strangely," Morag continued, sounding puzzled, "and she hath wondrous strange clothing—and black hair and blue eyes. Are you certain that she is my sister?"

"Quite certain," the voice said. "It is time that I explained matters to Princess Sharon."

There were no chairs in the room, and Sharon had the feeling this was going to be a long story. She shrugged and flopped into a sitting position on the floor, leaning back against the wall opposite the skull. Morag, who was standing facing the skull with her hands clasped loosely together in front of her, cast Sharon a scandalized glance.

Sharon concluded that, once again, she had done something un-princess-like. So far the list seemed to include crying, dressing in clothing warm enough to prevent frostbite, and sitting on the floor. When she was growing up, Sharon had always dreamed of being a princess and living in a castle. Now she was rapidly concluding that being a princess was a drag and life in a castle was cold and uncomfortable. She wondered where the bathroom was, and if they ever ate around here. Probably the skull didn't, but Morag appeared to be a growing girl and thus presumably in need of food.

"Did Princess Morag tell you about the ice?" the skull asked.

"She said that it 'got' her mother and all the servants," Sharon replied. "That doesn't make sense to me."

Morag shuddered. "Ice is so strong and so smooth—there's nothing one can do to it."

Sharon giggled. "Strong and smooth? Ice?" She shook her head. "You've obviously never seen a rink after a freestyle session—between the toepick marks from jump takeoffs and the grooves in the ice from the landings, it's a real mess. I've seen little kids kick holes the size of my fist in the ice without even trying." She shrugged, and continued, "And, of course, heat will melt it right back into water."

"Unfortunately," the skull said, "we do not get enough heat here now to melt ice."

"You mean you're having an ice age?" Sharon asked. "Glaciers coming out of the north and stuff like that?"

"No," the skull said. "Once, long ago, that did happen here. But now we have a different problem. We have a mage who can control the ice."

"And he's using it to kill everyone?" Sharon asked. "Isn't that sort of wasteful? I mean, can he cook? If he kills all the servants, he'll have to, won't he? Cook,

and do his own laundry, and clean the castle . . ."

The skull interrupted her. "It is your destiny to stop him. That is why you were fostered in the other world, so that you would learn the powers needed to defeat him. The queen your mother foresaw this day."

"Thou hast twice my years," Princess Morag pointed out, "so thou must know many more spells than I do. I have studied all my life, but doubtless thou hast twice my knowledge."

"You mean magic?" Sharon looked at her incredulously. "We don't study magic in my world. Most people don't even believe it exists."

"Don't believe in magic?" Morag exclaimed in horror. "Ancient, how can a world without magic exist?"

"Calm yourself, Princess," the skull said sternly. Morag gulped and composed her features. "Princess Sharon's world has magic; they simply call it other things."

"Like what?" Sharon challenged it.

"Religion."

"You mean like witchcraft?" Sharon shook her head emphatically. "No way! I'm a Christian, not a witch."

"Do you attend Mass?" the skull asked.

"Of course I do!" Sharon said indignantly. "Every week."

"And you don't consider that to be magic? The Christian Mass is a very powerful act of ritual magic. Don't you feel different after receiving communion?"

Sharon had to think about that—she had always taken the effects of the sacrament for granted. "Well, yes, but—"

"Different how?" Morag asked eagerly.

"Stronger . . . happier . . . more in harmony with the world and the people around me . . . closer to God . . ."

147

Sharon had never tried to put it into words before. "I just feel better, that's all."

"Then you do know what magic is and what it feels like," the Ancient said. "With that and the physical strengths and skills you have, you can accomplish the task before you."

"What task is that?" Sharon asked warily.

"When the Queen died," the skull explained, "the mage took her orb. He cannot use it, but as long as he keeps it away from Princess Morag, she cannot use it either. And she needs it if she is to survive."

"What's an orb?" Sharon asked.

"It is what gives the queen her power," the skull explained. "It is what makes her the queen."

"What about the king?" Sharon enquired.

"What is a king?" Morag asked.

I've heard of sheltered childhoods, Sharon thought, but this is ridiculous. "The queen's husband," she said. Morag still looked blank. "Our father. What happened to him?"

"Father?" Morag didn't seem to know that word either.

"You don't have a father," the skull informed Sharon. "The queen bears her daughters alone."

"Parthenogenesis?" Sharon asked incredulously.

"Yes," the skull replied.

"So that's why my hair and eye color bothers you," Sharon said, turning to Morag. "I'm supposed to look exactly like you, just older, right?"

"Yes," Morag said nervously. "Why dost thou not?"

"I'm a skater," Sharon explained, "and I skate in competitions, where part of what they judge you on is how you look. So I changed my hair and eye color to be more striking, and I work really hard to stay thin so

that I'll look good in my costumes. If I didn't dye my
hair and wear lenses that change my eye color, I would
look just like you."

"Truly?"

"Yes, truly. When I was ten, I looked exactly the
way you do now."

"So thou truly art my sister." Morag sounded im-
mensely relieved.

"It looks that way." Sharon smiled reassuringly at
the child.

"If you look unlike Princess Morag and the queen,"
the skull said, "that should help in your quest. The
mage will not immediately recognize you for what
you are."

"Probably not," Sharon said. "Is he likely to try to
kill me if he does?"

"He will try to kill you in any case," the skull said.
"He has killed everyone who has left this Tower. But
his powers are weaker during the day, so if you can get
the orb back here by nightfall, you should survive."

This is definitely the strangest dream I've ever had
in my life, Sharon thought. "Where is the orb and
what does it look like?" she asked.

"The queen our mother took it to the Temple,"
Morag said. "Yesterday was the longest day, when the
orb is taken to the Temple to soak in the sunlight. The
orb is a sphere, about this big," she held up her small
hands, indicating something about two inches in di-
ameter, "and it is made of translucent green stone."

"So you think the orb is still at the Temple?" Sharon
asked.

Morag nodded. "I know it is. I can feel it; I have
been able to ever since Mother died. I would know if it
had been moved."

"So how do I find the Temple?" Sharon asked. "How far away is it?" She moved to look out of the small window. The Tower was surrounded by a sea of ice as far as she could see, as if it were set in the middle of an enormous rink.

"I do not know." Morag looked confused. "Canst thou not feel it?"

"Feel what?" Sharon asked, feeling as confused as Morag looked. "The Temple? The orb?" She frowned. "If you can't tell me how to find it, you'll have to come with me and show me. Can you skate?"

"What is skating?" Morag asked.

"The Princess Morag cannot leave the Tower," the skull said firmly. "I shall have to link you together. Princess Sharon, come touch the top of my skull, right behind my eye socket."

Sharon looked dubiously at it, then shrugged. What can an old skull do to me, even if it can talk? She gingerly touched the tip of her index finger to the skull. It felt as if a strong electric current was running through her, from the top of her head and the soles of her feet through her finger and into the skull. She tried to pull her hand away, but she couldn't move at all. Suddenly this seemed less like a dream and more like a very strange reality.

"Princess Morag," the skull said. Its voice seemed to echo inside Sharon's head. Then Morag touched the skull, and Sharon abruptly realized what it had meant by "link together." She was looking at this skull through two sets of eyes, until she hastily squeezed her own shut, leaving her looking across the skull from Morag's viewpoint and giving her an excellent view of her terrified face.

"Fear not, Sharon." She heard Morag's voice in her

head, and she knew that neither of them was moving her lips. "Open thine eyes."

Sharon cautiously opened her eyes to narrow slits. As she did so, her vision through Morag's eyes went away. She opened her eyes the rest of the way, and discovered that the feeling in her body was returning to normal and she could move again. She backed cautiously away from the skull.

"The link is in place." Morag said. "Thank you, Ancient." She bowed slightly to the skull.

"Uh, thanks," Sharon added. *I think.*

"Come, Sharon," Morag took her hand and dragged her toward the stairs. "If thou art to return by dark, thou must leave very soon."

The girls went down the stairs together, much faster than they had come up them. Morag was obviously in a hurry now. "Canst thou feel the orb now?" she asked.

Sharon concentrated as much as she could while hurrying down the stairs. "I can feel something out that way," she admitted, pointing, "but I'm not sure what it is."

"That is the correct direction," Morag said. "And now I can see what thou seest and speak to thee without speaking aloud, so I can tell thee the way if thou loseth it."

"About this wizard—" Sharon began.

"Mage," Morag corrected her.

"Whatever. What are his weaknesses? Is there any way to kill him?"

"He likes not sunlight and warmth," Morag said, "but, beyond that, I do not know." She looked anxiously up at Sharon. "I hope that thou wilt not encounter him."

"Me too." They reached the room where Sharon's bed was. "I'm going to get dressed," she said. "Can you fix me some food to take with me? I haven't had anything to eat since dinner last night, and I'm starved!"

"Fasting makes our link stronger," Morag said.

"Skating with no food makes me fall down a lot," Sharon pointed out. "You can fast if you want, since you're staying here, but I'm going to be out there moving around and using energy. I need food."

"Very well," Morag agreed. "I shall fetch thee some bread." She left the room and continued down the stairs.

"Well, bread is better than nothing," Sharon sighed, "but it's certainly enough to make me appreciate the food back at the training center. I wonder if they can send me back when I've got the orb for them." She dropped the shawl on the bed and tried to get out of the dress. "For that matter, I wonder if I can unlace this wretched dress." She struggled unsuccessfully with it for several minutes before Morag came back with a tray.

"Here," she said, handing Sharon a hunk of bread. It was lumpy and coarse, but Sharon was too hungry to care. "I'll unlace the dress for thee," Morag continued. She had it undone before Sharon could take more than three bites of bread.

Sharon set the bread aside, dumped her skate bag on the bed, and began to select and hastily put on clothing. Even though it must be almost noon, it was still very cold in the room. She pulled on a pair of beige tights and a skating dress that so horrified Morag by its short skirt and bright colors that her thoughts came through to Sharon even though she wasn't deliber-

ately projecting them. "No, Morag," Sharon explained, "a virgin in my world can wear colors other than white. The color of my clothing says nothing at all about my character or my morals."

She put on the hooded sweatshirt with a pocket across its front, shoved her gloves in the pocket for the moment, and sat down on the edge of the bed to lace on her skates. Since the blades were covered by plastic guards, she could walk on them indoors, and it was certainly easier to put them on while sitting on a bed than it would be sitting on the ice outside the Tower door.

She shoved her water bottle, which was almost completely full, and all the bread she could fit into the pocket, picked up the piece she had been eating, and headed toward the stairs. "All right, Morag, show me the way out of here."

Morag led her down the rest of the stairs to a small door at the base of the Tower. She opened it, and the ice stretched out in front of Sharon. In spite of the seriousness of the situation, Sharon smiled. The ice was flat and smooth, just the way she liked it. She removed her blade guards and crammed them in next to her water bottle as she stepped carefully onto the ice. She skated a few curves to see how this ice felt against her blades, and smiled at Morag. "It's good ice," she said reassuringly, "hard and fast. I should be able to make good time to the Temple."

"I'll stay linked and keep watch," Morag promised. "Be careful."

Sharon stroked toward the Temple. The land was almost completely level, so it wasn't very different from being on a rink, except that this "rink" really did seem to go on forever. She looked back at the Tower to see how far she had come and gasped in surprise. She knew that Tower. It was part of an old ruin called the Castle, not far from the Training Center. The Tower was the only part of the ruin that still stood, and there were all sorts of rumors about the place: that it had been an insane asylum, or a sanitarium for patients with tuberculosis, or that satanists still used it for their rituals. Sharon had been there a few times with her boyfriend John, but only once at night. At night, it was a spooky place.

"Sharon?" Morag's voice whispered in her head. "Is something amiss?"

"Amiss?" It took Sharon a second to place the word. "No, Morag, it's okay. Nothing's wrong. The Tower just looks familiar, that's all—there's one like it in my world."

"It is probably one of the gates between our worlds," Morag thought calmly.

Sharon decided she didn't want to think about gates between worlds at the moment. She turned her back on the Tower and continued toward the Temple, chewing on another piece of bread as she skated. By the time she saw the Temple in front of her, she had finished all the bread and about half her water, but the food had made her feel better. Her legs ached slightly from all the stroking, but not enough to inconvenience her.

As she came to the final approach to the Temple, she heard a gasp of horror in her head. Looking at what lay ahead, she could understand it. There was a deep gorge between her and the Temple, and the only bridge across it was about three inches wide—and at least fifteen feet long. She could feel terror well up

inside her, but she realized that most of it was not hers. "Morag, relax," she thought at her little sister. "This is nothing to be afraid of."

"What if you fall?" It was the wail of a terrified child.

"I'm not going to fall. I've had to do harder things than this on beginning tests, and I've passed senior level." She backed up a bit so that she could get up to speed; there wasn't going to be any way to cheat on this maneuver. "I've had to do a spiral on a flat edge for at least four times my body length, and this is only about three."

"What's a spiral?"

"Just watch." Sharon pushed off strongly. Left, right, left, right. She hit the bridge in a perfect flat spiral position, right foot even on both edges of her skate blade, chest and left leg parallel to the ice, with the left leg turned out from the hip and the toe pointed, head up and facing into the breeze created by the air she was moving through, and arms outstretched to the sides, arching her chest slightly. It was definitely one of the best spirals she had ever done, and it carried her smoothly over the bridge in the space of a single breath. As soon as she reached the Temple entrance, an area about one meter square, she dropped her left foot to the ice, pulled her arms in, and converted her remaining momentum into a two-foot spin. She stopped it with a toe pick into the ice, and threw back her head, laughing softly in delight. "That felt good!" she thought.

"Yes," Morag's thoughts were wistful, "it did."

Sharon skated to the doorway and looked at the stone floor of the Temple, then up at the sun, which was halfway down to the horizon. I'd better hurry, she thought. Picking up her right foot, she ran her fingers along the blade to remove the excess ice, then pulled the blade guards from her pocket and fitted one over the right blade. She repeated the procedure with her left skate and walked into the Temple.

She passed through a small anteroom and into the main hall, which had a skylight in the center of the ceiling. On an altar under the skylight a woman lay on her back, holding a green sphere in her cupped hands. The sphere glowed faintly in the sunlight, despite the fact that both woman and sphere were covered with at least an inch of ice.

Sharon didn't need Morag's cry of "Mother" bouncing through her skull to recognize the woman. That's what I'd look like, she realized, if I weren't a skater. The woman's eyes were closed, but Sharon had no doubt they were the same pale gray as hers and Morag's. The brown hair, with a few strands of white mixed in, was parted in the center and coiled back as Morag had tried to do with Sharon's—which had come loose while she was skating and now hung every which way about her head. The woman looked peaceful, like an illustration of Sleeping Beauty or Snow White in a book of fairy tales.

"Are you sure she's dead?" Sharon wondered.

"Have thou never seen a dead body before?" Morag sounded surprised.

"Well, no, never," Sharon admitted.

"Look at her arms," Morag instructed. "See how her hands and forearms are white, but the backs of her upper arms look bruised? After death, the blood flows to the lowest part of the body and stays there. She's dead, and she's been dead since last night. I felt her die." Sharon felt a faint flicker of emotional pain,

quickly covered by annoyance. "Just get the orb and get out of there, before the mage finds you!"

Sharon frowned at the orb. The queen was not grasping it; it rested on top of her open hands, but it was still covered with ice, and there was nothing in the room to chip it out with. Nothing except my skate blades, Sharon thought. She removed the guard from her right blade, put her gloves on so that she could hold onto the ice-covered body for balance, and swung her leg over the body. A few good whacks with the heel of her blade chipped away the ice that held the orb in place at the bottom, but most of it was still covered with ice when she pulled it free. She shoved it into her pocket and put her blade guard back on. "What about our mother's body?" she thought to Morag.

"Leave it," Morag replied, "just get back here as quickly as thou canst!"

Nonetheless, Sharon bowed her head over the body for a moment and said a quick prayer for the repose of the queen's soul. Then she walked quickly out of the Temple.

She frowned as she looked at the bridge. With the small patch of ice on this side, she didn't think she could get up enough speed to be sure of getting back across it in a spiral. And it was too narrow to crawl along. A balance beam is wider, Sharon thought in disgust. How do people usually get in and out of here?

She would just have to sit straddled across it and pull herself along with her hands. That would be slow and a bit precarious, especially for the contents of her pocket. She pulled out the ice-covered orb and gritted her teeth. There was no help for it; the safest place for the orb was down the front of her skating dress. If she tied the neck of her sweatshirt tightly, the orb would stay with her even if she wound up hanging upside down. She loosened the neck of the sweatshirt and quickly shoved the orb down the front of her dress, tucking it under the waistband of her tights. The cold made her eyes fill with tears, but at least it was secure now. She pulled up the hood of her sweatshirt and tied the drawstring at the neck.

Dragging herself across the "bridge" seemed to take forever, but eventually she crawled onto the ice at the other side, moved away from the gorge, stood up, and started stroking back to the Tower.

The sun was halfway below the horizon as she approached the Tower, and Morag had been getting steadily more agitated for the past half-hour. Now she continually urged Sharon to hurry, and Sharon was getting a headache. "Can't you be quiet?" she thought, trying to project reassurance. "You're starting to make me nervous!"

"He's coming," Morag whispered. "I can feel him."

"Damn!" Sharon muttered. The ice was starting to crack around her, and a two-foot-wide fissure opened up in her path between her and the Tower.

She remembered her coach teaching her a jump called a Falling Leaf. "Pretend you're jumping over a mud puddle," he had said. She turned quickly to glide backwards on two feet toward the fissure, pushing a couple of times with the side of one foot to build up speed. Just before she reached it, she twisted her head and upper body to the left to look behind her and picked up her left foot and held it at the back of her right ankle. As she reached the very edge of the fissure, she jumped off her right foot, reaching out with her left foot and both arms. While she didn't think this

jump had quite the graceful floating quality of a falling leaf that its originator had in mind, it did get her safely into the Tower courtyard.

Then Morag's voice in her head said in warning, "He's here!"

The sun was almost completely below the horizon by now, but Sharon had excellent night vision. (The lamps on the stairway down from the rink were always getting broken, so she had plenty of practice in navigating hazardous terrain with almost no light.) She could see the man standing on the doorstep to the Tower, even though he was dressed in black. Black leather boots went up to his knees, black trousers were tucked into them, and he wore a black silk blouse slit open almost to his waist. Obviously the cold didn't bother him.

He looked to Sharon like a cross between the latest in teenage fashion and the cover of a romance novel, which meant that she didn't feel the automatic fear of him that Morag obviously did. Besides, it was late, she was tired, cold, and hungry; and he was between her and her dinner and bed. She pushed off hard onto her left foot on an outside edge, which started her arcing away from him to his left. She prayed that he didn't know enough about skating to realize that the track she was on was going to take her right to him. Although she was moving as quickly as she could, time seemed to slow down, as if she were doing this in slow motion. She leaned into her edge, bending her left knee as deeply as she could, and stretched forward into a position similar to the spiral she had used earlier, except that this time her left arm was directly in front of her left knee. She raised her head just enough to be sure that he wasn't trying to get out of her way, but he stood unmoving, looking amused. When she was almost close enough for her hand to touch him, she snapped her left arm back and rose up on her knee, putting her body into what would have been a beautiful camel spin—if she hadn't hit him squarely in the sternum with the toe picks of her right skate.

Sharp pointed stainless steel met bare flesh. His screams were deafening. Sharon had seen people get spiked with a skate blade before (it didn't happen often, thank God, but it did happen occasionally), but this was the first time she had ever heard anyone howl as if he were being burned alive.

She picked herself up from the ice, where she had landed on her hands and knees when her momentum was halted so abruptly, and twisted to look at him. Oddly enough, he did seem to be being burned alive. What she could see of his skin was crackling and bubbling, radiating out from where her skate blade had hit him. She watched in bewilderment as his screams died away and his entire body turned into a pile of ashes.

When she was certain he was no longer a threat, she put her blade guards back on, stepped over the pile of empty clothes, and went into the Tower, where Morag had been hovering just inside the door waiting for her.

"Is he dead?"

"It certainly looks that way." Sharon untied the neck of her sweatshirt and fished the orb out of the front of her skating dress. The ice covering it was down to a thin film in most places except for the bottom, which was bare.

"Here's your orb, little sister." She handed it to Morag, then stripped off her gloves. "Let's go upstairs; I want to get out of my skates and into some dry clothing."

She led the way up to her room. Morag followed her, cradling the orb and gazing at it as if it held the mysteries of the universe.

Sharon stripped off her skating clothes and, for lack of anything else to wear, put the white dress on again. Morag set the orb down long enough to lace the dress for her, then resumed her study of it. Sharon pulled her towel out of the pile of stuff on the bed and carefully dried her skate blades, then put terry-cloth soakers on them to keep them from getting nicked when she put them back in her bag. She hung her wet dress, tights, and sweatshirt over the footboard of the bed.

Morag stood up abruptly. "We have to see the Ancient."

"All right," Sharon said. "I want to ask if it knows

why the mage burned up like that."

She followed Morag up the stairs again, back to the room at the top of the Tower. By now the skull looked like an old friend. "Good evening, Ancient," she said. "Do you know what happened to the mage?"

"I could feel something," it replied. "Tell me."

Sharon described what she had seen to the best of her ability. "Why did he burn up like that?" she finished.

"What are your skate blades made of?" the skull asked.

"Stainless steel."

"Does this 'steel' have iron in it?"

Sharon frowned. "I think so. Why?"

"The mage must have had elven blood," the skull said. "Elves are the only creatures I have ever heard of that burn when exposed to iron. Did you hit him hard enough to draw blood?"

"I couldn't see blood through the burns," Sharon said, "but I must have. Toe picks are sharp and I hit him hard on bare skin."

"That would carry the iron burn through his entire body then," the skull concluded. "You did well."

Sharon bit her lip. "I've never killed anyone be-fore—and I didn't mean to kill him. Murder is a mortal sin."

"I think if you ask your priest, he will tell you that elves do not have souls," the skull said soothingly. "Therefore, killing him was no more murder than killing a venomous spider."

"Oh." That made Sharon feel a bit better. "So what happens to me now?"

"Do you wish to stay here?" the skull asked. "Now that the mage is gone, the ice should melt and the

land will be fair once again."

Sharon thought about it. She was a princess and she could stay here in the Tower and be a princess. But if the ice melted, she would have no place to skate, and even if it didn't, her coach and her friends were all back in her own world. And in this world she had no father and her mother was dead, and she had no memories of her mother save as a dead body. In her own world, she had parents who loved her, even if they weren't her biological parents. And in her own world she had her boyfriend, while here they would probably expect her to reproduce by parthenogenesis—assuming that she was allowed to have children at all. She might be a princess, but Morag was to be queen. Morag was a nice kid, but the idea of life with only Morag and a talking skull for company was a bit daunting. "I want to go home," Sharon said, "back to my own world."

"Very well," the skull replied. "Morag can send you back as soon as she masters the orb."

"How long will that take?" Sharon looked at Morag, who was frowning down at the orb.

"I fear it is broken," Morag said. "I cannot feel anything from it."

"What?" Sharon yelped. "After what I went through to get that thing, it had better not be broken! Let me see it." She lifted the orb out of Morag's unresisting hands—and nearly dropped it, as a flood of emotions and images swept through her. She shoved it back into Morag's hands and dropped to the floor, putting her head between her knees and hoping she wasn't going to faint. She had never felt so dizzy in her life, even when she first started learning to do spins.

"Morag," she said firmly. "That orb is not broken."

"Then why do I feel nothing from it?"

"Ancient?" Sharon appealed to the skull.

"I cannot help you with this," the skull replied. "Morag must master the orb herself—or you must."

Sharon frowned as she looked at Morag. "You don't feel anything from the orb?" Morag shook her head. "What do you feel?" Sharon asked. "Not from the orb—from anyplace, from inside yourself."

"Nothing." Morag looked blank and tired. "What am I supposed to feel?"

"What did you feel when you realized your mother was dead?"

"I knew I had to get the orb. That's why we brought you here."

"No," Sharon said. "You're missing the point. Not what did you do, what did you feel."

"A princess does not cry," Morag said, as if by rote. "A princess does not let feelings get in the way of what must be done."

"Maybe it's different for a queen," Sharon suggested. "Maybe your lack of feelings is what's keeping you from feeling the orb."

"So how am I supposed to feel?" Morag asked.

"You know," Sharon said. "You're just fighting it. Stop fighting your feelings, and the orb will work for you just fine." She fought unsuccessfully to keep from yawning. "I've had a long day," she said. "I'm going to bed. You might try that too; sleep might help you. Good night, Morag. Good night, Ancient."

"Good night, Princess Sharon," the skull said.

Sharon stumbled off to bed. She was too tired to struggle with the task of unlacing the white gown, so she slept in it.

Sometime in the early hours of the morning, Sharon woke up. Morag was standing next to the bed, crying her eyes out. "My mother is dead," she sobbed. Sharon sat up, reached out and put her arms around the child.

"I know," she said, starting to cry herself.

"I know how to use the sphere now," Morag sobbed. "But it hurts! And I shall have to use it to send thee home, and I shall miss thee!"

Sharon held Morag and rocked her in her arms until the girl fell asleep, then lay down next to her and went back to sleep herself.

Her alarm was ringing, and it was barely dawn. Sharon sat up in bed, switched off the alarm, and put saline solution in her eyes. Boy, that was a weird dream, she thought. Then she looked down at the white dress she was still wearing, at her skating clothes and sweatshirt hanging on the foot board of the bed, and at the mess that had been a neatly packed skating bag. It wasn't a dream, she realized, and I'm going to be late for my session if I don't hurry. And if I do hurry, I'll have time to eat breakfast first.

That was incentive. With concentration and the use of the large mirror in the bathroom, she managed to get out of the dress unaided. She threw on the first clean skating outfit that came to hand, ran a brush through her hair, and put a skirt over her skating dress so that she could go to breakfast. As she ate a double helping of pancakes with lots of syrup, she noted the date on the morning news show playing on the television. I haven't lost a day, she discovered with relief. That's good, I can explain why I'm so tired much more easily than I can explain why I was missing for twenty-four hours.

She dragged herself through her day's skating, then called John. "Can you take me over to the Castle this evening?" she asked him. "There's something I want to see there."

"Yeah, sure."

John came for her right after dinner, and they went to the old Tower. It was dark by then, so they didn't get too close. But they were close enough for Sharon to see Morag standing next to the window in the middle of the Tower, holding the orb and smiling down at her.

The Wild Hunt

IAN WATSON

As King Herla rode to his wedding feast, he met a dwarf who bargained, "Let us attend each other's festivals. Mine is a year hence; yours—I would judge from your gay bearing and those loaded horses—is not distant." The king feared to refuse, knowing the strange power of this race, and invited the dwarf to come along with him. But the dwarf said he

could make his own way there, and disappeared among the trees. On the wedding day he came with rich gifts, reminded the king of his promise, and went again to his own world, returning in due time to conduct the king and his men there. The king hated to leave, for his wife was in labor, but he could not do otherwise.

The company rode for many days through forests until they reached a tall cliff, where the dwarf pointed out an opening in the rocks. He rode into darkness and they followed. How many hours they passed in that dark of night, none could say; but at last they galloped into the light of many lamps hung along the cavern walls. Deep within the hill they came to the dwarf's home.

The festivities lasted for some time, and when they were over the dwarf led the king and his men back through the caverns to where the darkness began. There he presented them with a bloodhound, saying: "Let one of your men take it in his arms; it will point to the world. But be careful you do not alight until it has leapt down of its own accord!"

The horsemen passed into the darkness and again none could tell how long they galloped. When finally they reached the sunlight, the king's first thought was of his wife—and child, who must now be born. Seeing a swineherd in the forest, he called: "Do you have any news of Herla's queen—has she given birth?" But the peasant replied in a tongue that the king's men could barely understand: "I would not have answered you, being nobles, except that you seem, by your speech, of the old rulers in this land. They were good men—I thought they had all been slain. But, as to what you ask: I have heard of no Herla save one, that legend says rode into this very rock two hundred years ago."

At that, one of the king's men leapt down, believing that the peasant mocked them. As soon as his feet touched the earth, his whole body crumbled into dust.

When Herla saw that, he drew his horsemen about him. "We have been tricked!" he cried. "None of us can dismount until that dog springs from our arms. Yet I imagine that it never will—"

And they rode on as the hound directed.

The Door to Dark Albion

CHERITH BALDRY

Tom heard the shouting before he saw the reason for it. He had been riding all morning, taking supplies and news to the shepherds on the downs above the village near Guildford where his father was bailiff. Now he was returning home, whistling cheerfully and looking forward to the meal his mother would have waiting. His whistling died away as the noise broke out ahead of him.

Along the track from the village a dark figure appeared at a stumbling run, head down and lurching from side to side. Behind him, a rabble of the village boys were jostling each other in their efforts to come up with him. They were throwing stones, brandishing staves, yelling their threats.

A stone struck the fugitive on the shoulder; he staggered, and pitched to the ground at the feet of Tom's pony. Another stone thudded beside him, and the pony, startled, skittered into the bracken at the side of the path.

Tom soothed the animals and brought its head around, thrusting himself between the prone figure and his pursuers.

"What's going on?"

The boys crowded to a halt. The shouting died, but Tom could see they were still hostile.

"What's it to you?" one said.

"Think you're better'n us, because your father's the bailiff?"

"Get out of the way!"

"Mind your own business!"

They pressed around him threateningly. Tom thought fast. Most of the boys were about his own age, some of them he thought of as friends, and he had no authority over any of them. If they chose to ignore him he could do nothing, and by the time he could bring help it would be all over. He had to delay them until the killing rage was out of them. Calmly, he said,

"I thought we welcomed strangers here." He caught the eye of the leader, the boy who had first spoken. "What did he do to make you so angry?"

The boy's gaze slid aside.

"He came begging at the door," he said. "We told him to be off, and he called us clods. Ignorant peasants."

"I heard him," another said. "He threatened to set banefire in our thatch."

Tom's hands tightened on the reins. Sorcery? Nothing was feared more. If the boys' victim had really threatened sorcery, Tom could understand their anger.

"Did he do it?" he asked.

"No."

"Then haven't you punished him enough?" Tom said. "You've driven him off. If you kill him, there'll be questions asked. Do you want that?"

Relief washed over him as he realized they were listening. A few of them dropped the stones they held. At the back of the crowd, one or two were already starting to edge away. Others followed. As the leader realized his support was melting away, he took a pace or two backward, raising his staff.

"He'd better not come back!" he said, and fled after the rest.

Tom waited until the last of them had disappeared among the trees, and then dismounted. The fugitive was still lying on the track. As Tom approached warily, half expecting a shaft of magic hurled at him, he whimpered and shrank away, raising one arm as if to ward off a blow. Tom squatted at his side.

"I'm not going to hurt you," he said.

The arm was slowly lowered to reveal a pale face framed by curling dark hair, and enormous dark eyes. A boy no older than his persecutors, no older than Tom himself.

"Who are you?" he asked.

Tom grinned at him.

"Just another ignorant peasant," he said.

Color leapt into the boy's face, and his eyes flashed. He raised himself on one elbow.

"Fools!" he said. "They should have been proud to serve me, but they cursed me. I lost my temper."

And threatened them with sorcery, Tom thought, but did not say aloud. He was beginning to realize just how strange this was. The boy was no ordinary beggar. His clothes were torn and filthy, not just from the fall on the path, but the undershirt was silk, embroidered at the neck, the tunic of rich, heavy velvet. His boots—soft leather ankle boots—were in shreds. A lord's son? A king's son? But if so, what was he doing here, alone and in a state like this?

"Are you lost?" Tom said. "Will anyone be looking for you?"

The boy shuddered and caught his breath in a sob.

"Looking for me—don't!" he said.

Tom could see that he wanted to be proud and defiant, but he was almost at the end of his strength.

"It's all right," Tom said, reaching out to touch his shoulder. "You can come home with me. My mother will look after you."

He slid an arm around the boy, helping him to stand. The boy cried out in pain.

"What's the matter?"

"My feet," the boy gasped out. "I fled it for three days. I can't find the door—"

He sagged, a dead weight, in Tom's arms.

When Tom arrived home, with the boy slumped unconscious across the pony's back, his mother did not waste breath on questions. With Tom's help, she stripped off the ruined clothes, bathed the boy, salved and bandaged his feet, and settled him in Tom's bed. It was growing dark before he woke.

Tom was sitting by his bedside, watching. His eyes opened, vague and unfocused; then, as memory flashed into them, he sat up, drawing in a gasp of pure terror.

"Where is it?" he said. "Has it found me?"

Tom leaned over and gripped his arm.

"I don't know what you mean," he said, "but you're safe here."

The boy gazed around wildly at the sloping rafters and the tiny window opposite the bed, the stool and clothes chest that were the only other furnishings of the room.

"I can't stay here," he said.

"You're in no state to go anywhere."

For a moment the boy was silent, frowning slightly, examining Tom.

"You saved me on the road," he said. "Thank you." He sounded as if he found the words difficult. A moment later he repeated, "I can't stay here. I have to find the door."

He had mentioned the door on the road, Tom remembered. Tom still did not understand what he meant.

"You can find it later," he promised. "Wouldn't you rather have something to eat first?"

At the mention of food the boy's eyes widened and his mouth began to tremble.

"I would be . . . grateful," he whispered painfully.

Tom smiled at him.

"I'll bring you some."

He was moving toward the door when the boy said, "Close the shutters."

The words were snapped out. Tom turned, amazed at the change, and met an imperious look from the dark eyes. The boy was the first to look away, his voice dropping.

"Please . . ."

Tom crossed to the window and did as he asked, leaving the room in near darkness.

"Are the doors barred downstairs?" the boy asked.

"Not yet. Don't worry," he went on, forestalling the protest, or command, that he knew was coming. "There are people down there. No one will get in."

He went out before the boy could ask anything more.

Downstairs, he brought a bowl so that he could dip up some soup from the pot on the fire. His mother sat there, stitching at the silk shirt she had already washed. At her feet Tom's baby sister was banging industriously at the hearthstones with a spoon.

"This stuff's too good to throw away," his mother

said, shaking out the folds and admiring the embroidery. "Is the lad awake?"

"Yes. He seems frightened. I'm not sure he's in his right mind."

"Well, he's safe enough here. Tomorrow we'll try to get word to his people, whoever they are."

Tom was putting the soup and some bread on a tray when his father came in.

"What's this I hear?" he asked Tom, shrugging out of his jerkin. "A sorcerer in the village?"

"A sorcerer in your house," Tom's mother said, nodding toward the stairs. "But he's no sorcerer, just a poor lad who's lost his way and his wits."

Tom's father grunted. Tom explained what had happened, while his mother got up and started to lay bowls and plates on the table for the evening meal. By the time Tom had finished, his father was thoughtful.

"I don't know about sorcery," he said. "Superstitious nonsense, to my mind. But just now, when I turned into the yard—I saw something, in the shadow by the barn."

"One of the cats," Tom's mother said.

"I know a cat, woman," his father said good-humoredly. "This moved—soft. Like water." His hand traced a wavy line in the air.

"Squirrel, then."

"Stoat, more like. But black. It was dead black." He shrugged, dismissively. "Whatever it was, it's gone now."

When Tom went back upstairs, he said nothing about the strange beast by the barn. He did not know what his father had seen, but he could be sure it was not a cat or a squirrel. His father had good eyesight and not

176

a shred of imagination. "Has it found me?" the boy had asked. Tom found he did not want to answer that question.

As well as the soup and bread, Tom had brought a taper in a wooden holder, which he set on the clothes chest. By its light he could see the boy lying down again, half buried in the sheepskin coverings. A tear had tracked a shining line across his face. When he saw Tom he sat up, scrubbing angrily at his eyes.

"You're . . . very kind," he said.

The words were forced out, as if he found it hard to express thanks for anything. He was shaking so much Tom had to help him with the bowl. He guessed it was days since he had eaten. Three days fleeing, he had said. Fleeing from whatever it was Tom's father had seen in the yard?

When the boy had finished the soup, Tom helped him to sit up with a pillow behind him.

"Feel better?" he asked.

A nod; no other reply.

"My mother says tomorrow we'll try to get word to your people."

The response astonished him. The boy let out a spurt of almost hysterical laughter, and then forced it back with a hand pressed to his lips.

"My people!" he said after a minute. "If only you could!"

Tom, sitting on the stool again, leaned over toward him.

"You don't have to tell me anything you don't want to," he said. "But if you don't tell me, I don't know how to help you. I don't even know your name. Mine's Tom," he added encouragingly. "My father's bailiff here."

"My name is Romaric." The boy was speaking slowly. "I am not of your kind. I come from—from Dark Albion."

He looked as if that ought to explain everything.

"I don't know what you mean," Tom said. "Dark Albion? It sounds an evil place."

"Evil? No!" Pride flashed in Romaric's eyes. "Beautiful . . ."

Tom began to feel suspicious. He remembered the rumors of sorcery, and Romaric's threats to burn the village with banefire.

"Are you a sorcerer?" he asked abruptly.

Romaric did not reply directly to his question.

"In Dark Albion, my father is an enchanter," he said. "One of the greatest, one of the Seven Lords. I was his student." He drew himself up against the pillow, with a haughty tilt of the head. "Dark Albion is the realm of magic," he said. "Enchantment belongs there. It's as natural as air or water. Here you call it evil, but you know nothing—nothing!"

"I know you threatened to burn the village," Tom said. "Is that nothing?"

Romaric stared at him for a minute, eyes bright with furious pride. Tom met the look steadily. At last Romaric flushed, ashamed.

"I did wrong," he admitted. His lips twisted bitterly. "And all for nothing. I could do nothing. My power is gone. My father took it when he banished me."

Now it was Tom's turn to stare. He had been longing for explanations, but now they were coming a bit too fast for comfort.

"Your father banished you?" he repeated. "Why?"

Romaric's look of shame deepened.

"I—lost my temper."

"You seem to do a lot of that."

The dark eyes flickered toward him and away again.

"My servants were slow . . . and I thought them insolent. I raised a charm against them. My father challenged me, and I was afraid. I lost control. The power spilled out. We might all of us have died if my father had not mastered it. He sent me here and said I must live without power until I found the way back."

"Well, that doesn't sound too difficult," Tom said. "Where is Dark Albion? Is it far from here?"

Romaric's head jerked around toward him. He looked furious again.

"You fool, it's not—" he began. He broke off. Half choking, he said, "I'm sorry."

Tom could guess that he had never apologized, or thanked anyone, so often in his life before. But at least he was learning. Swallowing, struggling to steady his voice, he went on,

"Dark Albion is here, is everywhere—it fits over this world like a—like a skin. You could travel for a lifetime and never find it, or step through a door and be there in seconds."

"Then where is the door?"

"I don't know." Romaric's hands clenched tightly. "I can't find the way back."

The taper was burning down. Shadows flapped and chased across the rafters. Tom tried to think about what Romaric had told him. The way back to his own world . . . Was it a real door he had to find, or something like a spell or a word of power that would take him back where he belonged? But he had lost the power he once had, so a spell might not be any use to him if he found it.

"And that's not all, is it?" Tom said. "What are you

frightened of? What are you running away from?"

Romaric fought to hold onto a show of courage, and failed. He began to tremble. Softly, horror shivering in his voice, he said,

"When my father sent me here, something else came with me. I don't know what it is, but I know of its kind. One of the creatures that lives in the deeper darkness that surrounds Dark Albion. It will run, and track, and tear. It never tires, or sleeps, or turns aside. It cannot be killed. It is hunting me down. If I cannot find the door . . ."

He broke off and hid his face. Tom began to say, "But if your father—" and stopped. Romaric must know very well that the creature could never have followed him into this world if his father had not allowed it. Tom was not sure what to say. He thought of his own father: warm, impatient, wholly trustworthy. Had Romaric trusted his father, before this?

"We'll do something," he said. "Somehow, we'll find the door to Dark Albion."

Later, when Romaric was asleep again, Tom slid into bed beside him. He hoped Romaric would not mind, but there was nowhere else; it was that or the cowbyre. In the middle of the night he was roused by Romaric crying out and tossing in an evil dream, and lay with an arm across his shoulders until he grew quiet again. He thought he could hear something outside that snuffled and whined and scratched against the door.

Next morning, his mother, going to feed the chickens, found two of them with their heads torn off. Blood was spattered on the stones of the yard; feathers clung stickily to it. The two dogs, who should have barked an alarm, were huddled in their kennel, whimpering. On the outside of the house door were scratch marks, as if claws had scored across it.

Tom thought of his baby sister, still sleeping contentedly in her cradle. He felt cold.

Romaric did not wake until midmorning. Tom's mother returned his clothes to him, clean and mended, and gave him soft woollen slippers that fitted over his bandaged feet. She assumed that he would stay until he was fit to travel.

He washed and dressed and Tom helped him downstairs where breakfast was waiting for him: oatcakes and butter, milk and fruit. They were alone. Tom's father had gone out to his work long before, and his mother could be heard faintly, singing in the yard.

Romaric had a haughty look about him this morning. Tom could almost believe that he was a nobleman's son, lost and wanting in his wits, and all his tale of Dark Albion no more than a tale. But there were those dead chickens.

He filched an apple from the plate of fruit, bit into it, and said,

"I've been thinking."

"Yes?"

"When your father banished you—he didn't mean forever? He must have meant you to get back home sooner or later. Didn't he give you any kind of clue?"

"What kind?" Romaric asked.

"A place to go—someone you could ask—"

"No, nothing. If he had, do you think I would be here now?"

His voice was scornful. Tom started to feel irritated, but he bit back a sharp reply. He wanted Romaric—

and his beast—away from there before nightfall. But he could not turn him out to face danger alone. He had to help him.

"Where's a good place to look?" he asked.

"All places are doors to Dark Albion," Romaric said. He looked disdainfully around the room. "Even here."

"Doors to Dark Albion," Tom repeated, ignoring the look. "It doesn't have to be a real door, does it? A door is anything you go through. But some places might be better than others, maybe?"

"What do you mean?"

"Well—where did your father send you? Mightn't you get back the same way?"

Romaric shook his head. He did not bother to explain why not.

"But you have to try something," Tom said.

Romaric let fall the piece of oatcake he was eating, and brought one hand down flat on the table.

"How can you know—what can you know of the Lords of Dark Albion?"

Tom could not repress a grin.

"I know a bit about this one."

Romaric's eyes blazed; his voice was shaking.

"How dare you laugh at me! Stop it!"

Peaceably, Tom reached out to him across the table.

"I'm sorry. I only want to help."

"I don't need your help! If you want to be rid of me, I'll go!"

He sprang up, but as soon as he put weight on his injured feet he gasped with pain, and had to cling to the edge of the table. Tom went around to him and eased him back onto the bench.

"Don't be so stupid," he said gently.

"I know what to do," Romaric said. His voice was

stifled. "But I don't know how, not anymore. It's like being blind, and deaf, and you all speak a different language . . ."

He sighed; briefly his head rested against Tom's shoulder, but as soon as he realized it he jerked away. Not looking at Tom, he said,

"I don't know where it was. I was fleeing from—from the beast. There was a hill, and trees—and a great rock heaving up out of the ground. I crossed a stream—"

"Castle Rock!" Tom breathed out.

"What?"

"There's a place a few hours' ride away," Tom explained. "Castle Rock, they call it. There are . . . stories about it. People don't go there at night. They say they've seen things. But if it took you three days to get here, you must have come a long way around."

Romaric was listening now, really taking Tom seriously, and beginning to look a little hopeful.

"If the boundaries are thin there . . ." he said.

"It's worth a try."

While Romaric finished his breakfast, Tom saddled his own pony and another, for Romaric still could not walk without pain. His mother did not question his going, only packed supplies of cheese and rolls and apples. Tom bundled up a couple of blankets as well, for by the time they were ready to set out it was midday, and he did not think they could reach Castle Rock before nightfall.

Romaric could not hide his nervousness as they rode through the village, but no one came out and challenged them. Tom was keeping watch for a black creature that looked a little like a cat or a squirrel or a stoat, but was none of those, and moved like the flowing of water. He saw nothing, but he was glad of the strong belt knife he carried.

For the next few hours they rode through the forest. Romaric grew more nervous still, starting at every unexplained noise, eyes darting from side to side. He scarcely spoke at all.

As Tom had feared, it began to get dark before they reached Castle Rock.

"We ought to make camp," he said.

"No!" Romaric said. "We must keep going. If the beast comes up with us by night . . ." He shuddered.

"If we try to go on in the dark," Tom explained, "we risk laming the ponies. We'll have to take our chance with the beast."

Romaric opened his mouth to protest, caught Tom's eye, and thought better of it.

Before it was quite dark they came to a clearing with a stream running through it, perhaps the stream that Romaric remembered crossing. Tom collected wood for a fire, while Romaric huddled with an enormous tree at his back, and scanned the undergrowth with wide, frightened eyes.

It came when they had finished their meal, and the fire was starting to burn down. Fronds of bracken at the opposite side of the clearing rustled and parted as something slid between them. A dark shape moved into the open.

Tom had not seen it before. His father had been right; it was like a stoat in its size and the sinuous way it moved, but its fur was matte black, as if light sank into it and was lost. Its eyes were flat circles, pale as water, but it moved its head back and forth with a ceaseless questing movement, as if it were blind. Tom thought it might be sniffing.

Beside him, Romaric shrank against the tree, catching back sobs of pure terror. Cautiously, not taking his eyes from the thing, Tom got to his feet. He slid the knife from the sheath at his belt, and grasped the unburned end of a branch from the fire. The ponies whickered and shifted uneasily.

The beast was beginning to cross the clearing in swift, darting movements, pausing every few steps to snuff the air. Tom stepped forward, holding the brand in front of him. As soon as he moved, the beast was aware of him, rearing onto its hind legs and whipping its head back and forth. Tom heard Romaric moaning,

"No—oh, no!"

Tom plunged forward, waving the brand. It scrawled searing lines in the darkness. The beast snarled, a low, drawn-out sound. Tom caught a glimpse of needle-sharp teeth. Then it was giving way, shrinking from the fire, and as Tom followed after it, thrusting the brand toward it at every step, it turned and vanished into the undergrowth.

Tom stood panting. After a minute, when he was sure it had really gone, he tossed the brand back on the fire and threw on more wood.

"We'll have to stay awake," he said. "And keep the fire from going out."

Romaric was still pressed back against the tree, hands over his mouth as if he were holding back a scream. As Tom spoke he began to relax, thrusting back disheveled hair. He looked exhausted. Tom sighed.

"All right," he said, though Romaric had not spoken. "Try to get some sleep. I'll keep watch."

There was no more disturbance that night. Early the next morning they came to Castle Rock. The road had been winding upward for some time, and the last part of the hill was so steep that they had to tether the ponies and climb a narrow, rocky path that tracked back and forth across the slope, between the trees. Even with Tom to help him, it was almost more than Romaric could manage.

At last the trees gave way, and they came out onto a smooth swell of turf. Beyond, at the summit, an outcrop of gray rock thrust up to more than three times the height of a man. It was easy to imagine that its broken crest was the towers and pinnacles of a castle.

Romaric sank down onto the turf with a weary sigh. His sleep did not seem to have done him much good. Tom felt just as tired, light-headed from fatigue, but he knew that he had to keep going. Perhaps it would not be for very much longer.

"Stay here," he suggested. "I'll go and search. If the

door is something real, then I should be able to find it."

Romaric looked up at him, frightened again.

"No, don't leave me."

He was white from the pain of his injured feet, and exhausted from the effort he was making, but he forced himself to stand again. He gazed up at the gray sweep of rock above his head.

"You're right," he said. "This is the place."

The final approach to the rock castle was real climbing over tumbled stones where spiny shrubs had rooted themselves. It was all Romaric could do to haul himself upward until he stood on the narrow path that surrounded the rock itself.

He and Tom started to search, examining each fold and crevice in the rock. Tom was not sure what he was looking for; he found nothing but stone and sparse grass and lichen. And at last they came to the place where they had started.

The rock was a rock, no more. If strange things had ever been seen, there was nothing here now. Swaying with weariness, Romaric reached out and steadied himself against the rock face.

"It's no use," he said.

His voice was shaking; he was not far away from collapse. Tom wondered what they could do now. It had been a long chance at best.

"Does your father know what you're doing?" he asked. Romaric looked at him, puzzled. "Can he watch you?"

"Yes, if he wants to." He still did not sound as if he understood the purpose of the question.

"Then speak to him," Tom said. "Perhaps he just wants you to say that you're sorry."

Romaric's head went up, with the look of imperious pride that was becoming familiar. Tom could almost understand what his father had done to him; anyone might find Romaric pretty exasperating.

"I will not plead with him," he said.

"Wouldn't it be worth it?"

Romaric shook his head. His mouth tightened.

"It would be no use," he said. "You don't know my father."

He turned toward the rock and laid both palms flat on the sheer face.

"I can't live in this world, I can't!" he said. Suddenly he flung back his head and cried aloud, "Let me through! I command it!"

Tom held his breath. Even though he did not expect to see the rock split open, or the sky darken and the Lord Enchanter, Romaric's father, sweep down in a whirlwind to carry off his son, he was disappointed when nothing happened.

The silence stretched out until Romaric sobbed out, "Please!" and flung himself at the rock, his fingers digging into tiny crevices as if he could tear it apart by force. Tom went to him and put a hand on his shoulder.

"Let's go home," he said. "We'll try something else tomorrow."

Romaric let out a long sigh and turned away. Tom took his arm to help him down the slope. Then they both froze. Below them, where the green turf met the forest, something moved in the shadows. Tom could not see it clearly, but he had no doubt what it was.

"Stay here," he said. He drew his belt knife. "I'll go down."

He moved forward cautiously, his eyes fixed on the

movement at the edge of the trees, but a stone shifted under his foot as he put his weight on it, and he fell, one leg twisted awkwardly under him. He dropped the knife and it clattered over the stones to lie some ways below him. As Tom tried to get up to retrieve it, pain from the twisted leg washed over him, and he sank back, panting, his vision blurring. As it cleared, he saw the beast, like a clot of darkness undulating over the turf, questing back and forth along his trail, but always drawing closer.

He looked up at Romaric, still leaning against the rock.

"Run!" he said. "I don't think it can see you. Go the other way—work around through the trees. Take one of the ponies. I'll try to hold it here."

He did not watch to see if Romaric would obey him. Instead he faced the beast. It was close now; swiftly it gathered itself and launched itself at him, striking him in the chest. Claws pierced his jerkin. He tried to ward it off and protect his face with his arms, expecting always to feel those fine teeth close in his throat. The soft weight of it was cutting off his breath.

Then he heard scrambling feet on the rocks beside him. The beast was wrenched away. Lowering his arms, Tom saw Romaric grappling with it on the ground, a few feet farther down the slope. The beast had fastened on his throat and across his face. His hands tore vainly at it. He cried out sharply once, and then was silent.

Desperately Tom struggled to reach him, but every movement brought a wave of pain and sickness. He had to give in, shivering in the icy sweat that covered him. Romaric and the beast, locked together in combat, rolled even farther away.

As Tom peered down through a haze of pain, he thought he could see a change. He rubbed a hand across his eyes. The beast seemed to have shrunk, so that Romaric could imprison it in his clasped hands. His figure was outlined with an edge of light. His spasmodic struggles died away. He sat up, and opened his hands. Cupped between them was a sphere of incandescent light.

As water washes away mud and shows what is beneath, so the light washed over the hill and the forest and the Castle Rock, revealing what lay behind or beneath their everyday appearance. Every blade of grass was furred with silver like a night frost. Flowers starred the grass. The trees at the foot of the slope shone with globes of golden fruit.

Tom twisted around to look at the rock behind him. It was a true castle now. The spires and pinnacles looked as if they were carved out of ice and silver. Beyond them the sky was only a dark background for a blaze of stars.

The rocky slope had now become a flight of steps curving up to a gate. In the gateway a man was standing. He was robed in dark velvet, and he had a silver ring on his hand. His hair was dark, streaked with silver. He looked very like Romaric.

Hesitantly, Romaric approached the bottom of the steps. The globe of light in his hands was dissolving now, as if its power had poured out to reveal everything else. His face was pale, shocked. He looked unhurt.

"Father?" he said uncertainly.

The Lord Enchanter held out a hand. Still more uncertainly, Romaric mounted the steps until he was close enough for his father to rest the hand on his

shoulder.

"Do you understand?" he asked.

Romaric shook his head. Tom saw a faint exaspera-
tion, just as he had imagined, cross his father's face.

"A Lord Enchanter of Dark Albion," Romaric's father said, "must be able to control himself. As you
failed to do. I banished you, but I sent with you the
way back from your exile, if only you could recognize
it."

"The beast . . ." Romaric breathed out.

"Yes. It would never have attacked you. Not until
you turned and faced it. That was the only way you
could find what you were seeking, for what you really
sought was courage, and courage is the door to Dark
Albion."

A faint smile warmed the frosty countenance. He
raised his son the last step that brought him to his
side, and caught him into an embrace. Tom watched,
silent, an ache in his throat.

At last the Lord Enchanter drew back.

"Aren't you forgetting something?" he said. "Your
friend?"

Romaric turned toward Tom. His face was joyful.

"May I?" he asked his father.

"Try."

With great concentration, Romaric raised his hands
as if he molded something between them. Then he
seemed to throw it toward Tom, though there was
nothing to be seen. Tom felt a tingling in his leg, and
the pain abruptly stopped. He got to his feet, feeling
slightly foolish.

"Thank you," he said.

"I should be the one thanking you," Romaric said,
laughing. All the pride and ill temper had dissolved

out of him. "Without you, I could never have faced the beast. Stay with us!" he begged. "We can show you wonders."

Tom looked up at Romaric and his father. They were very much alike. Power sang out of them both. Their eyes shone with it. It tugged at Tom, but he knew he could not live in Dark Albion, could not breathe in it, any more than Romaric could be at ease in his world. He wondered that he ever could have mistaken Romaric for one of his own kind.

"No," he said. "I'm sorry. I don't belong here."

Romaric looked disappointed, but his father bowed his head.

"You are wise," he said. "We follow a different road, and the end of our journey is elsewhere. But for all that, if you have need of Dark Albion, come here and call us, and we will answer."

He turned away, but Romaric ran lightly down the steps, caught at Tom's hand, and then embraced him. For all his happiness, there were tears in his eyes.

"Goodbye," he said. "Goodbye, my friend."

Tom raised a hand in farewell, as Romaric went back to his father, and the Lord Enchanter drew him through the gates into the castle. Romaric looked back, until they were lost in the light within.

The brilliance of Dark Albion sighed itself back into ordinary daylight. Tom drew in a long breath, let it out again, and went to look for the ponies.

Dusk was gathering as he drew near the village. Not far from his own home he met one of the boys who had stoned Romaric.

"Got rid of your sorcerer?" the boy asked, sneering.

"Yes," Tom said. "He went home. He found what he was looking for."

The Fairy Trap

PETER CROWTHER

A squirrel hopped across the path directly in front of Charles and Tom. It leapt into the stubbly grass and stopped, looking first one way and then the other, curling and flicking its tail like one of those dinosaurs in the movies they showed over at the drive-in. A brief investigation into a small piece of bracken and it was on its way, stopping and starting, staccato bursts of movement, tail stabbing the air, until it had disappeared completely from sight.

Tom smiled, casting a sideways glance at Charles, who was picking up a stone. "What we gonna do?"

Charles shrugged and, pulling back, threw the stone high into the sky, watching as it reached its zenith and then plummeted down into the undergrowth.

"Let's call on Robby," Tom suggested excitedly.

"And do what?" Charles kicked through the dust to find another stone.

Tom didn't rightly know, so he didn't answer. Instead, he just stood a few paces behind his friend and scanned the horizon. "Oh," he said at last, "I don't know . . . maybe we could go down—"

Charles had spun around, his finger raised to his mouth. "Hear that?" he shout-whispered.

Tom listened but he couldn't hear anything except the wind playing in the grass around them. "Nope, I don't hear nothing."

"There it goes again," hissed Charles, his eyes darting

from side to side. This time Tom *did* hear something but he didn't know what it was, exactly. It had sounded like someone shouting but he couldn't see anyone. Then, out of the trees to their left, a man appeared. It seemed he had been sitting down because he was in a crouched position and was beckoning them over to him. Tom stared at Charles, who shrugged and started off across the grass toward the man. Tom followed after a quick glance around them.

As they neared the trees the man started waving again, but this time it appeared he wanted them to stop. "I wish he'd make up his mind," Charles snarled.

"Get down!" the man snapped across the clearing. "Get down and keep perfectly still."

Tom was enjoying himself. The whole thing had an air of mystery about it and he stooped to a crouch and listened.

"Get up, stupid," Charles laughed, pulling at Tom's sweater.

"No!" The reply was emphatic.

Charles shook his head and walked over to the man, beaming a huge smile.

"You stupid little bas—" the man started. Then "—little heathens." He waved his fist first at Charles and then at Tom, who had almost caught up with him. Just then Tom heard a rustling from behind him and he turned as quickly and as noiselessly as he could, but all he saw was another squirrel that stopped as his eyes fell on it. Charles had stopped a few feet from the man, who was now muttering to himself and packing things away into a small sack that had been leaning against a nearby tree. "Damned fool kids," he spluttered. "Not fit to be let out . . . should be locked up . . ."

The two boys looked at each other and shrugged. The man swung the loaded sack over his shoulder and walked toward them. Tom started to back away but Charles held his ground, though his heart was thumping in his chest. He reached the boys and stopped, studying them for a few seconds. Then, craning his neck so far out that his face was about an inch or so from Charles, he said, "Should be locked up!" again, this time in a voice that was just this side of an all-out, gut-emptying holler that sprayed Charles with saliva speckles.

The man was old and scruffily dressed. Tom reckoned he hadn't seen soap and water that year—and here it was, November!—judging by the smell that hit his nostrils. He had on an old pair of sneakers and a mud-splattered raincoat tied with string. Perched on his head, rather precariously, was an old brown bowler hat with the remains of a battered beige velvet band crumpled and torn by the weather, all of which made him look like Spooky the Tuff Little Ghost.

His hair was dark and straggly, hanging over a bright red scarf wrapped several times around his dirty, scrawny neck and tied into a huge knot at the front. The scarf looked almost new and was totally out of context with the rest of the outfit, which included a pair of patched, stitched, grass-stained (and who-knew-what-else-stained!) very faded old work denims, which were many sizes too big and hung down over and even under his sneakers. The man shook his head and spat into the grass, making a sound with his mouth that resembled a pig removing its foot from a mudhole. He walked past the two of them without another word.

"What exactly did we do?" said Charles, feeling just

a little guilty after the man's outburst—though, for the life of him, he had no idea why.

The man just looked over his shoulder and grunted.

Charles shrugged and turned to Tom, who was still staring at the man. "Look," said Tom.

Charles followed his friend's gaze. The man had dropped his sack and was fumbling with something in the grass, still shaking his head slowly and mumbling all the while.

The boys walked over to him and stood. And watched. Finally Charles spoke. "What's that?"

The man was holding a tiny metal object, filled with small spokes and wheels, gleaming though the sun was only hazy. "Never you mind," came the snarled answer.

Tom looked closer over the man's shoulder. "Looks like some kind of trap to me."

Charles bent down for a closer look and then stood up, apparently satisfied, nodding in agreement to Tom. "It *is* a trap," he said. Then to the man, "What do you expect to catch with that? A few bugs?" And he sniggered.

"Can I have a look?" said Tom, holding out his hand.

The man looked at him suspiciously and then smiled, exposing blackened teeth. Laughing gently, he dropped the object into Tom's outstretched hand. "That there's a fairy trap," he said.

"Fairy trap?" said Tom, astonished.

"Fairies? As in Brothers Grimm?" Charles laughed and peered at the thing as Tom turned it over in his hand. "There's no such thing as fairies."

The man took back the object and dropped it into his sack. He pulled the string around the sack's neck

and closed it up. "You believe in God?"

Charles looked shocked for a moment but quickly regained his composure and nodded. "I guess," he said, and thrust his hands deep into the warming reassurance of his jeans pockets.

"How come? You seen him?"

Charles turned to Tom. "C'mon, Tom, let's be getting back—it's late." They turned to leave.

"Now hold on there," the man shouted after them. "S'posing I was to show you one?"

"A fairy?" said Tom in unashamed excitement. "Have you caught one already?"

"Well," came the answer, "I ain't exactly *caught* one . . . yet! But I'm 'specting to catch one right soon now." He hawked and spat into the grass, and hitched up his pants through his coat. "These here woods are crawling with them," he said, waving his arms about him.

"Won't it hurt them if you catch one?" said Tom.

The man rubbed his nose with his finger and sniffed. "Well, might bruise them a mite, but it won't break nothing, won't my trap."

Charles had walked off and was now quite a ways off. Tom looked after him anxiously. "I have to go now, but maybe tomorrow . . . if you're still here."

"I'll still be here."

"Where, exactly?"

The stranger smiled and pointed to the ground right where he was standing. "Right here," he said.

Tom nodded. "OK, I'll be back, but I don't know about him." He nodded to the dwindling figure kicking at the tall grasses by the side of the path. "I gotta go, see you tomorrow maybe." He turned and ran after Charles.

The man stared after them and shook his head. "Should be locked up," he said to nobody in particular. But this time, he was smiling.

The next day wouldn't come around quick enough for Tom. When it finally did come around, it was bleak and thick with November mists and a hazy dreamlike sunlight. A widespread dew covered the grass and the cold had settled in, ready for the onslaught of winter. Before he went out, Tom had to sit through a long lecture on self-preservation from his mother, the outcome being he had to wear a thick sweater under his baseball jacket. When he *did* leave, it was dull . . . almost as though sunset would follow within the hour. His first job was to call on Charles.

"I'm sorry, Thomas, he's out already," Charles's mother said with an apologetic smile.

"Did he say where he was going?"

She shook her head. "I guess not."

"Okay, thanks anyway." He turned and ran back down the path to the street. "Tell him I called," he shouted back at the gate.

"Will do."

He heard the door close behind him.

Out in the fields it seemed colder than in the town. With the wide-open spaces the wind built up more speed, and Tom felt cold even through the extra sweater. The trees were now completely bare. Winter had this part of the world securely in its jaws and had shaken all signs of life from it. As he walked through the grass, Tom found himself scrutinizing his steps so that he didn't crush anything. This made his journey considerably longer than usual. When he eventually got to the place where he'd last seen the old man, Charles was already standing in front of him.

"I knowed he'd come," said a voice behind him. "He had to come, see—he's not a hundred percent sure 'bout there being no fairies."

Tom turned to face the old man. He looked exactly the same; same clothes, same stubble on the chin, and the same dank, musty smell hovering all about him.

Charles looked around on hearing them talking, and waved. He ran over. "I wasn't going to come," he shouted as he ran. "But I had to . . . guess I'm just as curious as you," he said, slapping his friend on the shoulder.

"Okay, boys," said the old man. "First off we got to decide on the likeliest place for 'em." Breathing deep and loud, he surveyed the surrounding countryside.

"You said yesterday the woods," said Charles, suddenly feeling a little bit silly at taking part in the proceedings after airing his views so emphatically the previous day.

"So I did," the old man nodded. "Woods'll be where they live right enough, but we don't want to go in there after 'em—they'll see us before we've gone even two steps. And *we* won't see even hide nor hair of *them!*" He nodded with a very self-satisfied smile. "No, sir. Where we lay the traps has got to be the quietest, most unexpected place they go . . . or are likely to go. So, we'll have to bait 'em."

"What do we bait them with?" asked Tom, not at all sure that he could think of anything that a fairy might like.

"Apples!"

"Apples?" Charles laughed.

The man looked at Charles, who started to clear his throat. It was a tired look from an old man who was dedicated to a belief. There was no hostility in it, only a sense of resignation . . . and pity. "Apples," he repeated, nodding.

There were six apples, one of which Tom ate. The remaining five were peeled and sliced carefully into small pieces. Fairies, apparently, had "easily upsettable digestive tracks" that could not accommodate the leathery peel. Tom wondered how the old man knew so much about fairies, considering he'd never seen one (or wouldn't admit to it anyway), but he didn't bother asking.

Within an hour the baited traps were prepared and back in the old man's sack, and the trio moved to a large field that sloped down to the river. At the base of the field was a gathering of trees while the top just led into more fields and, eventually, over to the highway. The boys learned that seeing as how the fairies lived near the trees, chances were that if they laid the traps here then they wouldn't be seen. So, without further

discussion, the old man supervised the laying of the traps—three in all—at various points amid the scattered apple pieces. The entire operation only took about twenty minutes, but at the end Tom and Charles were exhausted, having had to walk around in a crouched position all the time. This was, they discovered, to avoid them being "Too conspicutive."

Time disappeared to wherever it is time goes when you're young and having fun, and it seemed to do it double quick, too. It was turned two o'clock when they realized they were late for lunch and, without much in the way of formal farewells, Tom and Charles hotfooted it for home and the inevitable harsh words.

The old man watched the boys disappear and, his coat flapping in the wind that had got up, he gave a wave that wasn't returned by either of them. Then he turned around and walked slowly back to where they had laid the traps.

During lunch, the snow came.

The sky turned a deathly black and the wind howled and the snow came.

It came in a thick, blustering shower that whirled and cascaded across the fine-mown lawns and swept down the street like a huge white tidal wave. Visibility dropped to a few meters and, outside, breathing was difficult. Neither Tom nor Charles could move away from the house, so they just sat inside and watched. And waited.

The snow was relentless and had covered the ground within a few minutes. Tom's father said it was the worst shower since 1933; Charles's mother said 1936.

Tom just sat.

Charles just sat.

Outside the window the foaming white curtains shrouded the ground and the trees and buffeted the house. Quite independently of each other, the boys thought of the old man out there in the fields, alone and unprotected.

"Damned weather!" the old man shouted up at the sky and pulled up his coat collar. "Damned stupid heathen weather!"

The snow had started without warning. It was hard, biting into his face, clouding his vision. He ran up the field, puffing, and sheltered under a young oak tree that, although it didn't stop the snow entirely, did manage to shield him from the worst of the wind. He stood, shivering slightly, and clapped his hands together to keep them warm.

All before him turned to white. Even as he watched, the last few green patches disappeared and were replaced with sheets of pure whiteness while, far above, the clouds—black and menacing—scudded across the sky showing no signs of the storm stopping. Everywhere was still and silent. No sound could be heard.

Then, as if from a dream, a noise echoed through the ghostly white stillness and disappeared.

The old man stopped clapping his hands and stared into the falling snow, hardly daring to breathe. He could see nothing, and, but for the gentle breath of the wind, the silence had returned.

Suddenly, it sounded again. Soft and distant, far, far away. He strained to hear.

A laugh?

Was it a laugh?

He listened again, refusing to move his legs, which had momentarily gone into cramp.

There it was again. Faint, muffled, way down in the distance . . . another laugh. It *was* a laugh . . . coming from where they had laid the traps.

The old man opened his eyes wide and crept forward, crouching, from beneath the protection of the oak tree and out into the full throes of the blizzard, down to the field, back to the apple bait and the traps.

On all sides the snow whirled, flying into his face one minute and battering his back the next. Visibility was virtually nil. The world had disappeared, to be replaced by this endless snow. He stopped to wipe his face and plodded on. He must be near now. His eyes strained through the falling flakes.

Then; voices!

He stopped. High in his throat a pounding started up. Just above the wind he could hear tiny voices . . . many voices. He couldn't understand what they were saying but they *were* there . . . laughing voices, floating on the breeze. He crept forward, slowly, each step seeming to take an hour, each breath seeming to sound like a waterfall.

Suddenly, out of the corner of his eye, he saw a movement and instinctively dropped to the ground without a noise save for a soft *flump!* that he felt rather than heard. There they were, seven of them—unless there were more out of sight somewhere—four sitting down and three standing. They were naked and laughing, plodding around in the snow without a care in the world.

The old man swallowed hard.

A female stood up and moved to a piece of apple. She had long blond hair that lay across her shoulders and rippled very gently in the breeze as she walked. They were all about the same height—eight or nine centimeters, he guessed—and slim, with brown, healthy-looking skins. She picked up the piece of apple with both hands and nibbled at it. Suddenly, one of the males ran over and snatched the apple and pushed her to the ground. They all laughed as she spluttered and coughed, and even *she* was smiling.

The old man smiled, too, and despite the cold he felt very warm. So warm, in fact, that he suddenly had a crazy notion to take off all of his clothes.

"Hel-lo," said a small voice behind him.

The laughing in front of him stopped and all of the little figures clustered together in panic. The old man turned around to face the tiny person smiling up at him. "Hello," he replied.

"Hey, look!" Charles shouted over to Tom, who was standing on the ridge searching the surrounding fields. "There's something over there."

Tom followed Charles's pointing finger and he saw it: something flapping in the wind down by the trees. He nodded and both boys started to run, down toward the river.

The snow had stopped as quickly and unexpectedly as it had started. All was peaceful. The covering had drifted in places, and running across these drifts created a weird sensation—Tom misjudged his speed and fell headlong into a large bank of snow. Charles, however, reached the trees and pulled the object down from the branches.

Tom ran up, puffing, covered in white from head to toe.

"It's his scarf!" said Charles.

"Mmmm." Tom looked around, still out of breath. "He probably dropped it in the storm."

Without adding anything, both knew that they didn't believe that.

Charles folded up the scarf and slipped it into his jacket pocket. "He'll probably be back for it tomorrow when he comes to collect his traps," he said, looking around on the ground and noting without surprise that none of the traps could be seen.

"They're covered by the snow," Tom said.

And they didn't believe that either.

Over the following three days the boys spent hours in the fields where they had met the old man. The weather grew milder and the snow disappeared almost everywhere except for a few small patches, mostly under the trees where what little sunshine there was didn't quite reach.

They searched the fields for hours but they could find no trace of the traps or the apple pieces. And they never saw the old man again.

The Dark Island

C. S. LEWIS

This story comes from The Voyage of the Dawn Treader. *It's one of the Narnia books by C. S. Lewis. Edmund and Lucy Pevensie and their cousin Eustace found themselves back in Narnia when they looked at a picture of a ship and suddenly found themselves in the picture, swimming beside the ship. The ship belongs to Prince Caspian, who is on a quest to find what has become of seven lost lords. Also on board is the swashbuckling mouse Reepicheep, whom they had met in the earlier book* Prince Caspian. *The following is just one of their many adventures.*

The *Dawn Treader* sailed on south and a little east for twelve days with a gentle wind, the skies being mostly clear and the air warm, and saw no bird or fish, except that once there were whales spouting a long way to starboard. Lucy and Reepicheep played a good deal of chess at this time. Then on the thirteenth day, Edmund, from the fighting top, sighted what looked like a great dark mountain rising out of the sea on their port bow.

They altered course and made for this land, mostly by oar, for the wind would not serve them to sail north-east. When evening fell they were still a long way from it and rowed all night. Next morning the weather was fair but a flat calm. The dark mass lay ahead, much nearer and larger, but still very dim, so that some thought it was still a long way off and others thought they were running into a mist.

About nine that morning, very suddenly, it was so close that they could see that it was not land at all, nor even, in an ordinary sense, a mist. It was a Darkness. It is rather hard to describe, but you will see what it was like if you imagine yourself looking into the mouth of a railway tunnel—a tunnel either so long or so twisty that you cannot see the light at the far end. And you know what it would be like. For a few feet you would see the rails and sleepers and gravel in broad daylight; then there would come a place where they were in twilight; and then, pretty suddenly, but of course without a sharp dividing line, they would vanish altogether into smooth, solid blackness. It was just so there. For a few feet in front of their bows they could see the swell of the bright greenish-blue water. Beyond that, they could see the water looking pale and gray as it would look late in the evening. But beyond that again, utter blackness as if they had come to the edge of moonless and starless night.

Caspian shouted to the boatswain to keep her back, and all except the rowers rushed forward and gazed from the bows. But there was nothing to be seen by gazing. Behind them was the sea and the sun, before them the Darkness.

"Do we go into this?" asked Caspian at length.

"Not by my advice," said Drinian.

"The Captain's right," said several sailors.

"I almost think he is," said Edmund.

Lucy and Eustace didn't speak but they felt very glad inside at the turn things seemed to be taking. But all at once the clear voice of Reepicheep broke in upon the silence.

"And why not?" he said. "Will someone explain to me why not."

No one was anxious to explain, so Reepicheep continued:

"If I were addressing peasants or slaves," he said, "I might suppose that this suggestion proceeded from cowardice. But I hope it will never be told in Narnia that a company of noble and royal persons in the flower of their age turned tail because they were afraid of the dark."

"But what manner of use would it be ploughing through that blackness?" asked Drinian.

"Use?" replied Reepicheep. "Use, Captain? If by use you mean filling our bellies or our purses, I confess it will be no use at all. So far as I know we did not set sail to look for things useful but to seek honor and adventure. And here is as great an adventure as ever I heard of, and here, if we turn back, no little impeachment of all our honors."

Several of the sailors said things under their breath that sounded like "Honor be blowed," but Caspian said:

"Oh, *bother* you, Reepicheep. I almost wish we'd left you at home. All right! If you put it that way, I suppose we shall have to go on. Unless Lucy would rather not?"

Lucy felt that she would very much rather not, but what she said out loud was, "I'm game."

"Your Majesty will at least order lights?" said Drinian.

"By all means," said Caspian. "See to it, Captain."

So the three lanterns, at the stern and the prow and the masthead, were all lit, and Drinian ordered two torches amidships. Pale and feeble they looked in the sunshine. Then all the men except some who were left below at the oars were ordered on deck and fully armed and posted in their battle stations with swords drawn. Lucy and two archers were posted on the fighting top with bows bent and arrows on the string. Rynelf was in the bows with his line ready to take soundings. Reepicheep, Edmund, Eustace and Caspian, glittering in mail, were with him. Drinian took the tiller.

"And now, in Aslan's name, forward!" cried Caspian. "A slow, steady stroke. And let every man be silent and keep his ears open for orders."

With a creak and a groan the *Dawn Treader* started to creep forward as the men began to row. Lucy, up in the fighting top, had a wonderful view of the exact moment at which they entered the darkness. The bows had already disappeared before the sunlight had left the stern. She saw it go. At one minute the gilded stern, the blue sea, and the sky, were all in broad daylight: next minute the sea and sky had vanished, the stern lantern—which had been hardly noticeable before—was the only thing to show where the ship ended. In front of the lantern she could see the black shape of Drinian crouching at the tiller. Down below her the two torches made visible two small patches of deck and gleamed on swords and helmets, and forward there was another island of light on the forecastle. Apart from that, the fighting top, lit by the masthead light which was only just above her, seemed to be a little lighted world of its own floating in lonely darkness. And the lights themselves, as always happens with lights when you have to have them at the wrong time of day, looked lurid and unnatural. She also noticed that she was very cold.

How long this voyage into the darkness lasted, no-

body knew. Except for the creak of the rowlocks and the splash of the oars there was nothing to show that they were moving at all. Edmund, peering from the bows, could see nothing except the reflection of the lantern in the water before him. It looked a greasy sort of reflection, and the ripple made by their advancing prow appeared to be heavy, small, and lifeless. As time went on everyone except the rowers began to shiver with cold.

Suddenly, from somewhere—no one's sense of direction was very clear by now—there came a cry, either of some inhuman voice or else a voice of one in such extremity of terror that he had almost lost his humanity.

Caspian was still trying to speak—his mouth was too dry—when the shrill voice of Reepicheep, which sounded louder than usual in that silence, was heard.

"Who calls?" it piped. "If you are a foe we do not fear you, and if you are a friend your enemies shall be taught the fear of us."

"Mercy!" cried the voice. "Mercy! Even if you are only one more dream, have mercy. Take me on board. Take me, even if you strike me dead. But in the name of all mercies do not fade away and leave me in this horrible land."

"Where are you?" shouted Caspian. "Come aboard and welcome."

There came another cry, whether of joy or terror, and then they knew that someone was swimming toward them.

"Stand by to heave him up, men," said Caspian.

"Aye, aye, your Majesty," said the sailors. Several crowded to the port bulwark with ropes and one, leaning far out over the side, held the torch. A wild,

white face appeared in the blackness of the water, and then, after some scrambling and pulling, a dozen friendly hands had heaved the stranger on board.

Edmund thought he had never seen a wilder-looking man. Though he did not otherwise look very old, his hair was an untidy mop of white, his face was thin and drawn, and, for clothing, only a few wet rags hung about him. But what one mainly noticed were his eyes, which were so widely opened that he seemed to have no eyelids at all, and stared as if in an agony of pure fear. The moment his feet reached the deck he said:

"Fly! Fly! About with your ship and fly! Row, row, row for your lives away from this accursed shore."

"Compose yourself," said Reepicheep, "and tell us what the danger is. We are not used to flying."

The stranger started horribly at the voice of the Mouse, which he had not noticed before.

"Nevertheless you will fly from here," he gasped. "This is the Island where Dreams come true."

"That's the island I've been looking for this long time," said one of the sailors. "I reckoned I'd find I was married to Nancy if we landed here."

"And I'd find Tom alive again," said another.

"Fools!" said the man, stamping his foot with rage. "That is the sort of talk that brought me here, and I'd better have been drowned or never born. Do you hear what I say? This is where dreams—dreams, do you understand—come to life, become real. Not daydreams: dreams."

There was about half a minute's silence and then, with a great clatter of armor, the whole crew were tumbling down the main hatch as quick as they could and flinging themselves on the oars to row as they had never rowed before; and Drinian was swinging round the tiller, and the boatswain was giving out the quickest stroke that had ever been heard at sea. For it had taken everyone just that half minute to remember certain dreams they had had—dreams that make you afraid of going to sleep again—and to realize what it would mean to land in a country where dreams come true.

Only Reepicheep remained unmoved.

"Your Majesty, your Majesty," he said, "are you going to tolerate this mutiny, this poltroonery? This is a panic, this is a rout."

"Row, row," bellowed Caspian. "Pull for all our lives. Is her head right, Drinian? You can say what you like, Reepicheep. There are some things no man can face."

"It is, then, my good fortune not to be a man," replied Reepicheep with a very stiff bow.

Lucy from up aloft had heard it all. In an instant one of her own dreams that she had tried hardest to forget came back to her as vividly as if she had only just woken from it. So *that* was what was behind them, on the island, in the darkness! For a second she wanted to go down to the deck and be with Edmund and Caspian. But what was the use? If dreams began coming true, Edmund and Caspian themselves might turn into something horrible just as she reached them. She gripped the rail of the fighting top and tried to steady herself. They were rowing back to the light as hard as they could: it would be all right in a few seconds. But oh, if only it could be all right now!

Though the rowing made a good deal of noise it did not quite conceal the total silence which surrounded the ship. Everyone knew it would be better not to listen, not to strain his ears for any sound from the darkness. But no one could help listening. And soon everyone was hearing things. Each one heard something different.

"Do you hear a noise like . . . like a huge pair of scissors opening and shutting . . . over there?" Eustace asked Rynelf.

"Hush!" said Rynelf. "I can hear *them* crawling up the sides of the ship."

"*It's* just going to settle on the mast," said Caspian.

"Ugh!" said a sailor. "There are the gongs beginning. I knew they would."

Caspian, trying not to look at anything (especially not to keep looking behind him), went aft to Drinian.

"Drinian," he said in a very low voice. "How long

did we take rowing in?—I mean rowing to where we picked up the stranger."

"Five minutes, perhaps," whispered Drinian. "Why?"

"Because we've been more than that already trying to get out."

Drinian's hand shook on the tiller and a line of cold sweat ran down his face. The same idea was occurring to everyone on board. "We shall never get out, never get out," moaned the rowers. "He's steering us wrong. We're going round and round in circles. We shall never get out." The stranger, who had been lying in a huddled heap on the deck, sat up and burst out into a horrible screaming laugh.

"Never get out!" he yelled. "That's it. Of course. We shall never get out. What a fool I was to have thought they would let me go as easily as that. No, no, we shall never get out."

Lucy leaned her head on the edge of the fighting top and whispered, "Aslan, Aslan, if ever you loved us at all, send us help now." The darkness did not grow any less, but she began to feel a little—a very, very little—better. "After all, nothing has really happened to us yet," she thought.

"Look!" cried Rynelf's voice hoarsely from the bows. There was a tiny speck of light ahead, and while they watched a broad beam of light fell from it upon the ship. It did not alter the surrounding darkness, but the whole ship was lit up as if by searchlight. Caspian blinked, stared round, saw the faces of his companions all with wild, fixed expressions. Everyone was staring in the same direction: behind everyone lay his black, sharply edged shadow.

Lucy looked along the beam and presently saw something in it. At first it looked like a cross, then it looked like an aeroplane, then it looked like a kite, and at last with a whirring of wings it was right overhead and was an albatross. It circled three times round the mast and then perched for an instant on the crest of the gilded dragon at the prow. It called out in a strong sweet voice what seemed to be words, though no one understood them. After that it spread its wings, rose, and began to fly slowly ahead, bearing a little to starboard. Drinian steered after it not doubting that it offered good guidance. But no one except Lucy knew that as it circled the mast it had whispered to her, "Courage, dear heart," and the voice, she felt sure, was Aslan's, and with the voice a delicious smell breathed in her face.

In a few moments the darkness turned into a grayness ahead, and then, almost before they dared to begin hoping, they had shot out into the sunlight and were in the warm, blue world again. And all at once everybody realized that there was nothing to be afraid of and never had been. They blinked their eyes and looked about them. The brightness of the ship herself astonished them: they had half expected to find that the darkness would cling to the white and the green and the gold in the form of some grime or scum. And then first one, and then another, began laughing.

"I reckon we've made pretty good fools of ourselves," said Rynelf.

Lucy lost no time in coming down to the deck, where she found the others all gathered round the newcomer. For a long time he was too happy to speak, and could only gaze at the sea and the sun and feel the bulwarks and the ropes, as if to make sure he was really awake, while tears rolled down his cheeks.

"Thank you," he said at last. "You have saved me

from . . . but I won't talk of that. And now let me know who you are. I am a Telmarine of Narnia, and when I was worth anything men called me the Lord Rhoop."

"And I," said Caspian, "am Caspian, King of Narnia, and I sail to find you and your companions who were my father's friends."

Lord Rhoop fell on his knees and kissed the King's hand. "Sire," he said, "you are the man in all the world I most wished to see. Grant me a boon."

"What is it?" asked Caspian.

"Never to bring me back there," he said. He pointed astern. They all looked. But they saw only bright blue sea and bright blue sky. The Dark Island and the darkness had vanished forever.

"Why!" cried Lord Rhoop. "You have destroyed it!"

"I don't think it was us," said Lucy.

"Sire," said Drinian, "this wind is fair for the south-east. Shall I have our poor fellows up and set sail? And after that, every man who can be spared, to his hammock."

"Yes," said Caspian, "and let there be grog all round. Heigh-ho, I feel I could sleep the clock round myself."

So all afternoon with great joy they sailed south-east with a fair wind. But nobody noticed when the albatross had disappeared.

A Pattern of Pyramids

LIONEL AND PATRICIA FANTHORPE

It was not one of my better craft lessons, and to make it worse the normally pleasant and helpful Mr. Wilkes was in awesome mode. He was limping badly after last night's Staff versus Old Boys match, and the word on the street connected that limp to my dad's tackling. I was, therefore, avoiding eye contact and trying to blend into the Craft Room wall like a chameleon.

The second problem was my Unfinished Project. It hung around my neck like the Ancient Mariner's albatross. I felt sorry for Schubert whenever I opened that folder and looked at the scrappy mess that was laughingly referred to as my "Preliminary Research." I wondered whether poor old Dickens had felt like this about *Edwin Drood*.

My so-called project was ambitiously entitled "A Pattern of Pyramids." Knowing my morbid interest in anything to do with ancient Egypt—especially if it were mummified—the normally encouraging Mr. Wilkes had approved the title. All I had in the folder were seven pathetic little cardboard cutouts that in more skillful hands would have been the nets of square-based pyramids of various sizes and colors. The way I'd cut them out and folded them, they looked more like the overflow from the litter bin outside the chippie.

I decided to take desperate measures on the way home. Yes! There was a skip today: and it was nearly full. I glanced quickly around, but the kids at the bus stop were so busy jostling and fighting to get on that no one was looking my way. Mum always told Samantha to make sure I got on the bus, but she was concentrating on getting a seat next to Phil (her steady boyfriend since the fourth year) and didn't see me slinking around the corner. If you turned left onto Museum Street on your way home from school it took a bit longer, but there was always the chance of finding a skip by the big, old Victorian gates. You couldn't do much at four o'clock on a *summer* afternoon, of course, but now that they'd changed the clocks during the Christmas term things were magic. Museum Street was narrow, with tall, derelict buildings on both sides: what was left of the late afternoon sun didn't penetrate there.

Samantha would be in trouble with Mum, which I wasn't happy about. As elder sisters at the same school go, Sam is definitely OK, but sometimes it's like having a spy satellite in your bag.

Conscience fell asleep in the muffled recess where I normally kept it, as I scrambled up the darkest side of the skip—the side nearest to the museum wall. It's a technique I'd learned with the Army Cadets. They used to take us on rock-climbing weekends up on the Roaches in Staffordshire. Our Lieutenant Instructor looked like a bald, bearded gorilla with shoulders so wide they frequently got stuck in rock chimneys, but he did teach us a bit about safety and how to climb overhangs—so the skip was easy.

It was a better Aladdin's cave than the last one had

been: most of that had been picture frames full of worm holes, and a lot of unreadable books, with pages mildewed solid. I moved some bits and pieces about: half a model ship, what looked like old plow handles (as riddled with woodworm as the picture frames had been last time); a broken washstand and chunks of a nondescript plaster statue . . . Ah! What was this?

I couldn't see any details in the gloom, but it was vaguely pear-shaped, about forty centimeters long by twenty wide—*and it was wrapped in what felt like linen that crumbled where I touched it.* There was a strange, sweet, musty smell to it—like something that had been stored in preservative herbs for a *very* long time. I felt a curious, almost frightening mixture of horror and excitement. Part of me wanted to drop it, run home and wash my hands several times with disinfectant soap. The other part—the part that tries to keep my conscience locked up in its muffled recess—kept thinking: *it's a mummified cat!* I crammed it into my bag, wedged it securely between trainers and lunchbox, and scrambled out of the skip. I tried to convince myself that I had some vague but noble motive of getting home before the bus and saving Sam from a row. I *really* wanted to get the mysterious bundle into the shed and examine it properly before Mum saw it and insisted on throwing it away for reasons of hygiene. *Could it really be a mummified cat?*

Through the kitchen window—despite its new double glazing—I could hear Mum and Sam having a battle royal about my probable whereabouts. I shivered with a mixture of guilt and anxiety, and ducked well below their observation level. I made it to the shed undetected, and checked that the sack curtains I'd nailed up for such occasions were still tightly over the window. Then I turned on the light. I took a fine-toothed saw from dad's tool rack and began work on the crumbling linen wrappings . . .

It was a mummified cat—but what a cat! I had never seen anything like it, and the preservation was incredible!

The linen bandages smelled ever more strongly of tanis leaves and other ancient Egyptian herbs as I got deeper. Then there was a layer of papyrus covered in weird hieroglyphics. Below that was some sort of soft, reddish clay—a bit of plasticine—that seemed to have acted as a flexible, waterproof, preservative seal around the remarkable cat itself.

The body seemed more like that of a miniature lion than any cat's body had the right to be, and the face was disturbingly human rather than feline. Uncannily, it looked as if it was only asleep and was going to stretch, yawn, and wake up at any moment.

Conscience was hammering as hard as a heavy metal drummer on the inside of its muffled recess: *take it back to the museum; they'd never have thrown this away if they'd known what it was.*

I heard Sammy's angry footsteps on the gravel path outside the shed. (I was always careful to walk down the grass verge myself when I didn't want them to know I was going there.) I doused the light immediately and stood very still, but the steps continued relentlessly. Sammy must have guessed I'd gone to look for a skip near the museum, and worked out that if I'd found anything interesting I'd be in the shed examining it. I groped for the cat and dropped it into the big plastic bin Dad kept below the workbench. There was a muffled thud as it landed on something soft—mainly the wrappings and tanis leaves that I'd tidied away into the bin after cutting them off.

Sammy blasted her way into the shed like a tornado looking for a flimsy building to demolish—and I felt about as stable and substantial at that moment as a cardboard replica of the Leaning Tower of Pisa. She swore at me for a full five minutes without repeating herself, but we both knew it didn't mean anything. Then she laughed and put her arms around me.

"You're the daftest and most irritating kid brother in the world, but Mum and I love you so much that we go scatty when we don't know where you are. That's why we blow up!"

"I know, and I'm sorry. It was just that I wanted to go down Museum Street, and you wouldn't have let me."

"You've got an obsession about skips!"

We both laughed again and went in for tea.

There was the usual unwelcome mound of largely pointless homework followed by a couple of good TV programs. I'd more or less forgotten the mummified Egyptian cat in the bin in the shed by the time I went to bed.

At this point, it's very important that I should explain the domestic arrangements relating to one Inky, a disreputable, old black tomcat whom we rescued from the RSPCA pound four or five years ago. He enjoys the double privilege of access to both the shed and the house via a couple of cat flaps that Dad installed for him when he came on board. Dad's not bad at things like that, but I've given up asking him to help with simultaneous equations since my last D minus grade. Sammy's no help either: she dropped math as soon as she got into year twelve to do English, French, and History at "A" Level. There must be *some-body, somewhere* who's on my side and who also knows

223

what *x* and *y* are equal to when *12x + 2y = 40* at the same time that *12x—2y = 32*.

I like to sleep with my bedroom door ajar, and there's usually a comforting glow around it from the landing light. Inky also likes to creep in and curl up on the duvet after his amorous adventures on the tiles.

Somewhere between midnight and one in the morning, Inky—or what I first *thought* was Inky, because that's his usual time—crept in discreetly and leapt up onto my bed. Unlike Inky, it didn't settle. It moved up slowly toward my face. The door was open wider than usual and I could see the intruder quite clearly.

It was the mummified cat I'd dropped into the bin in the shed!

I wanted to scream but couldn't. I tried to tell myself I was dreaming, but I wasn't very convincing. I wanted Sammy. I wanted Mum and Dad like a ten-day camel wants water on the eleventh day of a Sahara crossing. I wanted the SAS, the Paras, MI5, the Welsh Guards, the Big Bald Bearded Gorilla that taught me rock climbing in the Cadets. I wanted *anyone* and *anything* that would be brave enough to stand between me and this catlike creature that had been wrapped in bandages, clay, and tanis leaves for several thousand years.

How do you describe a thought that's as clear as day but doesn't have any words? Ideas were coming into my mind and I knew they were coming from *outside*. But they weren't in words, music, or pictures. They weren't even in those brain-deadening mathematical symbols that gave me my amazingly consistent D-minus grades. They weren't wrapped up in any kind of codes or symbols at all: they were just *pure thought*. They were similar to *electricity*, but without a light bulb, a heater, or a computer performing at the far end

of the wire. The strangest thing was *knowing* the essence of what was being transmitted but having to put it into words for yourself before you could really understand all of it. I can't explain it any better than that, but I know that that was what was happening inside my head. *It was some kind of telepathy—and it was coming from the cat with the strangely human face and miniature lion's body.* The two things that were reaching me most strongly were that this amazing little guy was about ten times more intelligent than I was and also that he was genuinely *friendly*. It was a bit like the way I felt about Mum, Dad, and Sammy, on the rare occasions when I tried to analyze it. They're OK people. They're honest with me. We trust each other. We *matter* to each other. I feel totally safe and relaxed with them. That was how I was starting to feel about this tiny catlike thing: I *knew* that he really liked me, and I was certainly starting to like him, too. You know how it is if you go to a new school, or move to a different neighborhood; one or two of the people you meet seem to give off exactly the right vibes—you make friends on sight and it lasts. It was like that with the tanis-leaf cat: we just seemed to be on the same wavelength.

"Don't be afraid. I won't hurt you or your family. I just need help with my quest." It was right up beside my face now, and a pair of the brightest, wisest little eyes you ever saw were looking into mine with all the appeal of a baby bird that wants a nice, juicy worm. Although he was one of the strangest creatures I'd ever seen, he was strange in an attractive sort of way. He was totally furry. Even his remarkably human-looking face was covered in very short, close-packed fur that made it look like a velvet mask. Despite being so small, his lionlike little body rippled with muscle, and I got the impression that those muscles were a lot stronger than those of normal animals. He moved in a very *confident* way, as if he knew he didn't have to worry about predators, yet there wasn't anything threatening or aggressive in his confidence. I tried to analyze my feelings again, and decided they were a mixture of affection and admiration: like I felt about my two-hundred-pound dad when he left poor Mr. Wilkes lying on the pitch after that hard—but perfectly fair—tackle. My conscience broke out of its muffled recess, and I've never quite been able to get it back since.

"What do you want me to do?" I whispered.

"I want to go home. That's my quest."

"Who are you and where are you from?" I asked, surprised at the way good old human curiosity had already overcome the worst of my amazement. Gradu-

226

ally, I felt as if something small and gentle was walking around inside my head. The *movements*—I can't think of a better word for them—were careful and delicate, but all the same it felt embarrassing and uncomfortable: as if someone (even someone you like and trust completely) was rummaging through your confidential files and reading your secret diary. Through all the discomfort and resentment that I couldn't help feeling, I knew why he was doing it, and I tried to understand. He couldn't begin to answer my question until he knew what I knew—and, more to the point, what I *didn't* know.

"Think about the Ice Age," he began. "Antarctica was inhabited long before that. My people lived there. We had a great civilization. We traveled. We traded with other nations. We shared our culture with them. We tried to help them, to teach them things. They were grateful. They liked us. They admired us. Some of them even built statues of us. The Egyptians did—and you've seen pictures of one."

I gave a sudden start that nearly dislodged him from the pillow.

"The Sphinx!" I shouted. *"You're a baby Sphinx!"*

Now I knew where I'd seen that curiously lionlike body with the human face before.

"My parents knew that this particular Ice Age was coming," he explained, "but with all our technology we couldn't prevent it, and when it did come it was more sudden and more terrible than we'd ever imagined. We couldn't save our magnificent civilization, but my parents wanted to save me—so they put me into something like a very deep sleep and sent me for safety toward friends in Egypt. They would never have known whether I got there ahead of the ice. I can't find the words or the background knowledge in your mind that would make sense of the state I was in: just try to imagine something like a coma, hibernation, or suspended animation." He paused to make sure I'd got the message right.

"The key to my waking up again lay in the tanis leaves, and that's where my parents were clever: they put me inside a protective, flexible cocoon. Once the sealed inner structure was opened, there was a strong probability that I'd be close enough to the tanis for it to revive me."

I experienced something different. The baby sphinx was *laughing* silently inside my mind.

"I woke up in what I now know is a rubbish bin surrounded by scraps of decaying linen and enough tanis leaves to revive a herd of frozen mammoths. After I'd struggled out of that lot and made my way through a couple of cute little doors that were just the right size, I made friends with the person you call Inky. I thought when I first saw him that he was the one who'd revived me. But I did a quick mind scan on him and found that although he's a lot more intelligent than you think he is, he wasn't the one I needed."

I felt a lot of sadness in the baby sphinx.

"My quest for *home* ..." he mused, "finding my people." The mind-voice was sharp with longing. I really wanted to help him, but I hadn't the faintest idea where to start. He picked up my feelings.

"It's all a question of patterns. From the little bit of science you've studied, you know something about crystals and the patterns they form, don't you?" If it's possible to give the telepathic equivalent of a nod, I gave one. "The right type of pattern," he went on, "is far more powerful than I can explain to you with the

concepts you've got in your memory. The shape that you call a pyramid is one of the most powerful patterns of all, and when a group of pyramids is arranged in the right order there's almost no limit to what can be achieved. Colors are vitally important as well, and so are the *vibrations* hidden in certain words—what witches and wizards used to call spells. We need the words from the papyrus that was wrapped up with me. They'll help to open the door in the pattern of pyramids."

It was obvious to him that I couldn't understand that bit at all. The phrase *pattern of pyramids* only served to remind me of today's unspeakable craft lesson.

"But how *can* you go home if your country in Antarctica was destroyed by the ice sheet?" I asked. "There can't possibly be any of your family left after all these years. *Or can there?*"

"We live a long time," he answered, "and my parents said they were going to try to escape to what you now call Egypt, once I was safely away ahead of them. They *might* have made it. They *might* still be hidden there. Many of our people used to gather for holidays at the Great Meeting Place."

"The Great Meeting Place?" I echoed. He projected a picture into my mind. I thought at first it was going to be the start of his family album. The picture was a gigantic blowup of the baby sphinx beside my pillow . . .

No, it wasn't. It was another one—the one I had previously thought of as the *real* Sphinx, the *only* Sphinx, the huge one in Egypt with its pattern of pyramids nearby. But there weren't any pyramids in this picture. The colors were vivid and lifelike. There was no weathering, no damage, none of the mysterious water erosion that Graham Hancock had found at the base. It looked brand-new and *perfect*.

So *that* solved one of the riddles of the Sphinx: it was the Egyptian meeting point for an old and brilliant race of catlike beings with human faces, a race whose original home in what was now the Antarctic-waste had been wiped out by the invading ice twenty thousand years ago. The Sphinx was their equivalent of "under-the-clock-at-Victoria-Station," or the Meeting Point at Heathrow.

"Below what you have just called the Sphinx is a doorway to one of our underground living places . . . perhaps it still survives. In any event, my quest is to try to get there, and for that I need the pattern of pyramids together with the papyrus that will open the door."

He was searching my mind again, going into its smallest nooks and crannies like Mrs. Tiggywinkle cleaning out her burrow.

Have you ever felt anyone jumping for joy inside your head? It's weird. I think maybe that's why elephants are supposed to be afraid of mice getting into their ears.

"Stop it. You're damaging what little brain I've got left!" I shouted.

The excited mental trampolining subsided a little.

"I've found it!" came the wildly triumphant thought. I felt now as if someone had laid out a miniature railway inside my head and was testing the points.

He leapt off my bed as if the duvet had suddenly become red hot, and I knew that he was heading for the shed. The instruction "Get your CDT folder . . ." wafted into my mind. By the time I had the disreputa-

ble little cardboard nets out on my desk, the Sphinxette was back . . . with Inky helping him to drag the papyrus, and looking amazingly pleased with himself because he was being useful.

The two of them went to work on the pyramid nets. Cats are meticulously neat when they want to be. My horrendous mess slowly turned into seven of the smartest little model pyramids you ever saw. The Sphinxette arranged them in a sort of rainbow pattern, with all the colors in the right order, yet the pattern also looked a bit like a hand: the two largest pyramids were the wrist and palm, the five smaller ones were the fingers. I remembered we'd seen the Arthur C. Clarke video "Colors of Infinity" about fractals and the Mandelbrot Set in a math lesson at the end of last term. I hadn't understood much of it, but I'd sat there absolutely quiet and breathless with admiration. The pattern the Sphinxette had just made was curiously like a Mandelbrot shape.

Then he started making funny little feline noises . . . miaowing at the hieroglyphics the way that Inky miaows at a tin of cat food when you don't fill his dish quickly enough.

There was a purring sound from the model pyramids in their Mandelbrot pattern. They vibrated gently and beams of softly colored light focused on the Sphinxette. Where those beams converged, they turned white. He was glowing in the center of them . . . *and very slowly fading.*

"Don't go!" I shouted. "Please don't go!"

I had a glimpse of something like a long, long tunnel through reality, down which he was scampering happily. Our telepathic link was still holding, but it was getting fainter, like a local station fading on a car radio as you get farther from the transmitter. He was letting me see things through his eyes, hear things through his ears ... I saw a broad river with papyrus boats sailing gracefully and majestically along it; I guessed it was the Nile as it had been millennia ago. The scene changed and I saw a broad expanse of bright, fertile fields and waving corn. I saw the huge triangle of the Nile delta and ships—very different from the slow, stately, papyrus boats plying up and down the great river. These were sturdy, clinker-built, sea-going, cedarwood jobs with many banks of oars. Somehow I felt that ships like these had once gone in search of the Golden Fleece or sailed to attack Troy. The insubstantial tunnel continued snaking its weird way through space and time, and I could sense the fearless little Sphinxette scampering boldly on. I hoped so much that it would hold together for him just a little longer ...

Then, hazy and indistinct at first, but growing clearer with each passing second, I saw the great, gleaming shape of the newly constructed Sphinx—and how like him it was!

I could also feel his growing excitement and wonder. Whatever that tunnel was made of it went on boring its way relentlessly through time and space ... I could scarcely believe that it was held together somehow by my little cardboard pyramids. My daring Sphinxette friend was like the Wright Brothers, or one of the First World War pilots defying gravity with something made from canvas, kindling, and wire. Despite the increasing faintness of the telepathic link, I could hear him shouting with joy ... and other voices, like his but louder and deeper, were answering. I picked up a great surge of wildly happy emotion, a tidal wave of joyful reunion . . . then the other voices—his parents', I think they must have been—hurling enormous, wordless gratitude down the collapsing tunnel. I got a final, fleeting glimpse of the brightly colored, newly constructed Sphinx, with three deliriously happy miniatures of it embracing one another and cavorting wildly around its great base, then, very slowly, the softly colored lights went out and I thought wistfully that I had seen my Sphinxette friend for the last time.

But although I could no longer see the ecstatically happy dancers, there was one more message from them: "We'll find a way to reach you again, somehow . . . just remember the Pattern of Pyramids."

Mr. Wilkes was delighted with "my" project. I got the only A-plus grade in CDT awarded in our class. But I took the greatest care to get my pyramids back after the examiners and moderators had finished with them. I keep hoping to hear from my Sphinxette pal again, and sometimes Inky curls up near the pyramids on my bedroom cabinet and purrs as if he's talking to someone I can't see.

The Closed Window

A. C. BENSON

The Tower of Nort stood in a deep angle of the downs; formerly an old road led over the hill, but it is now a green track covered with turf; the later highway choosing rather to cross a low saddle of the ridge, for the sake of the beasts of burden. The tower, originally built to guard the great road, was a plain, strong, thick-walled fortress. To the tower had been added a plain and seemly house, where the young Sir Mark de Nort lived very easily and plentifully. To the south stretched the great wood of Nort, but the Tower stood high on an elbow of the down, sheltered from the north by the great green hills. The villagers had an odd, ugly name for the Tower, which they called the Tower of Fear; but the name was falling into disuse, and was only spoken, and then heedlessly, by ancient men, because Sir Mark was vexed to hear it so called.

Sir Mark was not yet thirty, and had begun to say that he must marry a wife; but he seemed in no great haste to do so, and loved his easy, lonely life, with plenty of hunting and hawking on the down. With him lived his cousin and heir, Roland Ellice, a heedless, good-tempered man, a few years older than Sir Mark; he had come on a visit to Sir Mark, when he first took possession of the Tower, and there seemed no reason why he should go away; the two suited each other. Sir Mark was sparing of speech, fond of books and of rhymes. Roland was different, loving ease and wine and talk, and finding in Mark a good listener. Mark loved his cousin, and thought it praiseworthy of him to stay and help to cheer so sequestered a house, since there were few neighbors within reach.

And yet Mark was not wholly content with his easy life; there were many days when he asked himself why he should go thus quietly on, day by day, like a stalled ox; still, there appeared no reason why he should do otherwise; there were but few folk on his land, and they were content; yet he sometimes envied them their bondage and their round of daily duties. The only place where he could else have been was with the army, or even with the Court; but Sir Mark was no soldier, and even less of a courtier; he hated tedious gaiety, and it was a time of peace. So because he loved solitude and quiet he lived at home, and sometimes thought himself but half a man; yet was he happy after a sort, but for a kind of little hunger of the heart.

What gave the Tower so dark a name was the memory of old Sir James de Nort, Mark's grandfather, an evil and secret man, who had dwelt at Nort under some strange shadow; he had driven his son from his doors, and lived at the end of his life with his books and his own close thoughts, spying upon the stars and tracing strange figures in books; since his death the old room in the turret top, where he came by his end in a dreadful way, had been closed; it was entered by a turret door, with a flight of steps from the chamber below. It had four windows, one to each of the winds; but the window that looked upon the down was fastened up and secured with a great shutter of oak.

One day of heavy rain, Roland, being weary of doing nothing, and vexed because Mark sat so still in a

great chair, reading a book, said to his cousin at last that he must go and visit the old room, in which he had never set foot. Mark closed his book, and, smiling indulgently at Roland's restlessness, rose, stretching himself, and got the key; and together they went up the turret stairs. The key groaned loudly in the lock, and, when the door was thrown back, there appeared a high, faded room, with a timbered roof, and with a close, dull smell. Around the walls were presses, with the doors fast; a large oak table, with a chair beside it, stood in the middle. The walls were otherwise bare and rough; the spiders had spun busily over the windows and in the angles. Roland was full of questions, and Mark told him all he had heard of old Sir James and his silent ways, but said that he knew nothing of the disgrace that had seemed to envelop him, or of the reasons why he had so evil a name. Roland said that he thought it a shame that so fair a room should lie so nastily, and pulled one of the casements open, when a sharp gust broke into the room, with so angry a burst of rain, that he closed it again in haste; little by little, as they talked, a shadow began to fall upon their spirits, till Roland declared that there was still a blight upon the place; and Mark told him of the death of old Sir James, who had been found after a day of silence, when he had not set foot outside his chamber, lying on the floor of the room, strangely bedabbled with wet and mud, as though he had come off a difficult journey, speechless, and with a look of anguish on his face; and that he had died soon after they had found him, muttering words that no one understood. Then the two young men drew near to the closed window; the shutters were tightly barred, and across the panels was scrawled in red, in an uncertain hand, the words

CLAUDIT ET NEMO APERIT, which Mark explained was the Latin for the text, *He shutteth and none openeth*. And then Mark said that the story went that it was ill for the man that opened the window, and that shut it should remain for him. But Roland girded at him for his want of curiosity, and had laid a hand upon the bar as though to open it, but Mark forbade him urgently. "Nay," said he, "let it remain so—we must not meddle with the will of the dead!" and as he said the word, there came so furious a gust upon the windows that it seemed as though some stormy thing would beat them open; so they left the room together, and, presently descending, found the sun struggling through the rain.

But both Mark and Roland were sad and silent all that day; for though they spake not of it, there was a desire in their minds to open the closed window, and to see what would befall; in Roland's mind it was like the desire of a child to peep into what is forbidden; but in Mark's mind a sort of shame to be so bound by an old and weak tale of superstition.

Now it seemed to Mark, for many days, that the visit to the turret room had brought a kind of shadow down between them. Roland was peevish and ill-at-ease; and ever the longing grew upon Mark, so strongly that it seemed to him that something drew him to the room, some beckoning of a hand or calling of a voice.

Now one bright and sunshiny morning it happened that Mark was left alone within the house. Roland had ridden out early, not saying where he was bound. And Mark sat, more listlessly than was his wont, and played with the ears of his great dog, that sat with his head upon his master's knee, looking at him with liquid eyes, and doubtless wondering why Mark went not abroad.

Suddenly Sir Mark's eye fell upon the key of the upper room, which lay on the window ledge where he had thrown it; and the desire to go up and pluck the heart from the little mystery came upon him with a strength that he could not resist; he rose twice and took up the key, and, fingering it doubtfully, laid it down again; then suddenly he took it up, and went swiftly into the turret stair, and up, turning, turning, till his head was dizzy with the bright peeps of the world through the loophole windows. Now all was green, where a window gave on the down; and now it was all clear air and sun, the warm breeze coming pleasantly into the cold stairway; presently Mark heard the pattering of feet on the stair below, and knew that the old hound had determined to follow him; and he waited a moment at the door, half pleased, in his strange mood, to have the company of a living thing. So when the dog was at his side, he stayed no longer, but opened the door and stepped within the room.

The room, for all its faded look, had a strange air about it, and though he could not say why, Mark felt that he was surely expected. He did not hesitate, but walked to the shutter and considered it for a moment; he heard a sound behind him. It was the old hound who sat with his head aloft, sniffing the air uneasily; Mark called him and held out his hand, but the hound would not move; he wagged his tail as though to acknowledge that he was called, and then he returned to his uneasy quest. Mark watched him for a moment, and saw that the old dog had made up his mind that all was not well in the room, for he lay down, gathering his legs under him, on the threshold, and watched his master with frightened eyes, quivering visibly. Mark, no lighter of heart, and in a kind of fearful haste, pulled the great staple off the shutter and set it on the ground, and then wrenched the shutters back; the space revealed was largely filled by old and dusty webs of spiders, which Mark lightly tore down, using the staple of the shutters to do this; it was with a strange shock of surprise that he saw that the window was dark, or nearly so; it seemed as though there were some further obstacle outside; yet Mark knew that from below the leaded panes of the window were visible. He drew back for a moment, but, unable to restrain his curiosity, wrenched the rusted casement open. But still all was dark without; and there came in a gust of icy wind from outside; it was as though something had passed him swiftly, and he heard the old hound utter a strangled howl; then, turning, he saw him spring to his feet with his hair bristling and his teeth bared, and next moment the dog turned and leapt out of the room.

Mark, left alone, tried to curb a tide of horror that swept through his veins; he looked around at the room, flooded with the southerly sunlight, and then he turned again to the dark window, and putting a strong constraint upon himself, leaned out, and saw a thing that bewildered him so strangely that he thought for a moment his senses had deserted him. He looked out on a lonely, dim hillside, covered with rocks and stones; the hill came up close to the window, so that he could have jumped down upon it, the wall below seeming to be built into the rocks. It was all dark and silent, like a clouded night, with a faint light coming from whence he could not see. The hill sloped away very steeply from the tower, and he seemed to see a plain beyond, where at the same time he knew that the down ought to lie. On the plain there was a light,

like the firelit window of a house; a little below him some shape like a crouching man seemed to run and slip among the stones, as though suddenly surprised, and seeking to escape. Side by side with a deadly fear that began to invade his heart, came an uncontrollable desire to leap down among the rocks; and then it seemed to him that the figure below stood upright and began to beckon him. There came over him a sense that he was in deadly peril; and, like a man on the edge of a precipice, who has just enough will left to try to escape, he drew himself by main force away from the window, closed it, put the shutters back, replaced the staple, and, his limbs all trembling, crept out of the room, feeling along the walls like a palsied man. He locked the door, and then, his terror overpowering him, he fled down the turret stairs. Hardly thinking what he did, he came out onto the court, and, going to the great well that stood in the center of the yard, he went to it and flung the key down, hearing it clink on the sides as it fell. Even then he dared not reenter the house, but glanced up and down, gazing about him, while the cloud of fear and horror by insensible degrees dispersed, leaving him weak and melancholy.

Presently Roland returned, full of talk, but broke off to ask if Mark were ill. Mark, with a kind of surliness, an unusual mood for him, denied it somewhat sharply. Roland raised his eyebrows and said no more, but prattled on. Presently after a silence he said to Mark, "What did you do all the morning?" and it seemed to Mark as though this were accompanied with a spying look. An unreasonable anger seized him. "What does it matter to you what I did?" he said. "May not I do what I like in my own house?"

"Doubtless," said Roland, and sat silent with uplifted brows; then he hummed a tune, and presently went out.

They sat at dinner that evening with long silences, contrary to their wont, though Mark bestirred himself to ask questions. When they were left alone, Mark stretched out his hand to Roland, saying, "Roland, forgive me! I spoke to you this morning in a way of which I am ashamed; we have lived so long together— and yet we came nearer to quarreling today than we have ever done before, and it was my fault."

Roland smiled and held Mark's hand for a moment. "Oh, I had not given it another thought," he said; "the wonder is that you can bear with an idle fellow as you do." Then they talked for awhile with the pleasant glow of friendliness that two good comrades feel when they have been reconciled. But late in the evening Roland said, "Was there any story, Mark, about your grandfather's leaving any treasure of money behind him?"

The question grated somewhat unpleasantly upon Mark's mood; but he controlled himself and said, "No, none that I know of—except that he found the estate rich and left it poor—and what he did with his revenues no one knows—you had better ask the old men of the village; they know more about the house than I do. But, Roland, forgive me once more if I say that I do not desire Sir James's name to be mentioned between us. I wish we had not entered his room; I do not know how to express it, but it seems to be as though he had sat there, waiting quietly to be summoned, and as though we had troubled him, and—as though he had joined us. I think he was an evil man, close and evil. And there hangs in my mind a verse of Scripture, where Samuel said to the witch, 'Why hast thou dis-

242

quieted me to bring me up?' Oh," he went on, "I do not know why I talk wildly thus," for he saw that Roland was looking at him with astonishment, with parted lips, "but a shadow has fallen upon me, and there seems evil abroad."

From that day forward a heaviness lay on the spirit of Mark that could not be scattered. He felt, he said to himself, as though he had meddled lightheartedly with something far deeper and more dangerous than he had supposed—like a child that has aroused some evil beast that slept. He had dark dreams, too. The figure that he had seen among the rocks seemed to peep and beckon him, with a mocking smile, over perilous places, where he followed unwillingly. But the heavier he grew the lighter-hearted Roland became; he seemed to walk in some bright vision of his own, intent upon a large and gracious design.

One day he came into the hall in the morning, looking so radiant that Mark asked him half-enviously what he had to make him so glad. "Glad," said Roland, "oh, I know it! Merry dreams, perhaps. What do you think of a good grave fellow who beckons me on with a brisk smile, and shows me places, wonderful places, under banks and in woodland pits, where riches lie piled together? I am sure that some good fortune is preparing for me, Mark—but you shall share it." Then Mark, seeing in his words a certain likeness, with a difference, to his own dark visions, pressed his lips together and sat looking stonily before him.

At last, one still evening of spring, when the air was intolerably languid and heavy for mankind, but full of sweet promises for trees and hidden, peeping things, though a lurid redness of secret thunder had lain all day among the heavy clouds in the plain, the two dined together. Mark had walked alone that day, and had lain upon the turf of the down, fighting against a weariness that seemed to be poisoning the very springs of life within him. But Roland had been brisk and alert, coming and going upon some secret and busy errand, with a fragment of a song upon his lips, like a man preparing to set off for a far country, who is glad to be gone. In the evening, after they had dined, Roland had let his fancy rove in talk. "If we were rich," he said, "how we would transform this old place!"

"It is fair enough for me," said Mark heavily; and Roland had chided him lightly for his somber ways, and sketched new plans of life.

Mark, wearied and yet excited, with an intolerable heaviness of spirit, went early to bed, leaving Roland in the hall. After a short and broken sleep, he awoke, and, lighting a candle, read idly and gloomily to pass the heavy hours. The house seemed full of strange noises that night. Once or twice came a scraping and a faint hammering in the wall; light footsteps seemed to pass in the turret—but the tower was always full of noises, and Mark heeded them not; at last he fell asleep again, to be suddenly awakened by a strange and desolate crying, that came he knew not whence, but seemed to wail upon the air. The old dog, who slept in Mark's room, heard it too; he was sitting up in a fearful expectancy. Mark rose in haste, and, taking the candle, went into the passage that led to Roland's room. It was empty, but a light burned there and showed that the room had not been slept in. Full of a horrible fear, Mark returned, and went in hot haste up the turret steps, fear and anxiety struggling together in his mind. When he reached the top, he found the little door broken forcibly open, and a light within. He cast a haggard look around the room, and then the crying came again, this time very faint and desolate.

Mark cast a shuddering glance at the window; it was wide open and showed a horrible liquid blackness; round the bar in the center that divided the casements, there was something knotted. He hastened to the window and saw that it was a rope, which hung heavily. Leaning out he saw that something dangled from the rope below him—and then came the crying again out of the darkness, like the crying of a lost spirit.

He could see as in a bitter dream the outline of the hateful hillside; but there seemed to his disordered fancy to be a tumult of some kind below; pale lights moved about, and he saw a group of forms that scattered like a shoal of fish when he leaned out. He knew that he was looking upon a scene that no mortal eye ought to behold, and it seemed to him at the moment as though he was staring straight into hell.

The rope went down among the rocks and disappeared; but Mark clenched it firmly and, using all his strength, which was great, drew it up hand over hand; as he drew it up he secured it in loops around the great oak table; he began to be afraid that his strength would not hold out, and once when he returned to the window after securing a loop, a great hooded thing like a bird flew noiselessly at the window and beat its wings.

Presently he saw that the form that dangled on the rope was clear of the rocks below; it had come up through them, as though they were but smoke; and then his task seemed to him more sore than ever. Inch by painful inch he drew it up, working fiercely and silently; his muscles were tense, and drops stood on his brow, and the veins hammered in his ears; his

breath came and went in sharp sobs. At last the form
was near enough for him to seize it; he grasped it by
the middle and drew Roland, for it was Roland, over
the windowsill. His head dangled and drooped from
side to side; his face was dark with strangled blood and
his limbs hung helpless. Mark drew his knife and cut
the rope that was tied under his arms; the helpless
limbs sank huddling on the floor; then Mark looked
up; at the window a few feet from him was a face,
more horrible than he had supposed a human face, if
it was human indeed, could be. It was deadly white,
and hatred, baffled rage, and a sort of devilish malignity
glared from the white set eyes, and the drawn mouth.
There was a rush from behind him; the old hound,
who had crept up unawares into the room, with a
fierce outcry of rage sprang on to the windowsill; Mark
heard the scraping of his claws upon the stone. Then
the hound leapt through the window, and in a moment there was the sound of a heavy fall outside. At
the same instant the darkness seemed to lift and draw
up like a cloud; a bank of blackness rose past the
window, and left the dark outline of the down, with a
sky sown with tranquil stars.

The cloud of fear and horror that hung over Mark
lifted, too; he felt in some dim way that his adversary
was vanquished. He carried Roland down the stairs
and laid him on his bed; he roused the household,
who looked fearfully at him, and then his own strength
failed; he sank upon the floor of his room, and the
dark tide of unconsciousness closed over him.

Mark's return to health was slow. One who has
looked into the Unknown finds it hard to believe
again in the outward shows of life. His first conscious
speech was to ask for his hound; they told him that

the body of the dog had been found, horribly mangled as though by the teeth of some fierce animal, at the foot of the tower. The dog was buried in the garden, with a slab above him, on which are the words:

EUGE SERVE BONE ET FIDELIS

A silly priest once said to Mark that it was not meet to write Scripture over the grave of a beast. But Mark said warily that an inscription was for those who read it, to make them humble, and not to increase the pride of what lay below.

When Mark could leave his bed, his first care was to send for builders, and the old tower of Nort was taken down, stone by stone, to the ground, and a fair chapel built on the site; in the wall there was a secret stairway, which led from the top chamber, and came out among the elder bushes that grew below the tower, and here was found a coffer of gold, which paid for the church; because, until it was found, it was Mark's design to leave the place desolate. Mark is wedded since, and has his children about his knee; those who come to the house see a strange and wan man, who sits at Mark's board, and whom he uses very tenderly; sometimes this man is merry, and tells a long tale of his being beckoned and led by a tall and handsome person, smiling, down a hillside to fetch gold; though he can never remember the end of the matter; but about the springtime he is silent or mutters to himself; and this is Roland; his spirit seems shut up within him in some close cell, and Mark prays for his release, but till God call him. He treats him like a dear brother, and with the reverence due to one who has looked out on the other side of Death, and who may not say what his eyes beheld.

The Goatboy and
the Giant

GARRY KILWORTH

There was a giant, full-limbed and fabulous, sleeping in the sun. The goatboy approached him warily, standing half as high as one of the enormous feet, whose bare soles looked like the bottom of a dry river bed. When the young man walked past the towering feet, he observed that the translucent moons of the creature's toenails gleamed like topaz and the veins just beneath the surface of his delicate skin were rivers of the palest blue.

The youth began the journey from feet to head, marveling at the paleness of the giant's body, even though it had been exposed to the fierce Turkish sun, day over day, and the abrasive sandstorms of the Turkish wilderness, night under night.

When the goatboy reached the giant's head, by way of his muscled left leg and sinewy arm, he found it to be bald. This was an old giant, one who had lost his pigtail to the passing centuries. Such ancient titans passed their final years in sleep until death came to filigree their fingers with webs and powder their pates with fine dust.

The giant's face was turned toward the goatboy and though the creature's breath swhooshed over the wasteland, raising dustclouds and whirling widdershins, he could see it wore gentle features. The next time the

giant breathed in through his nose, the youth threw
sand up his nostrils in order to wake him.

The giant coughed, sat up, and rubbed his face. His
eyes opened wide, then they shut tight as he gave out
the most enormous sneeze, which ripped shrubs from
the earth and sent them rolling like tumbleweed across
the desert. Finally, the giant blinked twice and looked
around him.

"What time is it?" he asked, on seeing the goatboy.

"Almost the end of the century," said the lad.

And the giant said, "I've overslept again."

He rose and stretched himself, then began digging,
scooping out handfuls of desert sand each large enough
to bury a house. The hole grew to a great pit whose
sides kept flowing like a flood into its depths, but
finally the giant reached water and bent his great head
to suck the liquid into his mouth. When he had finished drinking, the giant pulled fistfuls of cactus from
the ground and chewed them to mush before swallowing. He gave one tremendous belch, wiped his mouth
on his arm, then smiled at the goatboy.

"That was good," he said, and then lay himself
down once more.

"Wait!" cried the goatboy. "You're not going back
to sleep again?"

The giant sat up and blinked.

"Well, I was thinking of it, yes. I've had food and
water, so what else is there to stay awake for? Can you
give me a shake if you come by here in a few decades?"

The goatboy folded his arms and shook his head.
His goats milled around his legs bleating, as he con-
templated one of the last giants left on the earth. In
fact, he told himself, no one had seen such a creature
for at least a hundred years. He himself was familiar

with them only through stories told him by his grandfather, back in the old township of Yozgat. He saw in this giant the potential to fulfil his ambition.

Now, the problem with goatboys was they had too much time to daydream. Once upon a century, way back before this goatboy's time, they had to fight with lion and bears, keep wolves from descending like Assyrians on the fold, defend their herd against lost armies of ravenous Greeks. When they were not looking after the goats, they were practicing with their slingshots or cutting new staves. Goatboys of old had no time to daydream.

Since lions, bears, wolves, and confused Greeks were no longer a threat, the goatboy idled his hours away wishing he was a great rock star, like Michael Jackson, who sang to the most primitive of bushmen through the medium of transistor radios. At night the goatboy would lie under heavens glistening with distant suns, and think not of the wonders of the universe, but of the marvelous world beyond Turkey where a boy with something unusual to offer might become rich and famous. Goats earned him a living, but they smelled and would never lead to the kind of life a rock star followed.

"Listen," said the goatboy to the giant, "you and I could make a team. I bet you're the last living giant on the earth. People would pay a fortune just to look at you. We could become rich and famous together."

"Rich and famous," repeated the giant, using the same tremulous tones employed by the boy, "is that a good thing?"

"Is it a *good* ? Why it's the *only* worthwhile ambition in this world. Once you're rich and famous you can do anything. I expect you could buy a bed to support

your weight and drift to your final rest on a raft of duck down and goose feathers."

The giant patted the desert sand.

"This is pretty soft," he murmured.

"Not as soft as a mattress stuffed with feathers," replied the boy.

"Well, what do we have to do to become rich and famous?" asked the giant. "Is it hard work?"

"Certainly not. You only earn a living by working hard, or providing the necessities of life, like food and water. To become rich you must peddle luxuries. You just find something people don't really need but *desire* above all else, then you sell to them at extortionate prices. I'm sure people would want to see *you*, because you're unusual in this day and age."

"Am I?"

"Yes, and if you like, I'll help you get your riches. I'll have to charge you, of course—being a professional giant manager is not an easy task. What do you say to something in the region of seventy percent of the gross receipts?"

The giant's brow furrowed and he hugged his knees.

"What's a receipt? How many's a gross? I don't know anything about percentages. Are they the same as fractions?"

"I'll explain all that later," said the goatboy, "but in the meantime how about it?"

"That seems fair," he said. "After all, I have no idea about how to get rich and famous, and you're an expert.

"Precisely," said the goatboy.

"However," said the giant, "I have no wish to leave this pleasant spot, even for a feather bed," and he bade the goatboy farewell.

Stunned for only a moment, the youth invented a tale that only giants, the most gullible creatures on the earth, would believe. Unfortunately it is a quirk of supernature, a paradox of the cruellest kind, that whatever giants believe becomes their truth.

"What was your last job?" asked the boy, knowing full well that giants never do manual work and haven't the intellect or dexterity required for other types of employment.

The giant shook his head.

"I've never had one of those."

The goatboy opened wide his eyes in mock concern.

"You mean you've never earned anything in your life?"

"Not a penny," confirmed the giant.

"Oh, that's really sad!"

"Now why should that be?"

"Because," lied the boy, "everyone knows that Og the King of Bashan, the first giant, who walked beside Noah's Ark with his head still above water, decreed that since giants were bound to be big, lazy fellows who lay around in the sun all day, those who did no work and earned nothing during their stay on earth would not be permitted to enter heaven."

"He said that?"

"Everyone knows."

The giant sat up and held his face in his great hands, looking down through his fingers at the tiny goatboy below. His eyes were like lakes with no finite depth. His brow was a furrowed field. His pink lips trembled with worry.

"I haven't earned a penny," he cried, "so I shall never get to heaven."

In believing the tale, it had become the truth.

"You still have time before you die," said the goatboy, "to redeem yourself. Follow me!"

So the giant got to his feet and carried the goatboy down to the coast, striding out across the wasteland, each stride being twenty-one miles in length. Once they reached the sea, the goatboy instructed the giant to go into the water and follow the shoreline around to Istanbul, where he hoped they would be able to start making their fortune. It was not possible for the giant to walk over the land because there were cities, towns, villages, and farms scattered all over the countryside, and there was a danger someone might be crushed beneath those great soles. Even so, they had to keep a sharp lookout for ships cruising along in the shallows and fisherfolk collecting their lobsterpots out on the mud.

When they reached Istanbul, the giant was amazed at the amount of building that had gone on while he had been away.

"This was only a village last time I was here," he said. "I can't even recognize it. Are you sure this is Byzantium?"

"It was called that," said the boy, "but they changed the name to Constantinople, and now it's Istanbul."

"I'd never have believed it," said the giant.

"What can I say?" replied the goatboy. "You've been a bit of a sluggard in the past."

"I suppose that's true, but I do like my sleep."

"Well, that's going to change for a while, but eventually it will be worth it. You'll have your feather bed to float to heaven on, and I can start my career as a rock star with a solid financial backing. What we'll do is sound out the city's businessmen. You'll have to wait here, while I go and make some arrangements."

"All right," said the giant, who was up to his waist in harbor water, the ships circumnavigating his girth. He folded his arms, to keep his hands from doing any damage, and set himself foursquare in the mud. It began to rain, something the giant had not experienced out in the desert, but he did not complain. He knew the goatboy was helping him to a better way of rest.

It drizzled for days on end and the winds were from the north, but the giant merely shivered and hugged his beautiful body with his arms, trusting that the boy would soon return and help him earn some money so that Og would let him into heaven.

The goatboy left his fabulous creature and went to the big corporations, saying he had something quite extraordinary to offer them in the way of show business. Eventually he found himself in a plush office confronted by an array of the most wealthy persons in Istanbul. He explained his proposition to them.

"What I have here is probably unique," he said. "A giant, ladies and gentleman, in an age when technology is becoming old hat. People are beginning to get bored with video games and computers and are starting to look to the past, the golden age, the antique era, the ancient civilizations. What we have here is a wonder of the old world, when fables and folktales were live entertainment."

He paused to see how his speech was affecting his audience.

They did not appear spellbound.

In fact, someone yawned.

"Just what," rumbled one bearded moneyman, "do you propose to *do* with your giant?"

"Why," cried the goatboy, "people will pay just to look at him."

The old gentleman nodded towards the window overlooking the harbor.

"Why should they? They can see him for free. You can't miss him, can you? He's the tallest thing for miles."

"Well, we have to hide him in a building, so that they can't see him for free," said the boy frantically, feeling that things were not working out as well as he had planned, and his millions were slipping away from him. "I mean, if they can't see him, they"ll pay then, won't they?"

"It'll take years to build something to contain your giant," snapped one of the other financiers in the room, "and where would we put him in the meantime? There'll be tourists descending on Istanbul like locusts before we get him hidden from sight, which will be good for the city but not for the owners of the giant. The Japanese and Americans and Germans will all have seen him by the time we get him under cover. The British think they've got the most interesting weather in the world, and don't bother with any other wonder of nature. The Scandinavians and Russians are too phlegmatic to concern themselves with fabulous creatures. The French don't like anything they haven't discovered themselves. The Koreans would pirate holograms of him all over the world. The Swiss prefer clockwork giants about six inches high that they can sell to the toyshops. The Chinese haven't got any money and the Africans don't like to travel. The rest of Asia is too busy trying to catch up with the century. That leaves the Australians and New Zealanders, who don't amount to more than a handful of backpackers who prefer cheap boarding houses and food from the stalls in the all-night markets. Need I go on? Good morning to you, young man."

And so, to his dismay, the goatboy was dismissed.

Instead of returning to the giant and reporting his failure to the creature, he went on a tour of all the major cities in Turkey, trying to drum up enough enthusiasm to take the giant on a roadshow. He wrote to the Rolling Stones, telling them the giant would make a wonderful backdrop to their next concert. He tried to call David Bowie, who might have been able to suggest some zany use for the muscled colossus. He visited local radio and TV stations and went on the air with news of his find. All ended in failure.

"Can he sing?" asked the agents. "What does he play?"

Finally, defeat bearing down on him with its distinctively heavy and lumpy form, the goatboy returned to the Istanbul harbor.

There he found that his living wonder had caught a cold from standing in the wet, in the wind and the rain, which had turned to pneumonia. The poor giant had expired, slipping down into the waters of the Bosporus and floating away on the tide out into the sea of Marmara, where he drifted finally into the Mediterranean itself. His beautiful, big body was washed up on the shores of a land whose inhabitants had stopped believing in giants, and they were both amazed and confounded by his presence on their beach. For a while the people took to traveling down to the coast to view his remains and have their photographs taken standing between his fingers. A famous writer came to write descriptive notes on how the drowned giant affected the local population.

In time, his great ribs were used as bridges to cross ornamental streams, his pelvis became a skateboard park for the young and agile, his spinal cord became a tunnel down which youngsters would slide, his legbones and armbones were trestles for swings, his hands and feet seats for the elderly.

There was a small charge for the use of these facilities.

Mirror, Mirror . . .

FRANCES M. HENDRY

Mum stood back from hanging the last picture, smiling. "There! All done at last. Isn't it lovely, pet? A real grown-up room for you. Real antiques, and original oil paintings, really good, and it'll all increase in value."

"Yeah. Thanks, Mum."

Mum sighed. She knew that Anna wasn't as pleased as she'd hoped—but she'd get used to it. Lovely mahogany, it was, and the deep carving, real quality. And such pretty flower pictures. So lucky, that old friend of Bob's boss dying just when Anna's room really had to be redone. Such a horrible tragedy, the old lady killing her grandson and then herself—really dreadful! But Anna didn't know about it, so it didn't matter. "You'll want to sort your things out. I'll leave you to it. Okay, pet?"

"Okay, Mum."

Anna stared around. Yucky dark wood and sickly pink paper. "Grown-up room." All her stepfather's idea. Trying to smarm up to her and dig at her at the same time. That was why he'd done it, getting rid of all the things she liked—so maybe her Japanese kites and posters had been tatty, but they were hers! Beastly Bob. He'd no right to make her swap them for stupid flowers. Well, okay, she'd agreed, but she hadn't known it would be as soppy as this!

She'd never call him Dad. "Dad" was her father, not him . . .

Angrily, Anna tugged at the wardrobe door. It stuck—useless thing! Her reflection, all greenish and wobbly, glared back at her as she struggled with the handle. "Oh, I hate this stuff! Look at this carving—all yucky little faces!" Bulging eyes and cheeks made of cherries and plums grinned wickedly back from the mirror frame, watching her, leering at her.

Going to and from the bed, rearranging things in the new-old drawers, she kept making faces at her reflection in the wardrobe mirror. "Hate him! I hate him!" she whispered to herself. Bulges in the glass twisted and exaggerated her expression. Intrigued, she leaned closer, made an even worse face; it looked really horrible, almost devilish.

"Dinner!" Mum called.

As Anna moved toward the door, something odd made her glance back, but she couldn't see anything wrong.

It was a difficult meal—well, they all were, with Bob there. Stiltedly, Anna praised the new furniture to keep Mum happy. Mum smiled as if she didn't notice the strain—marrying Bob seemed to have turned her stupid. Bob himself smiled a lot, and asked sensible questions about school. Sucking up to her, trying to get around her, but he wouldn't! She hated him till she could scarcely eat.

After dinner, she went up early to bed. "Lots of things still to sort out, Mum. Night, everybody!" That included Bob without naming him . . .

Oh, hate him hate him hate him!

Again, something twitched at the corner of her eye. A mouse? No, not a movement; an absence of movement. She walked into the middle of the room and looked around. Nothing wrong. Chest of drawers, dres-

sing table, wardrobe, bed—wait a sec. The wardrobe. There was definitely something odd about the wardrobe. What was it?

The glass was green and twisted, so that everything reflected in it was dingy and distorted. Well, it *was* old. She pulled down her sleeve and went over to give it a rub, try to brighten it. She reached out—

She had no reflection.

There were the pink walls, and the bed behind her, and the door . . . but not herself.

Her legs wouldn't hold her. She found herself sitting on the bed, her face covered by her hands. Dreaming. She must be.

Sure enough, when she dared to look again, there she was, peering nervously back at herself.

Boy, what a relief! How silly could you get! The door must have been a bit open or something, and she hadn't noticed . . . But no, it was tight shut.

Oh, well . . .

She kept a wary eye on it while she undressed. Nothing happened.

When she came back from the bathroom, the first thing she looked at was the mirror. Perfectly normal.

Oh, stop this nonsense! She got a book, switched off the main light, and climbed into the new-old bed with a grunt of annoyance. Far too hard. The pink bedside light reflected from the wardrobe mirror, making a queer pattern like water running down the wall.

She couldn't settle. Might as well lie on the floor. Finally, she tossed the book aside. "I hate this! I hate him!" She beat her fists on the quilt.

Something changed.

Nothing moved.

Something was missing.

The bedside lamp was still on, but the watermark on the wall had gone.

Her heart swelled to fill her chest till it hurt, and she couldn't breathe. What—what was it? A dream? A ghost? But ghosts didn't stop light, they shone in the dark . . .

The little pink lamp shone steadily. But there was no reflection of its light on the wall.

Nothing happened. Slowly Anna's terror faded. She started to breathe again. Call for help? What would she say? "The mirror's not reflecting"? And Bob would look, and it would be; and then what would he say? No way.

She slid quietly out of bed. Stalking it, she crept over to look in the mirror. It was reflecting the room—she could see more and more as she came up from the side—but it didn't reflect her.

She looked more closely. The room was all there, all wobbly, the pink even more ghastly through the greenish glass. The bedclothes were rumpled as she'd left them. Her slippers lay beside the bed, the book on the cover. Perfectly ordinary. But here she was, right in front of the mirror, and there was no sign of her reflection at all.

What could it be? She reached out to touch the glass.

Her hand went right through.

Yikes!

She whipped back and waggled her fingers. They looked okay. They felt okay. But . . . she'd put her hand through a mirror. She could see the surface of the glass, shining faintly. And her hand had gone right through.

She tried again, with one finger, in and out. No

tingling, nothing.

She started to feel excited. Alice through the looking-glass, only for real! Spooky!

What about going through? Right through? All of her?

Oh, wowee!

Yes, she must go. What an adventure! Couldn't miss this! She must go.

No, stop. Be sensible; go slow.

She stuck her hand in again, and left it for a minute. A bit cold. Out. No problem.

She drew a deep breath, took a firm grip of the mirror frame to pull herself back, and stuck her head through. It looked just like her own room, except the other way around. Slightly distorted, greenish. Yes, she could breathe. No problem.

The carving writhed under her fingers for a second, as if the tiny faces had grinned—but no, it was quite solid. Her fingers had just slipped on the polished wood.

She could go on. Must go on. It drew her on . . .

At last she stepped right into the mirror.

She was all right. She looked behind her. In the mirror mirror, the brighter pink of her own room in the real world shone clearly. Could she get out again? She tried; yes, she could. No problem.

The mirror lamp was a bit dimmer, but still pink. Everything was slightly off straight, a bit off-color, somehow, but generally the same, in reverse.

Except that she couldn't move anything. And she didn't cast a shadow. It was as if she wasn't really there.

How could she get out, to see what the rest of the house was like? After a moment's thought, she went back into her real room. She opened the door and checked. Yes, the mirrored door was open now as well. Great! She must go on!

The mirror hall was like the mirror bedroom, the reverse of reality, but askew. The walls and floor sloped oddly. The stair down was uneven, and steeper. She clutched the icy banisters to steady herself. But she had to go on. She couldn't stop now. She couldn't stop.

Down and down. The same number of steps, but somehow far deeper. Queer how they seemed to twist into a spiral, like going down into a seashell. The streetlight through the panes of the mirror front door was sickly orangey-brown. It was colder, darker. Potholing must be like this.

The mirror sitting room felt cramped, skewed, air-

less. Mum was sitting on the sofa, knitting as usual, staring blankly as a doll, a fixed, foolish smile on her face.

He was there, too. Bob. The intruder. The man who tried to take Dad's place. The man who had changed everything, taken over Mum, wrecked her room. His face was off-white, and his slitty eyes gleamed green, distorted, and uneven, like his sneering mouth, his sharp nose, everything about him. Here, he appeared the way she knew he was—horrible and crooked. Why couldn't Mum see it? Oh, how she hated him!

He laid down his newspaper and stretched, long spider arms uncurling, spreading his filthy web. "Cup of tea, love?" His voice was harsh and off-key, dragging, like when you touch the edge of a record with your finger. It scraped and echoed in the tightness of the room.

Anna stepped into the room. "Hi. I couldn't sleep."

They didn't look up. She stepped forward. "Hello! Hi! Can't you see me?"

No, they couldn't see or hear her. They didn't know she was there.

She could say anything, do anything. They'd never know!

She stood right in front of Bob, snarling down at him. "Rotten, greedy pig, coming in and taking Dad's place, as if I'd ever forget Dad!"

But Mum had. Traitor.

"You've no right here! This is our house, not yours! I hate you! I wish you'd go away! I wish you'd die! I could kill you!" She could hear her own voice repeating over and over, faster and faster, higher and higher, like a speeded-up tape.

Light and sound and space shrank even further. Bob's voice, the telly, the click of Mum's needles, every noise was pin-sharp, tiny.

In the suffocating dark, the only brightness was a greenish light beaming from the kitchen door. She was drawn over to it.

The walls had vanished into close, smothering black. The biggest knife, the long, heavy, sharp carver, lay on the worktop. Glowing.

She stretched out her hand. Could she touch the knife, lift it? Yes. A keen, whispery whine sang in her bones, raised the hairs on her head, drilled high and clear through her skull . . . Her own voice, tiny and shrill, echoing "Hate kill killhate killkill . . ."

This was the very tip of the spiral.

Back in the sitting room, Mum was dully putting away her knitting. "I think Anna's room was a mistake."

The mirror Bob nodded slowly. "I'm afraid so, love. She's so loyal to her father, she'll not accept anything from me."

Their voices were muffled, hard to make out below the high, cold humming of the knife, shrilling in Anna's own voice, "Killkillkillkillhatekill . . ."

Mum nodded. "I wish she could learn to love you, the way I do."

Love? Love him? Anna sneered. The knife burned like ice in her hand. Why wait? Mum deserved to see it, for loving somebody else, for forgetting Dad . . .

"Oh, my dear." It was muffled, stifled. Mum leaned over to rest her head on Bob's shoulder.

Traitor!

Slowly Anna raised her hand. The shining blade rose before her face.

Her reflection was bright and clear in the glossy steel.

She blinked.

Everything here was distorted. The mirror twisted everything.

Away beyond the back of her mind, she could sense it watching, tasting, sniggering, gloating. It watched the people outside, waiting for the right kind of angry feelings, waiting for her, lurking like an octopus in its crevice to draw her in, feel her emotions . . .

Feed on them.

It didn't lie—but it exaggerated everything. Everything. It reflected and reflected your feelings, spiralling them in and in on themselves, winding in, screwing tighter and tighter till your head was bursting . . . you were a fanatic, unthinking, deadly . . . ready to give it its final feast . . .

But you weren't seeing straight . . .

The knife screamed, "Killkillkill!"

But its blade, a mirror inside the mirror, reflected free and true.

And this was truly wrong.

"Killkillkillkill!"

No. Stop. Don't let it twist you. It wants you to . . .

Think straight. See straight.

What had Bob really done, except fall in love with Mum? And her with him. If she struck now, how would Mum feel? What would Dad have said? Was killing Bob really being loyal to Dad?

In that tiny point at the back of her mind there was shock, disbelief, a thrust of fury. The knife leapt like a snake's fang toward Bob's neck.

Just in time, Anna dragged her hand back. She'd nearly done it—so nearly—what it wanted . . .

One half of her wanted to stay, to finish it. The song of killing was high and wild in her, drowning the murmurs of Mum's love. In the dim green of the mirror room, Bob's face was devilish, evil, deserving to die . . .

Twisted in the mirror. Distorted by the mirror. Don't believe it!

She turned, forced herself away, and fled. In her ears the knife's song screeched and howled, she couldn't think, she didn't know what to do . . .

Escape. Run. Get back to her room . . . to the real world . . .

Out to the hall. She groped through a black fog for the banister . . . up the stairs . . . up the spiral . . . impossibly steep, cold, airless . . . gasping for breath . . . knees shaking, aching . . . on, go on, mustn't stop, force on, up . . . up . . . up again . . .

A light. A dim, pink light, far away, far at the end of a huge, echoing hallway, far longer and darker than reality, but the light was there, warmth, home, safety . . .

She dragged herself into the mirror bedroom. The welcoming light glowed from the wardrobe door. Miles of carpet around the mountain range of the bed . . . She reached out to the bright glow—

Her hand struck glass. She couldn't get through.

Whimpering, she scratched and beat at it. The glass was solid. On the far side was her own room, waiting, quiet and ordinary. She could see it. But she couldn't get through to it. She was trapped here, swallowed by the mirror . . .

No! No!

The knife was still in her hand, its blade glittering, its hilt heavy and burning, its song deafening, sicken-

ing, turn, killkillkillkill, go the easy way, go back, killkillkill . . .

No!

Shrieking in defiance, she smashed it down against the glass that imprisoned her—

She was through, in her own room, stumbling forward onto the bed, glass from the broken mirror tinkling around her feet, onto the carpet. The frame of the wardrobe door gaped, filled safely with wood.

The crash brought everybody running up to see what had happened. Whitefaced and shivering, Anna sobbed and gasped tearlessly. "I'm sorry, Mum. I didn't mean—I wouldn't—no, it was all twisted, that's why—all green—I wouldn't have done it. Honest, I wouldn't."

Sweeping up shards and sparkles of glass, Mum was angry. "What a mess! And look, the carving's damaged too. All chipped! All spoiled!"

It was Bob, hated Bob, who sat on the bed beside Anna and put an arm around her shoulders to comfort her shock. "It's okay, Anna. It wasn't your fault. You're quite right, the glass was uneven. Well, it was old. You must have had a nightmare, and sort of half-wakened, seen yourself without knowing who it was and hit out at the glass in fright, eh?"

It was nearly the truth. He wasn't all that bad. She nodded. He smiled down at her. "It's OK, honestly. I tell you what. I should have realized this furniture isn't what a youngster wants. But your mum and I, we like it, don't we, Greta? So we'll see about getting you something more suitable for your birthday next week. It'll not be good stuff like this, we can't afford it, but as long as it's cheap it'll be whatever style you choose. And we'll take this. Fair enough?"

Anna sniffed, and nodded. "Oh, thanks, Bob. That's really good of you."

Mum looked astonished. Anna had actually sounded as if she meant it! To show how pleased she was, she offered, "I know you didn't like the pink much, pet. You can choose your own wallpaper, as well as new furniture. I don't mind."

"Oh, no, Mum. Leave the paper. It's—it's warm. Friendly." And normal, and ordinary, and dull. But Mum was pleased all over again.

They tucked her in as if she were a baby, and went out.

Anna cuddled down and relaxed. It must have been just a nightmare, as Bob said. The world through the mirror, all twisted and evil, was just a dream. Even the carving didn't look like faces any more, just bumpy little fruits. Only a bad dream.

She'd put the knife back in the morning.

The Trolls

J.R.R. TOLKIEN

This story comes from early on in The Hobbit, *the novel by J.R.R. Tolkien that precedes his even more famous trilogy* The Lord of the Rings, *which some may claim is the greatest fantasy ever written. Hobbits are little people with furry feet and warm hearts. Bilbo is a hobbit, and at the start of the book he finds himself visited by Gandalf the wizard and a party of dwarfs led by Thorin Oakenshield. Gandalf has selected Bilbo to help them recover the dwarfs' homeland and their gold, which has been taken by the dragon Smaug. Bilbo finds himself captivated by the stories and adventures told by the dwarfs, and before he realizes it has let himself be talked into joining them. This episode starts the next morning.*

Up jumped Bilbo, and putting on his dressing-gown went into the dining room. There he saw nobody, but all the signs of a large and hurried breakfast. There was a fearful mess in the room, and piles of unwashed crocks in the kitchen. Nearly every pot and pan he possessed seemed to have been used. The washing-up was so dismally real that Bilbo was forced to believe the party of the night before had not been part of his bad dreams, as he had rather hoped. Indeed he was really relieved after to think that they had all gone without him, and without bothering to wake him up ("but with never a thank-you" he thought); and yet in a way he could not help feeling just a trifle disappointed. The feeling surprised him.

"Don't be a fool, Bilbo Baggins!" he said to himself, "thinking of dragons and all that outlandish nonsense at your age!" So he put on an apron, lit fires, boiled water, and washed up. Then he had a nice little breakfast in the kitchen before turning out the dining-room. By that time the sun was shining; and the front door was open, letting in a warm spring breeze. Bilbo began to whistle loudly and to forget about the night before. In fact he was just sitting down to a nice little second breakfast in the dining room by the open window, when in walked Gandalf.

"My dear fellow," said he, "whenever *are* you going to come? What about *an early start*?—and here you are having breakfast, or whatever you call it, at half-past ten! They left you the message, because they could not wait."

"What message?" said poor Mr. Baggins all in a fluster.

"Great Elephants!" said Gandalf, "you are not at all yourself this morning—you have never dusted the mantelpiece!"

"What's that go to do with it? I have had enough to do with washing up for fourteen!"

"If you had dusted the mantelpiece, you would have found this just under the clock," said Gandalf, handing Bilbo a note (written, of course, on his own note-paper).

This is what he read:

"Thorin and Company to Burglar Bilbo greeting! For your hospitality our sincerest thanks, and for

your offer of professional assistance our grateful acceptance. Terms: cash on delivery, up to and not exceeding one-fourteenth of total profits (if any); all traveling expenses guaranteed in any event; funeral expenses to be defrayed by us or our representatives, if occasion arises and the matter is not otherwise arranged for.

"Thinking it unnecessary to disturb your esteemed repose, we have proceeded in advance to make requisite preparations, and shall await your respected person at the Green Dragon Inn, Bywater, at 11 A.M. sharp. Trusting that you will be *punctual*,

> "*We have the honor to remain*
> "*Yours deeply*
> "*Thorin & Co.*"

"That leaves you just ten minutes. You will have to run," said Gandalf.

"But—" said Bilbo.

"No time for it," said the wizard.

"But—" said Bilbo again.

"No time for that either! Off you go!"

To the end of his days Bilbo could never remember how he found himself outside, without a hat, a walking stick or any money, or anything that he usually took when he went out; leaving his second breakfast half-finished and quite unwashed-up, pushing his keys into Gandalf's hands, and running as fast as his furry feet could carry him down the lane, past the great Mill, across The Water, and then on for a mile or more.

Very puffed he was, when he got to Bywater just on the stroke of eleven, and found he had come without a pocket handkerchief!

"Bravo!" said Balin who was standing at the inn door looking out for him.

Just then all the others came round the corner of the road from the village. They were on ponies, and each pony was slung about with all kinds of baggages, packages, parcels, and paraphernalia. There was a very small pony, apparently for Bilbo.

"Up you two get, and off we go!" said Thorin.

"I'm awfully sorry," said Bilbo, "but I have come without my hat, and I have left my pocket handkerchief behind, and I haven't got any money. I didn't get your note until after 10:45 to be precise."

"Don't be precise," said Dwalin, "and don't worry! You will have to manage without pocket handkerchiefs, and a good many other things, before you get to the journey's end. As for a hat, I have got a spare hood and cloak in my luggage."

That's how they all came to start, jogging off from the inn one fine morning just before May, on laden ponies; and Bilbo was wearing a dark green hood (a little weather-stained) and a dark green cloak borrowed from Dwalin. They were too large for him, and he looked rather comic. What his father Bungo would have thought of him, I daren't think. His only comfort was he couldn't be mistaken for a dwarf, as he had no beard.

They had not been riding very long, when up came Gandalf very splendid on a white horse. He had brought a lot of pocket handkerchiefs, and Bilbo's pipe and tobacco. So after that the party went along very merrily, and they told stories or sang songs as they rode forward all day, except of course when they stopped for meals. These didn't come quite as often as Bilbo would have liked them, but still he began to feel that

adventures were not so bad after all.

At first they had passed through hobbit-lands, a wide, respectable country inhabited by decent folk, with good roads, an inn or two, and now and then a dwarf or a farmer ambling by on business. Then they came to lands where people spoke strangely, and sang songs Bilbo had never heard before. Now they had gone on far into the Lone-lands, where there were no people left, no inns, and the roads grew steadily worse. Not far ahead were dreary hills, rising higher and higher, dark with trees. On some of them were old castles with an evil look, as if they had been built by wicked people. Everything seemed gloomy, for the weather that day had taken a nasty turn. Mostly it had been as good as May can be, even in merry tales, but now it was cold and wet. In the Lone-lands they had been obliged to camp when they could, but at least it had been dry.

"To think it will soon be June," grumbled Bilbo, as he splashed along behind the others in a very muddy track. It was after teatime; it was pouring with rain, and had been all day; his hood was dripping into his eyes, his cloak was full of water; the pony was tired and stumbled on stones; the others were too grumpy to talk. "And I'm sure the rain has got into the dry clothes and into the food bags," thought Bilbo. "Bother burgling and everything to do with it! I wish I was at home in my nice hole by the fire, with the kettle just beginning to sing!" It was not the last time that he wished that!

Still the dwarfs jogged on, never turning round or taking any notice of the hobbit. Somewhere behind the gray clouds the sun must have gone down, for it began to get dark as they went down into a deep valley with a river at the bottom. Wind got up, and willows along its banks bent and sighed. Fortunately the road went over an ancient stone bridge, for the river, swollen with the rains, came rushing down from the hills and mountains in the north.

It was nearly night when they had crossed over. The wind broke up the gray clouds, and a wandering moon appeared above the hills between the flying rags. Then they stopped, and Thorin muttered something about supper, "and where shall we get a dry patch to sleep on?"

Not until then did they notice that Gandalf was missing. So far he had come all the way with them, never saying if he was in the adventure or merely keeping them company for a while. He had eaten most, talked most, and laughed most. But now he simply was not there at all!

"Just when a wizard would have been most useful, too," groaned Dori and Nori (who shared the hobbit's views about regular meals, plenty and often).

They decided in the end that they would have to camp where they were. They moved to a clump of trees, and though it was drier under them, the wind shook the rain off the leaves, and the drip, drip, was most annoying. Also, the mischief seemed to have got into the fire. Dwarfs can make a fire almost anywhere out of almost anything, wind or no wind; but they could not do it that night, not even Oin and Gloin, who were specially good at it.

Then one of the ponies took fright at nothing and bolted. He got into the river before they could catch him; and before they could get him out again, Fili and Kili were nearly drowned, and all the baggage that he carried was washed away off him. Of course it was

mostly food, and there was mighty little left for supper, and less for breakfast.

There they all sat glum and wet and muttering, while Oin and Gloin went on trying to light the fire, and quarreling about it. Bilbo was sadly reflecting that adventures are not all pony-rides in May sunshine, when Balin, who was always their lookout man, said: "There's a light over there!" There was a hill some way off with trees on it, pretty thick in parts. Out of the dark mass of the trees they could now see a light shining, a reddish comfortable-looking light, as it might be a fire or torches twinkling.

When they had looked at it for some while, they fell to arguing. Some said "no" and some said "yes." Some said they could but go and see, and anything was better than little supper, less breakfast, and wet clothes all the night.

Others said: "These parts are none too well known, and are too near the mountains. Travelers seldom come this way now. The old maps are no use: things have changed for the worse and the road is unguarded. They have seldom even heard of the king round here, and the less inquisitive you are as you go along, the less trouble you are likely to find." Some said: "After all there are fourteen of us." Others said: "Where has Gandalf got to?" This remark was repeated by everybody. Then the rain began to pour down worse than ever, and Oin and Gloin began to fight.

That settled it. "After all we have got a burglar with us," they said; and so they made off, leading their ponies (with all due and proper caution) in the direction of the light. They came to the hill and were soon in the wood. Up the hill they went; but there was no proper path to be seen, such as might lead to a house or a farm; and do what they could they made a deal of rustling and crackling and creaking (and a good deal of grumbling and dratting), as they went through the trees in the pitch dark.

Suddenly the red light shone out very bright through the tree trunks not far ahead.

"Now it is the burglar's turn," they said, meaning Bilbo. "You must go on and find out all about that light, and what it is for, and if all is perfectly safe and canny," said Thorin to the hobbit. "Now scuttle off, and come back quick, if all is well. If not, come back if you can! If you can't, hoot twice like a barn owl and once like a screech owl, and we will do what we can."

Off Bilbo had to go, before he could explain that he could not hoot even once like any kind of owl any more than fly like a bat. But at any rate hobbits can move quietly in woods, absolutely quietly. They take a pride in it, and Bilbo had sniffed more than once at what he called "all this dwarfish racket," as they went along, though I don't suppose you or I would have noticed anything at all on a windy night, not if the whole cavalcade had passed two feet off. As for Bilbo walking primly toward the red light, I don't suppose even a weasel would have stirred a whisker at it. So, naturally, he got right up to the fire—for fire it was— without disturbing anyone. And this is what he saw.

Three very large persons sitting round a very large fire of beech logs. They were toasting mutton on long spits of wood, and licking the gravy off their fingers. There was a fine toothsome smell. Also there was a barrel of good drink at hand, and they were drinking out of jugs. But they were trolls. Obviously trolls. Even Bilbo, in spite of his sheltered life, could see that: from the great heavy faces of them, and their size, and the

shape of their legs, not to mention their language, which was not drawing-room fashion at all, at all.

"Mutton yesterday, mutton today, and blimey, if it don't look like mutton again tomorrer," said one of the trolls.

"Never a blinking bit of manflesh have we had for long enough," said a second. "What the 'ell William was a-thinkin' of to bring us into these parts at all, beats me—and the drink runnin' short, what's more," he said, jogging the elbow of William, who was taking a pull at his jug.

William choked. "Shut yer mouth!" he said as soon as he could. "Yer can't expect folk to stop here forever just to be et by you and Bert. You've et a village and a half between yer, since we come down from the mountains. How much more d'yer want? And time's been up our way, when yer'd have said 'thank yer Bill' for a nice bit o' fat valley mutton like what this is." He took a big bite off a sheep's leg he was toasting, and wiped his lips on his sleeve.

Yes, I am afraid trolls do behave like that, even those with only one head each. After hearing all this Bilbo ought to have done something at once. Either he should have gone back quietly and warned his friends that there were three fair-sized trolls at hand in a nasty mood, quite likely to try toasted dwarf, or even pony, for a change; or else he should have done a bit of good quick burgling. A really first-class and legendary burglar would at this point have picked the trolls' pockets—it is nearly always worthwhile, if you can manage it—pinched the very mutton off the spits, purloined the beer, and walked off without their noticing him. Others more practical but with less professional pride would perhaps have stuck a dagger into each of them before they observed it. Then the night could have been spent cheerily.

Bilbo knew it. He had read of a good many things he had never seen or done. He was very much alarmed, as well as disgusted; he wished himself a hundred miles away, and yet—and yet somehow he could not go straight back to Thorin and Company empty-handed. So he stood and hesitated in the shadows. Of the various burglarious proceedings he had heard of, picking the trolls' pockets seemed the least difficult, so at last he crept behind a tree just behind William.

Bert and Tom went off to the barrel. William was having another drink. Then Bilbo plucked up courage and put his little hand in William's enormous pocket. There was a purse in it, as big as a bag to Bilbo. "Ha!" thought he, warming to his new work as he lifted it carefully out, "this is a beginning!"

It was! Trolls" purses are the mischief, and this was no exception. "'Ere, 'oo are you?" it squeaked, as it left the pocket; and William turned round at once and grabbed Bilbo by the neck, before he could duck behind the tree.

"Blimey, Bert, look what I've copped!" said William.

"What is it?" said the others coming up.

"Lumme, if I knows! What are yer?"

"Bilbo Baggins, a bur—a hobbit," said poor Bilbo, shaking all over, and wondering how to make owl noises before they throttled him.

"A burrahobbit?" said they, a bit startled. Trolls are slow in the uptake, and mighty suspicious about anything new to them.

"What's a burrahobbit got to do with my pocket, anyways?" said William.

"And can ye cook 'em?" said Tom.

"Yer can try," said Bert, picking up a skewer.

"He wouldn't make above a mouthful," said William, who had already had a fine supper, "not when he was skinned and boned."

"P'raps there are more like him round about, and we might make a pie," said Bert. "Here you, are there any more of your sort a-sneakin' in these here woods, yer nassty little rabbit," said he looking at the hobbit's furry feet; and he picked him up by the toes and shook him.

"Yes, lots," said Bilbo, before he remembered not to give his friends away. "No none at all, not one," he said immediately afterwards.

"What d'yer mean?" said Bert, holding him right way up, by the hair this time.

"What I say," said Bilbo gasping. "And please don't cook me, kind sirs! I am a good cook myself, and cook

281

better than I cook, if you see what I mean. I'll cook beautifully for you, a perfectly beautiful breakfast for you, if only you won't have me for supper."

"Poor little blighter," said William. He had already had as much supper as he could hold; also he had had lots of beer. "Poor little blighter! Let him go!"

"Not till he says what he means by *lots* and *none at all*," said Bert. "I don't want to have me throat cut in me sleep! Hold his toes in the fire, till he talks!"

"I won't have it," said William. "I caught him anyway."

"You're a fat fool, William," said Bert, "as I've said afore this evening."

"And you're a lout!"

"And I won't take that from you, Bill Huggins," says Bert, and puts his fist in William's eye.

Then there was a gorgeous row. Bilbo had just enough wits left, when Bert dropped him on the ground, to scramble out of the way of their feet, before they were fighting like dogs, and calling one another all sorts of perfectly true and applicable names in very loud voices. Soon they were locked in one another's arms, and rolling nearly into the fire kicking and thumping, while Tom whacked at them both with a branch to bring them to their senses—and that of course only made them madder than ever.

That would have been the time for Bilbo to have left. But his poor little feet had been very squashed in Bert's big paw, and he had no breath in his body, and his head was going round; so there he lay for a while panting, just outside the circle of firelight.

Right in the middle of the fight up came Balin. The dwarfs had heard noises from a distance, and after waiting for some time for Bilbo to come back, or to

hoot like an owl, they started off one by one to creep towards the light as quietly as they could. No sooner did Tom see Balin come into the light than he gave an awful howl. Trolls simply detest the very sight of dwarfs (uncooked). Bert and Bill stopped fighting immediately, and "a sack, Tom, quick!" they said. Before Balin, who was wondering where in all this commotion Bilbo was, knew what was happening, a sack was over his head, and he was down.

"There's more to come yet," said Tom, "or I'm mighty mistook. Lots and none at all, it is," said he. "No burrahobbits, but lots of these here dwarfs. That's about the shape of it!"

"I reckon you're right," said Bert, "and we'd best get out of the light."

And so they did. With sacks in their hands, that they used for carrying off mutton and other plunder, they waited in the shadows. As each dwarf came up and looked at the fire, and the spilled jugs, and the gnawed mutton, in surprise, pop! went a nasty smelly sack over his head, and he was down. Soon Dwalin lay by Balin, and Fili and Kili together, and Dori and Nori and Ori all in a heap, and Oin and Gloin and Bifur and Bofur and Bombur piled uncomfortably near the fire.

"That'll teach 'em," said Tom; for Bifur and Bombur had given a lot of trouble, and fought like mad, as dwarfs will when cornered.

Thorin came last—and he was not caught unawares. He came expecting mischief, and didn't need to see his friends' legs sticking out of sacks to tell him that things were not all well. He stood outside in the shadows some way off, and said: "What's all this trouble? Who has been knocking my people about?"

"It's trolls!" said Bilbo from behind a tree. They had

forgotten all about him. "They're hiding in the bushes with sacks," said he.

"O! are they?" said Thorin, and he jumped forward to the fire, before they could leap on him. He caught up a big branch all on fire at one end; and Bert got that end in his eye before he could step aside. That put him out of the battle for a bit. Bilbo did his best. He caught hold of Tom's leg—as well as he could, it was thick as a young tree trunk—but he was sent spinning up into the top of some bushes, when Tom kicked the sparks up in Thorin's face.

Tom got the branch in his teeth for that, and lost one of the front ones. It made him howl, I can tell you. But just at that moment William came up behind and popped a sack right over Thorin's head and down to his toes. And so the fight ended. A nice pickle they were all in now: all neatly tied up in sacks, with three angry trolls (and two with burns and bashes to remember) sitting by them, arguing whether they should roast them slowly, or mince them fine and boil them, or just sit on them one by one and squash them into jelly; and Bilbo up in a bush, with his clothes and his skin torn, not daring to move for fear they should hear him.

It was just then that Gandalf came back. But no one saw him. The trolls had just decided to roast the dwarfs now and eat them later—that was Bert's idea, and after a lot of argument they had all agreed to it.

"No good roasting 'em now, it'd take all night," said a voice. Bert thought it was William's.

"Don't start the argument all over again, Bill," he said, "or it *will* take all night."

"Who's a-arguing?" said William, who thought it

was Bert that had spoken.

"You are," said Bert.

"You're a liar," said William; and so the argument began all over again. In the end they decided to mince them fine and boil them. So they got a great black pot, and they took out their knives.

"No good boiling 'em! We ain't got no water, and it's a long way to the well and all," said a voice. Bert and William thought it was Tom's.

"Shut up!" said they, "or we'll never have done. And yer can fetch the water yerself, if ye say any more."

"Shut up yerself!" said Tom, who thought it was William's voice. "Who's arguing but you, I'd like to know."

"You're a booby," said William.

"Booby yerself!" said Tom.

And so the argument began all over again, and went on hotter than ever, until at last they decided to sit on the sacks one by one and squash them, and boil them next time.

"Who shall we sit on first?" said the voice.

"Better sit on the last fellow first," said Bert, whose eye had been damaged by Thorin. He thought Tom was talking.

"Don't talk to yerself!" said Tom. "But if you wants to sit on the last one, sit on him. Which is he?"

"The one with the yellow stockings," said Bert.

"Nonsense, the one with the gray stockings," said a voice like William's.

"I made sure it was yellow," said Bert.

"Yellow it was," said William.

"Then what did yer say it was gray for?" said Bert.

"I never did. Tom said it."

"That I never did!" said Tom. "It was you."

"Two to one, so shut yer mouth!" said Bert.

"Who are you a-talkin' to?" said William.

"Now stop it!" said Tom and Bert together. "The night's gettin' on, and dawn comes early. Let's get on with it!"

"Dawn take you all, and be stone to you!" said a voice that sounded like William's. But it wasn't. For just at that moment the light came over the hill, and there was a mighty twitter in the branches. William never spoke for he stood turned to stone as he stooped; and Bert and Tom were stuck like rocks as they looked at him. And there they stand to this day, all alone, unless the birds perch on them; for trolls, as you probably know, must be underground before dawn, or they go back to the stuff of the mountains they are made of, and never move again. That is what had happened to Bert and Tom and William.

"Excellent!" said Gandalf, as he stepped from behind a tree, and helped Bilbo to climb down out of a thorn-bush. Then Bilbo understood. It was the wizard's voice that had kept the trolls bickering and quarreling, until the light came and made an end of them.

The next thing was to untie the sacks and let out the dwarfs. They were nearly suffocated, and very annoyed: they had not at all enjoyed lying here listening to the trolls making plans for roasting them and squashing them and mincing them. They had to hear Bilbo's account of what had happened to him twice over, before they were satisfied.

"Silly time to go practicing pinching and pocket-picking," said Bombur, "when what we wanted was fire and food!"

"And that's just what you wouldn't have got of those fellows without a struggle, in any case," said

Gandalf. "Anyhow you are wasting time now. Don't you realize that the trolls must have a cave or a hole dug somewhere near to hide from the sun in? We must look into it!"

They searched about, and soon found the marks of trolls' stony boots going away through the trees. They followed the tracks up the hill, until hidden by bushes they came on a big door of stone leading to a cave. But they could not open it, not though they all pushed while Gandalf tried various incantations.

"Would this be any good?" asked Bilbo, when they were getting tired and angry. "I found it on the ground where the trolls had their fight." He held out a largish key, though no doubt William had thought it very small and secret. It must have fallen out of his pocket, very luckily, before he was turned to stone.

"Why on earth didn't you mention it before?" they cried. Gandalf grabbed it and fitted it into the keyhole. Then the stone door swung back with one big push, and they all went inside. There were bones on the floor and a nasty smell was in the air; but there was a good deal of food jumbled carelessly on shelves and on the ground, among an untidy litter of plunder, of all sorts from brass buttons to pots full of gold coins standing in a corner. There were lots of clothes, too, hanging on the walls—too small for trolls, I am afraid they belonged to victims—and among them were several swords of various makes, shapes, and sizes. Two caught their eyes particularly, because of their beautiful scabbards and jeweled hilts.

Gandalf and Thorin each took one of these; and Bilbo took a knife in a leather sheath. It would have made only a tiny pocketknife for a troll, but it was as good as a short sword for the hobbit.

"These look like good blades," said the wizard, half drawing them and looking at them curiously. "They were not made by any troll, nor by any smith among men in these parts and days; but when we can read the runes on them, we shall know more about them."

"Let's get out of this horrible smell!" said Fili. So they carried out the pots of coins, and such food as was untouched and looked fit to eat, also one barrel of ale which was still full. By that time they felt like breakfast, and being very hungry they did not turn their noses up at what they had got from the trolls' larder. Their own provisions were very scanty. Now they had bread and cheese, and plenty of ale, and bacon to toast in the embers of the fire.

After that they slept, for their night had been disturbed; and they did nothing more till the afternoon. Then they brought up their ponies, and carried away the pots of gold, and buried them very secretly not far from the track by the river, putting a great many spells over them, just in case they ever had the chance to come back and recover them. When that was done, they all mounted once more, and jogged along again on the path toward the East.

"Where did you go to, if I may ask?" said Thorin to Gandalf as they rode along.

"To look ahead," said he.

"And what brought you back in the nick of time?"

"Looking behind," said he.

"Exactly!" said Thorin; "but could you be more plain?"

"I went on to spy out our road. It will soon become dangerous and difficult. Also I was anxious about replenishing our small stock of provisions. I had not gone very far, however, when I met a couple of friends

of mine from Rivendell."

"Where's that?" asked Bilbo.

"Don't interrupt!" said Gandalf. "You will get there in a few days now, if we're lucky, and find out all about it. As I was saying, I met two of Elrond's people. They were hurrying along for fear of the trolls. It was they who told me that three of them had come down from the mountains and settled in the woods not far from the road: they had frightened everyone away from the district, and they waylaid strangers.

"I immediately had a feeling that I was wanted back. Looking behind I saw a fire in the distance and made for it. So now you know. Please be more careful, next time, or we shall never get anywhere!"

"Thank you!" said Thorin.

Sun City

TANITH LEE

O nce, in a far sea, there lay a stretch of land of which no one remembers the name. This land was very neatly divided into three parts. In the north and west lay empty deserts where a burning hot wind blew itself about all day, and in the east lay green fertile hills, threaded by seven rivers, where men had built splendid cities, but in the south were rolling grassy plains, and this was where the Horse People lived with their herds.

The Horse People were very handsome to look at, and strong and clever besides, and there was nothing they disliked more than a roof over their heads. They said they had no need of a city.

They traveled the plains with their horses, to whom they could talk as easily as to each other, and which they rode without ever needing to put on a saddle or a bit or a bridle. If it was very hot or it rained, they would set up their dark blue tents, but generally they slept in the open, and the rest of the time they liked to rove from place to place, not carrying much with them, except a little food.

Now the Horse People had a king, though he was never called by anything other than his own name like everybody else. Nevertheless, he was their leader, and he inherited this from his father, who had been leader before him and passed it on to his son when he grew old, or died and had better things to do. At this time the king was called Zakonax.

Zakonax was very handsome indeed, and, no doubt, very strong and clever, too, but there was one very strange thing about him, and this was his hair. It wasn't fair and it wasn't dark, but it grew both shades at once, so that one strand would be yellow and one black and then two others yellow and then another one black, and so on. No one minded about it, in fact no one even noticed it anymore, though it had given Zakonax's mother quite a start when it had first begun to come out. However, it was Zakonax's hair that finally gave the Horse People a city of their own, whether they liked it or not.

All the horses of the plains were swift and beautiful, but the swiftest and the most beautiful of all was Zakonax's white mare, Feena. When she wanted she could run so fast all you could see was a streak of white on the plain, and if she jumped as she ran it was like lightning. But a time came when Feena did not run but stood very still, as if she were listening to something no one else could hear. The Horse People had been traveling for several days, and had at last set up their camp by the bank of a little stream under the spreading trees. It was very hot, and although the time of the rains was coming, not a drop fell. The horses seemed disturbed and hardly cropped at the grass. After a while, Zakonax went and found Feena and asked her what the matter was.

"That's easily told, Zakonax," she answered promptly. "We know that the rain won't come this season; we have read the signs as our mothers instructed us when we were foals. And, if the rain doesn't come, then the watering places will run dry and the green grass will burn up, and we shall go hungry and thirsty, and perhaps die."

Zakonax was troubled, but at first he didn't take too much notice of what Feena had said. The horses grew very self-important when they had something to tell the Horse People, and often they would build a dreadful calamity out of nothing at all, simply in order to make speeches about it.

However, the days wore on and, although the sky darkened and thunder rang in the clouds, no rain came. The little stream grew narrower and narrower until at last there was only the thinnest of trickles left, and the grass twisted and yellowed.

"Well, Feena," said Zakonax, "you were right."

"I am always right," said Feena.

"Then, wise one, you must tell me what to do," said Zakonax.

"We must journey eastward, toward the green lands with seven rivers. Even if there's drought there, the city storehouses will be full."

Zakonax knew very well this was all they could do, but he didn't want to go anywhere near the great cities, and neither did the Horse People. They put off the journey for fifteen days, and then the horses grew angry with them and tore down their tents and tried to eat them, and stamped mud into the trickle of the stream. So the People sighed, and packed up their few possessions, and set off for the east, most of them walking, because the horses were still too furious to be ridden. Feena, the white mare, led the way, her head in the air, and Zakonax walked very humbly behind her, occasionally cunningly remarking to no one in particular how brave and clever and beautiful she was, until finally she relented.

It was a long, hard journey nevertheless. With each red dawn they would set off, and keep going across the dried-out land, under the cruel white sun of the hot season. Each night they would make a camp, and the old men would tell stories about the rain gods, and the children would make noises with their mouths that sounded like streams running over cold stones, and that was as near as they got to water.

One evening, just as the sun was about to go down, Zakonax made out a small, dark figure coming toward them across the plain. It was unusual to find a solitary traveler, so Zakonax watched to see who it might be. The figure wore a long, dark cloak with the hood pulled well over its face. As it got closer, it didn't look up at Zakonax at all, and in another moment it had gone by without a greeting, and was walking away. It was then that Zakonax realized it was an old woman leaning on a staff, barefoot, and with tired, bowed shoulders, so he called out:

"Where are you going to, lady? And, wherever it is, can I help you on your way?"

At that the old woman turned and seemed to be looking back at him, though he couldn't see her face at all.

"I am not journeying on your road, Zakonax of the Horse People," she said. "I am going to the Western Desert for a reason I can't tell you."

"That doesn't bother me," said Zakonax, "but you must be tired and hungry. Stay with us and share our evening meal."

"You've little enough to share among yourselves, let alone to give to strangers," said she. "Your people will complain."

"Then you can have my supper," said Zakonax.

"I see you're a good king," said the old woman, "but you'll be a better king later, and look more like one too, if I know anything. Which I do," she added.

Zakonax said he didn't doubt it, and when the tents were up, he was as good as his word and gave her the portion of food and drink that should have been his. After that, he gave up his tent for her so that she could rest quietly. The old woman thanked him and went in and lay down. Zakonax stretched out under the stars and the round red moon and thought about the eastern lands until he fell asleep.

He was woken early, before the sun was even up, and it was the old woman gently shaking his shoulder.

"I must be on my way now," she said, "but first I want to thank you for your kindness. I am afraid I have nothing to give you in return but this piece of advice: you must remember three things. The first is a white flower, the second is a golden fish, and the third is a plait of woman's hair."

"Thank you, lady," said Zakonax politely. He could tell she was a wise woman, and the advice of a wise woman is always worth something, though what, at this moment, he couldn't precisely see.

"Just be certain you don't forget," said the old woman, and, leaning heavily on her staff, she set off. Zakonax watched her out of sight. The sun was only just over the edge of the plain, and he couldn't be sure, but at the last instant it looked very much as if the old woman disappeared, and some sort of bird—it might have been an owl—flew up into the lightening sky instead.

For several more days they traveled, and then the land began to change. The grass became fresher and the wind cooler, and they passed a little stream running along as if it knew just where it was going. It did, too. After they had followed it for a mile or so, it ran into a river, and across the river lay green hills and valleys, with a blue mountain or two standing up in the far distance.

Zakonax and the Horse People wasted no time in swimming across the river, and the horses put down their heads and began to crop the grass. After a moment, however, Feena looked up again and said to Zakonax:

"This grass is eatable, but the grass on the plains was sweeter and better. I don't think I shall want to make do with this grass for very long."

Some of the other horses heard her, and so they stopped eating, too. Soon all the horses had stopped and were staring at Zakonax reproachfully.

"Then we shall have to go on," said Zakonax.

The horses said yes, they thought they should. So there was no help for it, and in the morning the Horse People had to set off again.

They journeyed for two days, traveling over green hills and crossing another river, and the grass was never good enough for Feena. But on the third day they came to the banks of a third river which was very wide and wild, rushing along angrily over its stones. And on the far side of the river lay the greenest, sweetest grass in the world.

With a lot of difficulty they crossed the river, and it was sunset before they were all on the other side. Zakonax's people lit fires to dry out their wet clothes, and the horses ran about and shook the water off themselves into the fires and began to eat the grass.

And then there came a terrible noise. It was a kind

of grating and grinding like rusty metal cogs going around, and at the same time there was a sort of clanking like metal shields rattled against each other. And then, up over the hills beyond the river into the glare of the setting sun, came four enormous men. Each was twelve feet tall, each carried a huge spiked club in his right hand, and each was made entirely out of metal. Their hands and feet were iron, their legs and arms and bodies were bronze, their faces were silver and their helmets were gold.

Naturally the Horse People were frightened, and the horses sensibly ran away and tried to hide behind the Horse People. But Zakonax could see there wasn't much hope in flight, so he walked up to the four metal giants and shouted:

"Good evening, gentlemen! Can we help you in any way?"

At this the four metal men stopped. They peered down at Zakonax and the nearest said in a hoarse, metallic voice:

"The land on this side of the river belongs to King Kemen, the ruler of Solko, the City of the Sun. No man is allowed to settle here without the king's permission. Why have you come?"

"There is a drought on the plains," said Zakonax, "and our horses need green grass to eat, and we need water."

"You may stay, on one condition," said the giant.

"And what is that?"

"All who live on the king's land must pay him half of what they own in tax."

"We own nothing," Zakonax said. "Your King Kemen is welcome to half of that."

But the giant looked around him, and he saw the

horses hiding among the tents. So he said:

"You must give the king half your horse herds."

"No," said Zakonax, "we would rather cross back over the river."

"Too late," said the giant, and with a rusty roar, he and his three companions reeled over the grass, swinging their spiked clubs. There was nothing Zakonax or his people could do. They threw their spears at the giants and they bounced off, and they thrust their knives at the giants' legs, but the knives broke. And, worst of all, if the giants thought they were becoming troublesome, they would bring down their clubs. Half the horses were quickly rounded up and driven over the hills. The people tried to run after them, but the giants took huge strides and the horses fled in front of them, and they were all soon out of sight.

So it was a dismal first night the Horse People spent in the land of King Kemen. The half of the horses who were left huddled together and would speak to no one, except Feena, who had escaped the giants by running so fast they simply couldn't catch her. She came and stood by Zakonax with her nose resting on his shoulder, and finally he said:

"Tomorrow you and I must ride to Solko, the king's city, and try to persuade him to let us have the horses back. Possibly there is something he would rather have instead."

And Feena didn't argue at all.

In the dawn Zakonax and Feena set out. They went the way the giants had taken, and by mid-morning they were over the hills, and had come to a broad, paved road. It was the kind of road men always build to take other men to their city, so Zakonax knew it

must lead to Solko. But before they came to the city, the road took them over a rise, and beyond this lay the sea. There was a broad bay and the road ran along above it. Behind them, at one end of the bay, was a dark, ragged mountain, and ahead, at the other end, lay a tiny, bright dab of light.

"That must be the city," said Zakonax. "I wonder what makes it shine?"

Just then there was a flapping of wings, and Zakonax looked up and saw what he thought to be a large black crow high up in the sky. It wheeled overhead, then turned and made for the crag behind them, and he had soon forgotten all about it.

What Zakonax didn't know was that this was not a crow at all, but the sorceress who lived on the dark mountain. Her name was Haxaretl, and from the moment she was old enough to walk, she had gone about the world making trouble, because misery and wickedness and death pleased her no end. The people who knew of her thought she must be a hideous old woman, but one of Haxaretl's powers was that she could be anything to anyone—animal, bird, or human; young, old, ugly, or beautiful. Men called the crag where she lived Crow Mountain because they had often seen what they took to be a large black crow circling around it. But this was really Haxaretl herself in her long black dress, with a pair of black wings on her back, flying home after some evil magic somewhere or other. No man could kill Haxaretl, but since her birth there had been a prophecy about her, which Haxaretl herself had never forgotten. The prophecy said that she would one day meet a man who would take away all her magic powers for good, and she would not be able to kill him or thwart him, and this man would have hair that was neither fair nor dark, but grew both yellow and black at once.

The moment Haxaretl saw Zakonax, her jet-black heart stopped like a clock with fright, but after a moment or so she recovered herself, and thought she had better find out some more about this dangerous stranger. So she flew down to earth about half a mile ahead of Zakonax, and changed herself into a fat, brown-skinned market woman with an empty basket on her arm. Then she waited by the roadside, and after a while, Zakonax came riding along on Feena.

"Good morning, sir," called out Haxaretl.

"Good morning," said Zakonax. "Can you tell me if that bright thing on the horizon is the City of Solko?"

"Indeed it is," said Haxaretl, "I've just come from there myself. A vile city, it is, too, with a greedy, grasping king. What a tax he puts on everything! Half the price of my goods gone before I've even sold them," for the sorceress knew very well how Kemen went about things, and be sure she liked it very much.

"Well," said Zakonax, "the king took a tax on half my horses. I'm riding to ask him for them back, but it seems unlikely I'll get them."

"Oh, sir," cried Haxaretl, clutching his arm, "don't go to the king empty-handed, whatever you do! He'll have you beheaded at once."

Zakonax thought about this, wondering whatever he could take the king, and while he sat thinking, Haxaretl crept behind him and drew a knife from her belt, and tried to stab him in the back. But somehow the blade went in and came out and did Zakonax no harm, and Haxaretl could see that this part of the prophecy was true.

Zakonax turned around in surprise to ask the market woman why she had suddenly slapped him on the back, but there was no sign of her. He rode Feena off the road and down a little path to the bay. Here he sat on a rock and looked hard at the sea. It was very calm and blue, though once or twice a peculiar roaring came from far out across the water. He thought it must be thunder.

He racked his brains for something he could give the king, but he could think of nothing, and eventually he gave it up and they set off along the beach, which Feena preferred to the hard road, making for Solko.

They had not gone very far when Zakonax made out a girl standing at the edge of the sea, her arms full of white flowers. She was a very beautiful girl with long fair hair. Her dress was blue like the water, and she wore a necklace and bracelets of beaten gold. Zakonax couldn't resist saying good morning to her.

"Oh, stranger," cried the girl joyfully, "I'm so happy! My mother, a great lady, has lain sick in her palace, near to death, for three days, and all that could save her were the white flowers that men call 'Fortune'; and they have not been seen in the land for hundreds of years. But then I walked by the seashore and I asked the sea god for help—and look! I found these same flowers growing in a little cave. They bring good luck, health, and happiness to all who touch them, and they never wither or die."

Zakonax was delighted that the girl's mother would be cured, but also he could not help thinking that one of these flowers, which were so rare and had such useful properties, would be an ideal gift to take the king. So he asked the girl if there were any more flowers growing in the cave.

"I picked them all," said the girl, "but as you're the first to share my joy, please, take one of these."

Zakonax thanked her, took one of the flowers and, wrapping it in a piece of cloth, put it in his belt. He then watched the girl, who was, naturally, Haxaretl, run up the beach, singing like a bird.

"Such a girl as that, I should one day like as a wife," Zakonax said to Feena, who tossed her head and snorted disdainfully.

Zakonax reached Solko, the City of the Sun, at noon. He had never seen a city before, and it made a great impression upon him, and also upon Feena, though she scoffed loudly at everything she saw.

First there were high walls and then, in the high walls, a high gate, and beyond the high gate, flights of many steps leading to huge palaces with high towers. Zakonax could see at once why the city had shone in the distance, for it seemed almost entirely made of white marble and polished bronze, and the tops of the walls and the gates and the towers were plated with gold. They rode through the wide streets and finally they reached an enormous palace, more splendid than any of the others, for this one was built entirely of gold, the steps leading up to it were laid with emeralds, and diamonds flashed from the roofs. Twenty guards in golden armor stood at the bottom of the steps, and forty at the top. The guards at the bottom had twenty fierce, slavering black wolves on golden leashes, and the guards at the top had forty ferocious, snarling orange tigers on golden leashes studded with sapphires. Zakonax and Feena stopped at the foot of the steps and looked at it all, and listened to the atrocious din all the wolves and tigers were making trying to get at them.

The captain of the guard came striding up to Zakonax.

"Be off!" he shouted. "No one is allowed to look at the king's palace without his permission. If you don't move, I shall behead you with my sword."

"Kindly tell the king," said Zakonax, giving the captain a look that made him uneasy despite all he had said, "that I bring him a rare and precious gift." He thought that greedy Kemen would not be able to resist this, and he was quite right. The captain went up the stairs and inside, and after a little wait came down again and said, "Come with me," and took Zakonax and Feena in through a side door, up several stairs, and through many corridors, each more splendid than the last, until they reached the king's throne room.

And there Kemen sat, a big, gross man, covered in cloth-of-gold and jewels, eating grapes and sweets out of golden bowls, and surrounded by a lot of frightened-looking people, who bowed or fell on their knees whenever he turned to them.

"Well!" roared Kemen when he saw Zakonax.

"Your Majesty," Zakonax said, "I bring you a gift—"

"Wine!" interrupted the king. A man filled the king's goblet. "Are *you* still here?" the king asked him. "Never liked you. Behead him," he added absently. Ten guards leapt from nowhere and carried the unlucky courtier off.

Zakonax hastily took the flower from his belt, unwrapped it, and held it out to Kemen.

Kemen peered at it a moment, and then he turned ashen. Recoiling in his chair, while his court cringed in horror, he croaked at Zakonax:

"You dare—you dare to bring such a thing to me!"

Zakonax was bewildered. He didn't know that the flower Haxaretl had given him was really called "*Ill Fortune*"; that it had not grown for hundreds of years because people had dug it up and burned it, and that it was supposed to bring misery, sickness, and death to whoever touched it.

"Take him away," shouted the king, recovering, "beheading's too good for him. Put him in the dungeons. We'll have a beast show tomorrow, and the tigers can have him." Out leapt ten more guards and seized Zakonax. "And I'll keep that white horse," the king added, pointing at Feena. But she was too quick for him. She sprang from the room, through the corridors and down the stairs and out of the palace and away like the wind, and nobody could catch her.

When Feena was sure they had all given up trying, she stopped galloping and looked around her. She had come to part of the city that was not nearly so splendid as Kemen's palace. There were hovels and dirty little alleys, and a muddy, bad-smelling canal. Feena went to the canal, and rolled herself thoroughly in the mud until she looked quite unlike herself, and then set off through the streets to find the king's dungeons.

They were, in fact, at the back door of the palace, and sunk low in the ground so that the prisoners could only see a scrap of daylight by climbing up the pitted stone walls and clinging to the little grating near the ceiling, which was what Zakonax was doing when Feena found him. She put her nose to the bars and stared in at him.

"Who are you, gray horse?" asked Zakonax.

"I am Feena," said Feena testily. "I rolled in the mud so they wouldn't know me."

"Well, wise one," said Zakonax, "you'd better run away before someone guesses. Kemen has offered a reward for your capture. I can hear the gaoler coming, so I won't talk anymore."

But Feena whispered her plan to him, and Zakonax changed his mind about that. He waited until the gaoler was right outside his cell and then he cried out:

"Oh, Feena, the gray mud can't disguise you—and you're limping! The king will catch you."

The gaoler, who knew about the reward, too, heard this and put one eye to the spyhole in the cell door, and when he saw the horse at the grating, he realized it must be Feena.

"If I can only catch her for the king," he muttered to himself, "I can live in luxury for the rest of my days." So he crept up the stairs and came out through a door not far from where Feena was standing, the keys clinking at his belt.

Feena spun around and began to run away, but very awkwardly, as if she were lame. The gaoler, all but the reward forgotten, ran after her. Out of the dungeon yard, down the narrow streets hobbled Feena, the gaoler running behind, never quite able to catch up with her, though he was certain he soon would. Yet the farther from the dungeons they went, the less Feena's lameness seemed to trouble her. Soon she was galloping and the gaoler was puffing and holding his side. What a dance she led him in, up and down the back streets of Solko. Until at last, she turned around and ran at him and knocked him over, and, as he lay on the ground quite breathless, she pulled the keys from his belt and ran back to Zakonax, too fast for the gaoler to follow, even if he had had any breath left.

She dropped the keys in to Zakonax through the

grating, and after that he let himself out of the cell, and also unlocked the doors of several other unfortunate prisoners. Soon he jumped on her back and they galloped out of Solko by another gate, and into the hills behind.

King Kemen was beside himself with anger and so, for that matter, was Haxaretl. Knowing she couldn't kill Zakonax herself, she had hoped the king would do it for her. Now, while Kemen proclaimed a reward for the capture of both horse and rider, Haxaretl scoured the city and the countryside, searching for Zakonax. And, because she could change herself into so many different shapes, and could therefore get into so many places that no one else could enter, and understand the language of any animal or bird she became, she finally found him.

He was in a bear's cave, high in the hills. Haxaretl changed herself into an old shepherdess and got into the king's throne room and told him where Zakonax was hiding. The king was very pleased, particularly when Haxaretl said she didn't want the reward—to serve her king had been reward enough. He sent a hundred soldiers with swords and bows into the hills toward the cave from the west, and the four terrible metal giant-men from the south, and Haxaretl flew overhead on her black wings to see Zakonax taken.

But when Zakonax heard the metal men coming, he thought they were on their own. He went out of the cave and lay along a ledge, and saw them striding toward him up the slope, so he found a large boulder and rolled it over on top of them. One of them was smashed into pieces, and the other three staggered into each other, and fell over and rolled down the hillsides into the valleys below, because they were too heavy to stop themselves. By the time they reached the bottom, they were broken into pieces also. And that was the end of King Kemen's metal men.

But Feena meanwhile had heard the tramp of the soldiers' feet, and she ran out of the cave to warn Zakonax.

Haxaretl was very angry with Feena for rescuing Zakonax, and now she swooped low on her black crow's wings and, pointing one long finger at the mare, she changed her into milk-white stone.

No sooner had Zakonax turned and seen this, than the soldiers of King Kemen were on him, and he was dragged back to the city.

The king had intended to kill him immediately, but now a very unexpected thing happened. None of the people of Solko had much liking for their king, and they couldn't help admiring the stranger who had come so insolently and brought him the flower of death. When Zakonax escaped from the king's dungeons, and let out the other prisoners as well, they admired him even more, and now that he had destroyed the four hated metal giants, their admiration knew no bounds. An ugly rumbling and threatening rose from the city, and the king began to be afraid of what the people would do to him if they rebelled. So he decided he couldn't kill Zakonax just then, and he sat on his throne, brooding about it.

On Crow Mountain, Haxaretl was brooding also; she did so want Zakonax safely dead, and she saw the king was afraid to do it. And then, one morning, an idea came into her wicked head.

She turned herself at once into a beautiful young

girl, even more beautiful than when she had given the flower to Zakonax. Next she got out an iron bucket and tied two grass snakes to it by a piece of cord, and this she changed into a splendid chariot drawn by two black horses, still with the heads of serpents, but this only made them look more impressive. And lastly she picked up all the stones she could find and arranged them in neat rows behind and before the chariot, and then she spat on each and every one, and they became fearsome soldiers in coal-black armor.

So, with this entourage, Haxaretl rode into Solko, where the people stared at her in astonishment, wondering who this important person could be.

The king was only too delighted to receive her; he even forgot Zakonax for a while. He feasted the beautiful princess, and every time the king drank a cup of wine, Haxaretl spoke words over him, which she said were a toast to his good health, but which were really spells to bind him to her will. Finally, dazzled by her beauty, and made stupid by the magic, the king begged her to become his wife.

"Nothing would please me better," said Haxaretl, "but first you must give me a suitable marriage gift."

"Anything!" cried the king.

You might think she would have asked for Zakonax's head at once, but she was too subtle for that, knowing Kemen's fears. She put her hand on the king's shoulder.

"I want," said she, "the Golden-Fish-Beyond-Price."

The court gasped and the king stared at her.

"How can I get you such a thing?"

"I have been told," said Haxaretl, "that you have a prisoner in your dungeons who is worth little to you. Send him on the dangerous quest. If he dies it will not be your hand that killed him, and no one will blame you. If, however, he can get the Golden Fish, I will become your wife."

King Kemen was very pleased. Zakonax's death was no longer so important to him as the strange princess, and he had a feeling that the young man's good luck might enable him to succeed. Haxaretl, however, was determined that he shouldn't.

The king had Zakonax brought in.

"I have decided," said the king, "that I will graciously pardon you, providing you will undertake a quest for the Golden-Fish-Beyond-Price."

Zakonax, who had liked the king's dungeons even less on the second visit, looked at Kemen with angry contempt. And then his eyes strayed to the beautiful princess, and he had the strangest feeling that he had seen her somewhere before.

"Well?" demanded the king.

"Well," said Zakonax, "I know nothing about any Golden Fish."

The king pushed one of his courtiers forward.

"Explain!" he barked.

The courtier obeyed.

"Long before this city was built, another city lay on the shore, Old Solko it is called. A tidal wave came and drowned it, and swept the ruins several miles out to sea where they now lie buried. In the ruins lives the monster Gorramatzi. Most of the time he sleeps, but he suffers from a pain in his belly, and sometimes he wakes and roars with discomfort and anger." The courtier stopped and turned pale. Far out at sea had sounded a dreadful roar, as if Gorramatzi had heard his name spoken and did not like it. "Inside the ruins also," went on the courtier, remembering he feared the king more than Gorramatzi, "behind four gates of iron, bronze, silver, and gold, lies the Golden-Fish-Beyond-Price. It is believed to be as long as a man, and seven feet high, and to be made of solid gold."

"And that is what I want," added the king. "Go and get it."

Zakonax looked hard at the king, and he recalled the wise woman in the plains. She had told him to remember a white flower, but he hadn't, and she had told him to remember a golden fish, and now he did.

"Very well," said Zakonax, "I'll try to find the fish. But first, I have a condition of my own."

The king looked furious, but he saw he would have to listen.

"If I succeed," said Zakonax, "you will give me back the half of my horses that you stole from me, and also Feena, my mare." For Zakonax hadn't seen Haxaretl, she had been too quick for him, and he thought one of the king's magicians had turned Feena to stone as a punishment.

"Oh, very well," said the king.

"Swear it," said Zakonax sternly.

So King Kemen had to swear before all his court and by the gods of Solko to give Zakonax what he wanted. Then Zakonax said:

"Now tell me how I can breathe under the sea, and I will go."

There was some confusion, as no one had thought of this, no one, that is, except Haxaretl. Smiling sadly at Zakonax, she held out a little silver thimble full of liquid.

"It is an elixir my grandmother gave me," she lied. "Drink it, brave warrior, and you will be able to breathe in the water as easily as a fish." Which was true. What

311

Haxaretl didn't tell him was that the magic in the elixir only lasted for three hours, and, as she well knew, it would take Zakonax much longer than that to accomplish the task—even supposing he escaped from Gorramatzi.

Zakonax thanked her, drank the liquid, and set off. When he reached the shore, he waded into the sea and then swam, with strong, sure strokes, out toward the ruins of Old Solko.

Haxaretl was certain he would not come back, but she couldn't resist the opportunity of seeing her enemy perish. So she told the king she was very tired, and shut herself away in her chamber. Then she changed into a black gull and flew out of the window, across the city, and came down on the waves just as Zakonax dived beneath them.

Here she turned herself into a shark, slid under the water, and followed him like an evil shadow.

The water melted from blue to turquoise, and from turquoise to jade green. Zakonax swam through great forests of dark weeds, where striped fish hunted, and glared at him with glassy eyes.

At first there was no sign of a drowned city, but in a little while he passed a pillar of stone, and soon after that, a whole colonnade. Under the green water Old Solko stretched before him, towers and terraced buildings and broken roads, full of shadows and silence.

Zakonax didn't like the feel of the city, but he searched thoroughly for the four gates, his knife in his hand in case he met Gorramatzi.

Two hours passed, and Haxaretl glided behind him unseen, full of triumph.

At last Zakonax came to a fallen place where

anemones clung on to the walls, and, through a gap in the stone, he made out the dull shine of metal. He swam through and, sure enough, there was the first gate, which was made of iron. But when he tried to push it open a terrible blow fell on his shoulders and almost stunned him.

"You cannot enter here," boomed a hollow voice, and he realized it was the gate that had spoken.

"Let me through," said Zakonax.

"No."

"Isn't there any service I can do for you?" said Zakonax, who had learned the ways of the cities by now.

"If you give me something, I will let you through," said the gate.

"What? Do you want my knife? That's all I have of any worth."

"You have other things of worth. Those are what I want. Give me your good looks and I will let you by."

Zakonax was amazed. He didn't doubt that the gate could take them if it wanted them, but why it wanted them and what it would do with them were a mystery. Also, without being vain of his handsomeness, Zakonax could see that it might be a disadvantage not to have it. But he reasoned with himself:

"I can get by in life without it, and find a good wife, too, when I want one, despite what I look like."

So he turned to the gate and he said:

"Take what you want."

An unpleasant sucking sound came from the gate, just as if it were eating something, and suddenly handsome Zakonax was very ugly, and the gate had rolled open.

He went on, up a steep paved pathway, and soon he

had come to the second gate, which was made of polished bronze, and in which he caught a glimpse of himself. He didn't try to push the gate open, he simply called out:

"Let me through."

"No," clanged the bronze voice of the gate.

"I'll give you whatever you ask if you do," said Zakonax.

"Then give me your youth," cried the gate at once.

Zakonax hesitated, but then he thought of the horses, and of Feena.

"I should have been an old man one day in any case," he said to himself, "besides, I shouldn't have had much of a life, looking as I do now." So he said to the gate:

"Take what you want," and the awful sound came again, and Zakonax felt his body shrivel and wither, his strange hair turn gray, and his eyes dim, and his teeth feel unsteady in his mouth. But the gate opened and he went through.

Farther up the path gleamed the third gate, of silver.

"What do I have to give you to make you let me through?" he asked in his old man's quaver.

"Your strength," said the gate, in a cruel, chiming voice.

"Now, this is bad," thought Zakonax. "Supposing I meet Gorramatzi. I'm so ugly now it's possible I might frighten him off, but if I don't, I'm already old and slow, and if I'm weak as well—" But he could see Feena turned to stone, so he said:

"Very well. Take it."

And the sound came, and his limbs felt as if they were filled with water, not bones and blood, and he bowed over, and he staggered, trembling, through the

gate and up the path, groping with his hands.

He could barely see the fourth gate, made of gold, only a shining blur, and he said to it sourly:

"What now?"

The gate laughed like a great bell.

"Your wits," said the gate.

Zakonax sat down on the sea bottom by the gate, because he was so weak he could hardly stand up, but he said to himself:

"After all, if I had my wits I would never go through the gate, knowing I might meet Gorramatzi without any strength at all. If I had any wits left, I'd run away as fast as I could—which wouldn't be very fast, either." So he called out to the gate:

"You're welcome."

And the sound came, and there stood Zakonax, an ugly, weak, and witless old man, who didn't know why he was there for the life of him. But he tottered through the gate because it opened.

He was in a dark cavern, though he couldn't really see it. All around lay piles of gold and silver, precious chains, scepters and armor, and heaps of jewels every color of the rainbow, but there was no large fish made of gold, though he couldn't see that, either. He sat down on a gigantic topaz, and bumbled and mumbled to himself, trying to remember what he was doing there.

Suddenly there was a resounding roar.

"Thunder?" asked Zakonax. "Thought I felt some rain."

Into the cavern from a large hole near the roof swam a huge black shadow. It was fifteen feet long or more, and it was shaped rather like a whale, except that it had many tentacles like an octopus, three tails and two heads. It opened its two mouths, and rows and rows of yellow teeth glittered. Its four little cold eyes stared into Zakonax's, and it roared with fury.

"You have woken me," cried Gorramatzi, in his two voices, "and when I'm woken, I remember the pain in my belly. I shall tear you into small pieces and feed you to the fish." And he grasped Zakonax in his tentacles and clasped him to his belly.

Zakonax was too stupid to be afraid, but he felt something hard pressing into him, and it made him uncomfortable. So he drew his knife and stabbed at the thing until he could get it free and throw it away somewhere. Gorramatzi roared and bellowed, and then was suddenly very still. Out of his belly Zakonax pulled the thing that had bothered him, and it was a small golden fish. Long ago, Gorramatzi had eaten it, thinking it to be a real one, and it had hurt inside him ever since. But Zakonax had killed Gorramatzi, and he had forgotten the pain.

Zakonax drew the fish close to his eyes so that he could see it. It was hanging from a thin golden chain. He was just about to throw it away, when he seemed to recall that once, long ago in his youth, someone had told him to remember a golden fish. So, instead of throwing it away, he put it around his neck.

And abruptly he grew strong, and straight, his years dropped away, and he was young and handsome again, and his teeth were sound, and he said:

"I seem to have killed the monster, even though I didn't have my wits, *and* I found the fish. And I see now why it's beyond price—because of its magic, not its size."

And this was true, for the Golden Fish of Old Solko brought to whoever wore it everything he needed for himself, and returned to him everything that he had ever lost.

Then he turned and walked out of the cavern, not troubling about the treasure, and the four gates had to open for him, and soon he was swimming shoreward through the green water.

The shark, who was Haxaretl, was still behind him, however, and she waited to see if he would drown, because the elixir had long since worn off. But because the fish brought to its wearer whatever he needed, it brought him the ability to go on breathing under the sea. And when she saw that he wasn't going to die, Haxaretl swam around in front of him, and attacked him, trying to bite him with her sharp shark teeth.

But an invisible shield surrounded Zakonax and she could do him no harm, and Zakonax reached out and stabbed her with his knife. Now, no man could kill Haxaretl, but he could kill the shape she took. And so, as Zakonax's knife entered her heart, the shark vanished. He caught a glimpse of a woman throwing herself up through the water, but, although he followed her, he was not quick enough. As they broke the surface, she grew a pair of black crow wings and flapped off toward the shore.

Zakonax could have followed her, with the help of the fish, but instead he swam very slowly toward Solko, thinking. And after a while, when he had put everything together in his mind, he began to wonder if he were dealing with a sorceress, and if that sorceress might be the beautiful princess in King Zemen's palace.

By the time Zakonax reached Solko, a golden sun was falling from the yellow sky beyond the hills.

He walked to the palace, and when he got to the steps the twenty wolves cowered away from him, and the forty tigers lay down and purred ingratiatingly as he passed. He went straight to the throne room, and there sat the king with the beautiful princess on his right wearing a dress of vermilion velvet, with diamonds in her hair.

"Here is the Golden-Fish-Beyond-Price," said Zakonax, though he didn't take it off.

"But it's only the size of my thumb," grumbled the king. "Still, my dear," turning to the princess, "it's what you wanted."

But the princess jumped up and pointed at Zakonax.

"No! He's cheated you!" she screamed. "Kill him!"

"Oh, very well then," said the king.

Out rushed ten guards, but when they ran at Zakonax they fell dead on the ground. Out rushed another ten, but they fared no better.

"You," cried the princess, thrusting at the king in fury, so he drew his dagger and went at Zakonax also, and fell down among all the others.

The Haxaretl let out a terrible screech of anger and fear. Turning into a hawk, she flew out of the window. But Zakonax ran after her down the stairs, seizing a bow and a sword from one of the soldiers as he went, and in the courtyard he shot the hawk down. However, she only became a princess once more, and leaping into her chariot, drawn by serpent-headed horses, she fled up the road to Crow Mountain.

Zakonax now knew she was a sorceress for sure, and he knew he must catch her. He wished he had Feena, who was so swift she could outrun the wind, and no sooner had he wished this than the magic of the Golden Fish broke the spell of stone on the white mare, and she came flying down from the hills, in at the back gate of Solko, through the streets to where Zakonax was standing.

Zakonax gave a cry of joy, jumped on her back, and they were off after Haxaretl in a moment.

Although her chariot went very fast, Feena went faster, and Zakonax called to the sorceress's horses, telling them to run slowly. They were more snake than horse, but the bit of horse blood in them obeyed Zakonax, so that he caught up with Haxaretl just as she jumped from her chariot and set one foot on the base of Crow Mountain. He seized her long hair sparkling with diamonds, and he swung the sword to cut off her head and be rid of her once and for all. But the blade passed clean through her flesh and nothing happened to her.

Haxaretl laughed nastily at him.

"No man can kill me," she said.

"Then, if I can't kill you," said Zakonax, still holding her firmly by the hair, "I must take away your magic powers, since you do nothing but wickedness with them."

Haxaretl paled.

"You can only take my powers if you can find out where they are, and destroy that part of me," she said.

"Then that's easy," said Zakonax. "We've had the white flower and the Golden Fish. And the last thing the wise woman told me to remember was a plait of woman's hair."

But Haxaretl had many plaits, and a good deal of hair.

"If you cut off the wrong plait," said she, "you will be in my power, for I have one foot on Crow Mountain, which is mine, and my magic is strongest here."

Zakonax thought for a moment, and then he grinned, for there was no problem after all. With one stroke of the sword, he lopped off Haxaretl's hair, plaits and all, and when it lay around her on the ground, the chariot and horses vanished, and so did her fine clothes and jewelry, though she kept her beauty—for that was different—and he knew he had succeeded, and she was a sorceress no longer.

Once the citizens of Solko had made the Horse People welcome, they begged Zakonax in turn to be their king. To which he modestly agreed.

But Haxaretl he shut in a comfortable enough palace, with a fine garden, all surrounded by a high wall. And every month he had her hair cropped by the barber to stop the dangerous plait from growing in again.

Yet sometimes Zakonax would go and climb the wall, and sit on its top, watching Haxaretl as she paced angrily among the flowers.

The truth was, Zakonax had always wanted a beautiful wife, and Haxaretl, even bald, still looked to him the most beautiful girl any man had ever seen.

One day he told Feena of his problem, and Feena sighed and put her jealousy away. "Remember again the Golden Fish," said Feena.

So Zakonax went back to Haxaretl's prison-palace, and, walking into the room where she sat scowling, he remarked, "How I wish you could be as good and loving as you're beautiful, dear Haxaretl. And that you would then be mine."

At which her wickedness and all her sins vanished like the dew, and with shining eyes full of true happiness, she put her hand in his.

She was to him the best wife in the world, and he to her the best of husbands.

But Feena wed a stallion of Solko, and their descendants run and jump like lightning on the hills to this day.

Brother Kenan's Bell

JANE YOLEN

Brother Kenan woke in the night. He had had the most wondrous dream. An angel with a great smile of joy had come to him and said:

Take you a bell into the wilderness, a bell without clapper or tongue. And when that bell shall ring by itself—there build a house of God.

When morning prayers were over, Brother Kenan hurried along the stone hall to the abbot's cell and told him of the dream.

"It *is* a strange dream," the abbot said, "for what is a bell without clapper or tongue?"

"A piece of metal?" asked Kenan.

"Just so," said the abbot with a smile. "A piece of metal. And do you think that I would send any of my monks into the wilderness with just a piece of metal to guide him? I am supposed to be a father to you all. What kind of father would I be to let you go because of a single strange dream."

Brother Kenan went into the monastery garden where he was to work that day. There he saw Brother David and Brother John, and told them about his dream.

Brother David, whose clever hands were never still, said, "Perhaps it was something you ate. Dreams often proceed from the stomach."

So Brother Kenan said no more.

But that night he dreamed again. This time the angel was not smiling, and said:

Take your bell into the wilderness, a bell without clapper or tongue. And when that bell rings by itself—there build a house of God with Brother David and Brother John.

Brother Kenan did not even wait for the morning prayers to be rung. He put on his sandals and hurried off to the abbot's cell, where he roused the good father with a shake. The abbot was annoyed to be awakened before the bells, but he did not show it with his words or eyes. Only his mouth was angry and drawn into a hard line.

"It is certainly another strange dream," admitted the abbot. "But I myself have had many such dreams. Perhaps you are working too hard."

"But the angel knew Brother David's name," protested Kenan. "And he knew Brother John's name, too."

"Then he read your heart," said the abbot. "Surely an angel could do that." Then he turned over on his side and said, "Go back to bed, Brother Kenan."

After prayers Brother Kenan went to work in the monastery kitchen with Brother David and Brother John. He told them of his second dream.

Brother John, who could heal any ache with his herbs, said, "I have a simple that will help you sleep. And in *that* sleep you will not dream."

So Brother Kenan said no more.

But that night he dreamed again. This time the angel came and took him by the shoulder and shook him hard and said:

> Take you a bell into the wilderness, a bell without clapper or tongue. And when that bell rings by itself—there build a house of God with Brother David and Brother John. AND DO IT SOON!

Brother Kenan did not even stop to put on his sandals. He hurried down the dark corridor to the abbot's cell. He burst in, and was surprised to see the abbot sitting up in his bed. By his side were David and John.

"I have had yet another dream," began Kenan.

"Come," said the abbot with a great smile, and opened his arms. "So have we all. In the morning we must search for a piece of iron for your quest."

In the morning, after prayers, the three monks and the abbot looked all around the monastery for metal for the bell. But except for small nails and smaller needles, the pots and pans to cook the monastery meals, some rakes and hoes in the garden, and a knocker on the door, no metal could be found.

The abbot gave a large sigh. "I suppose I must give you our only bell," he said at last. "Come up with me to the bell tower."

So the four climbed to the top of the tower, high up where only Brother Angelus, the bell master, went. And there, lying under the chapel's bell, was an iron bar.

"I have never seen it before," said Brother Angelus with awe. "It is a miracle."

The abbot merely nodded and sighed again, this time in thanks. Such miracles, he knew, often occurred when one was as old and as forgetful as the bell master. Still, when the four had descended the stairs,

the abbot blessed the bar and gave it to Kenan.

"Go you must," he said, "so go with God."

The three monks left the monastery and took the road going north. Only to the north was the land empty of towns.

Brother Kenan was in the lead, carrying the iron bar like a banner before them.

Brother David was next, his pack filled with bread and cheese and string with which to practice knots, for his fingers always had to be busy with something.

Brother John was last, his basket filled with herbs and simples in case of any accidents or ills.

The three monks traveled for nearly three weeks. Their food ran out, and John found berries and mushrooms and roots. Their wine gave out, and David found a fresh, flowing spring. Their spirits ran low, and Kenan cheered them on with a psalm. And always the silent iron bar went before.

One day, though, Brother David grew weary. He thought to himself, "Perhaps it was not a holy dream after all. I swear that that bell will never ring on its own. I must make the miracle happen." So that night his clever fingers fashioned a sling of the strings. And in the morning, as they marched along, he walked behind and aimed several small stones at the iron bar. But the stones went left or the stones went right. Each shot missed, and Brother Kenan marched on with the bell as silent as ever.

The next day Brother John grew weary. He thought to himself, "All dreams do not come from God. That bell will never ring by itself. Sometimes one must help a miracle along." So he waited until he found a bush with hard, inedible berries growing along the path. He grabbed up a handful and threw the lot of them at Kenan's back. But the berries went left or the berries went right. Not one of them struck the bar, and Brother Kenan marched on with the bell as silent as ever.

The next day the monks came upon a broad meadow that stretched down to the banks of a tumbling stream.

"This would be a lovely place to build a house of God," thought Kenan with a sigh, for he, too, was weary. But, putting such a thought behind him as unworthy of his dream, he shouldered the iron bar and walked on.

Just then, a small brown bird flew across the meadow, fleeing from a hawk. The little bird ducked and dived to escape its pursuer, and in its flight it flew straight toward the three monks. At the last minute, noticing them, it turned sharply and rammed into the iron bar. It broke its wing and fell.

As the hawk veered off into the woods, the iron bar sang out from the collision with a single clear and brilliant tone.

"The bell!" cried David and John as one.

"The bird!" cried Brother Kenan. He jammed the iron bar into the soft sod of the meadow and took up the wounded bird. And when he picked the bird up, the iron bar standing straight and true in the meadow grass rang out again and again and again. Each note was like a peal of hosannas to the Lord.

So the monks built their house of God in the meadow by the river. Brother David's wonderful hands and Brother John's wonderful simples cured the wounded bird. And with patient care, Brother Kenan melted down the iron bar and cast a perfect bell.

Ever after, the little brown bird sang outside Brother Kenan's window to call the many monks who worked in the abbey to their prayers. And its voice was as clear and as loud and as pure as the monks' own iron bell.

The Last Card

STEVE LOCKLEY

The common was busy with the clatter of metal on metal. Loud voices rang out as well-practiced routines were carried out. Slowly but surely the fairground began to form in the same way it had in one town after another on its annual tour. At the end of the year there would be a break for the winter when everything went into storage before the whole thing started again. In the distance the Brecon Beacons looked down on the ground of the open land as a constant reminder that this was one of the last towns before the semi wilderness of mid-Wales.

The common had become a focal point for boys looking for jobs while the fair was in town. Each of them wanted to ride on the back of dodgem cars or the waltzers collecting fares, but knew in their heart that the best they could hope for was to help set up some of the rides. More likely they would do no more than fetch and carry bags of nuts and bolts, or peel onions for the hamburger stalls.

Tony and Chris were no different from the others who had started to hassle the ride owners, except that their determination was perhaps less than the others'. For them the break from school and the sunny weather were enough, although as the summer progressed they looked forward to the chance of mis-directing backpacking tourists who could not read maps.

"Five quid?" Tony said in disbelief. "You've got to be joking."

"But I've been after it for three months and not even had a sniff of it," replied Chris. "A fiver's well worth it."

"It's still more than I would pay for a poxy card," said Tony.

His friend was obsessed with collecting. Chris would start saving something, anything, and just keep going until he had a full set. Then he would start again with something else. Sometimes it did not even seem to matter what it was he was collecting.

His dad had tried to get him interested in stamps, but Chris found no point to it. There was never an end. At the moment he was saving picture cards from boxes of tea bags showing a series of American astronauts. All that was missing was John Shepherd.

"So who's got it?" Tony asked.

"Vinnie."

"You sure?" Tony could not believe that Chris was having anything to do with the worst thug in school.

Chris nodded, "Yeah. He showed it to me yesterday. Said it was mine for a fiver but I had to get the money today."

"Where the hell did you get the cash from. You were skint two days ago."

"I had a couple of quid tucked away. The rest I got from Mam's purse."

"Does she know?" It was a stupid question. Tony knew things had been tight since Chris's dad left. He also thought it unlikely his friend had any money of his own, not even two pounds.

"You've got to be joking. She'd kill me if she knew."

"So when you meeting him?"

Chris looked at his watch, "Any minute now."

Behind them the final touches were being made to the giant dragon swing. Tony had seen the same sort of ride at numerous fun fairs, although they usually took the form of large ships. He suspected the paintwork was intended to look fearsome, but it did not work on him. Beyond it a large shed was being assembled. On the ground stood the sign that would appear above its entrance, declaring it to be Morgan's Maze of Mirrors.

"You looking for me, girls?" said a voice from behind them. Vinnie Daniels leaned over the side of the dragon, laughing down at them, while Tony and Chris could only gawp.

"Come up here," he said. "We need to balance the weight so we can test this thing.

"Ain't that right mate?" he said, winking at a young man in grease-stained jeans and T-shirt, who nodded back. The man wiped his neck with an equally oily rag, and the spider tattoo beneath his ear seemed to move.

"And what's that? You two engaged now?" Vinnie said as Tony and Chris sat down on the bench seats that ran from one side of the dragon to the other. He pointed at the gold ring Tony was wearing on his middle finger. His grandfather had given it to him on his last birthday. It was a plain band when you first looked at it, but examine it more closely, and you could see a thin vein of a different color running through it.

"Let us have a look then," said the man with the tattoo, reaching over and taking a firm grip on Tony's wrist. "That's pretty special, that is. Welsh gold running through it. I suppose you could say it's at home here. I'll give you thirty quid for it."

"No, thanks," said Tony, pulling his hand away and

hiding his arm behind his back. "It's an heirloom."

"Forty?"

"No. It's important."

The man laughed and stepped down. "I don't think you know just how important, boyo."

Tony watched him warily as he walked away toward the caravans. He whistled, and a young boy came running toward him in a strange, half-crouching run. The man bent down and said something to the boy while nodding in their direction. A cold shiver ran down Tony's spine along with a strong desire to be somewhere else. Anywhere else.

"You got the money?" Vinnie said.

Chris nodded. "Yeah," he said, his voice trembling. "You got the card?"

Tony could not believe what they were doing. They spent all of their time at school trying to keep out of Vinnie's way. Half the kids in the school did the same, while the other half gave him money to avoid getting beaten up. Now here they were giving him money by choice.

"Yeah. I've got your poxy card. Now show us your money, girls." His voice became more menacing as Chris fumbled in his jeans for the five one pound coins.

Vinnie stepped out of the ride and onto the steps. He held the card in his fingertips at arm's length, tantalizingly out of reach, while the coins were dropped into his hand. Then, as his fingers closed around the money and Chris reached out, he let go of the card. A gust of wind took hold of it and swept it out of the ride and into the longer grass on the edge of the common.

"You sod!" said Chris.

Vinnie just laughed and pushed him away. "Get lost, you creep."

Chris was reaching too far over the side, and what appeared to be no more than a light push caused him to overbalance. He fell headlong out of the dragon and banged his head with a sickening thud on the steps.

Vinnie walked away, shaking the coins in his cupped hands, while Chris lay unmoving in the grass and weeds.

That was yesterday. Now Chris lay unmoving in a hospital bed with tubes and wires linking him to a battery of machines. The doctors had said tonight would probably be the crucial time and Tony felt he had to do what he could. The only thing he could think of doing, the one thing he knew Chris really wanted, was to try and find the missing card.

It was late and the common was quiet when Tony arrived back at the fairground. He had waited until he was sure his parents were asleep then slipped out of the house. A dog barked outside one of the caravans at the far side of the common. A voice shouted at it to be quiet, and after whimpering for a moment it fell silent again. All Tony could hear was the beat of his own heart, afraid that it was so loud it would be heard by anyone still awake in any of the caravans.

He looked around for one last time and felt a shiver run up his spine. The hairs on the back of his neck stood on end as he stepped out of the protective glow of the streetlight.

The dragon ride creaked as he approached, and Tony felt an involuntary gulp echo around his chest. Then he saw movement somewhere beyond the metal structure. A cat? No, too big. A dog? Whatever it was, it was hiding in the long grass somewhere near where the card had fallen. Tony gave a soft whistle in the hope it was a dog, but nothing moved. He took a few tentative steps forward. Then, remembering he had the torch, he flicked it on and flashed it in the animal's direction.

He almost dropped the torch after the fleeting glimpse he caught of the shape. It was not a dog, but the boy he had seen talking earlier to the man with the spider tattoo. The first thing the torchlight caught was a crumpled piece of card in the boy's hand. Tony knew without even seeing it properly that it was the card he was looking for. All he had to do was get it from the boy. He had not dreamed the search would be so easy.

In one instant Tony was about to call out to the boy to tell him not to be afraid, but in the next he was full of fear himself as the boy's eyes shone back a violent red in the torchlight. This time he did drop the torch.

The boy darted away, keeping low to the ground, almost as if he were on all fours. Even in the dark, Tony could see him moving swiftly to the now fully built maze of mirrors before disappearing inside. Tony scrambled around in the grass to find the torch before following to the square structure the boy had entered. At first he pushed against the unmoving turnstile, then crawled underneath rather than risk making a noise by trying to climb over.

Inside Tony felt strangely safe, as if the world outside could not hear him. At first he flashed the torch around in an arc but the beam reflected wildly from one distorting mirror to the other.

"Are you there?" he half-whispered. There was no reply, but he heard scuffling and laughter and knew the boy was in there somewhere. Maybe the boy was more frightened than he was himself. Feeling his way

rather than relying on the torch, Tony moved from one section of the maze to the next until he heard more laughter. He flashed the torch ahead and found the boy crouching against a mirror. The boy held the card out tauntingly as if he knew what Tony was looking for, then crawled through the mirror. At least that was how it seemed to Tony. He stepped forward to the glass and pushed, but it was solid enough. He even crouched down where the boy had been, but still the mirror would not budge. He turned his torch on the floor in the hope it would reveal some sort of trapdoor, but there was nothing. Then the boy's face appeared in the mirror, grinning broadly at him. An arm reached out through the glass, waving the card in temptation, teasing Tony to try and take it. As he stretched for it the card was dropped to the ground, and the hand took a grip of iron on Tony's arm that even in his panic he could not shake loose, and he found himself being pulled through the glass.

Despite having seen the boy pass through the mirror, Tony still expected the glass to smash as he pressed against it. Instead the sensation was like breaking through the surface of the swimming pool. As he stepped through, the grip on his arm was released and Tony stumbled on loose ground under his feet. Confused, he found himself falling, then rolling, down a rocky bank. When he came to rest he found himself too dazed to move until he found himself being dragged along the ground.

"Over here, you prat!" said a voice that had haunted his worst nightmares. Vinnie.

Vinnie half pulled, half dragged him for a few paces before dumping him to the ground again. When Tony could focus again he shuffled along the ground to press himself against a boulder in fear. Through his jeans he could feel the deep grazes caused by his fall. He had not had time to think about what lay beyond the mirror, but could not have expected what he now saw.

The sky, which had been dark, with clouds blotting out even the moon and stars, was now red and glowing, yet there was no sign of a sun. As he stared at it, unable to drag his eyes away, he realized that it was not a sky but the roof of a cavern that seemed to stretch for as far as the eye could see. There were no buildings or vegetation to form a skyline, only rocks and distant mountains.

"Where are we?"

"Good question," said Vinnie. "You could say we're on the other side of the looking glass."

He laughed, obviously pleased at a joke Tony would not have expected him to make. More than that, Tony could see that Vinnie was not afraid, even if his own pulse was pounding in his head.

"It looks to me," said Vinnie, "as if this thing is running the show. All these kids seem to do whatever he asks."

Tony scrambled to his feet, and half crouching peered over the top of the boulder. Ahead of them, the boy he had chased was standing with his back to them. Beyond him stood the rocky mound Tony had fallen down, and on top of that a rough stone structure. Shimmering through this arch Tony could see his torch, still lying where he had left it in the maze of mirrors. Vinnie was looking to the left of these, where there was something that made Tony want to slide back to his place of safety behind the boulder. Looking straight at him, with one red eye in the side of its

head, was the largest lizard Tony had ever seen. Beyond it, although Tony barely noticed, stood hundreds of ragged children, all waiting for something.

"Plant yr Ddraig," said Vinnie. "That's what they call themselves."

Tony stared at the creature's eye, neither of them blinking. He did not claim to be fluent in Welsh but he understood this. Plant yr Ddraig: the children of the dragon.

"What do they want?" asked Tony.

"Search me," laughed Vinnie. "I heard them saying that the wait was almost over. Something about something coming home, and then they would all be able to return. That dragon thing was roaring away at the time and it was not that easy to hear. All I wanted was that damn card so I could flog it to your mate again, but this is more fun than taking him for another fiver."

Chris. For a moment, Tony had forgotten about him and why he was here. Chris could be dead by morning, could be dead already, and the one thing that could save him had slipped through his fingers. Now the card was lying on the other side of the mirror and yet he could not get to it.

"Fun! You think this is fun! Have you tried to get out of here?"

"Only a couple of steps, but the dragon doesn't seem too keen to let me go."

The boy ahead of them turned to face them, and an inner lid flicked across eyes that Tony could now see resembled those of the dragon.

"Let us have the gold and you can leave," said the boy. "No one will try to stop you."

"That's it, is it?" said Vinnie, and thrust his hand in

his pocket. He held out the five pound coins and the dragon flicked out its huge tongue. As they disappeared Vinnie set off on a run toward the stone arch. Before he had taken the first step up the mound the dragon had sent flame high into the air in anger, caught Vinnie hard in the chest with its tail, then turned its breath on the fallen body.

Without hesitating Tony ran to Vinnie's side. "Wait," called the boy. "Don't test the dragon's patience. The boy is dead."

Dead. Vinnie was dead and all Tony could concentrate on was the pound coins that had fallen to the ground in front of him. Five pieces of molten, twisted metal, still smoking with the heat. He wanted to pick them up, take them back to Chris along with the card in order to put things right, but his fingertips burned before they had even closed around the first coin. He felt a tear start to trickle down his cheek, but he was not sure whether this was for Vinnie, that the chance to return the money had slipped away, or that anyone should lose their life so cheaply.

"If you had given us the gold he could have left with you."

"What gold? I don't know what you mean."

"Yes, you do. We just want the ring. It has come home. Give it to us and we will be able to return after centuries of exile."

"I still don't understand," said Tony, already slipping the ring from his finger while trying to move closer to the mound. With each half-pace the dragon rumbled threateningly and twitched its tail.

"The ring is the only thing we have been waiting for. It is the last of our ancient treasures. Return it to us and the gateway to the world that was once ours will

open wide enough for the Ddraig to pass through. We have been waiting here in this twilight world for centuries, waiting for the chance, the one chance. The mirror acts as a gateway between this world and the one you have claimed for your own. We have friends beyond the mirror who keep the gateway open. But that will all change as soon as we have the ring. That is why the children have gathered here."

"Why don't you just take it?"

"If it is not given freely then it is worthless. That is why we took the card. It seems to be the only thing you would be prepared to exchange it for."

"But it is still in the mirror maze."

"Give us the ring and you will be able to collect it. Follow the torchlight."

Tony stared at the light, then at Vinnie's lifeless body, then the torch again. "How do I know you won't do to me what you did to Vinnie?"

"You don't," said the boy. "Sometimes you have to take things on trust. But what other choice do you have?"

Tony slipped the ring off his finger and hoped his grandfather would understand. The creature's eyes seemed to open even wider, flooding Tony with a red light, then its tongue flicked out and stung Tony's hand with its touch. Then the ring was gone, leaving in its place an angry patch of burned flesh.

Ahead he could see the mirror in full view. Despite the pain in his hand, Tony ran as fast as he could toward it and threw himself through the arch. Then he was through and lying on the floor of the mirror maze. Beside him lay the rubber torch where it had fallen, its bulb only glowing dimly.

Through the mirror he could see the red lights of the dragon's eyes growing larger beyond his own reflection. Tony knew that before long the dragon and the children would be coming, and he knew he had to stop them. Without thinking he picked up the torch and threw it with all his might at the mirror. With a crash that caused Tony to clutch his ears despite the pain in his hand, the mirror shattered into a million pieces, leaving him covered in tiny shards of glass.

As the last piece of glass fell to the floor and silence returned, he could see in the middle of the debris the face of John Shepherd. Where the mirror had stood there was nothing but the wooden frame and backing that had supported it. The gateway had been closed.

It was late by the time Tony limped into the streetlight again. His watch showed five minutes to three,

although he always kept it ten minutes fast so that he was never late for school. Someone had once told him that this was the real witching hour. That more people died at three o'clock in the morning than at any other time of the day. He had to get there before three o'clock, had to. The hospital was only a short distance away, and he would normally be able to reach it in plenty of time. With the pain in his hand burning deep inside him, making him feel light-headed, he was not sure he would make it. And yet he did.

His watch showed eight minutes past three by the time he was halfway along the corridor to the Intensive Therapy Unit. On the road, as he had hobbled along despite the pain, he had been rehearsing what he would say if anyone stopped him. He could not believe his luck. No one had asked him what he was doing there at that time of night, despite his dirty appearance. His luck ran out as he was about to enter the room.

"Can I help you?" asked a nurse who left her desk in the corridor as he looked through the glass.

"I've brought something for Chris. Can I go in?" He could see the clock inside the ward ticking toward three o'clock.

"I'm sorry," she said. "It will have to wait until morning. His mother's with him at the moment. Besides, shouldn't you be back at home in your own bed?"

He had not noticed Chris's mother in the corner of the room, half hidden by a curtain. "It can't wait," he said and brushed past the nurse, determined to finish what he had started.

"Wait," she shouted after him, but it was too late. He was through the door in an instant and was at

Chris's side. His mother looked at him in obvious surprise; her mouth opened but no words came out. He glanced up at the clock. Fifteen seconds to go. Tony fumbled in his trouser pocket, found the crumpled card, and pressed it into Chris's hand just as the second hand clicked to three o'clock.

"I got it for you, Chris. The last card."

"What is it, Tony?" Chris's mum said. "Why are you here so late? Your mum and dad must be worried sick."

"I had to bring something for Chris," he said.

The nurse tried to usher him out, apologizing that he had been able to get past her. Then Chris opened his eyes. "Thanks, Tony," he said. "I thought you'd never get here."

Tony squeezed Chris's hand and muttered words that had no meaning, while Chris's mum blubbered something equally unintelligible through her sobs. The nurse busied herself with checking the monitors that Chris was still hooked up to.

It was over now, and Tony could let the pain in his hand take over. It was all he could do to stop himself from cracking his head as he fell to the ground.

Atlantis

EDITH NESBIT

This adventure comes from The Story of the Amulet. *It's the third book in a series that Edith Nesbit wrote about a group of children—Robert, Cyril, Anthea, and Jane—and the sand fairy that they found, which was called a Psammead, and which could grant them one wish a day (the wish becomes ungranted at the end of the day). The first two books are* Five Children and It *and* The Phoenix and the Carpet, *and all three are well worth reading. In* The Story of the Amulet *the children buy an ancient amulet, or rather half of one, which if made whole will grant them their hearts' desires. Even the half-amulet is powerful as it allows them access to the past. They've already visited ancient Egypt and Babylon, and this time they return to fabled Atlantis.*

It was an old house; it had once been a fashionable one, and was a fine one still. The banister rails of the stairs were excellent for sliding down, and in the corners of the landings were big alcoves that had once held graceful statues, and now quite often held the graceful forms of Cyril, Robert, Anthea, and Jane.

One day Cyril and Robert, in tight white underclothing, had spent a pleasant hour in reproducing the attitudes of statues seen either in the British Museum, or in Father's big photograph book. But the show ended abruptly because Robert wanted to be the Venus of Milo, and for this purpose pulled at the sheet that served for drapery at the very moment when Cyril, looking really quite like the Discobolos—with a gold and white saucer for the disc—was standing on one foot, and under that one foot was the sheet.

Of course the Discobolos and his disc and the would-be Venus came down together, and everyone was a good deal hurt, especially the saucer, which would never be the same again, however neatly one might join its uneven bits with Seccotine or the white of an egg.

"I hope you're satisfied," said Cyril, holding his head where a large lump was rising.

"Quite, thanks," said Robert bitterly. His thumb had caught in the banisters and bent itself back almost to breaking point.

"I *am* so sorry, poor, dear Squirrel," said Anthea; "and you were looking so lovely. I'll get a wet rag. Bobs, go and hold your hand under the hot water tap. It's what ballet girls do with their legs when they hurt them. I saw it in a book."

"What book?" said Robert disagreeably. But he went.

When he came back Cyril's head had been bandaged by his sisters, and he had been brought to the state of mind where he was able reluctantly to admit that he supposed Robert hadn't done it on purpose.

Robert replying with equal suavity, Anthea hastened to lead the talk away from the accident.

"I suppose you don't feel like going anywhere through the Amulet," she said.

"Egypt!" said Jane promptly. "I want to see the pussy cats."

"Not me—too hot," said Cyril. "It's about as much as I can stand here—let alone Egypt." It was indeed hot, even on the second landing, which was the coolest place in the house. "Let's go to the North Pole."

"I don't suppose the Amulet was ever there—and we might get our fingers frost bitten so that we could never hold it up to get home again. No, thanks," said Robert.

"I say," said Jane, "let's get the Psammead and ask its advice. It will like us asking, even if we don't take it."

The Psammead was brought up in its green silk embroidered bag, but before it could be asked anything the door of the learned gentleman's room opened and the voice of the visitor who had been lunching with him was heard on the stairs. He seemed to be speaking with the door handle in his hand.

"You see a doctor, old boy," he said; "all that about thought transference is just simply twaddle. You've been overworking. Take a holiday. Go to Dieppe."

"I'd rather go to Babylon," said the learned gentleman.

"I wish you'd go to Atlantis sometime, while we're about it, so as to give me some tips for my *Nineteenth Century* article when you come home."

"I wish I could," said the voice of the learned gentleman.

"Good-bye. Take care of yourself."

The door was banged, and the visitor came smiling down the stairs—a stout, prosperous, big man. The children had to get up to let him pass.

"Hullo, kiddies," he said, glancing at the bandages on the head of Cyril and the hand of Robert, "been in the wars?"

"It's all right," said Cyril. "I say, what was that Atlantic place you wanted him to go to? We couldn't help hearing you talk."

"You talk so very loud, you see," said Jane soothingly.

"Atlantis," said the visitor, "the lost Atlantis, garden of the Hesperides. Great continent—disappeared in the sea. You can read about it in Plato."

"Thank you," said Cyril doubtfully.

"Were there any Amulets there?" asked Anthea, made anxious by a sudden thought.

"Hundred, I should think. So *he's* been talking to you?"

"Yes, often. He's very kind to us. We like him awfully."

"Well, what he wants is a holiday; you persuade him to take one. What he wants is a change of scene. You see, his head is crusted so thickly inside with knowledge about Egypt and Assyria and things that you can't hammer anything into it unless you keep hard at it all day long for days and days. And I haven't time. But you live in the house. You can hammer almost incessantly. Just try your hands, will you? Right. So long!"

He went down the stairs three at a time, and Jane remarked that he was a nice man, and she thought he had little girls of his own.

"I should like to have them to play with," she added pensively.

The three elder ones exchanged glances. Cyril nodded.

"All right. *Let's* go to Atlantis," he said.

"Let's go to Atlantis and take the learned gentleman with us," said Anthea; "he'll think it's a dream, afterward, but it'll certainly be a change of scene."

"Why not take him to nice Egypt?" asked Jane.

"Too hot," said Cyril shortly.

"Or Babylon, where he wants to go?"

"I've had enough of Babylon," said Robert, "at least

344

for the present. And so have the others. I don't know why," he added, forestalling the question on Jane's lips, "but somehow we have. Squirrel, let's take off these beastly bandages and get into flannels. We can't go in our unders."

"He *wished* to go to Atlantis, so he's got to go sometime; and he might as well go with us," said Anthea.

This was how it was that the learned gentleman, permitting himself a few moments of relaxation in his chair, after the fatigue of listening to opinions (about Atlantis and many other things) with which he did not at all agree, opened his eyes to find his four young friends standing in front of him in a row.

"Will you come," said Anthea, "to Atlantis with us?"

"To know that you are dreaming shows that the dream is nearly at an end," he told himself; "or perhaps it's only a game, like 'How many miles to Babylon?' "

So he said aloud: "Thank you very much, but I have only a quarter of an hour to spare."

"It doesn't take any time," said Cyril; "time is only a mode of thought, you know, and you've got to go sometime, so why not with us?"

"Very well," said the learned gentleman, now quite certain that he was dreaming.

Anthea held out her soft, pink hand. He took it. She pulled him gently to his feet. Jane held up the Amulet.

"To just outside Atlantis," said Cyril, and Jane said the Name of Power.

"You owl!" said Robert, "it's an island. Outside an island's all water."

"I won't go. I *won't*," said the Psammead, kicking and struggling in its bag.

But already the Amulet had grown to a great arch. Cyril pushed the learned gentleman, as undoubtedly

the first-born, through the arch—not into water, but
onto a wooden floor, out of doors. The others followed.
The Amulet grew smaller again, and there they all were,
standing on the deck of a ship whose sailors were busy
making her fast with chains to rings on a white quay-
side. The rings and the chains were of a metal that
shone red-yellow like gold.

Everyone on the ship seemed too busy at first to
notice the group of newcomers from Fitzroy Street.
Those who seemed to be officers were shouting orders
to the men.

They stood and looked across the wide quay to the
town that rose beyond it. What they saw was the most
beautiful sight any of them had ever seen—or ever
dreamed of.

The blue sea sparkled in soft sunlight; little white-
capped waves broke softly against the marble break-
waters that guarded the shipping of a great city
from the wilderness of winter winds and seas. The
quay was of marble, white and sparkling, with a vein-
ing bright as gold. The city was of marble, red and
white. The greater buildings that seemed to be
temples and palaces were roofed with what looked
like gold and silver, but most of the roofs were of
copper that glowed golden-red on the houses on the
hills among which the city stood, and shaded into
marvelous tints of green and blue and purple where
they had been touched by the salt sea spray and the
fumes of the dyeing and smelting works of the lower
town.

Broad and magnificent flights of marble stairs led up
from the quay to a sort of terrace that seemed to run
along for miles, and beyond rose the town built on a
hill.

The learned gentleman drew a long breath. "Wonderful!" he said, "wonderful!"

"I say, Mr.—what's your name?" said Robert.

"He means," said Anthea, with gentle politeness, "that we never can remember your name. I know it's Mr. De Something."

"When I was your age I was called Jimmy," he said timidly. "Would you mind? I should feel more at home in a dream like this if I—Anything that made me seem more like one of you."

"Thank you—Jimmy," said Anthea with an effort. It seemed such a cheek to be saying Jimmy to a grown-up man. "Jimmy, *dear*," she added, with no effort at all. Jimmy smiled and looked pleased.

But now the ship was made fast, and the captain had time to notice other things. He came toward them, and he was dressed in the best of all possible dresses for the seafaring life.

"What are you doing here?" he asked rather fiercely. "Do you come to bless or to curse?"

"To bless, of course," said Cyril. "I'm sorry if it annoys you, but we're here by magic. We come from the land of the sun-rising," he went on explanatorily.

"I see," said the captain; no one had expected that he would. "I didn't notice at first, but of course I hope you're a good omen. It's needed. And this," he pointed to the learned gentleman, "your slave, I presume?"

"Not at all," said Anthea; "he's a very great man. A sage, don't they call it? And we want to see all your beautiful city, and your temples and things, and then we shall go back, and he will tell his friend, and his friend will write a book about it."

"What," asked the captain, fingering a rope, "is a book?"

"A record—something written, or," she added hastily, remembering the Babylonian writing, "or engraved."

Some sudden impulse of confidence made Jane pluck the Amulet from the neck of her frock.

"Like this," she said.

The captain looked at it curiously, but, the other three were relieved to notice, without any of that overwhelming interest that the mere name of it had roused in Egypt and Bablyon.

"The stone is of our country," he said; "and that which is engraved on it, it is like our writing, but I cannot read it. What is the name of your sage?"

"Ji—jimmy," said Anthea hesitatingly.

The captain repeated, "Ji—jimmy. Will you land?" he added. "And shall I lead you to the kings?"

"Look here," said Robert, "does your king hate strangers?"

"Our kings are ten," said the captain, "and the Royal line, unbroken from Poseidon, the father of us all, has the noble tradition to do honor to strangers if they come in peace."

"Then lead on, please," said Robert, "though I *should* like to see all over your beautiful ship, and sail about in her."

"That shall be later," said the captain; "just now we're afraid of a storm—do you notice that odd rumbling?"

"That's nothing, master," said an old sailor who stood near; "it's the pilchards coming in, that's all."

"Too loud," said the captain.

There was a rather anxious pause; then the captain stepped onto the quay, and the others followed him.

"Do talk to him—Jimmy," said Anthea as they went; "you can find out all sorts of things for your friend's book."

"Please excuse me," he said earnestly. "If I talk I shall wake up; and besides, I can't understand what he says."

No one else could think of anything to say, so that it was in complete silence that they followed the captain up the marble steps and through the streets of the town. There were streets and shops and houses and markets.

"It's just like Babylon," whispered Jane, "only everything's perfectly different."

"It's a great comfort the ten kings have been properly brought up—to be kind to strangers," Anthea whispered to Cyril.

"Yes," he said, "no deepest dungeons here."

There were no horses or chariots in the street, but there were handcarts and low trolleys running on thick log-wheels, and porters carrying packets on their heads, and a good many of the people were riding on what looked like elephants, only the great beasts were hairy, and they had not that mild expression we are accustomed to meet on the faces of the elephants at the zoo.

"Mammoths!" murmured the learned gentleman, and stumbled over a loose stone.

The people in the streets kept crowding around them as they went along, but the captain always dispersed the crowd before it grew uncomfortably thick by saying—

"Children of the Sun God and their High Priest— come to bless the city."

And then the people would draw back with a low murmur that sounded like a suppressed cheer.

Many of the buildings were covered with gold, but the gold on the bigger buildings was of a different color, and they had sorts of steeples of burnished silver rising above them.

"Are all these houses real gold?" asked Jane.

"The temples are covered with gold, of course," answered the captain, "but the houses are only oricalchum. It's not quite so expensive."

The learned gentleman, now very pale, stumbled along in a dazed way, repeating:

"Oricalchum—oricalchum."

"Don't be frightened," said Anthea; "we can get home in a minute, just by holding up the charm. Would you rather go back now? We could easily come some other day without you."

"Oh, no, no," he pleaded fervently; "let the dream go on. Please, please do."

"The High Ji—jimmy is perhaps weary with his magic journey," said the captain, noticing the blundering walk of the learned gentleman; "and we are yet very far from the Great Temple, where today the kings make sacrifice."

He stopped at the gate of a great enclosure. It seemed to be a sort of park, for trees showed high above its brazen wall.

The party waited, and almost at once the captain came back with one of the hairy elephants and begged them to mount.

This they did.

It was a glorious ride. The elephant at the zoo—to ride on him is also glorious, but he goes such a very little way, and then he goes back again, that is always dull. But this great hairy beast went on and on and on along streets and through squares and gardens. It was a glorious city; almost everything was built of marble, red, or white, or black. Every now and then the party crossed a bridge.

It was not till they had climbed to the hill that is the

center of the town that they saw that the whole city was divided into twenty circles, alternately land and water, and over each of the water circles were the bridges by which they had come.

And now they were in a great square. A vast building filled up one side of it; it was overlaid with gold, and had a dome of silver. The rest of the buildings around the square were of oricalchum. And it looked more splendid than you can possibly imagine, standing up bold and shining in the sunlight.

"You would like a bath," said the captain, as the hairy elephant went clumsily down on his knees. "It's customary, you know, before entering the Presence. We have baths for men, women, horses, and cattle. The High Class Baths are here. Our Father Poseidon gave us a spring of hot water and one of cold."

The children had never before bathed in baths of gold.

"It feels very splendid," said Cyril, splashing.

"At least, of course, it's not gold; it's or—what's its name," said Robert. "Hand over that towel."

The bathing hall had several great pools sunk below the level of the floor; one went down to them by steps.

"Jimmy," said Anthea timidly, when, very clean and boiled-looking, they all met in the flowery courtyard of the public baths, "don't you think all this seems much more like *now* than Babylon or Egypt—? Oh, I forgot, you've never been there."

"I know a little of those nations, however," said he, "and I quite agree with you. A most discerning remark—my dear," he added awkwardly; "this city certainly seems to indicate a far higher level of civilization than the Egyptian or Babylonish, and—"

"Follow me," said the captain. "Now, boys, get out of

351

the way." He pushed through a little crowd of boys who were playing with dried chestnuts fastened to a string.

"Ginger!" remarked Robert, "they're playing conkers, just like the kids on Kentish Town Road!"

They could see now that three walls surrounded the island on which they were. The outermost wall was of brass, the captain told them; the next, which looked like silver, was covered with tin; and the innermost one was of oricalchum.

And right in the middle was a wall of gold, with golden towers and gates.

"Behold the Temples of Poseidon," said the captain. "It is not lawful for me to enter. I will await your return here."

He told them what they ought to say, and the five people from Fitzroy Street took hands and went forward. The golden gates slowly opened.

"We are the Children of the Sun," said Cyril, as he had been told, "and our High Priest, at least that's what the captain calls him. We have a different name for him at home."

"What is his name?" asked a white-robed man who stood in the doorway with his arms extended.

"Ji—jimmy," replied Cyril, and he hesitated as Anthea had done. It really did seem to be taking a great liberty with so learned a gentleman. "And we have come to speak with your kings in the Temple of Poseidon—does that word sound right?" he whispered anxiously.

"Quite," said the learned gentleman. "It's very odd that I can understand what you say to them, but not what they say to you."

"The Queen of Babylon found that, too," said Cyril; "it's part of the magic."

"Oh, what a dream!" said the learned gentleman.

The white-robed priest had been joined by others, and all were bowing low.

"Enter," he said, "enter, Children of the Sun, with your High Ji—jimmy."

In an inner courtyard stood the Temple—all of silver, with gold pinnacles and doors, and twenty enormous statues in bright gold of men and women. Also an immense pillar of the other precious yellow metal.

They went through the doors, and the priest led them up a stair into a gallery, from which they could look down onto the glorious place.

"The ten kings are even now choosing the bull. It is not lawful for me to behold," said the priest, and fell face downward on the floor outside the gallery. The children looked down.

The roof was of ivory adorned with the three precious metals, and the walls were lined with the favorite oricalchum.

At the far end of the Temple was a statue group, the like of which no one living has ever seen.

It was of gold, and the head of the chief figure reached to the roof. That figure was Poseidon, the Father of the City. He stood in a great chariot drawn by six enormous horses, and round about it were a hundred mermaids riding on dolphins.

Ten men, splendidly dressed and armed only with sticks and ropes, were trying to capture one of some fifteen bulls who ran this way and that about the floor of the Temple. The children held their breath, for the bulls looked dangerous, and the great horned heads were swinging more and more wildly.

Anthea did not like looking at the bulls. She looked about the gallery, and noticed that another staircase led up from it to a still higher story; also that a door led out into the open air, where seemed to be a balcony.

So that when a shout went up and Robert whispered, "Got him," and she looked down and saw the herd of bulls being driven out of the Temple by whips, and the ten kings following, one of them spurring with his stick a black bull that writhed and fought in the grip of a lasso, she answered the boy's agitated, "Now we shan't see anything more," with—

"Yes we can, there's an outside balcony."

So they crowded out.

But very soon the girls crept back.

"I don't like sacrifices," Jane said. So she and Anthea went and talked to the priest, who was no longer lying on his face, but sitting on the top step mopping his forehead with his robe, for it was a hot day.

"It's a special sacrifice," he said; "usually it's only done on the justice days every five years and six years, alternately. And then they drink the cup of wine with some of the bull's blood in it, and swear to judge truly. And they wear the sacred blue robe, and put out all the Temple fires. But this today is because the City's so upset by the odd noises from the sea, and the god inside the big mountain speaking with his thunder-voice. But all that's happened so often before. If anything could make me uneasy it wouldn't be *that*."

"What would it be?" asked Jane kindly.

"It would be the lemmings."

"Who are they—enemies?"

"They're a sort of rat; and every year they come swimming over from the country that no man knows, and stay here awhile, and then swim away. This year they haven't come. You know rats won't stay on a ship that's going to be wrecked. If anything horrible were going to happen to us, it's my belief those lemmings would know; and that may be why they've fought shy of us."

"What do you call this country?" asked the Psammead, suddenly putting its head out of its bag.

"Atlantis," said the priest.

"Then I advise you to get on to the highest ground you can find. I remember hearing something about a flood here. Look here, you"—it turned to Anthea; "let's get home. The prospect's too wet for my whiskers."

The girls obediently went to find their brothers, who were leaning on the balcony railings.

"Where's the learned gentleman?" asked Anthea.

"There he is—below," said the priest, who had come with them. "Your High Ji—jimmy is with the kings."

The ten kings were no longer alone. The learned gentleman—no one had noticed how he got there— stood with them on the steps of an altar, on which lay the dead body of the black bull. All the rest of the courtyard was thick with people, seemingly of all classes, and all were shouting, "The sea—the sea!"

"Be calm," said the most kingly of the kings, he who had lassoed the bull. "Our town is strong against the thunders of the sea and of the sky!"

"I want to go home," whined the Psammead.

"We can't go without *him*," said Anthea firmly.

"Jimmy," she called, "Jimmy!" and waved to him. He heard her, and began to come toward her through the crowd.

They could see from the balcony the sea captain edging his way out from among the people. And his face was dead white, like paper.

"To the hills!" he cried in a loud and terrible voice.

And above his voice came another voice, louder, more terrible—the voice of the sea.

The girls looked seaward.

Across the smooth distance of the sea something huge and black rolled toward the town. It was a wave, but a wave a hundred feet in height, a wave that looked like a mountain—a wave rising higher and higher till suddenly it seemed to break in two—one half of it rushed out to sea again; the other—

"Oh!" cried Anthea, "the town—the poor people!"

"It's all thousands of years ago, really," said Robert but his voice trembled. They hid their eyes for a moment. They could not bear to look down, for the wave had broken on the face of the town, sweeping over the quays and docks, overwhelming the great storehouses and factories, tearing gigantic stones from forts and bridges, and using them as battering rams against the temples. Great ships were swept over the roofs of the houses and dashed down halfway up the hill among ruined gardens and broken buildings. The water ground brown fishing boats to powder on the golden roofs of palaces.

Then the wave swept back toward the sea.

"I want to go home," cried the Psammead fiercely.

"Oh, yes, yes!" said Jane, and the boys were ready— but the learned gentleman had not come.

Then suddenly they heard him dash up to the inner gallery, crying —

"I *must* see the end of the dream." He rushed up the higher flight. The others followed him. They found themselves in a sort of turret—roofed, but open to the air at the sides.

The learned gentleman was leaning on the parapet, and as they rejoined him the vast wave rushed back on

the town. This time it rose higher—destroyed more.

"Come home," cried the Psammead; "*that's* the *last*, I know it is! That's the last—over there." It pointed with a claw that trembled.

"Oh, come!" cried Jane, holding up the Amulet.

"I *will see* the end of the dream," cried the learned gentleman.

"You'll never see anything else if you do," said Cyril.

"Oh, *Jimmy*!" appealed Anthea. "I'll *never* bring you out again!"

"You'll never have the chance if you don't go soon," said the Psammead.

"I *will* see the end of the dream," said the learned gentleman obstinately.

The hills around were black with people fleeing from the villages to the mountains. And even as they fled thin smoke broke from the great white peak, and then a faint flash of flame. Then the volcano began to throw up its mysterious, fiery inside parts. The earth trembled; ashes and sulphur showered down; a rain of fine pumice stone fell like snow on all the dry land. The elephants from the forest rushed up toward the peaks; great lizards thirty yards long broke from the mountain pools and rushed down toward the sea. The snows melted and rushed down, first in avalanches, then in roaring torrents. Great rocks cast up by the volcano fell splashing in the sea miles away.

"Oh, this is horrible!" cried Anthea. "Come home, come home!"

"The end of the dream," gasped the learned gentleman.

"Hold up the Amulet," cried the Psammead suddenly. The place where they stood was now crowded

with men and women, and the children were strained tight against the parapet. The turret rocked and swayed; the wave had reached the golden wall.

Jane held up the Amulet.

"Now," cried the Psammead, "say the word!"

And as Jane said it the Psammead leapt from its bag and bit the hand of the learned gentleman.

At the same moment the boys pushed him through the arch and all followed him.

He turned to look back, and through the arch he saw

nothing but a waste of waters, with above it the peak of the terrible mountain with fire raging from it.

He staggered back to his chair.

"What a ghastly dream!" he gasped. "Oh, you're here, my—er—dears. Can I do anything for you?"

"You've hurt your hand," said Anthea gently; "let me bind it up."

The hand was indeed bleeding rather badly.

The Psammead had crept back to its bag. All the children were very white.

"Never again," said the Psammead later on, "will I go into the past with a grown-up person! I will say for you four, you do do as you're told."

"We didn't even find the Amulet," said Anthea later still.

"Of course you didn't; it wasn't there. Only the stone it was made of was there. It fell onto a ship miles away that managed to escape and got to Egypt. I could have told you that."

"I wish you had," said Anthea, and her voice was still rather shaky. "Why didn't you?"

"You never asked me," said the Psammead very sulkily. "I'm not the sort of chap to go shoving my oar in where it's not wanted."

"Mr. Ji—Jimmy's friend will have something worth having to put in his article now," said Cyril very much later indeed.

"Not he," said Robert sleepily. "The learned Ji—jimmy will think it's a dream, and it's ten to one he never tells the other chap a word about it at all."

Robert was quite right on both points. The learned gentleman did. And he never did.

The White Doe

KEITH TAYLOR

Waiting for Harry Silver was a nerve-twisting business. He moved so quietly you never knew he was there until he spoke to you. Tonight he did not even speak, just touched me on the shoulder with that slim, long-fingered hand. I jumped a foot, swearing. He grinned mockingly at me and lifted a pale eyebrow to my brother.

"Ready, are you, Caradoc Tanner?"

"Aye . . ."

"Then come," he said, easy as a lord. Rare cheek he had. "We're doing bigger things than poaching rabbits this time, and we are somewhat in a hurry. I want to be on the ridge above the lake before moonrise."

"Why do you talk only to Caradoc?" I said. "I am here, too."

He looked at me. I looked right back. Thirteen years old, this one, same age as my brother, but no taller than me, and slighter, with less muscle. And I was ten.

"I know you're here. Grateful I am that you came, too, for I need you both, and you could have stayed safe at home. You know the sort of quest this is?"

"It's the white doe," I said. "Sir Rauff and his guests mean to hunt her tonight, but you want to help her."

A fairy creature was running the woods and mountains of Carnarvon in those years. She would appear as a fallow deer, white as new cream, shining, lovely. People said she ran so lightly her hoofs did not flatten the grass. They said she would leap across a ten-yard chasm like blowing thistledown. Caradoc and I never believed the stories, mind . . . until we saw her.

Twilight, it was, warm and purple-shadowed. She was moving quick and light through the wheat fields outside Carnarvon Castle. After that first look we ducked low and held our breaths, for it can be bad, bad luck to stare at the fairy folk. More than one man has called out good-night to footsteps he thought were human, and broken his leg the next day.

We didn't talk about her, either, except to each other . . . and to Harry Silver.

Plenty of stories told about him in Gwynedd, too. People gave him that nickname for the color of his hair. Some said he was a changeling, a fairy child left in a human cradle, a creature with no soul. Caradoc reckoned he was a baron's son, once a page at Hereford Castle, who had run away for reasons too bad to mention. I hadn't any way of knowing about that. Hereford belonged to a whole other world, not only outside our province but right away east of the Marches. One thing was certain, this homeless English boy was the best poacher in Gwynedd.

Caradoc was the first of us to go out after rabbits and salmon with him. I stayed home to cover his absence while Dad and Mam slept, and let him back into the house on his return. After my tenth birthday, I got a turn once in a while, but this was only the second time that all three of us had been out in the woods together. Harry had summoned us on what he said was a quest of his own, and not to come unless we were ready to risk our necks against mounted knights, huntsmen, and dogs.

That meant Sir Rauff Cobden, master of Carnarvon Castle, and he was a rough lad, whose view of the Welsh had no room in it for patience or mercy. I did not want to go against him at all. Wasn't even sure I really liked Harry Silver, come to that, but the white doe was another matter. We'd seen her, Caradoc and I. We'd risk our necks for her.

"It's the white doe," I repeated. "Right? Sir Rauff is planning to hunt her tonight."

"Yes, the brute fool," Harry said bitterly. "We have to spoil his hunt, boys. It must go so badly that Sir Rauff will never try it again as long as he's in Wales. Else he might catch her next time."

"Tell us what to do," said I.

"First I will tell you what you are getting into. And what the white doe is. You have the right, now that you've come this far."

"She's a fairy beast," Caradoc said, puzzled. "We know that."

"She carries fairy blood, true for you, but she doesn't always run in the forest on four feet. The white doe is a shape-changer. When the moon is bright she leaves her home and turns skin to run wild in the woods, because she must. She cannot help it."

"In daylight she's a woman?"

"Indeed she's a woman. She's Lady Cobden, boys, Sir Rauff's own wife. The fool doesn't know."

"She can't be!"

"Lady Cobden?"

"She is." Harry's voice was worried and urgent. "There's fairy blood in that family. Her grandfather was kin to Queen Morgan. Her mother—well, never mind all her relatives."

"How do you know all this?"

Suspicious, me. It came a bit too readily from his lips. My mistrust of Harry Silver returned.

"Oh, Mathwyn, do not doubt me now." Appeal from this one was something new. "I'm also part of the family. Lady Cobden is a second cousin of mine. It's too long and tangled a story for telling in full."

"There must be fairy blood in you, too, then. Just as they say."

"A bit. It's not as strong in me. Listen, we cannot stand here wagging our tongues until morning! The hunting party is on its way! Are you with me?"

"We are with you." We said it as one, Caradoc and I.

"The heroes are not all dead, then," said Harry, laughing. "First we have to confuse Sir Rauff's dogs. I want false trails laid for them, fresh and hot."

Clear and bright and wild was that night. Wind hooted through the hard crags, scraped and ground by ancient ice. The treetops surged like waves of the sea. If the wild, beautiful old gods of Gwynedd were not stirring in their sleep, expecting to see rare things, then my name is not Mathwyn Tanner.

Harry, light-footed and quick, led us through the woods by twisting game trails. From their hiding place in a tumble of rocks he produced soft rags and skins on the end of ten-foot thongs, and a number of small clay bottles. Out with the stoppers, one after the other, soaking each rag. Fresh pig's blood went on one, valerian juice, roe deer's musk, other things I couldn't name but all smelling rankly potent, fit to send hunting dogs mad. Where Harry had got them, don't ask me. We took them and went to work.

Down through the woods, round about, dragging that scent-cloth and getting it caught in bushes a dozen times, up a slope of clear ground, around and

about and double back the way I'd come. I obeyed Harry's instructions to the letter. He'd been hard at work all day placing traps for the huntsmen, he said, and assured me I did not want to step in one.

Two other rags we dragged on different routes, then. As for Harry, he laid a twisting, roundabout trail that crossed all of ours, many times. He covered more ground than Caradoc and I together. Panting and sweating he was when we met him again, bare legs under his tunic scraped and scratched; his eyes glowing hotly.

"Now," he said, gasping, "the safe part is over. Here they come, boys."

Yes, there they came. Huntsmen, belling dogs, riders in leather, mounted on horses they prized more than any commoner's life. Creak and jingle and shouted commands, then a fearful quiet as they gathered on the bank of a stream crashing down from the heights.

Hell broke loose.

First the huntsmen cast about for the white doe's trail, and got more than they wanted. Dogs baying on a scent of crushed valerian, splitting to follow another trail and racing up a long, stony ridge that damaged their feet, before the huntsmen got them back together. Sir Rauff Cobden cursing and humiliated in front of his foreign guests. A knight can starve his tenants and get drunk every evening, but if he owns a pack of ill-behaved deerhounds, why, then he will be ashamed.

Down a forest path with them, Sir Rauff leading the hunt. Something big and gray swooped a foot in front of his face, shrieking like a demon. The horse reared high. Sir Rauff controlled it, of course, trained knight that he was, but banged his head on a branch first. He continued the hunt with blood trickling down his face. The huntsmen started muttering about spooks.

Spooks, nothing. Harry, in a wide-winged cloak and gargoyle mask, swinging across the path on a rope, having practiced the thing until he could do it in darkness. He vanished through the undergrowth where horsemen could not follow. Although the huntsmen gave chase on foot, they were not eager to catch him; frightened silly, rather. He drowned his scent in a stream and joined us.

The moon was up by then.

"Harry?" I whispered. "We have been watching the castle, see. Something pure white came out through the fields, then vanished among trees. We think it's the doe."

"Think?" said he with scorn.

"All right, we are sure. Nothing else can be that color."

"Then for now we just watch the fun. If we're lucky the lady will not need us further. But if she does . . . rest while you can, boys, rest while you can."

Fun there was. Harry's kind of wicked fun. What had happened before was just gentle joking, but now it grew rougher. Dogs ran their necks into choking snares. Horses put their feet down holes with sharpened sticks at the bottom. Rope, stretched chest-high between two trees, caught a man riding at a canter. Always there were the scent trails that led nowhere, tiring the dogs and men.

The strangest thing was that, with all their skill, the huntsmen raised no game. Not even a mountain hare! It took fairy magic, not mortal tricks, to explain that, and I began to believe Harry's story.

Then came the hour to pay, as Harry, I think, had

known it must. Even fairy luck cannot last forever against mounted knights, dogs, and cold iron. They caught the white doe's scent. The hounds raised a cry. We heard them clearly in the night air, and Sir Rauff's voice, loud with triumph.

"The true scent at last! Now I'll catch her if I must ride to the end of the Marches after her! Spur, gentlemen, spur and she's ours!"

And the quarry he hunted was his own part-fairy wife in a different shape. True for Harry that the knight was a fool. Small wonder, too, that she had never told him this quirk of her heritage!

The hunting horns blew, ragged and strident. Harry was up at once. Knowing the woods and mountains as we knew Dad's tannery, he saw what was likely to happen.

"If they chase her up there, she'll be trapped by the corrie and the waterfall! *Uffern dan*! You stay here."

Off with him at once. His quicksilver way of moving had a clumsy tarnish on it by then, though. Dead tired he was still, after two hours' rest. And why not? Driven himself hard all day and half the night, had Harry Silver, and wasn't in condition to run any longer. Or play tricks with hard men like Sir Rauff.

I paid no attention to what he said. Went after him at once. Bigger, me, with more strength and endurance. Soon left Caradoc gasping behind.

Saw the white doe. Saw her clear, lovely in moonlight, leaping like poured cream, the pack after her. Five dogs left, and one of them ran with a limp. They bayed as they caught sight of her. No false trails would have put them off then.

Something else did. Harry Silver rose out of the ground, it seemed, and shouted to Sir Rauff.

"I noosed your dogs! I staked your horses! The white doe is not your prey, mortal man!"

Mortal man. I liked the cheek of that. But Harry was mortal, too. Turning, he ran up a loose, scree-covered ridge toward the corrie and waterfall, the spot he had said was dangerous, the place they could trap her. Dogs, horses, and men went after him like a storm.

The white doe went the other way, to safety. Harry had been right, she was not their prey, but what about him? I circled around below the waterfall. It fell into a deep black pool with alders around the edge, and I squirmed through them, lying flat in the wet dark, praying hard.

Then I looked up.

High above I saw the rocky lip of the corrie, with the waterfall plunging over and the stars beyond. Harry appeared, slim against the sky, with the dogs at his heels. The moon gleamed on his hair.

He jumped, far out. Two of Sir Rauff's deerhounds were so close that they went over with him, twisting down through the air. One struck the rocks. The other made a mighty splash in that deep, dark pool, a second after Harry.

I slipped in and dived, kicking down, down, all the way to the bottom of the world, cold and secret, with a roaring in my ears. Groping over slippery rocks, through the weed, I touched something limp, but it was hairy and the limbs ended in paws. The deerhound. Twisting around, I sensed something adrift beside me, grabbed hard, and got a handful of sodden tunic. There was smooth human skin inside. Harry's fingers curled around my wrist, feeble and helpless, like a sleepy infant's. Even down there with my lungs bursting, I remembered the lordly airs, the cool self-posses-

sion, take him or leave him. The difference came near
breaking my heart.

I hauled him to the surface. In among the alders on
the brink, he lay head downward while I worked on
him, hoping Sir Rauff would think he was done for.
That was when I had the surprise of my life, too.

A while later, Harry coughed and spluttered. Water
came up, half a bucket, and he shivered like one with a
bad fever. Quite a while before he could speak.

When he did, "The white doe?"

"Safe."

"Hunting . . . party?"

"Went back to the castle, Harry. So I believe. Quiet,
now, you."

Not much more to tell. We had trouble with Dad
and Mam when we went home, but they were happy
to know nothing when they learned how someone

had raised the devil with Sir Rauff's chase. He never tried to hunt the white doe again.

Harry Silver was another matter. Had to leave Carnarvon, Harry, until some other knight was made master of the castle and its garrison. Then he came back.

I never did know if the story he told was true. Plenty of things I never did know about mysterious Harry Silver. Two things, though, I did learn. Discovered them down among the alders' roots, at the rim of the dark pool, while I labored to bring him round. One was the reason he called us "boys" so often. The other was his proper name. His true name. It wasn't Harry.

It was Harriet.

Creature of Darkness

NICHOLAS STUART GRAY

O ne evening, it was later than usual when
Muffler came back from the mountain pas-
tures. Meg grew anxious, and begged Simon
to go out in search. Then there was a thudding of
hoofs in the lane outside; the click and creak of a gate;
a voice calling good night. Muffler came into the
kitchen, wet with dew and apologetic. He said he had
forgotten the time in making a poem.

"Silly boy," said Meg, rumpling his hair. "You're
soaked to the skin! Oh my, you will get such a cold!"

And he did.

In the morning, he sneezed thirty times. And Meg
made him stay in bed, saying she had told him so. She
brought an extra blanket, and a hot brick to warm the
truckle bed, and she lit a fire in the attic, for the boy
seemed slightly feverish.

"Now you keep quiet," said she, "and sleep all day,
my dear."

"My goats—" said Muffler, hoarsely.

"They'll do well enough," she laid her hand against
his hot forehead. "Young Robin from up the lane can
see to them till you're better."

And she went away. And Muffler fell asleep, and the
day passed. Meg came several times with hot milk,
and, in the evening, a potion of herbs. It was not nice,

but she gave its recipient a spoon of honey to sweeten the taste.

"The goats have been so naughty," she told him. "They ran from Robin, and came back here. Did you hear 'em bleating under your window? They ate nearly all my daffodils, too! We've put 'em in the big meadow, and there they can stay till you're well enough to deal with them. Wicked things!" and she laughed.

Muffler watched her then, while she banked charcoal around the smoldering logs in the fireplace. His eyes felt heavy, his head ached, and his feet seemed to be pinned to the bed. Meg came and looked down at him kindly. Then a very disapproving expression crossed her face.

"Ah," said she, "we'll have that out of here, for a start! When did he sneak in?"

She scooped up a large black cat who had been sprawling over Muffler's feet, dropped him on the floor with a thud, and shooed him toward the door. He glanced at her remotely, and strolled without haste from the room.

"I didn't know he was there," wheezed Muffler.

"Nor I, my dear! He's a saucy brute, that one—not like my dear Dulcie," the farmer's wife was turning Muffler's pillows as she spoke. "He's been hanging about the farm all day. He must be a stray, though I've never seen him in the village before. And he's a big handsome beast. But cheeky! I don't know why I fed him!"

"I do," said Muffler. "He'd starve, otherwise."

"That one would never go hungry," smiled Meg. "He's a creature of darkness if ever I saw one! He can settle here, and work for his living, and welcome—but I think he'll go, as stealthy as he came."

She smoothed the hair from the boy's forehead, and stooped to kiss him.

"There's water by you, if you wake. But I hope you sleep quiet all night. Good dreams to you, my dear."

She blew out the candle and went away. The door closed softly behind her, leaving the room to twilight and the gentle flicker of the fire.

A heavy weight landed with a thump on the bed, and a husky voice spoke in the stillness.

"Might I have your attention?" it said.

Muffler stared at the big cat. The light from the fire showed gleaming black fur and the glint of bright green eyes.

"I thought Mother Meg put you outside."

"I came back. No one puts me where I do not choose to go."

The cat began to work his paws, busily pulling long threads from the coverlet.

"I never heard a cat talk before," said Muffler sleepily. "Are you really a stray?"

The cat's eyes slitted. He arched his neck and licked his chest. It seemed he did not mean to answer. Then he favored Muffler with an impassive stare.

"You are thinking of some other animal," said he, coldly. "In order to stray, one must first belong. I do not belong."

"I beg your pardon."

"Cats are not like other creatures," said the ebony beast. "They live in two worlds. One is the world of daylight. The other, the world of night."

His tone was slightly sinister, and Muffler was fascinated.

"Mother Meg was right, then," he said. "She called you a creature of darkness."

"I heard her," said the cat loftily. "And she doesn't know the half! For I am Grimbold."

Muffler pulled himself up higher against his pillow. His head throbbed. And the cat paced up the bed and sat bolt upright on the boy's middle. He was extremely heavy, but Muffler was too enthralled by him to protest. He held out his hand and Grimbold touched it delicately with the tip of his cool nose.

"I've heard that you are kind, as humans go," said he. "And that you make songs, and tell tales of magic. I thought you might give me a hand."

"Me?" said Muffler doubtfully, and sneezed three times. "I've got a cold, you know."

The cat eyed him from the very end of the bed, where he had retired in a flash.

"I know," he said. "Please give some warning before you do that again!"

"I had no idea I was going to," Muffler apologized. "I'll be glad to help you if I can. It'll be no trouble, I'm sure."

"Won't it, just!" said Grimbold darkly. "But your troubles don't concern me. Only those of my master."

"I thought cats didn't have masters?"

"A loose term," came the airy reply. "Put it like this —I have a *friend* in the night world. And he's in a frightful mess!"

The cat's eyes opened until they were like lamps against his dark fur. He looked most formidable. Muffler was enchanted.

"Who is your friend?" breathed the boy. "And what has he done?"

"He's the son of a great sorcerer and he has offended his father."

"Oh! And—and where is he?"

Grimbold closed his eyes. He said, in a slightly affected voice:

"Ectually—he's tied hand and foot in the middle of a block of ice!"

He scratched his left ear. But Muffler thought he was more anxious than he seemed.

"Well, what can *I* do about it?"

"You know your farmer's wife's cat?" said Grimbold. "A small fat gray female—"

"Dulcie?" said Muffler. "Oh, yes. She's sweet."

"That's as may be," purred Grimbold, deep in his throat. "Anyway, she told me that you once got up in the middle of the night and climbed the king oak in the meadow, because you heard her crying there—"

"As I reached her," said Muffler indignantly, "she went down the other side."

"A misunderstanding," said Grimbold, in a dry voice. "She was not calling for help—but for me. And it isn't the point. You don't fear the dark, and you're good at climbing. And you're kind. Come with me."

The big cat stared at him compellingly and the boy got out of bed.

For a moment, his head whirled like a top and his knees buckled. He shivered with cold. But he managed somehow to get to a stool where his clothes were folded. He began to dress, putting on his old woollen tunic and belting it.

"How can I leave the house without being seen?" said Muffler. "Mother Meg would never let me out."

"Easy," said the cat.

He stretched his gleaming body, limb by limb. He sprang from the bed and strolled over to the fireplace.

"You're shivering," said he. "Are you cold?"

"I *have* a cold."

"Ah, then you mustn't risk further chills. Have a word with the fire."

"A word with *what?*"

"How dull can humans be?" wondered Grimbold. "All living things speak, don't they? The fire is alive. Stoop close, boy, and listen to it."

Muffler blinked and obeyed. He knelt on the rag rug and leaned down toward the bars of the grate. He heard the crack and rustle of the little flames as they licked in and out of the charcoal. The warmth brought a flush to his cheek, though his hands and feet were cold as snow. Then he heard small voices whispering together.

"What's it like outside?" they hissed softly.

"Who knows?"

"We'll know soon. When we turn to smoke and fly away."

"Will it be frightening?"

"Will it be fun?"

"If we've been good, shall we be happy?"

"Who knows?"

"We'll know soon."

This conversation went on and on. For the flames were turning into smoke, even while they questioned, and went singing up the chimney. And new flames formed, wondered, and became smoke in their own turn. And, behind all the smaller voices, a vast, soft, faraway song was sighing:

"Out and away— away I go—
Now I am smoke, and now I know—"

The boy listened with a catch in his breath to hear so sad and so happy a thing. The cat stirred by his side.

"Speak to them," he murmured. "Ask them for

warmth. Preferably in rhyme. It always goes down well when there's magic in the air."

Muffler looked dubious, but he thought for a moment and then said timidly:

"Smoke and flame, gray and gold,
Help me, for I've got a cold."

He glanced at the cat.

"Go on," prompted that dark creature. "Ask for heat to take away with you. It's very important."

The boy hesitated and then spoke again to the fire:

"Here I kneel and make a plea;
Give me warmth to take with me."

"Oh, jolly good!" said the cat. "For the spur of the moment."

The flames went on rustling and whispering together.

"What's it like outside?"

"Who knows?"

"Did you hear what I heard?"

"Yes, if you heard what I did."

"Someone spoke to us."

"What's it like outside?"

"He fears it will be cold, from what he said."

"And he spoke so gently. Give him what he asks."

The voices in the fire seemed suddenly to fuse together and spoke in one soft murmur:

"Flame and smoke, gold and gray
In your hands their magic lay;
Take the gift that you desire,

With the friendship of the fire:
Warmth of heart you had before;
Warmth go with you evermore."

And Muffler stopped shivering. A gentle glow started at his fingertips and crept all through him from head to foot. He felt like purring. For a moment he thought he was. But it was the cat.

"Now follow me!" cried Grimbold.

And sprang up the chimney. After a moment he came down again.

"Aren't you coming?" he said crossly.

"Up there?" faltered Muffler. "But—the fire—"

"Don't tread on it!" snapped the cat. "Use your brain! The chimney is wider than you think, and it's as easy to climb as a tree."

He vanished again in one huge bound. Muffler followed with some misgiving.

Being banked low, the fire was not much of an obstacle. By taking a deep breath before starting up, the boy escaped suffocation in the smoke. But the brick chimney was not as easy to climb as the cat seemed to think. Soot was everywhere, falling abut in soft, fluffy lumps. But finally Muffler emerged into the moonlight and gasped and coughed. Luckily for him, the chimney pot and part of the old stack had been blown away in a gale long ago. He scrambled out onto the roof and took a long breath of cool night air.

He was in a realm of sloping thatch, angled roofs, gables, and curly chimneys; for the farm was an old and rambling building. A bat sidestepped past his head; and owls were crying around the barns below. Grimbold was sitting like a black statue on the roof ridge nearby, his ears alert, and his whiskers quivering with excite-

ment. His mouth opened in a silent laugh when he saw Muffler's soot-smeared face emerge into the open, and he started to pick his way delicately down a long slope of thatch.

"It's an easy jump at the bottom," said he, and leapt into darkness.

This also was not quite such an easy business for the boy. He tried to clamber down slowly, but the pitch of the roof was too steep. He lost his footing, rolled over on his back, and slid down—faster and faster—until he shot over the eaves, with a startled squeak, and landed neck-deep in a full rain tub.

Grimbold minced away from the splash.

"That's one way of doing it," he commented.

Muffler dragged himself out of the big barrel. He stood in a growing pool of water, but still felt as warm as toast. He said so, and the cat gave him a wondering glance.

"Surely you understood the spell of the fire?" he said. "You'll never be cold again. Which is as well," he added, "considering how you come off roofs."

"I'm not in practice—"

But the cat was out of earshot and the boy limped quickly after him.

"Where are we going?" he called.

"To the nearest gap," came back the voice of the cat.

He led the way, by winding brick paths, through the moonlit garden to the stone wall at the end; here were fruit trees, blackcurrant bushes, gooseberries, and rhubarb, and herbs; and here the cat paused. He twitched his tail and vanished. Muffler waited patiently until he reappeared.

"Why must I always come back for you?" snarled Grimbold.

"You never explain where you're going."

"This time, into the night-world." The cat's teeth glinted as he drew back his lips. He said loftily, "All cats know the gaps. You must have noticed how they can disappear before your eyes when they choose. But I suppose it will take magic to get *you* through!"

He sniffed disparagingly and said something that sounded regrettably like:

"Barriers of earth and sky,
Let this hulking human by!"

And the ground shivered under Muffler's feet. A mist blew around him, and cleared. He blinked and saw that he was standing in the same place—but it was not the same.

The stone wall looked transparent, as though made of glass. The trees had pale golden leaves and their trunks were dappled with shifting colors. Blossoms were like tiny lamps, alight. Even the rhubarb was ebony-black and powdered with bright specks. A white bat went flicking through the strangely scented air. And the thatch on the farmhouse roof was as green as emerald.

Something touched Muffler's hand and he glanced down. He sprang back with a cry. A black panther looked at him with eyes of fire.

"It's me, silly," said Grimbold.

Muffler recovered slightly.

"You're—bigger!" he said.

"In the night-world, cats grow to their full stature," said Grimbold impressively. "This is not the world you know."

"It's beautiful."

"But very dangerous. Like everything else that is truly beautiful," the cat told him. "Those who see the night-world can never again content themselves with the ordinary one. It changes them."

"Am I changed?"

An enigmatic expression flickered over the broad and whiskered face.

"I would not have brought you here," said the cat carefully, "but for what Dulcie told me. Poets and singers can wander in and out of the night-kingdoms, for they aren't quite like other humans, anyway."

"Do many people come here?" said Muffler, puzzled by all this.

"We try to stop them. But sometimes they slip through. Ordinary people who are never the same again. They become strangers to their own kind; and they are accused of witchcraft—madness . . . ! We discourage casual visitors," said Grimbold firmly.

"Except for poets."

"We can't stop those. They find the way for themselves. Once they reach *that* point," said the cat, "they hardly count as human anymore! Now, do stop gossiping and come along."

He sped toward the stone wall and shot through as though it had been made of mist. Muffler took a deep breath to encourage himself, and did the same. The wall *was* made of mist. On the far side was the duckpond. But not the duckpond as the boy knew it.

The trees at its margins had slender silver trunks and branches. Glass leaves tinkled in the night breeze. Underfoot, the grass was white, as though there was a heavy frost. And the pond water was like milky, gleaming ice. Grimbold skidded as he loped across it, and,

seeing the scratches left on the surface by his claws, Muffler realized that it *was* ice. He limped gingerly after the cat, and found him in the very center, crouching until his nose almost touched the crystal coldness.

"There he is," said Grimbold.

It gave Muffler quite a shock to look down and see a young man lying still and rigid some ways beneath them, frozen into the solid ice. His hands and feet were tied with cords and his eyes were shut.

"Oh . . . " breathed Muffler, "is he dead?"

"No," said the cat. "But he's pretty cold! Mind you," he went on disapprovingly, "it's entirely his own fault. He will argue with his father, and the old man has some unbeatable back-answers!"

"He must be very cruel," said Muffler, "to treat his son like this."

"Ectually," said the cat, "it's six of one and half a dozen of the other. Sometimes, I could wash my paws of the pair of them!"

"I don't consider this a fatherly way to behave, whatever the cause!"

"You" said Grimbold, "are not a sorcerer! He lost his temper. He said Gareth must find his own way out, and he set a spell on the ice so that *I* could not open it. Gareth's been there for a whole week now."

"And what am I supposed to do? Chip him out?"

In answer to his question, Grimbold asked another. "Is it cold?"

"Not very," said Muffler, surprised. "In fact, considering all this ice—oh, it's the fire spell! I wish I could share it with your Gareth."

"Try," suggested Grimbold.

Muffler looked as doubtful as he felt. But he knelt on the ice and laid both hands on its surface. A pleasant glow tingled through his palms.

"I thought so! I thought so!" cried the cat.

Below them the sorcerer's son stirred. His pale hair floated around his face. Bubbles drifted from his lips. And the ice cracked across in thousands of fine, hair like lines. A deep pool of water spread in the middle of the pond and Muffler found himself elbow-deep in the warmth of it.

"Get to the side!" hissed Grimbold. "You're melting the lot!"

There was crackling all around and more bubbles underneath. The young man floated to the surface, and Grimbold stretched a huge paw to drag him up on to the crumbling ice. Then, with Muffler's assistance, he slid him across it and safely onto the soft white grass. They all tumbled there in a damp heap, and the duckpond turned blue as the last of the ice vanished.

The son of the sorcerer sat up stiffly and shook back his wet hair.

"You were long in coming," he said to Grimbold.

"Serves you right," said the cat.

"Who's the boy?"

"Muffler. He got you out of that coil."

"Speaking of which," said Gareth, "it would be kind if someone untied me."

Muffler always carried a small knife in his belt and now he used it to saw through the cords. The sorcerer's son rubbed his wrists and shivered.

"Chilly for the time of year!" said he.

Then he gave his hand to Muffler. It was slender and wet, and without the fire spell Muffler would have found it very cold. In the moonlight the eyes of Gareth were golden, and he was extremely handsome. But it was an unreliable sort of beauty and his smile was perfunctory.

"I'm most grateful," he said, and laughed. "The old man will be livid!"

"With me?" said Muffler, in some alarm.

Gareth gave him a flashing grin.

"With everyone!" said he, lightly.

"Oh, surely he will forgive you, if you apologize—"

Grimbold gave a small snigger, and the young man widened his strange and slanting eyes.

"Apologize?" said he, and turned to the cat. "You know that spell he's working at—to turn tadpoles into sponge cakes?"

The cat nodded.

"I," said Gareth, "have thought how to turn the whole thing to froth and frogs! It took some working out, but it kept me happy this last week."

He got to his feet, ran his hands down his wet tunic, and gave Muffler another of his careless smiles.

"You are welcome to this world," he said. "Do come again."

He turned on his heel and went lightly away under the trees. Muffler shook his head admiringly.

"You can't help liking him," he said. "But surely he's asking for more trouble with all that tadpole stuff?"

"Oh, he's a madman," said Grimbold.

A faint golden light began to creep up the sky. The breeze freshened and the glass leaves rang like little bells. The cat yawned.

"You'd better get back," he said. "Time flies fast in your world and the dawn is breaking."

He scratched his jaw so that a few shining hairs drifted to the ground. He turned a thoughtful stare on the boy.

"If the opportunity occurs for you to return to this

world," he said, very seriously, "think twice before doing it. So far, no harm is done. But the knowledge of magic and mystery may change your life, if you let it. You're only a boy—and you might grow out of your singing and your rhymes. Be careful, Muffler—be very careful, and very sure, before you settle for poetry."

"Well," said the boy, "I love the daylight world, but magic draws me. If I never saw this place again, I would always dream of it."

The cat's eyes slitted to slanting lines of fire.

"I've warned you," said he.

He gave another yawn that curled his tongue like a pink petal in his mouth.

"You'll never get back up that roof," he stated. "But there's another gap somewhere hereabout."

He waved his tail, and said:

"Barriers of earth and sky,
Let the boy go safely by."

Muffler blinked. The mist cleared. The ground steadied. He was looking at the duckpond that he knew. Green with water weeds and gently rippling, and apple trees leaning over to look at their morning reflections in it. A large white duck came stumping from the stable, plopped into the water, shouting raucously with pleasure, and stood on his head.

Something moved by Muffler's ankle. The boy stooped to stroke Grimbold, who was his daytime size again. The cat moved away, then relented and rubbed his head on the friendly hand.

"Doubtless we shall meet again," said he.

He minced away a few paces and turned.

"Must go, now," he said. "Gareth will have the old

386

man hopping mad by breakfast time. Good-bye, and thank you. And remember what I told you."

He twitched his tail and vanished.

Muffler limped to the gate of the meadow behind the barn. The goats stopped everything that they were doing and crowded around, bleating affectionately.

"Hallo, you woolly wickeds!" said Muffler.

The farmer's wife came from the house, carrying a trug of chicken food. She saw the boy and let it fall. And a fluster of hens came rushing from barns and stables, to fall on the scattered grain.

"Muffler!" cried Meg."What are you doing out of bed!"

"I'm quite all right, Mother Meg. I went up the chimney and into a world of—"

"You've certainly been messing with the fire," she scolded. "Look at you—all over soot! But your cold—!"

"It's gone. And I'll never have another," said Muffler hopefully. "The fire gave me a spell to keep me warm."

Meg was holding his hand very closely in her own.

"You're certainly warm enough," said she, wonderingly. "And not in fever. You've made a quick recovery, and no mistake! It must have been that potion I gave you. Never mind your tales of magic and your dreaming! You come along and have your break-fast!"

Chorus for a Cat

I will never subject be,
I am free.
Try to curb me and, no doubt,
You'll find out
Just exactly what a claw

Is for!
Or I'll dematerialize
Before your eyes:
Ere you lay a hand upon
Me, I'm gone!
You may think I'm in the lane;
Think again.
You may guess I'm on the roof;
Any proof?
I am not to hold or bind,
Or find.

I will hunt and sing and fight
In the night;
All day long I lie and doze,
Comatose:
Never answer when you call
And bawl.
If to order me you choose,
You will lose.
Try to understand my mind,
Then you'll find
Truest friendship I will give
While I live;
Kindly amiability,
And sympathy.
If subservience you prefer,
Buy a cur!

Troll Bridge

NEIL GAIMAN

They pulled up most of the railway tracks in the early sixties, when I was three or four. They slashed the train services to ribbons. This meant that there was nowhere to go but London, and the little town where I lived became the end of the line.

My earliest reliable memory: eighteen months old, my mother away in the hospital having my sister, and my grandmother walking with me down to a bridge and lifting me up to watch the train below, panting and steaming like a black iron dragon.

Over the next few years they lost the last of the steam trains, and with them went the network of railways that joined village to village, town to town. I didn't know that the trains were going. By the time I was seven they were a thing of the past.

We lived in an old house on the outskirts of the town. The fields opposite were empty and fallow. I used to climb the fence and lie in the shade of a small bulrush patch and read; or, if I were feeling more adventurous, I'd explore the grounds of the empty manor beyond the fields. It had a weed-clogged ornamental pond, with a low wooden bridge over it. I never saw any groundsmen or caretakers in my forays through the gardens or woods, and I never attempted to enter the manor. That would have been courting disaster, and, besides, it was a matter of faith for me that all empty old houses were haunted.

It is not that I was credulous, simply that I believed in all things dark and dangerous. It was part of my young creed that the night was full of ghosts and witches, hungry and flapping and dressed completely in black.

The converse held reassuringly true: daylight was safe. Daylight was always safe.

A ritual: on the last day of the summer term, walking home from school, I would remove my shoes and socks and, carrying them in my hands, walk down the stony, flinty lane on pink and tender feet. During the summer holiday I would only put shoes on under duress. I would revel in my freedom from footwear until the school term began once more in September.

When I was seven I discovered the path through the woods. It was summer, hot and bright, and I wandered a long way from home that day.

I was exploring. I went past the manor, its windows boarded up and blind, across the grounds, and through some unfamiliar woods. I scrambled down a steep bank and found myself on a shady path that was new to me and overgrown with trees; the light that penetrated the leaves was stained green and gold, and I thought I was in fairyland.

A stream trickled down the side of the path, teeming with tiny, transparent shrimps. I picked them up and watched them jerk and spin on my fingertips. Then I put them back.

I wandered down the path. It was perfectly straight and overgrown with short grass. From time to time I would find these really terrific rocks: bubbly, melted things, brown and purple and black. If you held them up to the light you could see every color of the rainbow. I was convinced that they had to be extremely valuable, and stuffed my pockets with them.

I walked and walked down the quiet, golden-green corridor, and saw nobody.

I wasn't hungry or thirsty. I just wondered where the path was going. It traveled in a straight line and was perfectly flat. The path never changed, but the countryside around it did. At first I was walking along the bottom of a ravine, grassy banks climbing steeply on each side of me. Later the path was above everything, and as I walked I could look down at the treetops below me, and the roofs of occasional distant houses. My path was always flat and straight, and I walked along it through valleys and plateaus, valleys and plateaus. And eventually, in one of the valleys, I came to the bridge.

It was built of clean red brick, a huge curving arch over the path. At the side of the bridge were stone steps cut into the embankment, and at the top of the steps, a little wooden gate.

I was surprised to see any token of the existence of humanity on my path, which I was by now certain was a natural formation, like a volcano. And, with a sense more of curiosity than anything else (I had, after all, walked hundreds of miles, or so I was convinced, and might be *anywhere*), I climbed the stone steps and went through the gate.

I was nowhere.

The top of the bridge was paved with mud. On each side of it was a meadow. The meadow on my side was a wheat field; the other was just grass. There were caked imprints of huge tractor wheels in the dried mud. I walked across the bridge to be sure: no trip-trap, my bare feet were soundless.

Nothing for miles; just fields and wheat and trees.

I picked a stalk of wheat and pulled out the sweet

391

grains, peeling them between my fingers, chewing them meditatively.

I realized then that I was getting hungry, and went back down the stairs to the abandoned railway track. It was time to go home. I was not lost; all I needed to do was follow my path home once more.

There was a troll waiting for me under the bridge.

"I'm a troll," he said. Then he paused and added, more or less as an afterthought, "Fol rol de ol rol."

He was huge: his head brushed the top of the brick arch. He was more or less translucent: I could see the bricks and trees behind him, dimmed but not lost. He was all my nightmares given flesh. He had huge, strong teeth, and rending claws, and strong, hairy hands. His hair was long, like one of my sister's plastic gonks, and his eyes bulged.

"I heard you, Jack," he whispered, in a voice like the wind. "I heard you trip-trapping over my bridge. And now I'm going to eat your life."

I was only seven, but it was daylight, and I do not remember being scared. It is good for children to find themselves facing the elements of a fairy tale—they are well-equipped to deal with these.

"Don't eat me," I said to the troll. I was wearing a striped brown T-shirt and brown corduroy trousers. My hair also was brown, and I was missing a front tooth. I was learning to whistle between my teeth, but wasn't there yet.

"I'm going to eat your life, Jack," said the troll.

I stared the troll in the face. "My big sister is going to be coming down the path soon," I lied, "and she's far tastier than me. Eat her instead."

The troll sniffed the air, and smiled. "You're all alone," he said. "There's nothing else on the path.

Nothing at all." Then he leaned down and ran his fingers over me: it felt like butterflies were brushing my face—like the touch of a blind person. Then he snuffled his fingers and shook his huge head. "You don't have a big sister. You've only a younger sister, and she's at her friend's today."

"Can you tell all that from smell?" I asked, amazed.

"Trolls can smell the rainbows, trolls can smell the stars," it whispered, sadly. "Trolls can smell the dreams you dreamed before you were ever born. Come close to me and I'll eat your life."

"I've got precious stones in my pocket," I told the troll. "Take them, not me. Look." I showed him the lava jewel rocks I had found earlier.

"Clinker," said the troll. "The discarded refuse of steam trains. Of no value to me."

He opened his mouth wide. Sharp teeth. Breath that smelled of leaf mold and the underneaths of things. "Eat. Now."

He became more and more solid to me, more and more real; and the world outside became flatter, began to fade.

"Wait." I dug my feet into the damp earth beneath the bridge, wiggled my toes, held on tightly to the real world. I stared into his big eyes. "You don't want to eat my life. Not yet. I—I'm only seven. I haven't *lived* at all yet. There are books I haven't read yet. I've never been on an aeroplane. I can't whistle yet—not really. Why don't you let me go? When I'm older and bigger and more of a meal, I'll come back to you."

The troll stared at me with eyes like headlamps.

Then it nodded.

"When you come back, then," it said. And it smiled.

I turned around and walked back down the silent, straight path where the railway lines had once been.

After a while I began to run.

I pounded down the track in the green light, puffing and blowing, until I felt a stabbing ache beneath my ribcage, the pain of a stitch, and, clutching my side, I stumbled home.

The fields started to go as I grew older. One by one, row by row, houses sprang up with roads named after wildflowers and respectable authors. Our home—an aging, tattered Victorian house—was sold, and torn down; new houses covered the garden.

They built houses everywhere.

I once got lost in the new housing estate which covered two meadows I had once known every inch of. I didn't mind too much that the fields were going,

though. The old manor house was bought by a multi-national, and the grounds became more houses.

It was eight years before I returned to the old railway line, and when I did, I was not alone.

I was fifteen; I'd changed schools twice in that time. Her name was Louise, and she was my first love.

I loved her gray eyes, and her fine, light brown hair, and her gawky way of walking (like a fawn just learning to walk, which sounds really dumb, for which I apologize). I saw her chewing gum when I was thirteen, and I fell for her like a suicide from a bridge.

The main trouble with being in love with Louise was that we were best friends, and we were both going out with other people.

I'd never told her I loved her, or even that I fancied her. We were buddies.

I'd been at her house that evening: we sat in her room and played *Rattus Norvegicus*, the first Stranglers LP. It was the beginning of punk, and everything seemed so exciting: the possibilities, in music as in everything else, were endless. Eventually it was time for me to go home, and she decided to accompany me. We held hands, innocently, just pals, and we strolled the ten-minute walk to my house.

The moon was bright, and the world was visible and colorless, and the night was warm.

We got to my house. Saw the lights inside, and stood in the driveway, and talked about the band I was starting. We didn't go in.

Then it was decided that I'd walk *her* home. So we walked back to her house.

She told me about the battles she was having with her younger sister, who was stealing her makeup and perfume. Louise suspected that her sister was sleeping with boys. Louise was a virgin. We both were.

We stood in the road outside her house, under the sodium-yellow streetlight, and we stared at each other's black lips and pale yellow faces.

We grinned at each other.

Then we just walked, picking quiet roads and empty paths. In one of the new housing estates a path led us into the woodland, and we followed it.

The path was straight and dark; but the lights of distant houses shone like stars on the ground, and the moon gave us enough light to see. Once we were scared, when something snuffled and snorted in front of us. We pressed close, saw it was a badger, laughed and hugged and kept on walking.

We talked quiet nonsense about what we dreamed and wanted and thought.

And all the time I wanted to kiss her.

Finally I saw my chance. There was an old brick bridge over the path, and we stopped beneath it. I pressed up against her. Her mouth opened against mine.

Then she went cold and stiff, and stopped moving.

"Hello," said the troll.

I let go of Louise. It was dark beneath the bridge, but the shape of the troll filled the darkness.

"I froze her," said the troll, "so we can talk. Now: I'm going to eat your life."

My heart pounded, and I could feel myself trembling.

"No."

"You said you'd come back to me. And you have. Did you learn to whistle?"

"Yes."

"That's good. I never could whistle." It sniffed and nodded. "I am pleased. You have grown in life and

experience. More to eat. More for me."

I grabbed Louise, a taut zombie, and pushed her forward. "Don't take me. I don't want to die. Take *her*. I bet she's much tastier than me. And she's two months older than I am. Why don't you take her?"

The troll was silent.

It sniffed Louise from toe to head.

Then it looked at me.

"She's an innocent," it said. "You're not. I don't want her. I want you."

I walked to the opening of the bridge and stared up at the stars in the night.

"But there's so much I've never done," I said, partly to myself. "I mean, I've never . . . Well, I've never had sex. And I've never been to America. I haven't . . ." I paused. "I haven't *done* anything. Not yet."

The troll said nothing.

"I could come back to you. When I'm older."

The troll said nothing.

"I *will* come back. Honest I will."

"Come back to me?" said Louise. "Why? Where are you going?"

I turned around. The troll had gone, and the girl I had thought I loved was standing in the shadows beneath the bridge.

"We're going home," I told her. "Come on."

We walked back, and never said anything.

She went out with the drummer in the punk band I started and, much later, married someone else. We met once, on a train, after she was married, and she asked me if I remembered that night.

I said I did.

"I really liked you, that night, Jack," she told me. "I thought you were going to kiss me. I thought you were going to ask me out. I would have said yes. If you had."

"But I didn't."

"No," she said. "You didn't." Her hair was cut very short. It didn't suit her.

I never saw her again. The trim woman with the taut smile was not the girl I had loved, and talking to her made me feel uncomfortable.

I moved to London, and then, many years later, I moved back again, but the town I returned to was not the town I remembered: there were no fields, no farms, no little flint lanes; and I moved away as soon as I could, to a tiny village, ten miles down the road.

I moved with my family—I was married by now, with a toddler—into an old house that had once, many years before, been a railway station. The tracks had been dug up, and the old couple who lived oppo- site us used it to grow vegetables.

I was getting older. One day I found a gray hair; on another, I heard a recording of myself talking, and I realized I sounded just like my father.

I was working in London, doing scouting for one of the major record companies. I was commuting into Lon- don by train most days, coming back some evenings.

I had to keep a small flat in London; it's hard to commute when the bands you're checking out don't even stagger onto the stage until midnight.

I thought that Eleanora—that was my wife's name; I should have mentioned that before, I suppose—didn't know about the other women; but I got back from a two-week jaunt to New York one winter's day, and when I arrived at the house it was empty and cold.

She had left a letter, not a note. Fifteen pages, neatly typed, and every word of it was true. Including the P.S.

which read: *You really don't love me. And you never did.*

I put on a heavy coat, and I left the house and just walked, stunned and slightly numb.

There was no snow on the ground, but there was a hard frost, and the leaves crunched under my feet as I walked. The trees were skeletal black against the harsh, gray winter sky.

I walked down the side of the road. Cars passed me, traveling to and from London. Once I tripped on a branch, half hidden in a heap of brown leaves, ripping my trousers, cutting my leg.

I reached the next village. There was a river at right angles to the road and a path I'd never seen before beside it, and I walked down the path and stared at the river, partly frozen. It gurgled and plashed and sang.

The path led off through fields; it was straight and grassy.

I found a rock, half buried, on one side of the path. I picked it up, brushed off the mud. It was a melted lump of purplish stuff, with a strange rainbow sheen to it. I put it into the pocket of my coat and held it in my hand as I walked, its presence warm and reassuring.

The river meandered across the fields, and I walked on in silence.

I had walked for an hour before I saw houses—new and small and square—on the embankment above me.

And then I saw the bridge, and I knew where I was: I was on the old railway path, and I'd been coming down it from the other direction.

There were graffiti painted on the side of the bridge: *Barry Loves Susan* and the omnipresent *NF* of the National Front.

I stood beneath the bridge, in the red brick arch,

stood among the ice-cream wrappers and the crisp packets and watched my breath steam in the cold afternoon air.

The blood had dried into my trousers.

Cars passed over the bridge above me; I could hear a radio playing loudly in one of them.

"Hello?" I said, quietly, feeling embarrassed, feeling foolish. "Hello?"

There was no answer. The wind rustled the crisp packets and the leaves.

"I came back. I said I would. And I did. Hello?"

Silence.

I began to cry then, stupidly, silently, sobbing under the bridge.

A hand touched my face, and I looked up.

"I didn't think you'd come back," said the troll.

He was my height now, but otherwise unchanged. His long gonk hair was unkempt and had leaves in it, and his eyes were wide and lonely.

I shrugged, then wiped my face with the sleeve of my coat. "I came back."

Three kids passed above us on the bridge, shouting and running.

"I'm a troll," whispered the troll, in a small, scared voice. "Fol rol de ol rol."

He was trembling. I held out my hand, and took his huge, clawed paw in mine. I smiled at him. "It's okay," I told him. "Honestly. It's okay."

The troll nodded.

He pushed me to the ground, onto the leaves and the wrappers. Then he raised his head, and opened his mouth, and ate my life with his strong, sharp teeth.

*   *   *

When he was finished, the troll stood up and brushed himself down. He put his hand into the pocket of his coat, and pulled out a bubbly, burnt lump of clinker rock.

He held it out to me.

"This is yours," said the troll.

I looked at him: wearing my life comfortably, easily, as if he'd been wearing it for years. I took the clinker from his hand and sniffed it. I could smell the train from which it had fallen, so long ago. I gripped it tightly in my hairy hand.

"Thank you," I said.

"Good luck," said the troll.

"Yeah. Well. You too."

The troll grinned with my face.

It turned its back on me and began to walk back the way I had come, toward the village, back to the empty house I had left that morning; and it whistled as it walked.

I've been here ever since. Hiding. Waiting. Part of the bridge.

I watch from the shadows as the people pass: walking their dogs, or talking, or doing the things that people do. Sometimes people pause beneath my bridge. And I watch them, but say nothing; and they never see me.

Fol rol de ol rol.

I'm just going to stay here, in the darkness under the arch. I can hear you all out there, trip-trapping, trip-trapping over my bridge.

Oh yes, I can hear you.

But I'm not coming out.

Acknowledgments

Grateful acknowledgment is made for permission to reprint previously published material.

"A Harp of Fishbones" from *A Harp of Fishbones and Other Stories* by Joan Aiken (London: Jonathan Cape, 1972). Copyright © 1972 by Joan Aiken. Reprinted by permission of Joan Aiken.

"The Door to Dark Albion" copyright © 1996 by Cherith Baldry. Printed by permission of Cherith Baldry.

"The Closed Window" from *The Hill of Trouble* by A.C. Benson (London: Isbister, 1903).

"The Pit of Wings" by Ramsey Campbell from *Swords Against Darkness* no, 3, edited by Andrew J. Offutt (New York: Zebra Books, 1978). Copyright © 1978 by Ramsey Campbell. Reprinted by permission of Ramsey Campbell.

"The Bone Beast" copyright © 1996 by Simon Clark. Printed by permission of Simon Clark.

"The Fairy Trap" copyright © 1996 by Peter Crowther. Printed by permission of Peter Crowther.

"The Hoard of the Gibbelins" by Lord Dunsany from *The Sketch* (January 25, 1911), reprinted in *The Book of Wonder* (London: William Heinemann, 1912). Copyright © 1911 by Lord Dunsany. Reprinted by permission of Curtis Brown, Ltd.

"A Pattern of Pyramids" copyright © 1996 by Patricia and Lionel Fanthorpe. Printed by permission of Patricia and Lionel Fanthorpe.

"Troll Bridge" by Neil Gaiman from *Snow White, Blood Red*, edited by Ellen Datlow and Terri Windling (New York: AvoNova, 1993). Copyright © 1993 by Neil Gaiman. Reprinted by permission of the author.

"A Spell for Annalise" by Parke Godwin from *Marion Zimmer Bradley's Fantasy* magazine (winter 1993). Copyright © 1993 by Parke Godwin. Reprinted by permission of Parke Godwin.

"Creature of Darkness" by Nicholas Stuart Gray from *Grimbold's Other World* (London: Faber & Faber, 1963). Copyright © 1963 by Nicholas Stuart Gray. Reprinted by permission of Mrs. Fiona Carton.

"Mirror, Mirror . . ." copyright © 1996 by Frances M. Hendry. Printed by permission of Frances M. Hendry and Laurence Pollinger, Ltd.

"The Green Stone" by Diana Wynne Jones from *Gaslight & Ghosts*, edited by Stephen Jones and Jo Fletcher (London: World Fantasy

Convention, 1988). Copyright © 1988 by Diana Wynne Jones. Reprinted by permission of Diana Wynne Jones and Laura Cecil Literary Agency.

Introduction: "Into Your Dreams" copyright © 1996 by Garry Kilworth. Printed by permission of Garry Kilworth.

"The Goatboy and the Giant" copyright © 1996 by Garry Kilworth. Printed by permission of Garry Kilworth.

"The Invisible Kingdom" by Richard Leander from *The Strand* (March 1896).

"The Selkie's Cap" copyright © 1996 by Samantha Lee. Printed by permission of Samantha Lee and Dorian Literary Agency.

"Sun City" by Tanith Lee from *Young Winter's Tales*, no. 5, edited by Marni Hodgkin (London: Macmillan, 1974). Copyright © 1974 by Tanith Lee. Reprinted by permission of Tanith Lee.

"The Dark Island" from *The Voyage of the Dawn Treader* by C. S. Lewis (London: Geoffrey Bles Ltd., 1952). Copyright © 1952 by C. S. Lewis. Reprinted by permission of HarperCollins Publishers, London.

"The Secret of Faërie" copyright © 1996 by Paul Lewis. Printed by permission of Paul Lewis.

"The Last Card" copyright © 1996 by Steve Lockley. Printed by permission of Steve Lockley.

"The Back of the North Wind" from *At the Back of the North Wind* by George Macdonald (London: Alexander Strahan, 1870).

"Atlantis" from *The Strand* (November 1905), reprinted in *The Story of the Amulet* by Edith Nesbit (London: T. Fisher Unwin, 1906).

"The White Doe" copyright © 1996 by Keith Taylor. Printed by permission of Keith Taylor.

"The Trolls" from *The Hobbit* by J. R. R. Tolkien (London: Allen & Unwin, 1937). Copyright © 1937 by J. R. R. Tolkien. Reprinted by permission of HarperCollins Publishers, London.

"Ice Princess" by Elisabeth Waters from *Marion Zimmer Bradley's Fantasy* magazine (summer 1994). Copyright © 1994 by Elisabeth Waters. Reprinted by permission of Elisabeth Waters.

"The Wild Hunt" by Ian Watson from *Darlite* (September 1966) (Tanzania). Copyright © 1966 by Ian Watson. Reprinted by permission of Ian Watson.

"Brother Kenan's Bell" from *Tales of Wonder* by Jane Yolen (New York: Schocken Books, 1983). Copyright © 1983 by Jane Yolen. Reprinted by permission of Jane Yolen and Curtis Brown, Ltd.

400 PAGES OF FANTASTIC STORIES
BY SOME OF THE WORLD'S BEST WRITERS

☐ **The Random House Book of Dance Stories**
Including stories by Joan Aiken, Louisa May Alcott, Hans Christian Andersen, Alexandre Dumas, Rudyard Kipling, Margaret Mahy, E. Nesbit, Noel Streatfeild, and Oscar Wilde
(0-679-88529-3) $9.99

☐ **The Random House Book of Science Fiction Stories**
Including stories by Piers Anthony, Arthur C. Clarke, John Christopher, H. B. Fyfe, Douglas Hill, Samantha Lee, and William Temple
(0-679-88527-7) $9.99

☐ **The Random House Book of Horse Stories**
Including stories by Louisa May Alcott, Lewis Carroll, Arthur Conan Doyle, Nathaniel Hawthorne, James Herriot, Andrew Lang, C. S. Lewis, Jonathan Swift, Anna Sewell, and Patricia Wrightson
(0-679-88530-7) $9.99

Available wherever books are sold ...

OR

You can send in this coupon (with check or money order)
and have the books mailed directly to you!

Subtotal .... $ _____
Shipping and handling .... $ 3.00
Sales tax (where applicable) .... $ _____
Total amount enclosed .... $ _____

Name _____

Address _____

City _____ **State** _____ **Zip** _____

Make your check or money order (no cash or C.O.D.s)
payable to Random House, Inc., and mail to:
Random House Mail Sales, 400 Hahn Road, Westminster, MD 21157.

Prices and numbers subject to change without notice. Valid in U.S. only.
All orders subject to availability. Please allow 4 to 6 weeks for delivery.

Need your books even faster? Call toll-free 1–800–795–2665
to order by phone and use your major credit card.
Please mention interest code 049–13 to expedite your order.